澄清聲明

親愛的讀者：

倍斯特出版事業有限公司鄭重聲明，大陸中國紡織出版社與本社無業務往來。

近來發現本社之公司Logo，出現於中國紡織出版社之貝斯特英語系列書籍，該出版社自 2012年11月1日起之所有出版品與本社並無任何關係；鑑於此事件，懷疑有人利用本社之商業信譽，藉此誤導大眾，本社予以高度關注。特此聲明，以正視聽。

倍斯特出版事業有限公司　敬啟

倍斯特出版事業有限公司
Best Publishing Ltd.

Awesome!
It's to
Easy
Learn!

漸進式
句型完全 英文文法
KO版

免驚啦!
句型學通不再怕文法,
學以致用,一次就全盤掌握!

1	**紮下實力基礎**	從五大句型的介紹開始,了解英語句子的基本結構,對句型不再害怕。
2	**通透正確觀念**	強化文法概念的認識,經由解說後,清楚明白各句型的用法。
3	**活用好學句型**	舉常用的文法句型加以剖析,讓讀者更熟稔英語句型的應用。
4	**加強實際演練**	有充分的練習題與精闢的解答,讓你學得通達,學得精。
5	**糾正常犯錯誤**	有對和錯相互類比的解析,提醒您要注意的文法陷阱。
6	**句例多易上手**	每個章節都有詳盡地舉例說明,讓你觸類旁通,舉一反三。

黃亭瑋 ◎ 著

作者序

文法是每個英文學習者感到最痛苦的一環，但不能否認的是，文法也是了解一個語言最有系統的方法，而句型是實踐文法最有效的方式。本書即以這此為著力點，希望可以用最深入淺出的方法，讓學習英文一點也不難。

本書分為兩個部分，第一部分著重於句子的基本結構，分析句子的構成因素；第二部分針對各種語氣的句型進行探討。每一篇主要分為三個章節：概念篇、句型篇和文法糾正篇，也有生活實用小短句和好學的諺語，希望可以透過文法的概念解釋和實用的句型練習，加強讀者於生活中應用英文的能力。

在本書的寫作過程中，謝謝倍斯特出版社全體同仁，除了給予本次寫作的機會，並多次針對架構和內容提出更好的方向，使本書得以順利完成，內容也更加豐富。

謝謝家人、老公和朋友的支持，提供我許多寫作的靈感，也不厭其煩的和我辯論更好的寫作方式。

謝謝購買這本書的您，語言日新月異，學習語言是一個漫長的旅途，但絕對不是痛苦的，Seek mickle, and get something; seek little, and get nothing.(尋找得多，就能得到一些；尋找得少，什麼也得不到。) 但願這本書除了能讓您對英文的文法句型有更深入的了解，也能帶給你對於語言學習的啟發。

黃亭瑋

好學易上手的英語句型>即將要出版了！作者和編者希望經由本書的寫作，可以幫助讀者，快速的搞懂英語句型。特別是在閱讀寫作上，如何能有效的分析文章，幫助自己學習，以及用正確的句型和文法，寫出正確的英文文章，不但有利於讓讀者的英語程度，藉由了解句子的功能與使用，可以整體提升與進步，這是倍斯特編輯部編著此書的目標。從句子的基本結構的了解，到分章節解析英語句型的分類與用法，本書用心的協助讀者，搞懂觀念，多多練習，因而達到讓讀者可以善用句型結構的變化，使讀者在使用本書學習時，訓練自己運用英語句型的靈活度，因而讓您的英語讀寫更加熟稔，也讓您的英語聽說更加有自信。

倍斯特編輯部

目次

PART I ｜句子的基本結構｜

CONTENTS

PART **1**

句子的
基本結構

01
CHAPTER
五大基本句型和句子的十二種時態

一、五大基本句型

‖ 句子的構成要素 |

　　構成句子的基本要素為主詞、動詞、受詞和補語。最簡單的句子僅僅由主詞和動詞組成，同時，根據動詞的不同，也會適時加入受詞和補語。

(1) 主詞

　　在句子裡扮演主角的，我們稱為主詞。一個主詞是一個句子中的靈魂人物，如果沒有主詞，我們就無法知道這個句子要表達的主題是什麼。主詞必須是名詞、代名詞、動名詞、不定詞或是由名詞所組成的相關語，例如：

Japan is my favorite country.（日本是我最喜歡的國家。）
→ 名詞做主詞。

She is very nice.（她人很好。）
→ 代名詞做主詞。

Swimming is good for health.（游泳有益健康。）
→ 動名詞做主詞。

To swim is good for health.（游泳有益健康。）
→ 不定詞做主詞。

(2) 動詞

　　句子中只有主角，還不能構成一個完整的句子。有了主題，我們還需要知道發生什麼事。動詞在句子中扮演的角色，就是要明確表示出主詞的動作與狀態，經由動詞變化，也可以表示動作發生的時間。有了主詞和動詞，就可以構成一個完整的句子，但是也並非所有的句子中一定都會有動詞，有些句型，例如感嘆句，就完全沒有動詞，例如：

She ate a sandwich for breakfast.（她早餐吃了三明治。）
→ 句子中有動詞，表示主詞的動作，也可以表示發生的時間。
What a wonderful day!（多美好的一天呀！）
→ 句中雖然沒有動詞，但也可以構成句子。

(3) 受詞

　　受詞是句子中受到動作影響的語詞。一般而言，可以做為主詞的語詞，例如名詞、代名詞、動名詞、不定詞和名詞相關語，皆可以做為受詞。有時，疑問詞和副詞有時也可以當作受詞使用，例如：

I don't know why.（我不知道為什麼。）
→ why 是疑問詞，在這個句子中做為 know 的受詞。
He always knows all the ins and outs.（他總是能知道內線消息。）
→ ins and outs 為副詞組合，表示「內情」，在這裡做 know 的受詞。

　　受詞可以細分為直接動詞和間接動詞。直接受詞是直接接受動作的語詞。間接受詞為非直接接受動作，但卻受到動作影響的語詞，例如：

He wrote me a letter.（他寫一封信給我。）
→ letter 是受到 wrote 動作的受詞，為直接受詞；me 沒有直接受到 wrote 動作的影響，為間接受詞。

通常，一個動詞後面會銜接一個受詞，但有些動詞後面會分別出現直接受詞和間接受詞。

⑷ 補語

補語分為主詞補語和受詞補語。主詞補語在句子中用來補充說明主詞，受詞補語則是用來補充說明受詞，也就是說，如果一個句子中有兩個語詞的關係或狀態可以畫上等號，那這兩個語詞就是主詞和主詞補語、受詞和受詞補語的關係。因此，可以做為主詞或是受詞的語詞，也可以用來當作補語使用。不僅如此，因為補語具有修飾主詞或是受詞的功能，形容詞也可以做為補語。

She is a Chinese teacher.（她是一位國文老師。）
→ she = Chinese teacher。she 是主詞，Chinese teacher 為主詞補語。

He makes me happy.（他使我開心。）
→ me 是 make 的受詞，me 的狀態是 happy，happy 為受詞補語。

・換你試試看，是主詞、動詞、受詞還是補語？

1. They elected the man their chairperson.
   (A)   (B)   (C)   (D)

2. She practices the piano every day.
   (A)   (B)   (C)

3. Debby found a little cat in the box.
   (A)   (B)   (C)

4. Monica became a famous musician.
   (A)   (B)   (C)

5. The teacher thinks her an honest girl.
   (A)   (B)   (C)   (D)

・你答對了嗎？

1. They elected the man their chairperson.
   (A)主詞 (B)動詞 (C)受詞   (D)受詞補語

2. She practices the piano every day.
   (A)主詞 (B)動詞 (C)受詞

3. Debby found a little cat in the box.
    (A)主詞(B)動詞(C)受詞

4. Monica became a famous musician.
    (A)主詞(B)動詞　(C)主詞補語

5. The teacher thinks her an honest girl.
    　(A)主詞　(B)動詞(C)受詞 (D)受詞補語

瞭解了句子的構成要素後，我們來看看這些要素是如何構成句子。

‖ 句子的結構 ‖

單獨學習句子的構成方式，老實說是有點沉悶的。在一般生活對話中，我們不會需要特別去判斷句子是何種結構，就算不了解句子的構造，也不會影響對話內容的理解。但是當我們開始閱讀，甚至練習寫作時，如果對這些基本句型有一定程度的熟悉，有助於理解較長的句子，或是掌握寫作的語感。

英文的結構可以區分為五大類，不論多長的句子，都可以逐步拆解為這五大句型中的一種。這五大句型分別為：

五大基本句型
(1) 主詞 S＋動詞 V
(2) 主詞 S＋動詞 V＋受詞 O
(3) 主詞 S＋動詞 V＋主詞補語 SC
(4) 主詞 S＋動詞 V＋受詞補語 OC
(5) 主詞 S＋動詞 V＋間接受詞 IO＋直接受詞 DO

(1) 主詞＋動詞（S＋V）
這類句型的動詞皆為不及物動詞，後面不需銜接受詞或補語，就能表達完整的意思，例如：

He walks.（他走路。）
→ 動作可以單獨出現，不用牽涉其他的人事物句意也完整。

儘管這個句型不需要受詞或補語，但我們也可以在句子中加入副詞或副詞片語，讓句子的涵義更完整：

He walks quickly.（他走路很快。）
→ quickly 是副詞，修飾動詞 walk。

He walks to school every day.（他每天走路上學。）
→ to school 是方向副詞片語，every day 是時間副詞片語，皆用來修飾動詞。

不及物動詞即使在後面接上副詞，形成片語動詞，還是屬於不及物動詞，可以單獨使用。常見的不及物片語動詞如 go ahead（繼續）、fool around（閒晃）、clear up（天氣放晴）、pass away（過世）、pass out（昏倒）、die down（減弱）等。

但是，並非不及物動詞永遠都是不及物動詞，有些不及物動詞搭配介係詞，就會具有及物動詞的功能，後面要接受詞。這類的動詞，我們歸類於第二類句型進行討論。

⑵ 主詞＋動詞＋受詞（S＋V＋O）
這個句型中的動詞為及物動詞，需要在後面加上受詞：

He made a cake.（他做了一塊蛋糕。）
→ 動詞 made 後面要有承受動作的受詞 cake。

有些及物動詞後面加上受詞還不足以將動詞的意思充分表達，而需要副詞幫忙，例如：

He put a cake on the table.（他放一塊蛋糕在桌上。）
→ on the table 是修飾 put 的動作，讓動作完整。

　　如果這一個句子只有 He put a cake，而沒有後面說明 put 動作的 on the table，是不是邏輯很奇怪呢？好像句子沒有結束。因此，遇到這類句型時，要小心不要受到副詞片語的影響而誤判句子的結構。

　　和第一類句型的不及物動詞類似，及物動詞加上副詞，還是及物動詞，這類的片語動詞例如：hand sth. out（發送某物）、call sb. up（打電話給某人）、put on（穿上）、take off（脫掉）、take out（拿出去）、make sth. out（明白某事）等。

　　有些不及物動詞搭配介係詞後，形成介係詞動詞，或是搭配副詞和介係詞，構成片語動詞，具有及物動詞的作用，這些動詞常見的有：

不及物動詞轉為及物動詞使用				
不及物動詞＋介係詞	call for	要求	persist in	堅持
	yield to	屈服	live on	存活
	depend on	依賴	dispose of	廢棄
不及物動詞＋副詞＋介係詞	look back on	回想	watch out for	小心
	come up with	想出	stand up for	維護
	catch up with	趕上	come down with	染病

(3) 主詞＋動詞＋主詞補語（S＋V＋SC）

　　在這個句型中，動詞扮演將主詞和主詞補語連接起來的作用。視動詞的不同，可以細分為兩種類型。

　　若動詞為 be 動詞，主詞補語有很多類型，請看下面的例子：

She is beautiful.（她很漂亮。）
→ 形容詞做主詞補語。

She is a Chinese teacher.（她是一位國文老師。）
→ 名詞做主詞補語。

The truth is that she doesn't want to be a teacher.（真相是，她不想當老師。）
→ that 領導的子句做主詞補語。

The problem is <u>how to tell</u> her parents
（問題是，她不知道怎麼跟她的父母說。）
→ 疑問詞＋不定詞做主詞補語。

The most important thing is <u>what she thinks</u>.（最重要的是她怎麼想。）
→ what 領導的子句做主詞補語。

She is <u>in the bedroom</u>.（她在臥室裡。）
→ 地方副詞做主詞補語。

To see is <u>to believe</u>.（眼見為憑。）
→ 不定詞做主詞補語。

Seeing is <u>believing</u>.（眼見為憑。）
→ 動名詞做主詞補語。

然而，有些動詞只能用形容詞當作主詞補語，我們稱這類的動詞為連綴動詞。連綴動詞包含和感官或狀態改變相關的動詞，例如：

The coffee <u>smells good</u>.（咖啡聞起來很香。）
→ 和感官有關的連綴動詞 smell 後面接形容詞 good。

Her dream <u>came true</u>.（她的夢想成真了。）
→ 表示狀態改變的連綴動詞 came 後面接形容詞 true。

常用的連綴動詞有：

連綴動詞	
感官相關	look、taste、sound、smell、feel
狀態	become、get、remain、stay、keep、

但並非所有的連綴動詞後面只能接形容詞，例如 become，也可於其後加名詞做主詞補語：

She has <u>become an English teacher</u>.（她成為了英文老師。）

(4) 主詞＋動詞＋受詞補語（S＋V＋OC）

　　主詞補語為主詞的補充，一樣的概念，受詞補語也是補充說明受詞。受詞補語多為名詞或形容詞。

He makes me happy.（他使我開心。）
→ 形容詞補充說明受詞的心情狀態。

We named our *cat Mi-mi.*（我們把貓咪取名叫 Mi-mi。）
→ 名詞補充說明受詞的身分。

(5) 主詞＋動詞＋間接受詞＋直接受詞（S＋V＋IO＋DO）

　　這類句型的動詞為及物動詞，會有兩個受詞，一個是直接受詞，通常為事物，另一個是間接受詞，通常是人，例如：

My dad gave me the pen.（我的爸爸給了我這支筆。）
→ 動詞 gave 先接表示人物的間接受詞，再接表示事物的直接受詞。

　　動詞本身具有「給予」的涵義，受到給予動作影響的是 the pen，受到動作間接影響的為 me。

　　但是並非所有的間接受詞都是人，例如：

He gave his bike a wash.（他洗他的腳踏車。）
→ his bike 是事物而非人物，做間接受詞使用。

　　是不是被搞糊塗了呢？如果你真的搞不清楚到底哪一個才是直接受詞，哪一個才是間接受詞，你可以想成：被給的東西是直接受詞，接收到東西的是間接受詞。

　　這類句型中的動詞，例如 give（給）、bring（帶來）、offer（提供）、send（寄送）、buy（買）、show（展示）、lend（借）、tell（告訴）、read（閱讀）、pay（付費）、hand（傳遞）、pass（傳遞）、leave（留給）、sing（唱歌）等，多半具有「一方給予一方」的意味，有些文法書中將之稱為授與動詞。

　　這個句型也可以轉換成＜主詞＋動詞＋直接受詞＋for / to＋間接受詞＞，以上面的句子為例：

My dad gave me the pen.

= *My dad gave the pen to me.*

→ 間接受詞和直接受詞的位置交換，並在中間加入 to。

有些動作，例如 write 或 sing，介係詞 to 或是 for 都可以使用。差別在於，for 表示「為了…」，而 to 僅僅具有動作方向的意思。試比較下列句子語氣的不同：

He wrote me a love letter.（他寫了一封情書給我。）

He wrote a love letter for me.（他為了我寫了一封情書。）

He wrote a love letter to me.（他寫了一封情書給我。）

・換你試試看，把相同的句型配成對！

1. Jane sings well. ＿＿＿＿＿＿

2. The boy looks happy. ＿＿＿＿＿＿

3. I want a hamburger. ＿＿＿＿＿＿

4. My mom bought me a new dress. ＿＿＿＿＿＿

5. They dubbed him Fatty ＿＿＿＿＿＿

a. The waiter brought me a cup of coffee.

b. You need to keep your T-shirt clean.

c. He doesn't know how to swim.

d. They will go shopping tomorrow.

e. The chicken tastes bad.

・你答對了嗎？

1. Jane sings well.

   應搭配 d. They will go shopping tomorrow.

   句子的結構是＜主詞＋動詞＞

2. The boy looks happy.

   應搭配 e. The chicken tastes bad.

   句子的結構是＜主詞＋動詞＋主詞補語＞

3. I want a hamburger.
   應搭配 c. He doesn't know how to swim.
   句子的結構是＜主詞＋動詞＋受詞＞

4. My mom bought me a new dress.
   應搭配 a. The waiter brought me a cup of coffee.
   句子的結構是＜主詞＋動詞＋間接受詞＋直接受詞＞

5. They dubbed him Fatty.
   應搭配 b. You need to keep your T-shirt clean.
   句子的結構是＜主詞＋動詞＋受詞＋受詞補語＞

二、句子的十二種時態

在中文的句型中，只要知道事件發生的時間，就可以判斷出是過去、現在或是未來，在動詞上也不需要有特別的變化。英文則是利用動詞的變化來表示某個動作何時發生。

表示過去、現在和未來的時間關係，稱為時態。時態分為四種:簡單式、進行式、完成式和完成進行式。每種時態又可以依發生的時間不同，分為過去、現在和未來。

簡單式

簡單式		
(1) 過去簡單式	主詞＋過去式動詞	He ate an apple yesterday. （他昨天吃了一顆蘋果。）
(2) 現在簡單式	主詞＋動詞	He eats an apple every day. （他每天都吃一顆蘋果。）
(3) 未來簡單式	主詞＋will＋動詞原形	He will eat an apple tomorrow. （他明天將要吃一顆蘋果。）
(4) 簡單式的否定句	主詞＋助動詞＋not＋原形動詞	He didn't eat an apple yesterday. （他昨天沒有吃蘋果。） He doesn't eat an apple every day. （他沒有每天都吃蘋果。） He won't eat an apple tomorrow. （他明天將不會吃蘋果。）
(5) 簡單式的問句	助動詞＋主詞＋原形動詞…？	Did he eat an apple yesterday？ （他昨天有吃蘋果嗎？） Does he eat an apple every day？ （他每天有吃蘋果嗎？） Will he eat an apple tomorrow？ （他明天會吃蘋果嗎？）

(1) 過去簡單式

　　表示某動作發生在過去的時間中，因此要將動詞變為過去式。大部分的動詞加上 ed 即為過去式，有些動詞則是不規則變化。動詞的變化方式，可以參考第二篇名詞與動詞。

　　過去簡單式除了表示過去時間發生的動作，也可以表示過去的狀態或是習慣的動作：

He used to go to work by MRT.（他之前習慣搭捷運上班。）

　　在過去簡單式的句型中，除了明確點出過去的時間點，ago（之前）也常常放在一段時間之後使用，例如：

I left school at four o'clock.（我四點鐘離開學校。）
→ 點出過去的時間點。

She left school ten minutes ago.（她十分鐘之前離開學校。）
→「十分鐘之前」也是明確的過去時間點。

(2) 現在簡單式

　　這個時態大多用來表示事實、習慣或真理。be 動詞根據主詞的不同而改變。若主詞為第三人稱單數，則後面的動詞字尾加 s 或 es。

　　有些動作時間確定的動詞，例如：arrive（到達）、begin（開始）、end（結束）、finish（結束）、leave（離開）、open（開始）、close（關閉）、start（開始）和表示狀態的 be 動詞等，可以用現在簡單式代替未來式。例如：

She plays the piano.（她彈鋼琴。）
→表事實、習慣
There will be an English class tomorrow afternoon.（明天下午有英文課。）
＝*There is an English class tomorrow afternoon.*

The English class will start at ten o'clock tomorrow morning.
＝*The English class starts at ten o'clock tomorrow morning.*
（英文課在明天早上十點開始。）

(3) 未來簡單式：

　　未來簡單式表示在未來時間所發生的動作，這個時態要在動詞前加 will，

後面銜接的動詞則要使用原形動詞。

I will finish his homework tomorrow.（我明天將會完成作業。）

在正式的文法中，如果主詞是 I 或是 We，會用 shall 代替 will，可以說，shall 是比 will 正式的用法。現在多將 shall 用於問句或是附加問句中，表示詢問或是提議，例如：

Shall we go to the party together?（我們一起去派對如何？）

關於 shall 和附加問句的使用，可以參閱第七篇的問句和附加問句。

另一個表示未來簡單式的句型是＜主詞＋be 動詞＋going to＋動詞原形＞。

在這個句型中，be 動詞要隨主詞而變化。will 和 be going to 的差別在於，will 用於預測或是敘述未來會發生的事情，通常後面會伴隨著未來的時間；而 be going to 除了根據可知事實進行預測，也可以用於表示個人的計畫或是用途，試比較下列兩句：

He will mop the floor this afternoon.（他下午會拖地。）
He is going to mop the floor this afternoon.（他下午會拖地。）

這兩句的中文意思都一樣，但第一句使用 will，聽起來像是個承諾「他保證下午會拖地」，而第二句用 be going to，則感覺是「他在計畫下午要做的事。」

(4) 簡單式的否定句

當句子裡有動詞，想要改寫成否定句型時，可以找助動詞幫忙；依人稱和時態的不同，要使用不同的助動詞。

助動詞＋not		
第一人稱、第二人稱、複數	do not	= don't
第三人稱單數	does not	= doesn't
過去式	did not	= didn't
未來式	will not	= won't

例如：

I don't believe you anymore.（我再也不相信你了。）

He doesn't wear glasses.（他沒有戴眼鏡。）

They didn't go to the movies last week.（他們上星期沒有去看電影。）

She won't have dinner with us this Friday.
（這周五她將不會和我們共進晚餐。）

(5) 簡單式的疑問句

　　將助動詞置於句首，即可構成簡單式的疑問句，主詞的人稱和時態不同，助動詞也要跟著做變化：

Do you believe me?（你相信我嗎？）

Does he wear glasses?（他有戴眼鏡嗎？）

Did they go to the movie last week?（他們上星期有去看電影嗎？）

Will she have dinner with us this Friday?
（這周五她將會和我們共進晚餐嗎？）

　　若有 What、When、Where、How、Who 等疑問詞，則將疑問詞置於助動詞前即可，例如：

He drinks black tea every day.（他每天都喝紅茶。）
變成疑問句 → *Does he drink black tea every day?*（他每天都喝紅茶嗎？）
加入疑問詞 what → What does he drink black tea every day?

　　但是因為句子的目的在問主詞喝的飲料是什麼，所以不能說出喝的東西，要把 black tea 省略。寫成：What does he drink every day?（他每天喝什麼？）

・換你試試看，什麼時態的簡單式才對呢？

1. Dad _____ (read) newspaper at the table every day.
2. He _____ (play) video game with Emma last night.

3. She _____ (decide) to make chicken soup for dinner.

4. It _____ rain, you need to take an umbrella with you.

5. I don't know how to use it, but Lisa _____ (tell) me she _____ show me.

・你寫對了嗎？

1. Dad reads newspaper at the table every day.

2. He played video game with Emma last night.

3. She decided to make chicken soup for dinner.

4. It will rain; you need to take an umbrella with you.

5. I don't know how to use it, but Lisa told me she will show me.

進行式

進行式		
(1) 過去進行式	主詞＋be 動詞＋動詞 ing（be 動詞用過去式）	He was eating an apple last night.（他昨晚正在吃蘋果。）
(2) 現在進行式	主詞＋be 動詞＋動詞 ing	*He is eating an apple now.*（他現在正在吃蘋果。）
(3) 未來進行式	主詞＋ will be＋動詞 ing	He will be eating an apple tomorrow morning.（他明天早上將會正在吃蘋果。）
(4) 進行式的否定句	主詞＋be 動詞＋not ＋動詞 ing（be 動詞依人稱和時態變化）	*He is not eating an apple now.*（他現在沒有吃蘋果。）（be 動詞依人稱和時態變化）
(5) 進行式的問句	be 動詞＋主詞＋動詞 ing…?（be 動詞依人稱和時態變化）	*Is he eating an apple now?*（他現在正在吃蘋果嗎？）（be 動詞依人稱和時態變化）

　　be 動詞隨著主詞和時間而改變，在「現在」的時間裡，第一人稱為 am，第二人稱和複數為 are，第三人稱單數為 is；在「過去」的時間裡，第一人稱和第三人稱單數，要用 was，第二人稱和複數則用 were；若是「未來」的時間，不論人稱，皆於 be 動詞前加 will，同時 be 動詞變成原形 be。

　　關於動詞變化為動詞 ing 的形式，有四項原則：
1. 動詞直接加 ing：*walk*→ *walking*
2. 動詞結尾是 e，去 e 加 ing：*make*→ *making*
3. 動詞結尾是母音加子音，要重複子音加 ing：*run*→ *running*
　但是如果動詞的結尾是母音+母音+子音，則直接加 ing 即可：*eat*→ *eating*
4. 動詞結尾是 ie，去 ie 加 ying：*lie*→ *lying*

(1) 過去進行式：
　　過去進行式，主要在說明過去的某一段時間正在進行的動作。如果是第一人稱和第三人稱單數，要用 was，第二人稱和複數則用 were。
　　過去進行式常常會和 when 帶領的句子一同出現，例如：

I was taking a shower when Jim called.（當我正在沖澡時，*Jim* 打電話來。）
→ when 連接兩個過去發生的動作，過去進行式用來表示具有持續性的動作，簡單過去式表示瞬間發生的動作。

We were waiting for the bus when the car bumped into the tree.
（當這輛車撞上樹時，我們正在等公車。）

(2) 現在進行式：
　　現在進行式用來表示此刻正在進行的動作，例如：

They are watching TV.（他們正在看電視。）

　　有時，我們也會用現在進行式表示近期內即將發生，或是未來已經安排好要做的事。這樣的用法，常常與表示往來、停留的動作如 go（去）、come（來）、leave（離開）、start（開始）、arrive（抵達）、stay（停留）或是可以表示社交活動的 do（做）、have（有）一起使用，為了避免和現在進行的動作混淆，通常會在句尾加上未來的時間，例如：

I am going to Japan next month.（我下個月要去日本。）
→ 雖然動詞變化為現在進行式，但因為時間是未來的時間，所以這句話可以表示未來即將發生的事。

Are you doing anything on Sunday night?
（你星期六晚上有計畫要做什麼嗎？）

I am having a party on Saturday night.（我星期六晚上舉辦派對。）

(3) 未來進行式：

未來進行式表示未來某個時刻正在進行的動作。

我們也可以用未來進行式表示某件事情的可能性，語氣會比未來簡單式較為婉轉與客氣：

Will you come with me?（你可以跟我一起來嗎？）
=*Will you be coming with me?*（可以請您跟我一起來嗎？）
→ 用未來進行式，語氣比較委婉。

(4) 進行式的否定句

進行式的否定句，只要在 be 動詞後面加上 not 即可。

be 動詞 are、is 和 not 可以縮寫成 aren't 和 isn't；過去式的 be 動詞 was、were 和 not 可以縮寫成 wasn't 和 weren't，例如：

She isn't talking on the phone.（她沒有在講電話。）

He wasn't running when he saw Helen in the park.
（當他看到 Helen 時，他沒有正在跑步。）

(5) 進行式的問句

將 be 動詞放在句首，句號改為問號，即構成問句，同時也要根據人稱和時態的的不同來選擇 be 動詞。

I am eating a hamburger.（我正在吃漢堡。）
→ *Are you eating a hamburger?*（你正在吃漢堡嗎？）

若有疑問詞，只要將疑問詞置於 be 動詞前面。

What are you eating?（你正在吃什麼？）

· 換你試試看，用進行式完成對話！

1. Sam: Where are you _____ (go)?

   Lisa: I am _____ (go) to the library. I want to rent some books.

2. Jimmy: What is Mom _____ (do)?

   May: I don't know. Let's ask her.

3. Tracy: Are Tom and you _____ (do) anything on Friday?

   Anna: Oh, we plan to go to the movies.

   Tracy: Well, I am _____ (have) a party at Friday night. Will you be _____ (come)?

4. James: Why didn't you answer my phone yesterday?

   Kevin: Oh, I am sorry. I was _____ (take) a shower at that time.

· 你完成了嗎？

1. Sam: Where are you going?

   Lisa: I am going to the library. I want to rent some books.

2. Jimmy: What is Mom doing?

   May: I don't know. Let's ask her.

3. Tracy: Are Tom and you doing anything on Friday?

   Anna: Oh, we plan to go to the movies.

   Tracy: Well, I am having a party at Friday night. Will you be coming?

4. James: Why didn't you answer my phone yesterday?

   Kevin: Oh, I am sorry. I was taking a shower at that time.

完成式

完成式		
(1) 過去完成式	主詞＋had＋過去分詞	He had eaten an apple before he went to school.（他去學校前已經吃了一顆蘋果。）
(2) 現在完成式	主詞＋have＋過去分詞（第三人稱用 has）	He has eaten an apple for half an hour.（他已經吃蘋果吃了半小時。）
(3) 未來完成式	主詞＋ will have＋過去分詞	He will have eaten an apple by 2:00.（到兩點時，他將已經吃完蘋果了。）
(4) 完成式的否定句	主詞＋have not＋過去分詞（have / has / had 根據人稱或時態的不同而變化）	He has not eaten an apple.（他還沒吃完蘋果。）（have / has / had 根據人稱或時態的不同而變化）
(5) 完成式的問句	Have＋主詞＋過去分詞…?（have / has / had 根據人稱或時態的不同而變化）	Has he eaten the apple?（他已經吃完蘋果了嗎？）（have / has / had 根據人稱或時態的不同而變化）

　　過去分詞可以分為規則動詞和不規則動詞的變化。一般規則動詞的過去分詞在字尾加 ed 即可，不規則動詞的過去分詞可以區分為四種類型：
　　ABC 型：即原形、過去式、過去分詞皆不同，例如 begin-began-begun。
　　ABB 型：即過去式和過去分詞相同，例如 find - found - found
　　ABA 型：即原形和過去分詞相同，例如 run - ran - ran
　　AAA 型：即三態皆相同，例如 cost- cost- cost。

(1) 過去完成式
　　過去完成式表示某動作在過去時間開始，持續一段時間，並於過去時間結束。

過去完成式很少單獨於句子中使用，多用於想要明確指出過去的某件事情比另一件事情更早發生，也就是說，若有兩個動作於過去的時間內發生，則先發生的動作用過去完成式，例如：

He had eaten an apple before he went to school.
（他去學校前，吃了一顆蘋果。）
→ 吃蘋果的動作在去學校前先發生，所以用過去完成式。

　　在正式的文法裡，如果句子中出現 after 或 before，則用過去簡單式即可，因此，上面的例句也可以改寫成：

He ate an apple before he went to school.

　　當然，這個句型除了可以用 before 和 after 表示動作的先後關係，也可以用代表因果關係的從屬連接詞來表示動作的先後，例如：

I didn't sleep well because I had drunk an espresso.
（我沒睡好，因為我喝了一杯濃縮咖啡。）
→ because 也可以清楚表達動作的前後順序。

　　在口語或是非正式的文章中，我們也可以將主詞和 had 縮寫，例如 I'd、You'd、She'd、He'd、We'd 和 They'd。

(2) 現在完成式
　　現在完成式主要表示過去某時發生的動作持續到現在時間的狀態。
　　我們可以將現在完成式的概念，想成是過去簡單式+現在簡單式。

I started to learn English ten years ago.（我十年前開始學英文。）→ 過去式

+ *I still learn English.*（我現在還在學英文。）→ 現在式

= *I have learned English for ten years.*（我學英文已經十年了。）
→ 現在完成式

上述的例句中，第一句表示過去時間開始的事件，第二句表示現在仍在持續的狀態，將兩句合併，表示過去發生但和現在產生關聯的動作。

若想強調動作已經完成，可以在 have 和過去分詞中間加入 already 或 just，強調「已經完成」或「剛剛完成」，例如：

I have already finished my work.（我已經完成了我的工作。）

I have just finished my work.（我剛剛才完成我的工作。）

already 除了表示「已經」，也有強調「某動作不用再重複」的涵義，例如：

You do not need to call John. I have already called him.
（你不需要打給 *John*，我已經打給他了。）

since 和 for 常常和現在完成式一起使用，表示發生在過去時間，但一直持續到現在的動作或狀態。for 和 since 的用法很容易被混淆，for 後面加上時間的總數，since 則是加時間的起點：

I have studied English for one year.（我已經學英文一年了。）
→ for + 總數

I have studied English since ten years old.（我從十歲開始學英文。）
→ since + 時間起點

現在完成式常常被用於表示經驗，多與時間副詞連用。這些可以表示經驗的時間副詞有：ever、never、before 和表示次數的 once、twice 等。

I have been to Japan before.（我之前曾經去過日本。）
I have been to Japan twice.（我曾經去過日本兩次。）
→ 表示次數的 once、twice、⋯times 和 before 多置於句尾。

I have never been to Japan before.（我從來沒去過日本。）
→ never 用於否定句，放在 have 和過去分詞中間。

Have you ever been to Japan?（你曾經去過日本嗎？）
→ ever 用於疑問句，放在主詞和過去分詞中間。

(3) 未來完成式

　　未來完成式主要表示在目前尚未發生的事件，但在未來某個時刻前已經發生或完成的動作，因此，常常在會句子中加入「by+時間點」或是 by the time 表示未來的某時，例如：

I will have studied English for one year by next month.
（到了下個月，我就學了一年英文了。）
→ 未來完成式代表目前為止還沒有滿一年，但到了下個月，就會滿一年。

(4) 完成式的否定句

　　完成式的否定句，只要在 have、has 或 had 後面加上 not 即可，依據人稱和時態選擇適合的語詞。Have、has 和 had 可以與 not 縮寫為 haven't、hasn't 和 hadn't。

　　若想強調動作尚未完成，可以在過去分詞前加上 yet。完成式中的 yet 多用於否定句或疑問句，表示「尚未…」，例如：

He hasn't left yet.（他還沒離開。）

　　若表示經驗的否定，則在 have 和過去分詞中加上 never，有時為了加強語氣，我們可以在句子的最後加上 before，但是要小心，若使用 never，就不會再使用 not：

I have never heard it before.（我之前從來沒聽過。）

(5) 完成式的疑問句

　　將 have、has 或 had 置於句首，就是完成式的疑問句。
　　若有疑問詞，將疑問詞放在 have、has 或 had 的前面即可，例如：

What have you done?（你做了什麼？）

　　完成式強調動作的延續性，若要詢問事件持續的時間，我們要用 How long 做為疑問詞，例如：

How long have you finished your homework?（你花多久完成家庭作業？）

若是表示經驗，可以在 have 和過去分詞中間加上 ever，句尾加上 before，例如：

Have you ever been to Seattle before?（你之前曾經去過西雅圖嗎？）
→ 句尾的 before 也可以省略不用。

若要詢問次數，可以在 have 前加上 How often 或 How many times，例如：

How often have you been to Japan?（你多久去一次日本？）
→ How often 詢問頻率。

How many times have you been to Japan?（你去過日本多少次？）
→ How many times 詢問次數。

・換你試試看，利用提示寫出完成式句型！
1. Amanda / ride / bicycle / half an hour
2. Vicky / not / be / New York / before
3. Mickey / drink a cup of tea / before / go to work
4. Tim / never / play chess / before

・你完成了嗎？
1. Amanda / ride / bicycle / half an hour
   Amanda has ridden this bicycle for half an hour.
2. Vicky / not / be / New York / before
   Vicky hasn't been to New York before.
3. Mickey / drink a cup of tea / before / go to work
   Mickey had drunk a cup of tea before he went to work.
4. Tim / never / play chess / before
   Tim has never played chess before.

完成進行式

完成進行式		
(1) 過去完成進行式	主詞 + had been + 動詞 ing	He had been eating an apple for half an hour before he went to school. （他在上學前，吃了半小時的蘋果。）
(2) 現在完成進行式	主詞 + have been + 動詞 ing （第三人稱用 has）	He has been eating an apple for thirty minutes. （他已經吃蘋果吃了三十分鐘。）
(3) 未來完成進行式	主詞 + will have been+ 動詞 ing	He will have been eating an apple for thirty minutes by 1 o'clock. （到了一點，他吃蘋果就要吃了三十分鐘了。）
(4) 完成進行式的否定句	主詞 + have been + not + 動詞 ing （have / has / had 根據人稱或時態的不同而變化）	He has not been eating an apple. （他還沒有吃完蘋果。） （have / has / had 根據人稱或時態的不同而變化）
(5) 未來完成進行式的問句	Will + 主詞 + have been + 動詞 ing…?	Will he have been eating the apple for thirty minutes by 1 o'clock? （到了一點，他吃蘋果就要吃了三十分鐘了嗎？）

(1) 過去完成進行式

　　過去完成進行式，表示在過去的時間裡，某動作發生且持續一段時間後結束。

　　過去完成進行式和過去進行式有點類似，通常不會單獨一個句子出現，而是與其他句子一起使用，強調在過去時間中，所發生兩個事件之間的延續性與關聯性，也就是說，過去時間內發生的兩件事情，比較早發生的要用過去完成進行式，例如：

I had been waiting for a long time before the bus came.
（公車來之前，我已經等了好長一段時間。）

⑵ 現在完成進行式

　　現在完成進行式，可以用來描述兩種狀況的發生。第一種表示從過去開始的動作，直到現在仍然在進行，這樣的句型多半與 since、for 和 how long 等表示時間的語詞連用，例如：

It has been raining for two hours.（已經下雨下了兩小時了。）
→ 兩小時前開始下，到現在還在下。

　　第二種用於剛剛停止的動作，這個停止的動作會對現在的動作或狀態產生影響，例如：

The ground is wet. It has been raining.（剛剛下過雨，所以地上是溼的。）
→ 剛剛停止的雨造成現在地板是濕的狀態。

　　有時，我們也會使用現在完成進行式描述持續了一段時間的動作或暫時性的動作，一般會將這種句型用於描述最近的活動、重複一段時間的動作和持續的動作，例如：

He has been studying for a while.（他唸書已經一陣子了。）
→ 說明最近的活動。

He has been calling his girlfriend.（他一直打電話給他的女友。）
→ 表示一直重複的動作。

He has been studying Japanese for six months.（他已經學了六個月的日文。）
→ 代表持續的動作。

　　那麼，這個句型和現在完成式有什麼不同呢？
　　現在完成式表示到現在的時間為止，已經完成的動作或經驗。
　　現在完成進行式則是表示到現在仍在進行的動作。
　　兩者後面都可以用 for 或 since 表示持續多久的時間，只是在意義上有點不同：

I have studied English for three hours.（我已經念了三個小時的英文。）
→ 但是現在我沒有要繼續念英文。

I have been studying English for three hours.（我已經念了三個小時的英文。）
→ 但是我現在還正在念英文。

⑶ 未來完成進行式

　　未來完成進行式，表示從過去的時間開始，持續到未來某個時刻且仍然持續的動作。和未來完成式一樣，未來完成進行式常常在會句子中加入「by + 時間點」或是 by the time 表示未來的某時，例如：

By 2014, I will have been living here for four years.
（到了 2014 年，我在這裡就住了四年了。）

⑷ 完成進行式的否定句

　　完成進行式的否定句，只要在 had、have、has 後面加 not 即可，若是未來完成進行式，not 要放在助動詞 will 的後面，例如：

I won't have been reading the newspaper for too long by the lunch time.
（到了午餐時間，我不會花太久的時間閱讀報紙。）

⑸ 完成進行式的問句

　　只要將 had、have、has 放在句首，最後的標點符號改成問號，就可以構成完成進行式的問句，同樣地，未來完成進行式的問句，是要將助動詞 will 做變化，將 will 移到句首。

　　若有疑問詞，則將疑問詞放在 have 的前面，例如：

How long have you been waiting here?（你在這裡等了多久了？）

・換你試試看，把兩個句子用完成進行式合併！

1. They are waiting for Nancy.
   They started waiting 10 minutes ago.
2. Daniel is working in the company.
   He started working there since February.

· 你完成了嗎？

　1.　They have been waiting for Nancy for 10 minutes.

　2.　Daniel has been working in the company since February.

· 換你試試看，劃線部分是什麼時態呢？

　1.　Joyce has been studying English for three years.

　2.　I am singing.

　3.　Gina gets up at six o' clock.

　4.　I saw Eliza who was jogging in the park last night.

　5.　She had made the cookie before she went to work.

　6.　While Helen was waiting in front of the shop, she noticed a new restaurant.

　7.　Winnie will go to America this summer.

　8.　Albert is going to buy a new video game.

　9.　Have you finished your report yet?

　10.The child has been asking his teacher questions.

· 你答對了嗎？

　1.　Joyce has been studying English for three years.
　　　→ 現在完成進行式。

　2.　I am singing.
　　　→ 現在進行式。

　3.　Gina gets up at six o' clock.
　　　→ 現在簡單式。

　4.　I saw Eliza who was jogging in the park last night.
　　　→ 過去簡單式；過去進行式。

　5.　She had made the cookie before she went to work.
　　　→ 過去完成式；過去式。

　6.　While Helen was waiting in front of the shop, she noticed a new restaurant.
　　　→ 過去進行式；過去式。

　7.　Winnie will go to America this summer.
　　　→ 未來簡單式。

　8.　Albert is going to buy a new video game.
　　　→ 現在進行式。

9. <u>Have</u> you <u>finished</u> your report yet?

　→ 現在完成式。

10.The child <u>has been asking</u> his teacher questions.

　→ 現在完成進行式。

三、文法糾正篇：常常混淆的時態句型

> 1. have been to＝曾經去過…
>
> 　 have gone to＝已經去了…

　　have been to 表示曾經去過某地的經驗，have gone to 則是表示某人已經去了某地，，因此，have gone to 前面的人稱只有第三人稱是合理的，例如：

I <u>have been to</u> Japan.（我曾經去過日本。）→（ O ）

I <u>have gone to</u> Japan.（我已經去了日本。）

→ (X)不合理，「我」不可能同時去日本，同時也在這裡說話。

He <u>has been to</u> Japan.（他曾經去過日本。）→（ O ）

He <u>has gone to</u> Japan.（他已經去了日本。）→（ O ）

·換你試試看，把情況換句話說！

1. Jason has ever gone to Japan for three times.

2. Steven went to America six days ago.

3. I have never gone to Thailand before.

4. David is in Italia now.

·你寫對了嗎？

1. Jason has ever gone to Japan for three times.

　→ <u>Jason has been to Japan for three times.</u>

2. Steven went to America six days ago.

　→ <u>Steven has gone to America since six days ago.</u>

3. I have never gone to Thailand before.

    → I have never been to Thailand before.

4. David is in Italia now.

    → David has gone to Italia.

---

2. 主詞+ used to + 動詞原形 = 過去習慣…

   主詞+ be used to + 動詞 ing =現在習慣…

這個句型很容易產生混淆，如果沒有加上 be 動詞的 used to 後面動詞要使用原形動詞，表示過去習慣做某事，但現在已經沒有這個習慣；有加 be 動詞的 used to 後面動詞要使用動名詞，強調現在仍然習慣，例如：

He used to go to work by the MRT.（他之前習慣搭捷運上班。）

He is used to going to work by the MRT.（他現在習慣搭捷運上班。）

· 換你試試看，利用單詞練習兩種句型！

1. I / drink a cup of coffee / every morning

2. He / read / after dinner

3. They / play tennis / on Thursday

· 是不是很簡單呢？

1. I / drink a cup of coffee / every morning

    →（過去習慣）I used to drink a cup of coffee every morning.

    →（現在習慣）I am used to drinking a cup of coffee every morning.

2. He / read / after dinner

    →（過去習慣）He used to read after dinner.

    →（現在習慣）He is used to reading after dinner.

3. They / play tennis / on Thursday

    →（過去習慣）They used to play tennis on Thursdays.

    →（現在習慣）They are used to playing tennis on Thursdays.

3. have 和 think 的進行式

　　have 和 think 用於簡單式和進行式中，所表達的意思不同。

　　have 若表示「擁有」，是屬於表示狀態的動詞，不可以有進行式的型態。但若作「享用、吃」，則可以有進行式。例如：

I am having lunch now.（我現在正在吃午餐。）

　　think 可以表示「認為、想」。若作「認為」解釋，表示的是心裡長期的想法，不可以有進行式，相反地，若表示「想」，則可以有進行式。

I think she is pretty.（我認為她很漂亮。）→ 心裡長期的想法
Be quiet! I am thinking.（安靜！我正在思考。）→ 現在正在做的動作

4. just 和 just now 的誤用

　　just 可以用於完成式中，表示「剛剛完成」，但 just now 卻只能接過去式，表示「剛才」。兩者在中文的意思上差不多，但英文的語法上卻不同。試比較下列兩句：

I have just finished my work.（我剛剛完成工作。）
→ just 強調剛剛做完的動作。

I finished my work just now.（我剛剛才做完工作。）
→ just now 是強調剛剛做完的時間

5. 不能用在完成式的時間副詞

　　可以明確表示時間的副詞，不能用在現在完成式，例如: last month、yesterday、this morning 等，只能用過去式。

　　同樣的道理，詢問某特定時間點的 when 和 what time 也不能使用於完成式句型。

　　但是，如果在特定的時間點前加上 since，便可以用完成式：

I have drunk three cups of coffee <u>since</u> this morning.
（從早上以來，我已經喝了三杯咖啡。）

6. 不能使用進行式的動詞

有些動詞不能使用進行式，這些動詞通常具有「繼續」的涵義，或是表示狀態、心理情感及知覺，例如：exist（存在）、own（擁有）、need（需要）、prefer（比較喜歡）、hear（聽）、see（看）、forget（忘記）、remember（記得）、belong（屬於）、like（喜歡）、love（愛）、hate（恨）、know（知道）和 want（想要）。以 want 為例：

I <u>want</u> a toy car.（我想要一台玩具車。）→*(O)*

I <u>am wanting</u> a toy car. →*(X)*

雖然「現在想要」，但 want 是屬於心理情感欲望的動詞，所以沒有進行式的形態。

7. be going to 和 be 動詞 + V-ing 的混淆

I <u>am going</u> to school.（我正要去學校。）
→ go 是動詞，am going 是現在進行式。

I <u>am going</u> to go to school.（我將要去學校。）
→ be going to 等於 will，後面的 go 才是這個句子的動詞。

談論到未來確定會發生的活動或事件時，可以用現在進行式代替未來式，但是記得後面要接有未來的時間，否則句子的意思會不一樣。

・換你試試看，這個句子寫錯了嗎？

1. I have eaten an apple pie just now.
2. The apple pie makes me thirsty.
3. I am wanting to have some tea.
4. Eric is going to visit Johnson this Friday.

5. They haven't met each other last month.

6. They will play basketball on Friday.

7. They are liking spend time getting along each other.

8. Bob has just finished his homework.

9. He wants to play the computer game.

10. He's owning this computer.

11. His dad has bought him this computer 2 months ago.

・你找到了嗎？

1. I have eaten an apple pie just now.

　→ just now 和完成式不能一起使用，此句應改成 I have just eaten an apple.

2. The apple pie makes me thirsty. → (O)

3. I am wanting to have some tea.

　→ want 不能使用進行式，本句應改成 I want to have some tea.

4. Eric is going to visit Johnson this Friday. → (O)

5. They haven't met each other last month.

　→ last month 若和完成式一起使用，應加上 since，本句應寫成 They haven't met each other since last month.

6. They will play basketball on Friday. → (O)

7. They are liking spend time getting along each other.

　→ like 不能使用進行式，應將此句改寫為 They like to spend time getting together.

8. Bob has just finished his homework. → (O)

9. He wants to play the computer game. → (O)

10. He's owning this computer.

　→ own 不能使用進行式，本句正確寫法為 He owns this computer.

11. His dad has bought him this computer 2 months ago. → (O)

O2
CHAPTER
名詞和動詞

一、概念篇

‖ 名詞 ‖

什麼是名詞

名詞在句子中，扮演主詞、受詞或補語的角色。

　　名詞涵蓋的範圍很廣，可以細分成普通名詞、專有名詞、抽象名詞、物質名詞、集合名詞等等，當然也有可以代替上述名詞的代名詞，就連動詞也可以經由改變後成為動名詞。這麼多類型的名詞，聽起來似乎很嚇人，但其實都是我們生活中時常接觸到的。

名詞的總類	
(1) 普通名詞	cat、dog、room、school、coat、hour、man、book 等
(2) 集合名詞	group、family、enemy、public、herd、media、team 等
(3) 專有名詞	March、Taiwan、Monday、Renaissance、Christian 等
(4) 物質名詞	beer、coffee、poison、iron、soup、wool、wood 等
(5) 抽象名詞	wisdom、knowledge、happiness、freedom、courage 等
(6) 代名詞	I、you、he、she、it、this、that、who、oneself 等

(1) 普通名詞

一般普通的物件，稱為普通名詞。

(2) 集合名詞

集合名詞是對某種類型的統稱，以 bread 為例，麵包的種類很多：土司麵包、法國吐司、紅豆麵包…等不勝枚舉，但是我們在句子描述中不可能一一列舉出來，便用一個統稱的字代替全部。

使用集體名詞做主詞時，動詞用單數形和複數形的意思略有不同；如果將某個群體視為整體，動詞應該用單數，但若將之視為整體中的若干個體，則動詞可以用複數形，例如：

My family has its own farm.（我家有自己的農場。）
→ 用單數動詞表示整體。

My family are all nearsighted.（我的家人都近視。）
→ 用複數表示群體中的個體。

有時，將 the 加上形容詞，也可以表示特定的人群、抽象概念或是任何事物。例如: the poor（窮人）、the wrong（錯誤）或是 the blue（藍天）。

(3) 專有名詞

專門稱地名、人名、事件或名稱的用語，這類名詞的第一個字母都是大寫。

(4) 物質名詞

能表示出物體特質或材質，稱為物質名詞。

(5) 抽象名詞

舉凡抽象的概念，例如…等沒有具體形象，只是表達一種概念的語詞，就叫做抽象名詞。

(6) 代名詞

代名詞，即**代替名**詞的**詞**。在和別人聊天時，我們會時常省略句子中重複出現的字眼，改用代名詞代替。代名詞又可以分成：

代名詞的種類	
人稱代名詞	I、you、he、she、it、we、you、they 等
指示代名詞	this、that、these、those 等
疑問代名詞	who、which、what、whose、whom 等
不定代名詞	one、some、someone、nobody、anyone 等
關係代名詞	who、that、which、whom、whose 等
反身代名詞	myself、yourself、himself、herself、itself、ourselves、yourselves、themselves

什麼是名詞片語和名詞子句？

名詞片語的形態是＜疑問詞＋不定詞＞。

名詞子句多為 that、疑問詞做為開頭的句子，例如：

How to be a good teacher is very important.（如何當個好老師非常重要。）
→ How to be a good teacher 為名詞片語。

She is the one who I love.（她是那個我深愛的人。）
→ who I love 為名詞子句。

什麼是動名詞？

　　有時在閱讀文章時，會發現教科書都把主詞講的很簡單，就像是只有一個簡單的詞彙，但在文章裡卻可能是好幾個字構成的，也有可能是看起來像是動詞或是形容詞的字。其實這樣的情形在中文也很常發生。比如說，「唱歌是我最喜歡的事。」這個句子想表達「唱歌」這件事是「我」最喜歡做的事，並且把唱歌這件事簡化為「唱歌」兩字。唱歌原本也是動作，卻在這裡變成了代表唱歌這件事的概念。

　　英文裡，只要在動作後面加上 ing，就可以代表動作所指涉的事，文法概念裡稱為動名詞，即是將動作轉化成名詞，具有名詞的功能。例如，唱歌的英文是 sing，於其後加上 ing，變成 singing，指唱歌這件事。

　　因此，我們可以說，動名詞是由代表某種動作涵義的語詞，具有名詞的功用，可以做句子中的主詞、受詞和補語。

容易和動名詞混淆的，叫做現在分詞。現在分詞也寫作 V-ing 的型態，具有形容詞的功能，可以用來修飾名詞。例如，a running rabbit（一隻正在奔跑的兔子）。但是，動名詞有時也會被用來修飾名詞。試比較下列兩者：

a sleeping baby（一個正在睡覺的嬰兒）
→ 用於修飾嬰兒的 sleeping，是現在分詞，表示被修飾名詞的狀態。

a sleeping bag（一個睡袋）
→ 用於修飾 bag 的 sleeping，是動名詞，表示被修飾名詞的用途。

在句子中，如果出現連續兩個動詞，我們會在兩個動詞之間加 to，或是將第二個動詞轉變為動名詞。但是，有些動詞後面一定要加動名詞，這些動詞常見的有：
Finish（結束）、practice（練習）、enjoy（享受）、quit（戒除）、mind（介意）、spend（花費）、avoid（避免）、complete（完成）、give up（戒絕），例如：

Tom finished doing his homework.（*Tom* 完成了他的功課。）
→ finish 後面的動詞 do 要轉變為動名詞的形式。

Jack tries to give up drinking.（*Jack* 試著要戒酒。）
→ give up 後面加動名詞 drinking。

什麼是不定詞？
動詞轉化成名詞，還有另一種方式，就是在動詞前面加上 to，構成不定詞，也可以表示動詞所指涉的事，可以在句子中扮演主詞、受詞或補語的角色。
不定詞最常見的表達方式為＜to ＋ 原形動詞＞，主要用來表示目的，例如：

He wants to eat a hamburger.（他想要吃一個漢堡。）
→ to eat 是不定詞，扮演名詞的角色做為動作 want 的受詞，亦表示出最終的目的是 eat。

句子中若有兩個動詞相連，一定要將動詞做變化。有些動詞只能接續不定詞，常見的有: agree（同意）、decide（決定）、except（反對）、wish（希望）、hope（希望）、ask（詢問）、appear（顯現）、arrange（安排）、beg（請求）、claim（主張）、choose（選擇）、desire（要求）、dare（膽敢）、expect（盼望）、happen（碰巧）、learn（學習）等，而 want（想要）和 need（需要）這兩個字在大部分句子中，都接續不定詞，若接續動名詞，則帶有被動的涵義。在稍後的好學句型中，我們會針對這兩個字進行探討。

不定詞的否定變化和一般句子的否定變化很容易產生混淆。試比較下列句子：

My mom didn't ask me to do the dishes.（我媽媽沒有要求我洗碗。）
My mom asked me not to do the dishes.（我媽媽要求我不要洗碗。）
→ 如果要表示不定詞的否定，應將表示否定的 not 置於不定詞前。

名詞怎麼變成複數形？
名詞的複數形可以分為規則和不規則兩種。

名詞的複數形	
⑴ 直接 + s	cats、dogs、books、pencils、movies 等
⑵ 結尾是 s、ss、sh、ch、x、o，+ es	buses、glasses、brushes、watches、boxes、mangoes 等
⑶ 子音加 y，- y + ies	babies、flies、cities 等
⑷ 母音加 y，直接 + s	toys、keys、boys 等
⑸ 字尾是 f 或 fe，去 f 或 fe + ves	leaves、knives、wives 等

不規則複數名詞雖然稱為不規則，但可以區分為三種類型：

不規則複數名詞		
(1) 母音改變	man → men woman → women tooth → teeth goose → geese	mouse → mice foot → feet louse → lice cactus → cacti
(2) 字尾加上 en 或 ren	ox → oxen	child → children
(3) 單複數同形	deer	sheep
	結尾為 ese，表示人的名詞，例如 Taiwanese	
	數量 + hundred、thousand、million 等	

可數名詞使用單數的時候，前面要有冠詞 a、an 或 the。有些單數名詞和 the 一起使用，可以表示某件獨特的事物，例如 the sun（太陽）、the moon（月亮）。

· 換你試試看，練習名詞的複數變化！

1. bus
2. walrus
3. elephant
4. dress
5. mango
6. mouse
7. tooth
8. knife
9. witch
10. lady
11. child
12. monkey

· 你完成了嗎？

1. bus → buses
2. walrus → walruses
3. elephant → elephants
4. dress → dresses
5. mango → mangoes
6. mouse → mice
7. tooth → teeth
8. knife → knives
9. witch → witches
10. lady → ladies
11. child → children
12. monkey → monkeys

怎麼表達名詞的數量？

表達名詞數量的方法，可以大致分為兩種，一種是表達數量的多寡程度，另一種使用不同的量詞做為單位詞。

表達數量的多寡程度		
	可數名詞	不可數名詞
一些	a few、some	a little、some
很少	few	little
不夠	not enough	not enough
很多	many、a lot of	much、a lot of
太多	too many	too much

使用量詞做為單位詞時，後面銜接的語詞多為表示物質的名詞或是和食物有關的名詞。

量詞做為單位詞	
＋表示物質的名詞	a piece of paper a bottle of water a sheet of snow
＋表示食物的名詞	a cup of tea a packet of potato chips a loaf of bread

當我們使用量詞做為單位詞時，後面可以接可數名詞或不可數名詞。若想要改變量詞的數量，要記得量詞本身要做複數的變化，例如：

I would like a cup of coffee.（我想要一杯咖啡。）
→ 單數不用變化。

We would like two cups of coffee.（我們想要兩杯咖啡。）
→ 兩杯以上單位詞要變為複數。

· 換你試試看，這句英文怎麼說？

1. 我有很多朋友。
2. Jimmy 的朋友很少。
3. Mandy 沒有很多錢。
4. 請給我一些牛奶。
5. 罐子裡只有一點點果醬。
6. 請給我一瓶柳橙汁。
7. 桌子上的湯匙太多了。
8. 教室裡的椅子不夠。
9. 碗裡面的冰淇淋不夠。
10.瓶子裡的水太多了。

· 你寫對了嗎？

1. 我有很多朋友。

   I have many / a lot of friends.

2. Jimmy 的朋友很少。

   Jimmy has few friends.

3. Mandy 沒有很多錢。

   Mandy doesn't have much money.

4. 請給我一些牛奶。

   I would like some milk, please.

5. 罐子裡只有一點點果醬。

   There is little jam in the jar.

6. 請給我一瓶柳橙汁。

   Please give me a bottle of orange juice.

7. 桌子上的湯匙太多了。

   There are too many spoons on the table.

8. 教室裡的椅子不夠。

   There are not enough chairs in the classroom.

9. 碗裡面的冰淇淋不夠。

   There is not enough ice cream in the bowl.

10.瓶子裡的水太多了。

   There is too much water in the bottle.

01 CHAPTER
02 CHAPTER
03 CHAPTER
04 CHAPTER
05 CHAPTER
06 CHAPTER
07 CHAPTER
08 CHAPTER
09 CHAPTER
10 CHAPTER

你有沒有發現，not enough 雖然可以用在可數名詞和不可數名詞，但可數名詞要使用複數形，同時，動詞也要跟著做變化。

名詞的所有格

名詞的所有格主要分為兩種：

名詞的所有格		
人或動物	字尾 +'s	Sally's、cat's、children's
	字尾 s 或 es +'	girls'、ladies'
無生命的物體 of 擁有者		the pencil of Steve the mouth of Eric

雖然我們習慣用 of 表示無生命物體的所有格，但也有例外的情況，例如和時間或價值相關時，一般會使用's：today's news（今日新聞）、forty minutes'class（四十分鐘的課）、two week's vacation（兩星期的假期）、one dollar's worth（一塊錢的價值）等。

‖ 動詞 ‖

什麼是動詞

看看下面這個句子，你可以找出動詞嗎？

Mary walks.（*Mary* 散步。）

沒錯，walk 這個動作就是動詞。動詞在一個句子中，扮演表達主詞動作或狀態的角色，更重要的是，可以表現出句子發生的時間，也就是「時態」，可以說是句子裡重要的靈魂人物。

動詞的種類

動詞根據用途和表達方式的不同，可以區分為七種類別：

動詞的種類	
⑴ be 動詞	be、am、are、is、was、were、been、being
⑵ 一般動詞	walk、run、eat、write、sweep、mop 等
⑶ 連綴動詞	look、sound、taste、smell、feel、become、get、appear 等
⑷ 助動詞	do、does、did、will、have、may、would、should 等
⑸ 授與動詞	give、bring、write、pass、send、show 等
⑹ 感官動詞	look at、see、watch、smell、listen to、hear 等
⑺ 使役動詞	make、let、have

⑴ be 動詞

　　be 動詞可以表示主詞呈現於某種狀態中的情況：

I am a teacher.（我是一位老師。）
→「我」和「老師」指的都是自己，也是表示自己的身分。

　　在這樣的句子中，be 動詞扮演的是使主詞等於受詞的角色。
　　如果將 be 動詞加上動詞 ing，代表時態中的現在進行式，表示主詞正在做某件事：

I am going to the theater.（我正要去電影院。）

⑵ 一般動詞

　　一般動詞又分為及物動詞與不及物動詞。不及物動詞的概念是，其後不用加上受詞。不及物動詞後面沒有受詞，句意也可以完整表達。例如：

I walk.（我散步。）
→ 散步本身就是完整的動作，不需要一定要在後面加上受詞。

及物動詞，顧名思義，動詞後面還要加上受詞句意才會完整。例如：

Mary takes.（*Mary* 拿。）
→ take 什麼東西沒有交代清楚

上述句子中，應於 take 後加上拿的東西語意才完整，可以判斷 take 為及物動詞。這句在 take 後面加上受詞才是完整的句子：

Mary takes a shower.（*Mary* 沖澡。）

我們可以藉由其他語詞幫忙，讓這句話的意思更加豐富，也可以透露更多資訊。

Mary takes a shower in the morning every day.（*Mary* 每天早上沖澡。）
→ in the morning every day 即便從句子中刪去，也不影響結構，但卻讓整個句子的意思更加完整。

及物動詞又可以再細分為完全及物動詞和不完全及物動詞。
完全及物動詞只要後面有受詞，就可以構成完整的句子，但不完全及物動詞還需要有補充受詞狀態的受詞補語才能使句子清楚。試比較下列兩個句子：

Mary takes a shower.（*Mary* 沖澡。）
→ take 後面加上受詞 a shower，語意完整。

Mary named her dog.（*Mary* 幫她的小狗取名為。）
→ dog 是 name 的受詞，Mary 幫小狗取名，但我們不知道取什麼。

Mary named her dog Poppy.（*Mary* 幫她的小狗取名為 *Poppy*。）
→ Poppy 是補充說明 dog，為受詞補語。

上述句子中，name 後面要加受詞，是及物動詞，但要再加入 Poppy 之後，整個句子的意思才可以清楚表達，所以 name 是不完全及物動詞。

(3) 連綴動詞

連綴動詞真正要描述的是主詞，而不是強調動詞本身的動作，所以連綴動詞本身雖有意義，但並不完整，應於後面加形容詞或名詞，作為修飾主詞的補語。

The coffee smells.（咖啡聞起來。）
→ 只有動作 smell，語意不完整。

The coffee smells great.（咖啡聞起來好香。）
→ smell 後加上形容詞修飾，語意完整。

連綴動詞後若要接名詞，中間要加入 like，例如：

This soap smells like an apple.（這塊肥皂聞起來像蘋果。）

有些動詞可以同時當一般動詞和連綴動詞，試比較下面的句子：

Willie suddenly appeared in the classroom.（*Willie* 突然出現在教室。）
→ appear 做一般動詞使用，表示「出現」。

It appeared impossible.（這似乎不太可能。）
→ appear 做連綴動詞使用，表示「似乎」。

判斷動詞是否為連綴動詞，可以用 be 動詞代換看看，如果可以用 be 動詞代換，這個動詞就是連綴動詞。

become（變成）和 get（變成）也屬於連綴動詞。我們習慣將這兩個字用現在進行式的句型表達，表示「漸漸變成⋯」。

This cup of coffee is getting cold.（這杯咖啡漸漸冷掉了。）

(4) 助動詞

用來協助動詞作時態或語氣變化的語詞，稱為助動詞。

助動詞常常被用來輔助疑問句或否定句的形成，例如：

Do you want a cup of tea?（你想要一杯咖啡嗎？）

I *don't want to go to school.*（我不想要去學校。）

do 是最常見的助動詞，根據人稱和時態的不同，要作適當的變化：第三人稱單數 does、過去式 did。

還有一種助動詞稱為情態助動詞，這類助動詞有：

情態助動詞	
表示確定性	must、will、shall、would、need
不確定的可能	may、should、ought to
較小的可能	could、might
理論或習慣上的可能	can

通常，助動詞後面加上原形動詞，不會銜接不定詞，遇到第三人稱單數時，助動詞也不用做任何變化，例如：

She will go hiking.（她將要去健行。）
will 後面直接加原形動詞 go，而不是不定詞 to go。

She ought to study hard.（她應該要認真念書。）
→ ought to 是唯一後面加上不定詞的例外。

這些助動詞除了具有輔助動詞的文法功能外，本身也可以是一般動詞，具備某種語意，例如 need，可以是一般動詞的「需要」，也可以是助動詞的「必須」，例如：

You needn't do the dishes.（你不需要洗碗。）
→ need 做助動詞使用。

You need to water the garden.（你該去花園裡澆花了。）
→ need 做一般動詞使用，可以銜接不定詞。

(5) 授與動詞

　　我們在句型的章節中有提到，有些動詞後面會先加間接受詞，才加直接受詞，這類的動詞因為具有「給予」的涵義，稱為授與動詞。這些動詞常見的有：bring（帶來）、buy（買）、give（給）、leave（留下）、read（閱讀）、show（展示）、take（拿取）、send（寄送）、write（寫）、make（製作）、pass（傳遞）等。

(6) 感官動詞

　　這類動詞包含 look at（看著）、see（看）、watch（看）、hear（聽）、listen to（聽著）、smell（聞）、feel（感覺）、notice（注意到）、observe（注意到）等和感官動作相關的動詞。

　　一般而言，接續在感官動詞後面的動詞形態有兩種，一種是原形動詞，另一種是現在分詞。兩者的差別在於，銜接原形動詞表示當主詞聽見或看見某件事發生的完整過程，而銜接現在分詞則強調主詞聽見或看見某件事正在發生的狀態，例如：

Jimmy saw May eat an ice cream cone.（*Jimmy* 看到 *May* 吃冰淇淋甜筒。）
→ 用原形動詞比較強調動作發生的事實。

Jimmy saw May eating an ice cream cone.
（*Jimmy* 看到 *May* 時，*May* 正在吃冰淇淋甜筒。）
→ 用現在分詞比較強調正在發生的動作。

(7) 使役動詞

　　使役動詞用於命令、要求的語氣。這類的動詞有: make（使）、let（讓）、have（使）和 get（使）。在使役動詞後面，要先接受詞，才接被命令的動作，同時，這個動詞要使用原形。例如:

My mom made me sweep the floor.（我媽媽叫我掃地。）
→ 使役動詞 make 先接受詞 me，後面的動詞 sweep 要用原形。

使役動詞的句型很容易和不定詞句型混淆，要特別小心。試比較下列兩句:

My mom made me sweep the floor.（我媽媽叫我掃地。）

My mom asked me to sweep the floor.（我媽媽要求我掃地。）

→ ask 並非使役動詞，所以當後面要接續 sweep 時，要用 to 將兩個動詞隔開。

· 換你試試看，這個句子用了什麼動詞？

1. His dad is so proud to have him study abroad.
2. Ivan is looking at the caterpillar crawling on the ground.
3. It seems amazing!
4. May is running on the playground.
5. Mom read my little brother a fairy tale.
6. Miss Yang is tall and thin.
7. I can play the drum well.

· 你判斷對了嗎？

1. His dad is so proud to have him study abroad. → 使役動詞
2. Ivan is looking at the caterpillar crawling on the ground. → 感官動詞
3. It seems amazing! → 連綴動詞
4. May is running on the playground. → 一般動詞
5. Mom read my little brother a fairy tale. → 授與動詞
6. Miss Yang is tall and thin. → be 動詞
7. I can play the drum well. → 助動詞

什麼是動詞片語和片語動詞？

動詞片語的型態為＜助動詞／副詞＋動詞＋受詞＞

I will go to school.（我將要去上學。）

→ will go to school 為動詞片語。

片語動詞指的是＜動詞＋介係詞或是副詞＞，本身具有意義，例如 pick up（拾起），有些片語動詞甚至不只一個意思，例如 get on（穿上、上車、應付）。

大部分的片語動詞可以將受詞放置於兩字中間或是片語後面，若受詞為代名詞只能放在兩個字之中：

I take the trash out.（我倒垃圾。）
= *I take out the trash.*
= *I take it out.*

有些片語動詞則不行被分離，不論名詞或代名詞都要放在後面：

I get on the bus. = I get on it.（我搭公車。）→ *(O)*
I get the bus on. → *(X)*
I get it on. → *(X)*

動詞怎麼變化？
　　動詞的變化形有：原形、第三人稱單數現在式、現在分詞、過去式和過去分詞。

⑴ 原形
　　為動詞的基本形式，沒有做任何的變化，例如：have（擁有）、make（製作）、sing（唱歌）等動詞。

⑵ 第三人稱單數現在式
　　第三人稱單數包含 he、she 和 it。只要主詞為這三個代名詞所指涉的人事物，其動詞都要變化。將動詞字尾加 s 即可，有些動詞結尾為 sh 或 ch，字尾加 es。
　　例如：make → makes（製作）、sing → sings（唱歌）、wash → washes（洗）、watch → watches（看）。

⑶ 現在分詞
　　將動詞轉化為現在分詞的方式有五種：
　　直接加 ing，例如：walk → walking（走路）
　　動詞結尾是 e 去 e 加 ing，例如：make → making（製作）
　　動詞結尾為子音加母音加子音，重複子音加 ing，例如：run → running（跑）
　　動詞結尾為母音加 y，直接加 ing，例如：play → playing（玩）
　　動詞結尾為 ie，去 ie 加 ying，例如：lie → lying（說謊、躺）

(4) 過去式

過去式為動詞的過去時態，分為規則動詞和不規則動詞。

將規則動詞轉化為過去式的方式有三種：

動詞結尾加 ed，例如：walk → walked

動詞結尾是 e，則直接加 d，例如：like → liked

動詞結尾是 y，則去 y 加 ied，例如：study → studied

(5) 過去分詞

過去分詞多用於被動語態和完成式句型。一般而言，將動詞後面加上 ed 即可構成過去分詞，有些動詞為不規則變化。

不規則動詞中，過去式和過去分詞的變化，可以歸類為四種類型：

ABC 型：即原形、過去式、過去分詞皆不同，例如 begin-began-begun（開始）。

ABB 型：即過去式和過去分詞相同，例如 find- found- found（找到）。

ABA 型：即原形和過去分詞相同，例如 run- ran- run（跑）。

AAA 型：即三態皆相同，例如 cost- cost- cost（花費）。

二、好學好用的句型

和名詞相關的句型

---

1. One … and the other … ＝一個… 而另一個…。

One …, another…, and the other … ＝一個…，一個…，另一個…。

例如：

Ivy has two sisters, one is a nurse and the other is a waitress.

（*Ivy* 有兩個姊姊，一個是護士，另一個是服務生。）

Steven has three cats, one is brown, another is black and the other is gray.

（*Steven* 有三隻貓，一隻是咖啡色的，一隻是黑色的，一隻是灰色的。）

　　這個句型也可以改為複數形＜some…and the others＞，若是有三者以上，可以改為＜some…others…and the others＞，例如：

There are many students in the classroom; <u>some</u> have black hair <u>and the others</u> have blonde hair.
（教室裡有很多學生，他們的頭髮有一些是黑色，另一些則是金色的。）

There are many students in the classroom; <u>some</u> have short hair, <u>others</u> have long hair <u>and the others</u> have curly hair.
（教室裡有很多學生，有些人是短髮，有些是長髮，還有一些的頭髮是捲的。）

　　也可以用 some of 來表示某群體中的一些：

<u>Some of these students</u> are from America, <u>others</u> are from Japan <u>and the others</u> are from China.
（這些學生有些來自美國，有些來自日本，另外一些來自中國。）

・我們可以這樣說
　　我們可以利用這個句型來向別人介紹自己的家人，如果你有兩個哥哥，你可以說：
I have two brothers. One lives in Tainan and the other lives in America.
（我有兩個哥哥，一個住在台南，一個住在美國。）

・換你試試看，寫出完整的句子！
1. There are three erasers in my pencil box, red / white / black.
2. Kitty has two books, novel / comic book.
3. There are ten children playing on the playground, play badminton / jump rope.

・你完成了嗎？
1. There are three erasers in my pencil box, <u>one is red, another is white and the other is black.</u>
2. Kitty has two books. <u>One is a novel and the other is a comic book.</u>

3. There are ten children playing on the playground. <u>Some of these children are playing badminton and the others are jumping rope.</u>

---

2. by oneself＝某人自己…

on one's own

---

by oneself 可以有兩種中文涵義，一種是表示某人自己獨力完成某件事，另一種則強調獨自一個人的意味，例如：

I made these cookies by myself.
= I made these cookies on my own.
（我自己獨力做完這些餅乾。）

I would like to <u>be by myself</u> for ten minutes.（我需要獨處十分鐘。）

這個句型時常和 of one's own 與 for oneself 混淆，of one's own 表示「屬於某人自己的…」，而 for oneself 表示「為了某人自己…」，例如：

There is a sport car <u>of my own</u>.（這是屬於我自己的跑車。）

You need to work hard <u>for yourself</u>.（為了你自己好，認真工作吧。）

・我們可以這樣說

如果同事被交付重要的任務，但卻沒有自信將工作完成，我們可以鼓勵地說：

You can do it by yourself!（你可以靠自己的力量完成的！）

・換你試試看，填入適當的反身代名詞！

1. Amanda finished washing the car by ＿＿＿＿＿＿.
2. Sam made this birthday by ＿＿＿＿＿＿.
3. I try to make dinner by ＿＿＿＿＿＿.
4. Nancy and Anna painted the wall of their bathroom by ＿＿＿＿＿＿.

・你寫對了嗎？

1. Amanda finished washing the car by <u>herself</u>.
2. Sam made this birthday by <u>himself</u>.
3. I try to make dinner by <u>myself</u>.
4. Nancy and Anna painted the wall of their bathroom by <u>themselves</u>.

---

3. 名詞 (1) is one thing, and 名詞 (2) is another. ＝…一回事，…又是另一回事。

例如：

To know is one thing, <u>to do</u> is another.（知道是一回事，做又是另一回事。）
→ 不定詞可以當作名詞使用。

・我們可以這樣說

　　當好朋友被戀愛沖昏了頭，不顧一切都要結婚時，我們除了表示恭喜，也要稍微提醒好友：

To be in love is one thing, to get married is another.
（談戀愛是一回事，結婚又是另一回事。）

・換你試試看，可以怎麼說？

1. see / believe
2. have a chat with foreigners / write an English essay
3. make money / save money

・你說對了嗎？

1. To see is one thing, to believe is another.
2. To have a chat with foreigner is one thing, to write an English essay is another.
3. To make money is one thing, to save money is another.

和動名詞相關的句型

---

4. 特定動詞＋動名詞

有些特定的動詞後面的動詞要變化為動名詞，這類的動詞常見的有：practice（練習）、finish（結束）、allow（同意）、keep（保持）、quit（戒除）、regret（遺憾）、mind（介意）、enjoy（享受）、avoid（避免）、consider（思考）、suggest（建議）等，例如：

Tom decides to quit drinking coffee.（*Tom* 決定戒掉喝咖啡的習慣。）
→ quit 後面的動詞要加 ing。

動名詞的主詞和句子的助詞不同時，可以在動名詞前加上所有格或受詞：

I appreciate his / him helping those students.
（我很感謝他對於那些學生的幫助。）
→ 用所有格或受詞表示動名詞的主詞。

想要寫成否定句時，只要在動名詞前面加 not 即可，例如：

The consulter suggested us not putting all eggs in the same basket.
（顧問建議我們不要把雞蛋都放在同一個籃子裡。）

· 換你試試看，試著造句！

1. Nancy / enjoy / read / detective novel
2. Do / you / practice / play the piano / every day
3. I / can't imagine / he / lie to me
4. You / not allow / smoke / in the lobby

· 你寫對了嗎？

1. Nancy enjoys reading detective novels.
2. Do you practice playing the piano every day?
3. I can't imagine his / him lying to me.
4. You are not allowed smoking in the lobby.

5. 接動名詞卻表示被動的動詞

　　大部分銜接動名詞的動詞，都帶有主動的意味，然而，有些動詞卻帶有被動的意涵，這些動詞有 need、want、require，例如：

The plants need watering.（這盆植物需要澆水了。）
→ need 加動名詞，表示被動。

這個句子也可以用不定詞改寫，一樣具有被動的涵義：

The plants need to be watered.

・我們可以這樣說

　　在辦公室處理文書相關的工作，很多時候都要用到影印機，但影印機卻常常在緊要關頭的時候卡紙，我們可以說：

This copy machine is broken again! It needs fixing!
（這台影印機又壞了，需要維修！）

・換你試試看，用動名詞翻譯出下面的句子！

1. 嬰兒都需要被保護。
2. 這隻鉛筆需要削一削了。
3. 你的短褲很髒，它們需要洗一下。
4. 你提到的問題需要仔細考慮一下。

・是不是很簡單呢？

1. Babies need protecting.
2. The pencil requires sharpening.
3. Your shorts are dirty. They need washing.
4. The question you mentioned requires considering.

---

6. 主詞 have + fun / problem + 動名詞＝對做…感到愉快 / 困難

如果在 have 後面加上 fun 或 good time，表示愉快；若接 difficulty、problem、trouble 或 a hard time，則表示困難，例如：

Alex has fun playing video games with his sister.
（*Alex* 對於和他妹妹一起打電動感到很愉快。）

Alex has problem writing an English article.
（*Alex* 對於寫一篇英文文章感到困難。）

如果想要表達愉悅或困難的程度，可以在這些語詞前加上 a lot of、some、great 或 no，例如：

He has a lot of difficulties speaking English.
（他對於說英文感到非常困難。）

·我們可以這樣說

當上司要求我們向國外客戶進行簡報，為了在上司面前展現出自信心，可以說：

I have no difficulty doing this presentation!（做簡報絕對難不倒我！）

·換你試試看，改寫下面的句子！

1. Mr. Smith is stubborn. Mrs. Smith can't get along with him.
2. Sandra can't communicate with her mom.
3. Jeff has been to China. He was happy there.
4. The mechanic fixes the printer easily.

·你完成了嗎？

1. Mr. Smith is stubborn that Mrs. Smith has problem getting along with him.
2. Sandra has trouble communicating with her mom.
3. Jeff has good time touring around China.
4. The mechanic has no difficulty fixing the printer.

7. 和時間相關的動名詞句型
主詞 + take one's time + 動名詞＝慢慢做…
主詞 + lose no time in + 動名詞＝馬上做…
主詞 + waste / spend time (in) + 動名詞＝浪費 / 花費時間做…

例如：

Take your time reading this magazine.（你可以慢慢讀這本雜誌。）

When she saw the accident, she lost no time in calling the police.
（當她看到這起意外時，她馬上打電話給警察。）

· 我們可以這樣說
小朋友放假的時候，一直賴在沙發上看電視，實在非常浪費時間，我們可以說：

Don't waste your time lying on the sofa and watching TV.
（不要浪費時間躺在沙發上看電視。）

· 換你試試看，將句子做適當的變化！
1. The housewife takes her time _____(do) this housework.
2. The little boy lost no time in _____(clean) his room.
3. The teacher spent a lot of time _____(prepare) the class.

· 是不是很簡單呢？
1. The housewife takes her time <u>doing</u> this housework.
2. The little boy lost no time in <u>cleaning</u> his room.
3. The teacher spent a lot of time <u>preparing</u> the class.

8. 主詞 + can't help + 動名詞＝忍不住…；不得已只好…

這個句型表示「忍不住做…」，例如：

After knowing the end of this movie, she can't help crying.
（在知道電影的結局後，她忍不住哭了起來。）

這個句型也可以用＜主詞＋can't help＋but＋原形動詞＞來改寫：

After knowing the end of this movie, she can't help but cry.
→ 要記得 *but* 後面的動詞要使用原形動詞。

・我們可以這樣說

　　這個句型也可以用 it、oneself 或名詞代替動名詞，表示「管不住自己…」，例如當另一半問你「為什麼又花錢買衣服啦？」，你就可以回答：

I can't help it!（我就是忍不住！）

・換你試試看，這句英文怎麼說？

　1. Justin 不得已只好揮動拳頭保護自己。
　2. Bill 不得已只好向朋友借錢。
　3. 這位主管為了降低成本不得已只好開除一些員工。

・你寫對了嗎？

　1. Justin can't help waving his fist to defend himself.
　2. Bill can't help borrowing money from his friends.
　3. The manager can't help dismissing some workers to reduce the costs.

和不定詞相關的句型

---

9. It is + 形容詞＋不定詞＝做某事太過…

例如：

It is cold to swim in winter.（在冬天游泳太冷了。）

我們可以將不定詞帶領的語詞置於句首，使不定詞成為句子的主詞，例如：

To swim in winter is cold.

→ To swim in winter 是這句的主詞，表示「冬天游泳」這件事。原句 It is cold to swim in winter. 中的 It，是代替 to swim in winter 的虛主詞

如果要強調是某個人做某事，可以在形容詞後面加上 for 某人，但是如果形容詞是和人的態度個性有關，就要將 for 改成 of，例如：

It is cold for me to swim in winter.（對我來說，在冬天游泳太冷了。）

It is nice of you to invite me to your party.
（你人真是太好了，邀請我參加你的派對。）

這個句型也可以在形容詞前加上 too，但是意思和原本的句型略有差異，表示「太過…以至於無法…」，例如：

The tea is too hot to drink.（這杯茶太燙了，以至於我還不能喝。）

通常這樣的句型也可以寫成＜not ＋ 形容詞 ＋ enough ＋ 不定詞＞：

The tea is not cold enough to drink.（這杯茶不夠冷，以至於我還沒辦法喝。）

・我們可以這樣說

當剛到新的工作環境時，有同事邀請你中午一起用餐時，你可以高興地說：

It's nice of you to invite me to have lunch with you.
（你人真好，邀請我一起吃午餐。）

・換你試試看，這個句子怎麼說？

1. 這本書讀起來太無趣了。
2. 這顆蘋果吃起來太酸了。
3. 這碗玉米濃湯喝起來太燙了。

・你完成了嗎？

1. This book is too boring to read.
2. This apple is too sour to eat.
3. This corn soup is too hot to drink.

---

10. ask / tell / want / allow + 受詞 + 不定詞

ask、tell、want、allow 等字具有命令的感覺，和不定詞連用，有要求某人去做某事的意味。

My mom asked me to do the dishes.（我媽媽要求我洗碗。）

・我們可以這樣說

除了表示命令，我們也可以用這個句型表示輕微的抱怨，例如：

My mom doesn't allow me to eat fast food. She thinks it is harmful to my health.
（我媽媽不准我吃速食，她覺得速食對我的健康不好。）

・換你試試看，這句話英文怎麼說？

1. 老師准許學生在考試的時候使用字典。
2. 總經理要求秘書針對這次會議整理一份報告。
3. 這位老太太准許他們在這間房間裡抽菸。

・你完成了嗎？

1. The teacher allowed the students to use the dictionary during the test.
2. The manager asked the secretary to write a report about this meeting.
3. This old lady allowed them to smoke in the room.

---

11. had better + 不定詞＝最好…

這個句型具有警告、建議或表示迫切期望的意味，例如：

You had better to put on your coat.（你最好把外套穿上。）

如果想要表示否定，則在 had better 和不定詞中間加 not 即可：

We had better not to tell mom that you broke the vase.
（我們最好不要告訴媽媽你打破了花瓶。）

‧我們可以這樣說

我們也可以將這個句型用在叮嚀，例如家人感冒了，但卻不肯吃藥時，我們可以說：

You had better to take some medicine, or you will get worse.
（你最好吃藥，不然你生病會更嚴重。）

‧換你試試看，遇到這種狀況要怎麼給建議？

1. It's going to rain.
2. Smoking is harmful to health.
3. Mrs. Lee is very punctual.

‧你完成了嗎？

1. It's going to rain.
   → You had better to take an umbrella with you.
2. Smoking is harmful to health.
   → You had better to stop smoking.
3. Mrs. Lee is very punctual.
   → You had better be there in time.

和動詞有關的句型

12. would rather + 動詞 + than + 動詞＝寧願做…也不要…

例如：

I would rather go to the movies than stay at home.
（我寧願去看電影也不要待在家裡。）

若是前後的動詞一樣，我們可以把第二次出現的動詞省略：

I would rather read newspaper than (read) this novel.
（我寧願看報紙也不要看這本小說。）

·我們可以這樣說

這個句型可以用來表達意願，假設你去餐廳吃飯，只有雞排和牛肉麵可以選擇，比起雞排，你比較不喜歡吃牛肉麵，那麼你就可以說：

I would rather eat chicken chop than beef noodles.
（我寧願吃雞排也不要吃牛肉麵。）

·換你試試看，這個狀況怎麼說？

1. 媽媽覺得掃地比倒垃圾有趣。
2. 唱歌和跳舞相比，Mia 比較喜歡唱歌。
3. 他們寧願住汽車旅館，也不願意住那間五星級飯店。

·你完成了嗎？

1. 媽媽覺得掃地比倒垃圾有趣。

   Mom would rather sweep the floor than take out the trash.
2. 唱歌和跳舞相比，Mia 比較喜歡唱歌。

   Mia would rather sing than dance.
3. 他們寧願住汽車旅館，也不願意住那間五星級飯店。

   They would rather live in the motel than that five-star hotel.

---

13. keep + 受詞 + from + 動名詞＝使免於…

這個句型中 keep 也可以代換為表示停止的 stop、prevent、prohibit，表示保護的 protect、save、rescue 或表示勸阻的 discourage，同時，from 為介係詞，所以後面銜接的動詞要轉換為動名詞的形態，也可以用名詞代替動名詞，如果句子有被動涵義，則以 being＋過去分詞代替動名詞。例如：

Dad discouraged me from buying that expensive computer.
（爸爸勸我不要買那台昂貴的電腦。）
→ from 加動名詞。

The umbrella keeps us from the rain.（雨傘使我們不會被雨淋濕。）
→ from 加名詞。

The police protected the hostages from being killed.
（警察保護人質不被殺害。）
→ from 加被動式。

· 我們可以這樣說

小朋友常常從冰箱拿飲料出來喝，卻忘了把飲料冰回去，你可以這樣叮嚀：

Don't forget to keep the milk in the refrigerator from rotting.
（別忘了把牛奶放回冰箱，以免壞掉。）

· 換你試試看，試著完成下面的句子！

1. The seat belt / protect / driver / injure
2. The lawyer / try to save / the woman / embarrassing situation
3. The bodyguard / stop / car / accident

· 你完成了嗎？

1. The seat belt protects the driver from being injured.
2. The lawyer tried to save the woman from this embarrassing situation.
3. The bodyguard stopped the car from an accident.

三、文法糾正篇

1. 搞不清楚什麼時候要大寫

什麼時候名詞要用大寫呢？

首先，特定的名稱要大寫，這包含了人名、公司品牌、稱謂、地方名稱、歷史事件、宗教、國籍、種族、行星等，例如 Jennifer、Apple、Mom、Japan、World War II、Christian、Chinese、Denmark、Mars。其中，如果稱謂前面有所有格，那麼稱謂就可以小寫，例如 my dad。

其次，單一字母開頭的字要大寫，例如 X-ray、T-shirt、U-turn。

最後，文章、電影、書籍等的標題和表示時間的星期、月份、假日要大寫，例如 Chapter one、Mansfield park、Monday、April、Christmas。但是季節不能大寫，例如 summer、winter。

2. 名詞單複數所有格的混淆

常常有人搞不清楚，究竟兩個人一起的所有格，要把's 放在後面還是兩個人名後面都放，試比較下面兩個句子：

Jason and Ella's bicycle is blue.（*Jason* 和 *Ella* 的腳踏車是藍色的。）
→ 兩個人一起擁有，腳踏車只有一台。

Jason's and Ella's bicycle are blue.（*Jason* 和 *Ella* 的腳踏車都是藍色的。）
→ 兩個人各自都有腳踏車，腳踏車有兩台。

你發現不同了嗎？當只有第二個人名後面加's，才是表示兩人共有的，因此動詞要用單數動詞，若兩個人名後面各自加's，那就表示兩個人都獨自擁有，所以用複數動詞。

3. 動名詞和不定詞混淆

不定詞和動名詞兩者都具有名詞的功能，可以做主詞、受詞或補語，例如：

To see is to believe.（眼見為憑。）
→ To see 是句子的主詞，to believe 為主詞補語。

Seeing is believing.（眼見為憑。）
→ seeing 是主詞，believing 是主詞補語。

She likes to read.（她喜歡閱讀。）
→ to read 做 like 的受詞。

She likes reading.（她喜歡閱讀。）
→ reading 做 like 的受詞。

但是只有動名詞可以做介係詞的受詞：

Eric doesn't want to spend time in playing computer games.
（Eric 不想花時間在打電腦遊戲上。）
→ 在介係詞 in 後面的 play 要改為動名詞

有些動詞後面接動名詞或不定詞，表達的意思不同。這些動詞如動詞 stop、remember 和 forget，後面接續動名詞時，分別表示停止正在做的事、記得做過的事和忘記做過的事；若接續不定詞，則代表停止原本做的事，去做另一件事、記得去做某事和忘記去做某事，例如：

I remember mopping the floor.（我記得我有拖地。）
→ remember + 動名詞，表示記得有做過。

I remember to mop the floor.（我記得要去拖地。）
→ remember + 不定詞，表示記得要去做。

有些動詞後面接動名詞或不定詞，表達的意思相同
love（喜愛）、like（喜歡）和 hate（恨）後接續動名詞或不定詞，意義大致相同，只是接續動名詞，語氣強烈程度會稍微比不定詞大，例如：

I love reading comic book.
= *I love to read comic book.*

　　兩者都是表示「我喜歡閱讀漫畫書。」，但第一句表達喜愛的程度會比第二句來的強烈與確定。

---

4. can't help 後面到底要用動名詞還是原形動詞

　　在前面的句型中，我們學到在 can't help 後面加上動名詞，可以表示「忍不住…」，但是如果在 help 後面加上 but，也具有同樣的意思，只是，這時候的動詞就不可以用動名詞，而必須用動詞原形，例如：

When Kim heard this news, she can't help but laugh.
（當 *Kim* 聽到這個消息，忍不住笑了起來。）

・換你試試看，找出文章中的錯誤！

　　Last Summer, my family and I went on a picnic there in mountain a-li. My Mom prepared some sandwiches, hot dogs and orange juice, but dad forgot putting them into the trunk. We were angry but can't do anything about it. Then, we decided to go hiking. My two sisters, Wendy and Stella, bought new shoes for this time. Wendy and Stella's shoes are pink and white.

・你找到了嗎？

　　Last summer , my family and I went on a picnic there in Mountain A-li . My mom prepared some sandwiches, hot dogs and orange juice, but dad forgot to put them into the trunk. We were angry but can't do anything about it. Then, we decided to go hiking. My two sisters, Wendy and Stella, bought new shoes for this time. Wendy's and Stella's shoes are pink and white.

NOTE

01
CHAPTER

02
CHAPTER

03
CHAPTER

04
CHAPTER

05
CHAPTER

06
CHAPTER

07
CHAPTER

08
CHAPTER

09
CHAPTER

10
CHAPTER

03
CHAPTER
介係詞

一、概念篇

▎什麼是介係詞│

　　介係詞，即介於句子中表示關係的語詞，可以使名詞、代名詞與動名詞等字，和句子中的其他單字產生關聯，主要用來表示地方、手段或時間，例如：

Kelly and Alvin went to the park.（*Kelly* 和 *Alvin* 去公園。）
→ to 用來連接 went 的動作和代表地方的 park，表示方向性。

The apple is on the table.（這顆蘋果在桌上。）
→ on 用來連接東西 apple 和地方 table，表示某物的位置。

My sister is sitting by me.（我妹妹正坐在我旁邊。）
→ by 用來連接兩個人物 my sister 和 me，表示兩者間的相對關係。

常見的介係詞有：
這些介係詞中，有很多不只有一個意思，僅列出最常見的涵義。

about 關於	Behind 在…後面	Despite 儘管	Off 離開	To 向
Above 在…上	Below 在…下面	Down 向下	On 在…上面	Toward 朝…去
Across 越過	Beneath 在…下面	Except 除了…	Onto 到…之上	Under 在…下面
After 在…之後	Beside 在…旁邊	For 為了	Out 通過…而出	Underneath 在…下面
Against 對著、違反	Besides 除…外	From 來自	Outside 在…之外	Until 直到
Along 沿著	Between 在…之間	In 在…裡	Over 越過	Up 向上
Among 在…之間	Beyond 超出	Inside 在…裡	Past 經過	Upon 在…之上
Around 環繞	But 除…外	Into 進到…裡	Since 自從	With 隨著…
At 在…	By 在旁邊	Like 像	Through 通過	Within 不超過…
Before 之前	Concerning 關於	Of …的	Throughout 遍及	Without 沒有

▌ 介係詞的位置

　　一般而言，介係詞出現在名詞、代名詞或動名詞的前面，但有時也會出現在後面：

She has few friends to talk with.（她幾乎沒有聊天的朋友。）
→ to talk with 是不定詞片語，用來修飾介係詞 with 的受詞 friend。

What is she looking for?（她在找什麼？）
→ what 為疑問詞，在這裡作為 look for 中介係詞 for 的受詞。

有時，我們也會將介係詞放在句子的最後面：

Kelly is the girl that Tom is sitting next to.（*Tom* 坐在 *Kelly* 的旁邊。）

這句話正確的寫法是：*Tom is sitting next to Kelly.*

在口語中，為了讓句子較為輕鬆，或是想要加強語氣，可以把介係詞放在句尾。

‖ 介係詞的受詞 ｜

什麼是介係詞的受詞呢？只要是在介係詞後面，接受介係詞作用的語詞，就是介係詞的受詞。不論是名詞、代名詞或是動名詞，只要可以作為名詞使用的語詞，都可以當成介係詞的受詞。

・換你試試看，找出介係詞的受詞

1. Can you wait for me?
2. There is a book on the sofa.
3. I am going to the school.
4. Whom did she go with?
5. Look at the sleeping baby.

・你找到了嗎？

1. Can you wait for me ?
2. There is a book on the beautiful sofa .
3. I am going to the school .
4. Whom did she go with?
5. Look at that sleeping baby .

你有沒有發現，這些介係詞的受詞中，可以分為兩類，即名詞和代名詞，舉凡像 sofa、school 和 baby，都是屬於名詞，它們的前面都要加上冠詞 the、指示形容詞 that / this 或是形容詞，例如第二題用 beautiful 來修飾 sofa 或是第五題中，用 sleeping 來修飾 baby；若是屬於人稱代名詞，則必須要以受格的形式出現：I 變成 me、who 變成 whom。

▌也可以作為副詞使用的介係詞

介係詞中有很多單字同時也可以作為副詞使用，例如 up、down、on、off 等，這類的介係詞，我們稱為介副詞。了解什麼是介係詞的受詞，可以幫助我們區分句子中的介係詞究竟是做介係詞還是副詞使用，看看下列的句子：

She took out the trash last night.（她昨晚倒垃圾。）

out 後面接 trash 作為受詞，看似介係詞，但是卻是作為修飾動詞 took 的副詞。大部分的片語動詞可以將受詞放在中間。因此這句可以寫成：

She took the trash out last night.

從這句可以看出，the trash 並非 out 的受詞，而是動作 took 的受詞。因此，我們可以判斷，out 是作為修飾動作狀態的副詞。一般而言，大部分由〈動詞 + 介副詞〉型態組合成的片語動詞，具有強調動詞的作用，介係詞為扮演修飾動詞的副詞。我們來比較另一個句子：

The little child fell down the chair.（這個小孩從椅子上掉下來。）

fell 本身就是具備完整「掉落」意思的動詞，不像上述句子中的 take 需要 out 才能組成完整的意思，而 down 只表示小孩、掉落和椅子之間的關係，是介係詞而非副詞。同時，若將 the chair 放在 fell 和 down 之間，也是錯誤的用法。

從上面的句子中，你有沒有發現，介係詞後面一定有受詞，但是要特別小心的是，有時介係詞的受詞不一定就在介係詞的後面。

・換你試試看，是副詞還是介係詞？

1. Kelly got on the train and went to Hualien.
2. Jimmie fell off the motorcycle last week.
3. My mom is chatting with her best friend on the phone.
4. Larry put on his favorite hat.
5. Could you turn on the light?

01 CHAPTER
02 CHAPTER
03 CHAPTER
04 CHAPTER
05 CHAPTER
06 CHAPTER
07 CHAPTER
08 CHAPTER
09 CHAPTER
10 CHAPTER

6. Whom did she talk <u>with</u>?

7. My brother gets <u>on</u> well <u>with</u> my new boyfriend.

· 你判斷出來了嗎？

1. Kelly got <u>on</u> the train and went <u>to</u> Hualien。
   → 這一句中的 got on，表示搭乘交通工具。on 和 to 後面分別銜接受詞 train 和 Hualien，兩者皆為介係詞。

2. Jimmie fell <u>off</u> the motorcycle last week.
   → off 連接掉落的動作和位置，後面的 motorcycle 是 off 的受詞，off 為介係詞。

3. My mom is chatting <u>with</u> her best friend <u>on</u> the phone.
   → with 和 on 後面都有受詞，兩者皆為介係詞。

4. Larry put <u>on</u> his favorite hat.
   → put on 是可以拆解的片語動詞，因此可以將 his favorite hat 放在 put 和 on 之間，on 是修飾 put 的副詞。

5. Could you turn <u>on</u> the light?
   → turn on 也是可以拆解的片語動詞，on 是修飾 turn 的副詞。

6. Whom did she talk <u>with</u>?
   → with 的受詞是位於句首的 whom，with 是介係詞。

7. My brother gets <u>on</u> well <u>with</u> my new boyfriend.
   → 這一句子中出現了帶有介係詞的片語動詞。這類片語動詞的結構為 <動詞＋介副詞＋介係詞>，on 是副詞，with 是介係詞。

▌是介係詞片語還是片語介係詞？

介係詞片語 = <介係詞＋受詞>
介係詞片語可以作為主詞、補語或是修飾語使用，例如：

After dinner is the time to take a walk.（晚餐過後是散步的時間。）
→ after dinner 作為句子的主詞。

My parents are not at home now.（我的父母現在不在家。）
→ at home 作為主詞補語。

Where is your desk in the classroom?（你的書桌在教室的那裡？）

→ in the desk 作為 desk 的修飾語。

片語介係詞＝＜單詞＋介係詞＞或是＜單詞＋單詞＋介係詞＞

單詞指的是什麼呢？例如動詞、連接詞、副詞、形容詞或是介係詞，後面接續介係詞，都可以組成片語介係詞。

常用的片語介係詞有

according to	根據	instead of	代替	in favor of	支持
ahead of	在…之前	thanks to	幸虧、由於	regardless of	不顧…
along with	和…一起	at the end of	在…結束時	in charge of	負責
because of	因為	for the sake of	由於	by means of	藉由
due to	由於	in front of	在…前面	by way of	經由
owing to	由於	in spite of	儘管	along with	與…一起
out of	因為、自…離開	in place of	代替	in honor of	紀念
as regards	至於、關於	in case of	萬一	in the face of	面臨

只要有＜介係詞＋受詞＞的結構出現，就可以構成介係詞片語，因此一個句子中，會有介係詞片語和片語介係詞同時出現的狀況，例如：

We can go to the park due to the rain.（因為下雨，所以我們不能去公園。）

→ 這個句子中，出現了兩個介係詞片語：to the park 和 to the rain；due to 是＜單詞＋介係詞＞組成的片語介係詞。

・換你試試看，可以找出介係詞片語嗎？

1. My cat is sleeping on my computer.
2. What is on the shelf?
3. She is the girl with black eyes.
4. He came here by taxi.

・找到了嗎？後面有受詞的介係詞就是介係詞片語。

1. My cat is sleeping on my computer.
2. What is on the shelf?
3. She is the girl with black eyes.
4. He came here by taxi.

・試試看找出片語介係詞！

1. I cannot go out because my homework.
2. Thanks to your help.
3. My dad stopped smoking for the sake of his health.
4. You must ask for help when you are lost.

・找到了嗎？

1. I cannot go out because of my homework.
2. Thanks to your help.
3. My dad stopped smoking for the sake of his health.
4. You must ask for help when you are lost.

當然，這些片語介係詞，也會和後面的受詞一起構成介係詞片語。

‖ 介係詞的功能 ‖

在了解了介係詞的種類和相關名詞之後，你應該會發現，介係詞具有副詞的作用和形容詞的作用。若作為副詞使用，目的在修飾動詞，通常會出現在句尾；若作形容詞使用，會接續在名詞的後面，例如：

He went to school by bus.（他搭公車上學。）
→ by bus 修飾動詞 went，說明方法，是介係詞片語作為副詞使用。

The cat on the sofa is Tabby.（在沙發上的貓叫做 *Tabby*。）
→ on the sofa 修飾名詞 cat，為介係詞片語作形容詞使用。

・換你試試看，是具備副詞還是形容詞的作用呢？

1. The comic book on my desk is so funny.

2. She went <u>down the hill</u> and gave her mom a big hug.
3. He picked up the key <u>on the floor</u>.
4. Jimmy is sitting <u>on the sofa</u> and reading the newspaper.

・判斷出來了嗎？

1. The comic book <u>on my desk</u> is so funny.
   → on my desk 修飾名詞 book，具有形容詞的作用。
2. She went <u>down the hill</u> and gave her mom a big hug.
   → down the hill 修飾動詞 went，具有副詞的作用。
3. He picked up the key <u>on the floor</u>.
   → on the floor 修飾名詞 key，具有形容詞的作用，在這個句子中，同時還出現了片語動詞 pick up，其中的 up 是介係詞作副詞使用的介副詞。
4. Jimmy is sitting <u>on the sofa</u> and reading the newspaper
   → on the sofa 修飾動詞 sit，具有副詞的作用。

二、好學好用的介係詞種類

　　介係詞主要可以分為表示地方、表示時間、其他作用和慣用語四種，以下一一針對每一種類別說明。

‖ 表示地方的介係詞 |

　　表示地方的介係詞中，又可以分為靜態和動態兩種。靜態的介係詞，主要表示位置的相對關係；動態的介係詞，表示動作的移動和移動的方向。

表示地方的介係詞			
靜態（表示位置）		動態（表示移動和方向）	
(1) 地點	at、in、on	(2) 上下關係	on、over、above、under、below
(3) 前後關係	in front of、behind	(4) 相對關係	between、next to、opposite、without

(5) 周邊關係	beside、by、near、around	(6) 在…之間	between、among
(7) 內外關係	into、out of	(8) 上下關係	up、down
(9) 平行關係	along	(10) 穿越關係	across、through
(11) 起訖點	from、for	(12) 方向性	to、toward(s)

(1) 表示地點：

    ＜at＋小地方＞，小地方包含地址、房子或是某事件發生的地點。

    ＜in＋大地方＞，大地方包含國家、城鎮或是大範圍的區域。

    ＜on＋特定地方＞，特定地方包含樓層、街道。

    有時，in 和 at 可以接續同一地點，但是表示的涵義略有不同，in 多半表示地點的大小或是內外關係，而 at 是強調在這個地點所發生的活動，例如：

I was in the supermarket.（我在超市裡面。）
→ 強調在超市的「裡面」。

I was at the supermarket.（我在超市這邊。）
→ 表示所在的位置，是在超市「這個地方」。

    in 常常被用來表示在某物體「裡面」，例如 in the water、in the cup。

    in 和 on 也可以接續交通工具，一般而言，in 接續 car 或是 taxi，而 on 則是用於 bike 和大眾交通工具，例如 in the car、on the bus。

(2) 上下關係：不論在物體的上面、側面或是下面，只要有接觸到物體表面的，就要用 on；above 表示的是某物位於物體上方的位置，其相反詞為 below；over 除了表示位於物體上方未接觸的位置，也具有兩件物體互相接觸，且有一方覆蓋於另一方之上的概念，其相反詞為 under。

(3) 前後關係：in front of 表示「在…前方」；behind 表示「在…後方」。

(4) 相對關係：between 表示「在…間」，只能接續數量為二的語詞；next to 表示「在…的旁邊」；opposite 則表示「在…對面」；without 表示「在…之外」，例如 without the village。

(5) 周邊關係：near 表示「靠近」；by 也是表示「在…旁邊」，但並非像字面上的意思，真的局限在左右兩旁，而是涵蓋前後左右的位置；beside 表示在左右的位置關係；around 則是具有環繞在周圍的意味。

(6) 在…之間：between 除了可以用於具體的地理位置，也可應用於個體之間的關係，例如：

There is something wrong between David and me.
（我和 *David* 之間有點怪怪的。）
→ David 和 me 是人物，而不是地理位置。

between 用於兩者之間；among 用於三者以上的之間：

There is something wrong among David , Lisa and me.
（*David*、*Lisa* 和我之間有點怪怪的。）
→ David、Lisa 和我有三個人，不能用 between，要用 among。

(7) 內外關係：into 表示 in 加上 to，表示「由外向內」，其相反詞為 out of。

(8) 上下關係：up 表示「向上」，down 為其相反詞，表示「向下」。

(9) 平行關係：along，具有「沿著…」的意味。

(10) 穿越關係：across 和 through 都表示「越過、穿過」，差別在於，across 是指平面的穿過，而 through 比較針對內部或是有經過遮蔽物的穿越，試比較看看：

They walked across the road.（他們越過了馬路。）
→ 從馬路一邊到另一邊，屬於平面性的穿越

They walked through the park.（他們穿越過了公園。）
→ 走進了公園又走出來，屬於內部的穿越

(11) 起訖點：form 表示「起點」，for 表示「目的地」。

⑿ 方向性：to 表示「終點、方向」；toward(s) 具有「朝…」的意思，表示動作的方向。

・換你試試看，填入適當的介係詞

1. The girl sitting _____ Sandy is my sister.
2. The label is _____ the bottle.
3. The old woman is standing _____ the desk.
4. The children are playing _____ the floor.
5. The cup is _____ a magazine and a vase.
6. I would like some milk _____ my coffee.
7. My brother went _____ his room after dinner.
8. The man got _____ the taxi and went _____ the post office.
9. The plane _____ Japan will take off at 11 o'clock.
10. The train drove _____ the tunnel.
11. The bookstore is _____ the street.
12. We are sitting _____ the tree.

・你填入正確的介係詞了嗎？

1. The girl sitting │by / beside / next to / in front of / behind / near│ Sandy is my sister.
   → girl 和 Sandy 的位置，可以有很多變化：by、beside 和 next to 表示旁邊的位置；in front of 和 behind 表示前後的位置；near 表示僅僅在附近而已。

2. The label is │on│ the bottle.

3. The old woman is standing │at / by / beside / next to / in front of / behind / on / under / near│ the desk.
   → 和第一句一樣，不同的介係詞具有不同的意義。

4. The children are playing │on│ the floor.

5. The cup is │between│ a magazine and a vase.

6. I would like some milk │in│ my coffee.

7. My brother went │to / into│ his room after dinner.
   → to 和 into 都表示方向，但 into 比 to 更具有「由外向內」的語感。

8. The man got │out of│ the taxi and went │to / into│ the post office.

9. The plane to Japan will take off at 11 o'clock.

10. The train went through the tunnel.

11. The bookstore is across the street.

　　→ 這句如果要使用 opposite，應該將 opposite 轉換為形容詞「對面的」，句子改寫成 The shop is on the opposite side of the street. 。opposite 主要強調兩個物體的相對位置，所以作介係詞使用時，兩個位置相對的物體要分別放在 opposite 的前後，例如 The bookstore is opposite the school. 。

12. We are sitting by / beside / next to / in front of / behind / under / near the tree.

　　你有沒有發現，有些空格可以填入好幾種介係詞? 使用不同的介係詞，就可以傳達不同的意思，是不是很好玩呢?

▌ 表示時間的介係詞 ▏

表示時間的介係詞	
(1) 時刻、星期和年月日	at、on、in
(2) 期間	for、during
(3) 時間先後順序	before、after、between
(4) 時間起點和完成期限	from、since、till、until、in、within、by

(1) 時刻、星期和年月日：

　　at、on 和 in，分別是表示從時間範圍小到時間範圍大的介係詞。

　　＜at + 時刻＞，例如 at ten o'clock。

　　＜on + 特定的日子＞，特定的日子包含某天、日期或是某天與時段的組合。

　　＜in + 年、月、季節或是一天的某時段＞，例如 in 1982、in November、in autumn、in the morning。

　　要特別注意的是，一天的時段中，晚上 night 前面要用 at，而不是用 in。但是，night 前面也有使用 in 的情況，試比較下面的句子：

He reads books at night.（他在晚上看書。）

　　→ at 表示晚上的「時刻」。

He woke up in the night.（他在半夜醒來。）
→ in 強調晚上的「期間」。

(2) 期間：
　　＜for＋時間的總數＞，例如 for three days、for several hours。
　　＜during＋表示特定期間的時間＞，例如 during summer vacation。
　　我們會以 how long 來詢問時間的總數，以 when something began 來詢問事情開始的時間，這樣的問句可以用 during 帶領的時間回答。

(3) 時間先後順序：before 表示「在…之前」；after 表示「在…之後」；
　　between 表示「在…時間之間」。

(4) 時間起點和完成期限：
　　from 表示「從…開始」，since 也表示「從…開始」，和 from 不同的是，since 帶有「從過去持續到現在」的意味，常常和完成式一起使用。
　　till 和 until 表示「直到…」，是動作或狀態持續的終點，until 比 till 更為正式。
　　in 和 within 均表示「在…內」，常常用於表示動作完成的期間，例如 in one hour、in ten minutes。within 在用法上，比 in 更強調「不超出…的範圍」。
　　by 用來表示動作完成的期限，試比較下列句子：

He will be back in one hour.（他大約一小時就會回來了。）
→ 表示回來的動作大約在一小時左右發生。

He will be back within an hour.（不超出一小時他就會回來了。）
→ 強調回來的動作在一小時之內完成。

He will be back by six o'clock.（到了六點，他就會回來了。）
→ 強調回來的動作是在六點發生。

・換你試試看，填入正確的介係詞！
　1. I will visit you ＿＿＿＿ Sunday.
　2. Jerry got married ＿＿＿＿ 2012.
　3. We have a couple of days off duty ＿＿＿＿ Chinese New Year.
　4. Leo works ＿＿＿＿ Monday to Saturday.

5. We have studied English _____ 3 hours.

6. We have studied English _____ ten o'clock.

7. We have studied English _____ three hours ago.

8. I need to hang out this report _____ half an hour.

9. He watched TV _____ midnight yesterday.

10. He needs to give the presentation to the boss _____ one o'clock.

·你填對了嗎？

1. I will visit you [on] Sunday.

2. Jerry got married [in] 2012.

3. We have couple of days off duty [during] Chinese New Year.

4. Leo works [from] Monday to Saturday.

5. We have studied English [for] 3 hours.

6. We have studied English [since] ten o'clock.

7. We have studied English [since] three hours ago.

8. I need to hang out this report [in / within] half an hour.

9. He watched TV [till / until] midnight yesterday.

10. He needs to give the presentation to the boss [by] one o'clock.

　　你有沒有發現，和表示地點的介係詞相比，表示時間的介係詞常常只有一種選擇，最多只有語氣上的差別，因此，在使用表示時間的介係詞時，要特別小心唷！

▌具有其他作用的介係詞

具有其他作用的介係詞	
(1) 表示工具、手段或方法	with、by、in
(2) 表示原因或理由	from、through、with
(3) 其他	with、without、of、by、for、like、about

(1) 表示工具、手段或方法：

　　＜with＋工具＞，例如 with a pen、with a hammer。

＜by ＋ 交通工具＞，例如 by bus、by car。
＜in ＋ 材料或是語言＞，例如 in wood、in Chinese。

(2) 表示原因或理由：from、through 和 with 都表示「因為…」，這三個字後面都可以接續名詞或是動詞，若接續動詞，要將動詞轉換為現在分詞，例如：

He is sick from eating too much.（他因為吃太多而感到不舒服。）
→ from ＋ 動作，動作要轉換成現在分詞的形式。

She lost her job through her rudeness.（她因為無禮而丟了飯碗。）
→ through ＋ 名詞。

They were crying with happiness.（他們因為高興而哭了。）
→ with ＋ 名詞。

(3) 其他：

with 表示「和、身上帶有…」，例如 talk with friend、have money with me，其相反詞為 without「沒有…」。
of 是表示所有的介係詞，具有「…的」意思，例如 the house of my grandparents，of 在使用上，語序和中文不同，中文先說祖父母，才說房子，但英文卻剛好相反。by 表示「依據…」，例如 by the rules；同時，當我們描述某件作品是由某人創作時，也會使用 by，而不是 of，例如 a book by Jane Austen。
for 表示「為了…」，例如 for you、for waiting her，因為 for 具有「為了…」的涵義，在英文的口語表達上，有時候也會在 for 後面加上原因，表示因果關係。
about 表示「關於…」，例如 the story about animals。
like 表示「像…」，在使用上常常和動詞的 like 混淆，動詞的 like 表示「喜歡」，比較看看下面兩個句子：

She likes her sister.（她喜歡她的姊姊。）
→ like 是動詞，表示喜歡。

She is like her sister.（她像她的姊姊。）
→ be 動詞 ＋ like，表示「像…」，like 是介係詞。

・換你試試看，填入適當的介係詞！

1. Kevin usually goes to work _____ MRT.
2. This movie is _____ the vampires in Germany.
3. Children need to learn how to eat _____ chopsticks.
4. She wrote her diary _____ Japanese.
5. Tim and Eric are _____ brothers.
6. He can't live _____ his wife.
7. Vicky drew a card _____ her mother.

・你寫對了嗎？

1. Kevin usually goes to work by MRT.
2. This movie is about the vampires in Germany.
3. Children need to learn how to eat with chopsticks.
4. She wrote her diary in Japanese.
5. Tim and Eric are like brothers.
6. He can't live without his wife.
7. Vicky drew a card for her mother.

是不是很簡單呢？

‖ 介係詞的慣用語 ‖

常用的介係詞慣用語

介係詞的慣用語		
＜動詞+介係詞＞	＜be 動詞+形容詞+介係詞＞	＜介係詞+名詞＞
agree with 一致	be absent from 缺席	at first 首先
agree to 同意	be afraid of 對…害怕	at least 最後
care about 關心	be different from 對…相異	at once 立刻
get on 上車	be fond of 對…喜歡	on time 準時
get off 下車	be kind to 對…好心	on the way 盛行
look for 尋找	be good at 擅長	for example 例如

look after 照顧	be bad at 拙於	for oneself 為了某人自己
look at 注視	be nervous of 緊張	by oneself 某人自己做的
apologize for 道歉	be scared of 對…害怕	in time 及時
arrive at 抵達	be angry with / about 對…生氣	of course 當然
believe in 相信	be polite to 對…禮貌	at the end 在…的結尾
borrow sth. from 借	be anxious about 為…擔心	in the end 終於
run into 撞到	be clever at 擅長	in one's opinion 認為
name after 以…命名	be upset with / about 對…難過	on the phone 講電話
depend on 依賴	be disappointed with / about 對…失望	at home 在家

　　這一類的慣用語非常多，平常在背誦單字時，就可以順便把搭配的介係詞一起記憶，有時，隨著介係詞的不同，整個片語表達的意思也會不同，要靠平時的慢慢累積字彙量與閱讀文章，久而久之，也會對該搭配什麼介係詞有一定程度的了解喔！

・換你試試看，判斷哪一個介係詞才是對的！

1. Ivy is good at / in playing the piano.
2. Garcia is not afraid of / to speaking English to foreigners.
3. Justin arrived in / to New York last night.
4. Jason borrowed an eraser from / to Eric.
5. Tim drove his competitor against / into a corner.
6. It is dependent of / on you.
7. This is an example for / of how prepositions are used.
8. Anna got married with / to Jason in 1982.
9. The boss divided the department into / in five groups.

・你選對了嗎？

1. Ivy is good at playing the piano.
2. Garcia is not afraid of speaking English to foreigners.
   → 這句也可以用介係詞 to，但應將後面的 speaking 改為不定詞 to speak。

3. Justin arrived in New York last night.

　→ 如果將 New York 換成小範圍的地方，例如 station，in 就要改成 at。

4. Jason borrowed an eraser from Eric.

　→ 這句也可以改寫成 Eric lent an eraser to Jason.

5. Tim drove his competitor into a corner.

　→ drive one into a corner 表示「把…逼入絕境」。

6. It is dependent on you.

　→ dependent 為形容詞，這句也可以改用動詞 depend，寫成 It depends on you.

7. This is an example of how prepositions are used.

8. Anna got married with Jason in 1982.

9. The boss divided the department into five groups.

三、好學好用的句型篇

‖ 和介係詞相關的句型 ‖

　　你是不是已經對介係詞的使用有一定程度的了解了呢？以下是介係詞的常用句型，多多練習這些句型，讓你的英文更加流利！

---

1. 介係詞 + 名詞

　＜ at + 名詞＞ = 處於某種狀態中

　＜ in + 名詞＞ = 處於某種情緒中

　＜ on + 名詞＞ = 在…中

　＜ under + 名詞＞ = 被…中

　　例如：

The skyscraper is still under construction. （這棟摩天樓仍在施工中。）

Albert goes to China on business every 2 months. （*Albert* 每兩個月去中國出差一次。）

He is always active at work.（他在工作方面總是很積極。）

Alvin said goodbye to Ella in joy.（*Alvin* 快樂的向 *Ella* 道別。）

·我們可以這樣用

這類的句型因為非常簡短，很容易在生活上使用。

在和別人交談但尚未達成共識時，我們可以說：

It is still under discussion.（事情還是有討論空間。）

→ 表示仍在被討論中。

被蜘蛛嚇到的時候，我們可以說：

I rushed out of my room in horror when the spider crawling on my desk.

（當那隻蜘蛛在我書桌上爬時，我嚇的衝出房間。）

→ 表示驚恐的情緒。

有時候想抱怨小孩念書的時候像一條蟲，玩樂的時候又像一條龍，我們可以說：

My little boy is alive at play but dead at study.

（我的兒子玩的時候很活潑，但一要念書就死氣沉沉。）

→ 表示玩樂和唸書的狀態

工作了一段時間，終於可以好好放個假。放假中不希望別人打擾時，我們可以說：

Don't call me on weekends. I am on vacation.

（周末不要打電話給我，我正在渡假。）

→ 表示在渡假中。

·換你試試看，改寫下面的句子

1. Everything is controlled.

　　= _____

2. Amanda yelled angrily when she saw the news on TV.

　　= _____

3. The life during the war is difficult.

　　= _____

4. The bodyguard is working.

　　= _____

・你寫對了嗎？

1. Everything is controlled.

　= Everything is under control.

2. Amanda yelled angrily when she saw the news on TV.

　= Amanda yelled in anger when she saw the news on TV.

3. The life during the war is difficult.

　= The life at war is difficult.

4. The bodyguard is working.

　= The bodyguard is on duty.

---

2. To one's + 表示情緒的名詞 = 令人感到…的是

　To one's knowledge = 就某人所知

　To the best of one's memory = 就某人記憶所及

例如：

To his surprise, the baby didn't cry when the driver stopped the bus suddenly.
（令他驚訝的是，嬰兒在公車司機緊急剎車後竟然沒有哭。）

To my knowledge, America is the most powerful country on earth.
（就我所知，美國是世界上最有權力的國家。）

To the best of her memory, her mom always makes apple pie on Sundays.
（就她所記得的，她的媽媽總是在星期天製作蘋果派。）

　　和情緒有關的名詞，常見的有：anger、delight、horror、sorrow、surprise、amusement、amazement、astonishment、disappointment、satisfaction、sadness...等。

·我們可以這樣用

你可以試著在生活中，以這樣的句型作為談話的開頭。

如果發生了幸運的事，比方中了樂透，我們可以說：

To my joy, I won the lottery!（令我感到快樂的是，我中了樂透！）

如果覺得語氣不夠強烈，可以在句首的地方加上 much：

Much to my joy, I won one hundred thousand dollars!
（令我大感高興的是，我中了十萬元！）

在和朋友討論到電影的主角時，我們可以說：

To my knowledge, Leonardo DiCaprio is the leading actor in Inception.
（就我所知，*Leonardo Di Caprio* 是全面啟動的男主角。）

開同學會和老朋友憶當年時，我們可以說：

To my best memory, Bella was talkative at that time.
（就我記憶，*Bella* 那時很愛說話。）

·換你試試看，這樣的狀況你會怎麼說？

1. When the boss appeared suddenly:

   _____

2. Einstein is the smartest person in the world:

   _____

3. My mom sang lullaby to me when I was a little child:

   _____

·你想到了嗎？

1. When the boss appeared suddenly:

   To my surprise, the boss appeared suddenly.

   → 如果你的老闆突然出現在你面前，不僅讓你感到驚訝，還感到驚恐的

話，也以把 surprise 改成 horror 囉！

2. Einstein is the most smartest person in the world:

   To my knowledge, Einstein is the smartest person in the world.

3. My mom sang lullabies to me when I was a little child:

   To the best of my memory, my mom sang lullabies to me when I was a little child.

---

3. Despite

   In spite of　＋名詞 / 動名詞 ＝ 儘管…還是…

   For all

這個句型在連接詞的單元裡，和 though / although 做了用法的比較，要特別記得，這個句型後面要接的是名詞或是動名詞，例如：

Despite his sadness, he tried to make us laugh.
= In spite of his sadness, he tried to make us laugh.
= For all his sadness, he tried to make us laugh.
（儘管他很憂傷，他還是盡力逗我們笑。）

・我們可以這樣用

在公司裡，對於下屬的報告感到滿意，但又希望對方不要得意忘形，還是要把工作做好時，我們可以說：

Despite your presentation is good, you have to work hard on it.
（儘管你的報告很好，你還是要在這方面多下功夫。）

・換你試試看，用提供的單字造句吧！

1. rain / James / went out

   _____

2. illness / Willie / finished this report

   _____

3. being very tired / Melody / went to work

   _____

·你寫好了嗎？

1. rain / James / went out

   Despite rain, James went out.

2. illness / Willie / finished this report

   Despite illness, Willie finished this report.

3. being very tired / Melody / went to work

   Despite being very tired, Melody went to work.

上面句子中的 despite 也可以改為 in spite of；這兩個語詞也可以放在句子中間。

---

4. Besides

   In addition to   + 名詞 / 動名詞 = 不但有…還有…

   Except +名詞 / 動名詞 = 沒有…

例如：

Besides Monica, everyone in his class was invited to the party.

= In addition to Monica, everyone in his class was invited to the party.

（除了 *Monica*，他班上的每個人也都受邀參加派對。）

Except Monica, everyone in his class was invited to the party.

（他班上的每個人都受邀參加派對，只有 *Monica* 沒有被邀請。）

這個句型要特別注意，besides 和 in addition to 後面接的名詞，是有被包含在裡面的，而 except 是把後面的名詞排除在外的；同時，beside 和 besides 只有一個字母 s 之差，前者是表示位置在旁邊的介係詞，後者是表示包含的介係詞，要區別清楚喔！

‖ 我們可以這樣用 |

去 3C 商店買東西時，如果有兩樣東西想買，我們可以說：

Besides the laptop, I also want a printer.（除了電腦，我也想要印表機。）

和朋友相約看電影，在討論要看什麼片時，我們可以這樣說：

Every movie will be fine except a horror film. （除了恐怖片，看什麼都好。）

・換你試試看，看看中文寫出英文！

1. 除了香蕉，我什麼水果都不喜歡。

2. 除了 Debbi，我還邀請了 Kevin。

3. 除了閱讀報紙，我很喜歡閱讀各式各樣的東西。

・你完成了嗎？

1. 除了香蕉，我什麼水果都不喜歡。
   I don't like any fruit except bananas.
2. 除了 Debbi，我還邀請了 Kevin。
   Besides Debbi, I invited Kevin.
3. 除了閱讀報紙，我很喜歡閱讀各式各樣的東西。
   Except the newspaper, I like to read everything.

---

5. Because of
   Owing to
   As a result of　＋ 名詞 = 因為…的緣故
   Due to

例如：

Because of different cultures, they have different opinions about cuisine.
= *Owing to different cultures, they have different opinions about cuisine.*
= *As a result of different cultures, they have different opinions about cuisine.*
= *Due to different culture, they have different opinions about cuisine.*
（因為文化的不同，他們在飲食的概念上也有不同的意見。）

01 CHAPTER
02 CHAPTER
03 CHAPTER
04 CHAPTER
05 CHAPTER
06 CHAPTER
07 CHAPTER
08 CHAPTER
09 CHAPTER
10 CHAPTER

在前面的章節中，我們提到了 because 和 because of 的不同，because 是連接詞，連接兩個具有因果關係的句子，because of 後面要接續名詞；as a result of 和 as a result 在使用上也常常混淆，前者是介係詞，後者是副詞，要獨立於句子外使用。

這幾種句型都可以表示「由於…」，其中又以 because of 較為常用，其他用法較為正式。比較特別的是，due to 是這幾種用法中，唯一可以放在 be 動詞後面，具有主詞補語的作用，例如：

The reason that he was fired is due to his carelessness.
（他被解雇的原因是因為他的粗心。）
→ due to 放在 be 動詞後面，作為主詞補語。

在使用 due to 或是 owing to 時，後面的動詞較加上 ing，因為這個句型中的 to 是介係詞，而不是不定詞中的 to，例如：

She is getting fat owing to eating too much candy.
（她變胖是因為吃太多糖果。）
→ owing to 後面動詞要加 ing。

She wants to eat candy.（她想要吃糖果。）
→ 兩個動詞 want 和 eat 中間加上 to，to 和第二個動詞構成不定詞，第二個動詞要用原形動詞。

如果常常搞不清楚 to 到底是介係詞還是不定詞，我們可以試著判斷 to 是和後面的動詞構成一組以表示目的，或是和前面的語詞構成一組具有獨立的意義。以上述的兩句為例，第一句中的 get fat 和 eat too much candy 具有因果關係，因此 to 後面如果加上原形動詞 eat，句意就會變成 get fat 是為了 eat too much chocolate，不是很沒有邏輯嗎?所以我們可以大膽推斷，這裡的 to 是和 owing 為一組的語詞，具有獨立的意義「因為…」；第二句中 to 和動作 eat 表示目的「要吃」，是不定詞的 to，後面的動詞使用原形。不過這樣的判斷方式，只是一個簡單的原則，平時還是要多熟記這類特別用法的片語唷!

・我們可以這樣用
有時候也要感謝家人對我們的鼓勵，我們可以說：

Because of your encouragement, I can make my dream come true.
（因為有你的鼓勵，我才可以實踐我的夢想。）

01 CHAPTER

02 CHAPTER

· 換你試試看，改寫下面的句子！

1. He can't walk. He fell down the stairs.

_____

2. She helps poor people. She is kind.

_____

03 CHAPTER

3. I enjoy reading this novel. The plot is so interesting.

_____

· 是不是很簡單呢？

04 CHAPTER

1. He can't walk. He fell down the stairs.
   He can't walk because of falling down the stairs.

2. She helps poor people. She is kind.
   She helps poor people because of her kindness.

05 CHAPTER

3. I enjoy reading this novel. The plot is so interesting.
   I enjoy reading this novel because of its plot.

上面的這些句子，也可以將 because of 用句型中的其他語詞代換。

06 CHAPTER

6.	result in + 結果 = 導致…的結果
原因 +	lead to
	contribute to
	bring about

07 CHAPTER

例如：

08 CHAPTER

Drinking too much coffee may <u>result in</u> insomnia.
= *Drinking too much coffee may <u>lead to</u> insomnia.*
= *Drinking too much coffee may <u>contribute to</u> insomnia.*

09 CHAPTER

= *Drinking too much coffee may <u>bring about</u> insomnia.*
（喝太多咖啡可能會導致失眠。）

10 CHAPTER

和 result in 很相似的 result from，也具有相似的意思，不同的是，前者後面要加上結果，後者後面則是加上原因。因此，上述這句話也可以寫成：

Insomnia <u>results from</u> drinking too much coffee.
（失眠起因於喝了太多的咖啡。）
→ 介係詞後面的動作，要加上 ing。

·我們可以這樣說

家人在外頭應酬時，難免會多喝幾杯，我們可以這樣表達提醒和關心：

Drunk driving might <u>lead to</u> car accidents. Don't drive after drinking alcohol, OK?
（酒駕有可能會導致車禍，喝完酒後不要開車好嗎？）

·換你試試看，利用單字照樣造句！

1. eat too much dessert / obesity

   _____

2. smoking / lung cancer

   _____

3. bankruptcy / waste

   _____

·你寫對了嗎？

1. eating too much dessert / may / obesity
   <u>Eating too much dessert may result in obesity.</u>
2. smoking / lung cancer
   <u>Smoking results in lung cancer.</u>
3. his bankruptcy / his waste of money
   <u>His bankruptcy results in his waste of money.</u>

7. nothing but = only 只有
   anything but = not... at all 一點也不…
   all but = almost 幾乎

　　我們在第二章提到，but 作為連接詞使用，具有語氣轉折的意味，但是，but 除了當作連接詞，也可以作為介係詞使用。作為介係詞的 but 和連接詞的使用方法很類似，前後連接的語感也是相對的。上面和 but 有關的三個句型，是生活中常常用到，但是很容易混淆，nothing but 表示「只有」，整句的重點是 but 後面的語詞，例如：

I can't do nothing but wait.（我能做的只有等待了。）
→ 重點是等待的動作，而不是前面的動詞 do。

She is nothing but an idiot.（她就是一個傻瓜。）
→ 強調她是傻瓜這件事。

　　anything but 表示「一點也不」，和前一個句型不同的是，nothing but 強調 but 後面的語詞，但是 anything but 卻要在 but 後面加上否定解釋，也就是將 anything but 視為 not，例如：

She is nothing but an idiot.（她就是一個傻瓜。）
→ 她是傻瓜。

She is anything but an idiot.（她絕對不是一個傻瓜。）
→ 她除了是一個傻瓜，什麼身分都有可能。
→ 她不是一個傻瓜。雖然 but 後面接 an idiot 沒有任何代表否定涵義的字，但卻要加上否定解釋。

　　all but 表示「幾乎」，例如：

She is all but an idiot.（她幾乎就是個傻瓜。）

・我們可以這樣用
　　生活忙碌，心中難免希望有幾天可以在家裡懶散一下，我們可以說：

What I need is nothing but a few days to stay at home.
（我需要的只是待在家裡幾天。）

朋友因為工作不如意，對自己很沒自信時，我們可以鼓勵他：

You are anything but a wimp.（你絕對不是一個沒用的人。）

・換你試試看，這種情形你會怎麼說？
1. 上司交代了一件你不想做的工作。
2. 和朋友抱怨另一半是一個懶骨頭。
3. 因為生病，只有吃了一點麵包。

・是不是很簡單呢？
1. 上司交代了一件你不想做的工作時。
   I can do anything but this.
2. 和朋友抱怨另一半是一個骨頭。
   He / She is nothing but a lazy bone.
   He / She is all but a lazy bone.
3. 因為生病，只有吃了麵包。
   I eat nothing but bread.

四、文法糾正篇

　　學了這麼多介係詞的慣用語和句型，你是不是對介係詞的使用得心應手了呢?如果可以避免以下常見的錯誤，相信遇到與介係詞相關的文法時，都可以輕鬆迎刃而解了！

1. at / in / on + 慣用的地方

　　在之前我們提到，這三個介係詞的基本原則為＜at + 小地方＞、＜in + 大地方＞而＜on + 特定地方＞，但有些地點沒有辦法使用這個原則，而是要搭配

特定的 at、in 或是 on，在使用上常常會造成混淆。這些地方如下表：

常被混淆的 at / in / on		
at +	in +	on +
(1) 某一點的位置	線狀地點中的一點	線狀地點
(2) 娛樂場所	有環繞感的環境	與垂直平面接觸的位置
(3) 讀書場所	獨立的環境	面部表情
(4) 活動的名稱	柔軟的身體部位	身體表面
(5) 地址的號碼	街道名稱（英式英文）	街道名稱（美式英文）
(6) 地址的街道和號碼	創傷	樓層

(1) 某一點的位置：at the crossroad、at the desk、at the door 等。

(2) 娛樂場所：at a pub、at a club、at a theater、at a restaurant 等。

(3) 讀書場所：at university、at school 等。

(4) 活動的名稱：at a concert、at a meeting、at a party、at a match 等。

(5) 地址的號碼：at number 50、at number 10 等。

(6) 地址的街道和號碼：只要有號碼出現，都要用 at，例如 at 11 Green Street。

(7) 線狀地點中的一點：the boy in the third row、the stone in the river 等。

(8) 有環繞感的環境：in the cupboard、in the house、in the grass 等。

(9) 獨立的環境：in the field、in the car park 等。

(10) 柔軟的身體部位：hit sb in the eye / mouth / stomach 等。

(11) 街道名稱（英式英文）：in Green street、in Red Avenue 等。

(12) 創傷：was hurt in the shoulder / head / leg 等。

(13) 線狀地點：on the row、on the river、on the road 等。

(14) 與垂直平面接觸的位置：on the table、on the sofa、on the floor 等。

(15) 面部表情：an expression of anger / cunning / eager on one's face。

(16) 身體表面：on the skin、on the shoulder、on the face 等。

(17) 街道名稱：on Black Road、on Purple Street 等。

(18) 樓層：on the second floor、on the tenth floor 等。

你是不是更清楚了呢？

1. There is a magazine _____ the desk.
2. The boat is _____ the river.
3. I live _____ 116 White Avenue.
4. We will have a dinner _____ the Steak House tonight.
5. The little boy has a wound _____ his right leg.
6. I am sorry the manager is _____ the meeting; would you like to leave the message?
7. The two rabbits are running happily _____ the grass.
8. The baby is sleeping _____ the bed.
9. There are many fast food restaurants _____ the train station.
10. We can meet _____ the bus station.
11. They went on a picnic _____ the lawn.

· 你寫對了嗎？

1. There is a magazine at the desk.
   → 某一點的位置用 at。
2. The boat is on the river.
   → 線狀地點用 on。
3. I live at 116 White Avenue.
   → 只要地址中有號碼的都要用 at。
4. We will have a dinner at the Steak House tonight.
   → 娛樂地點用 at。
5. The little boy has a wound in his right leg.
   → 表示受傷時，在受傷的身體部位前加 in。
6. I am sorry the manager is at the meeting ; would you like to leave the message?
   → 表示活動時要用 at。
7. The two rabbits are running happily in the grass.
   → 具有環繞感、立體感的場所要用 in。
8. The baby is sleeping in / on the bed.
   → in 和 on 都正確，但表達的語感不同。一般而言，在床上睡覺用 in the bed，表示睡在床的「裡面」，但若用 on，是強調身體和床之間的平面接觸，表示睡在床的「上面」，這和中文表達的方式不同，要特別小心。

9.　There are many fast food restaurants in the train station.

　　→ 這句想要表達的是，在火車站「裡面」有很多速食餐廳，所以用 in。

10.We can meet at the bus station.

　　→ 這句提到公車站，只是表示在公車站「這個地方」，和公車站內部沒有關係，所以要用 at。

11.They went on a picnic on the lawn.

　　→ 雖然 grass 要用 in，但是 lawn 卻是習慣使用 on，可以把這兩種固定用法牢記下來，以後就不會用錯了。

2. to 作介係詞使用時，後面的動詞要加 ing

　　一般而言，to 後面的動作要使用原形，但是作為介係詞使用的 to，後面的動詞卻要使用 V-ing 的形式，這一類型的片語常見的有：

to 後面要加 V-ing 的片語			
look forward to	期待	owing to	由於
in addition to	除…以外	due to	由於
with regard to	關於	as to	至於
with reference to	關於	be used to	（現在）習慣於
according to	根據	get used to	漸漸習慣於
compared to	相較而言	be accustomed to	習慣於
be a key to	為…的關鍵	be relative to	相關
be a way to	通往…的方法	be a pressure to	造成…的壓力

・換你試試看，改寫成正確的單字！

1.　I am looking forward to go to the movies with you.

2.　Ann is used to eat an apple every day.

3.　To work hard is the key to be the general manager.

4.　In addition to ride bikes, they also went mountain climbing.

・你完成了嗎？

1.　I am looking forward to go to the movies with you.

　　→ I am looking forward to going to the movies with you.

2. Ann is used to eat an apple every day.

→ Ann is used to _eating_ an apple every day.

3. To work hard is the key to be the general manager.

→ To work hard is the key to _being_ the general manager.

4. In addition to ride bikes, they also went mountain climbing.

→ In addition to _riding_ bikes, they also went mountain climbing.

---

3. 有些用語的介係詞不能使用或是可以省略

介係詞可以使句子中的各個語詞產生關係，但是卻不能濫用，有些用語是不能使用介係詞的，這些語詞有：

不使用介係詞或是介係詞可以省略的用語		
(1) to discuss ~~about~~（討論）	(4) ~~to~~ + home / here / there	(6) (in) the same / this way
(2) to marry ~~with~~（結婚）	(5) ~~on / in / at~~ + next / last / this / one / every / each / some / any / all	(7) (on) 一周七天
(3) to lack ~~of~~		(8) (at) what time

⑴ to discuss 不能加 about，但是 a discussion 卻要加 about：

They discussed the movie.（他們討論這部電影。）
We had a discussion about the movie.（我們針對這部電影進行討論。）

⑵ to marry 後面不能加 with，但是 get married 要加 to：

Henry married Jane.
= *Henry got married to Jane.*（Henry 和 Jane 結婚。）

⑶ to lack 不加 of，但是 a lack 後面加 of，也有 to be lacking in 的用法：

I don't lack anything.
= *I lack for nothing.*（我什麼都不缺。）
→ lack 不能加 of，但可以加 for。

Money is a lack for this family.
= *The family is lacking in money.*（這個家庭很缺錢。）

⑷ 在 home / here / there 前不能有 to：

I am going to home / there.（X）
應改成 *I am going home / there.*（我正要回家／去那裡。）

She is coming to here.（X）
應改成 *She is coming here.*（她正要來這裡。）

　　在正統文法裡，here 和 there 是地方副詞，前面不能加介係詞；在口語中，有時為了強調所在的位置，會在前面加上介係詞，但是這是非正式的用法。

⑸ next / last / this / one / every / each / some / any / all 的前面不加 in、at 或是 on，因為這些語詞並沒有特定點出明確的時間或地點，因此也無從判斷到底用哪一種介係詞，所以乾脆全部都不使用，例如：

We have an exam on next Monday.（X）
We have an exam next Monday.（O）
（我們下周一有考試。）

　　在⑹⑺⑻的用法中，這些介係詞可加，也可省略：

⑹ *My home is (in) this way.*（我的家在這個方向。）

⑺ *See you Friday.*（周五見囉！）

⑻ *What time do you watch TV?*（你什麼時候看電視？）

‧換你試試看，判斷要不要加介係詞呢？

1. At what time did Justin come last night?
2. We can't write our report in the same way.
3. He went to there and bought some cookies.

4. The young man is lacking of experience.

5. She doesn't want to marry to the old man.

1. At what time did Justin come last night?

   → （O）at 可加可不加。

2. We can't write our report in the same way.

   → （O）in 可加可不加。

3. He went ~~to~~ there and bought some cookies.

   → （X）there 前面不可以加 to。

4. The young man is lacking ~~of~~ experience.

   → （X）is lacking 後面要加介係詞，但是不是加 of，是加 in。

5. She doesn't want to marry ~~to~~ the old man.

   → （X）marry 後面不能加 with 也不加 to。

---

4. 常用字的混淆

有些用語在使用上容易產生混淆，這些用語有：

(1) during 和 while：

during 表示「…的期間」，後面接名詞；while 表示「當…」，後面加動作，例如：

Steven usually reads <u>during a meal</u>.（*Steven* 通常在吃飯時閱讀。）
→ during 加表示期間的名詞 meal。

Steven usually reads <u>while he is eating</u>.（當 *Steven* 在吃飯時，他通常會一邊閱讀。）
→ while 加表示動作的句子 he is eating。

(2) with 和 between：

表示關係中，單一對象用 with，兩個對象要用 between。

Her friendship <u>with</u> Mia is endless.（她對 *Mia* 的友誼永不止息。）

→ with 加單一對象 Mia。

The friendship between Mia and Ella is endless.
（*Mia* 和 *Ella* 之間的友誼永不止息。）
→ between 介於兩個對象 Mia 和 Ella 之間。

⑶ in the way 和 on the way：
　　in the way 表示阻擋；on the way 表示在某事在進行中，例如：

Sam wanted to go to the bathroom, but the chair was in the way.
（*Sam* 想去洗手間但椅子擋到他的路。）

Flu is on the way.（現在盛行流感。）

⑷ in the end 和 at the end：
　　in the end 表示「終於」，at the end 表示「在…結束時」。

Don't worry, you will be all right in the end.（別擔心，你最終會沒事的。）

He laughed himself hoarse at the end of this movie.
（在電影最後，他笑到嗓子都啞了。*)*

⑸ dream of 和 dream about：
　　dream of 表示「有…夢想」，dream about 除了表示夢想，還可以表示「夢見」。

I dreamed of being an astronaut.（我以前夢想當太空人。）

I dreamed about being rich last night.（我昨天夢見我變有錢了。）

⑹ in time 和 on time：
　　in time 表示「及時」，有比預定時間略早的語感，on time 表示「準時」，有在時間上剛剛好的感覺。

I will be home in time for lunch.（我會及時趕回家吃午餐。）

The 10:30 plane didn't take off on time.（這班十點半的班機沒有準時起飛。）

· 換你試試看，填入適合的用語！

1. The school bus is seldom late. It is usually _____.
2. The biker stopped his bike just _____.
3. They played cards _____ the party.
4. The relationship _____ you and I is wonderful.
5. I like going mountain climbing _____ the summer vacation.

· 你寫對了嗎？

1. The school bus is seldom late. It is usually <u>on time</u>.
2. The biker stopped his bike just <u>in time</u>.
3. They played cards <u>at the end of</u> the party.
4. The relationship <u>between</u> you and I is wonderful.
5. I like going mountain climbing <u>during</u> the summer vacation.

---

5. of / with + 抽象名詞，代表的詞性不同

　　of + 抽象名詞，具有形容詞的作用；with + 抽象名詞，具有副詞的作用。例如：

He is a man <u>of importance</u>.（他是一個很重要的人。）
→ of + 抽象名詞，具有形容詞的功能，修飾前面的名詞 man。

He teaches his students <u>with patience</u>.（他很有耐心地教導學生。）
→ with + 抽象名詞，具有副詞的功能，修飾前面的動作 teach。

· 換你試試看，要用 of 還是 with？

1. Claire always gives me suggestion of / with help.
2. Please read this article of / with great caution.
3. My brother vacuumed the floor of / with reluctance.
4. This is an experience of / with much value.
5. She is the woman of / with great beauty.

· 你選對了嗎？

1. Claire always gives me suggestion $\boxed{of}$ help.

→ of help = helpful，用來修飾前面的名詞 suggestion。

2. Please read this article ｜with｜ great caution.

　　→ with+ caution = cautiously，用來修飾動詞 read。

3. My brother vacuumed the floor ｜with｜ reluctance.

　　→ with+ reluctance = reluctantly，用來修飾動詞 vacuumed。

4. This is an experience ｜of｜ much value.

　　→ of+ value = valuable，用來修飾名詞 experience，如果想要加強語氣，可以在抽象名詞前加上 great、much、some、little 或是 no 來修飾感覺的程度。

5. She is the woman ｜of｜ great beauty

　　→ of+ beauty = beautiful，用來修飾名詞 woman。

---

6. 使用錯誤的介係詞

下列情況或用語中的介係詞，常常被誤用：

(1) good / bad 是用 at，不是用 in：

My Mom is good in playing the piano. →（X）
應寫成 *My mom is good at playing the piano.* →（O）
（我的媽媽很會彈鋼琴。）

(2) arrive 是用 at，不是用 in：

Eric finally arrived in school at ten o'clock. →（X）
應寫成 *Eric finally arrived at school at ten o'clock.* →（O）
（*Eric* 終於在十點鐘時抵達學校。）

(3) borrow 是用 from，不是用 to：

My sister borrows some books to me. →（X）
應寫成 *My sister borrows some books from me.* →（O）
（我妹妹向我借了一些書。）

若把動詞 *borrow* 換成 *lend*，就可以使用 *to* 作為介係詞，例如：*I lend some books to my sister.*（我借了一些書給我妹妹。）

⑷ bump / run / drive / crash 是用 into，不是用 against：

The sport car bumped against the tree. →（ X ）
應改成 *The sport car <u>bumped into</u> the tree.* →（ O ）
（這輛跑車撞上了這棵樹。）

⑸ 對於某件事的 idea 是用 of，不是用 to：

I have an idea to travel the world in 100 days. →（ X ）
應改成 *I have an <u>idea of</u> traveling the world in 100 days.* →（ O ）
（我想要在一百天內環遊世界。）

⑹ 音量是用 in，不是用 with：

The children are sleeping, please talk with a quiet voice. →（ X ）
應改成 *The children are sleeping, please talk in a quiet voice.* →（ O ）
（孩子們都睡了，請講話小聲一點。）

⑺ 收音機、電視、電話是用 on，不是用 in：

The music in the radio is beautiful. →（ X ）
應改成 *The music <u>on the radio</u> is beautiful.* →（ O ）
（收音機播放的音樂很優美。）

當 radio 與 telephone 和 on 一起使用時，要有定冠詞 the，例如 on the radio、on the telephone、on the phone，on TV 和 on the TV 卻有不一樣的解釋。on TV 表示電視正在播放的節目，on the TV 則表示在電視這件物體的上方，試比較下列兩句：

The show on TV is so funny.（這個電視節目真有趣。）

→ on TV 表示電視播出的節目。

The vase on the TV is colorful.（放在電視上的花瓶顏色珍鮮豔。）
→ *on the TV* 表示電視上方的位置。

・換你試試看，填入正確的介係詞！

1. Wen is good ＿＿＿ cooking.
2. When will you arrive ＿＿＿ home?
3. She borrowed some money ＿＿＿ her parents.
4. The actor lends some clothes ＿＿＿ his assistant.
5. He has the idea ＿＿＿ inviting the band to his party.
6. The singer ＿＿＿ TV is so pretty.
7. You have to report ＿＿＿ a loud voice.

・你答對了嗎？

1. Wen is good at cooking.
2. When will you arrive at home?
3. She borrowed some money from her parents.
4. The actor lends some clothes to his assistant.
5. He has the idea of inviting the band to his party.
6. The singer on TV is so pretty.
7. You have to report in a loud voice.

O4
CHAPTER
讓句子更完整：形容詞和副詞

一、概念篇

‖ 什麼是形容詞 ‖

形容詞在句子裡，扮演修飾名詞或代名詞的角色，可以說明所修飾語詞的狀態、性質和數量，例如：

She is hungry.（她餓了。）
→ hungry 說明 she 的狀態。

These apples are very sweet.（這些蘋果很甜。）
→ sweet 說明 apples 的性質。

There are some books on the table.（有一些書在桌子上。）
→ some 說明書的數量。

‖ 形容詞的種類 ‖

形容詞依照描述性質的不同，可以分為三種類別：

1. 性狀形容詞

　　性狀形容詞又可以細分為敘述形容詞、專有形容詞、分詞形容詞和物質形容詞。敘述形容詞，用來描述物體的性質，例如：good（好的）、new（新的）、cute（可愛的）、ugly（醜陋的）、convenient（方便的）、helpful（有助益的）等。

　　專有形容詞，是將專有名詞作形容詞使用，例如：Chinese（中國的）、Japan（日本的）、American（美國的）。

　　分詞形容詞可以分成現在分詞和過去分詞，現在分詞如：interesting（令人有趣的）、exciting（令人興奮的）、frightening（令人恐懼的）等；過去分詞如：interested（感到有趣的）、excited（感到興奮的）或 frightened（感到恐懼的）等。通常，現在分詞扮演主動的角色，而過去分詞帶有被動的意味。關於現在分詞和過去分詞的用法，可以參考第十篇被動句。

　　物質形容詞，是將物質名詞作形容詞用，例如：plastic（塑膠的）、wood（木製的）、gold（含金的）。有些物質名詞可以在字尾加上 y 或 en 成為形容詞，例如：rain（下雨）→ rainy（下雨的）、cloud（雲）→ cloudy（多雲的）、gold（黃金）→ golden（金黃色的）、wood（木頭）→ wooden（木製的）。

2. 數量形容詞

　　下面的表格，可以幫助我們對數量形容詞更加的了解：

	+ 可數名詞	+ 不可數名詞
一些	a few some	a little some
很少（幾乎沒有）	few	little
很多	many a lot of	much a lot of
任何 （用於否定句或疑問句。）	any	any

　　例如：

I have a few / some friends.（我有一些朋友。）

I have few friends.（我的朋友很少。）
→ 注意 few 的用法，和上一句的 a few 不一樣，是表示幾乎沒有。

There are many / a lot of people in the lobby.（大廳裡有很多人。）

Do you have any friends?（你有任何朋友嗎？）
→ 問句用 any 來表示數量，後面的可數名詞要使用複數。

I don't have any friends.（我們沒有任何朋友。）
→ 否定句用 any 來表示數量，後面可可數名詞要使用複數。

I have a little / some money.（我有一些錢。）

I have little money.（我幾乎沒有錢。）
→ 注意 little 的用法，和上一句的 a little 不一樣，是表示幾乎沒有。

There is much / a lot of money in the box.（盒子裡有很多錢。）

Do you have any money?（你有任何錢嗎？）

I don't have any money.（我沒有任何錢。）

我們可以用＜數字 + 單位詞 + 形容詞＞的結構，來修飾名詞的狀態，例如：

Diana is 168 centimeters tall.（*Diana* 有 *168* 公分高。）
→ ＜數字＋單位詞＋形容詞＞用來修飾 Diana。

The mountain is 3000 meters high.（這座山高三千公尺。）

The little girl is ten years old.（這位小女孩十歲大。）

3. 代名指示形容詞

將代名詞作形容詞使用，就稱為代名指是形容詞。這類的形容詞如：this（這些）、that（那些）、some（某些）、all（全部）、both（兩者）、my（我的）、your（你的）、his（他的）、which（哪一個）、what（什麼）等。

▮ 形容詞的位置 ｜

　　在句子中，形容詞會出現在三個地方，例如：

(1) 形容詞在名詞前，修飾名詞

　　a cute girl（可愛的女孩）
　　→ 形容詞 cute 在名詞 girl 前。

　　a useful tool（好用的工具）
　　→ 形容詞 useful 在名詞 tool 前。

(2) 形容詞在代名詞後，修飾代名詞

　　something new（某樣新的東西）
　　→ 形容詞 new 在代名詞 something 之後，直接修飾代名詞。

　　anything bad（任何一樣不好的東西）
　　→ 形容詞 bad 在代名詞 anything 之後。

(3) 形容詞在連綴動詞後，補充說明主詞的狀態或性質

　　She is pretty.（她很漂亮。）
　　→ 形容詞 pretty 在連綴動詞 is 之後。

　　He looks nice.（他看起來很好。）
　　→ 形容詞 nice 在連綴動詞 look 之後。

　　連綴動詞常見的還有：appear（顯露）、become（變成）、feel（感覺）、get（變成）、seem（似乎）、smell（聞起來）、taste（嘗起來）等，關於連綴動詞的用法，可以參考第二篇名詞和動詞。
　　大部分的形容詞都可以遵循上述的原則，但有些形容詞只能放在指定的位置，例如：

　　There is an indoor swimming pool.（這裡有一個室內游泳池。）
　　→ indoor 只能放在名詞的前面。

His former boss is retired.（他的前任老闆現在退休了。）
→ former 也是只能放在名詞前面的形容詞。

這類的形容詞如：main（主要的）、chief（主要的）、elder（年紀較大的）、inner（內在的）、outdoor（戶外的）、only（只有）、outer（外在的）、upper（上面的）等字，都只能放在名詞或代名詞的前面。

那有沒有只能放在連綴動詞後的形容詞呢？例如：

The baby is asleep.（小嬰兒睡著了。）
→ 形容詞 asleep 只能放在連綴動詞後。

She feels afraid.（她感覺很害怕。）
→ 形容詞 afraid 只能放在連綴動詞後。

類似這樣用法的形容詞如：alone（單獨的）、ashamed（羞愧的）、awake（清醒的）、glad（高興的）、fine（美好的）、pleased（高興的）、unwell（不舒服的）、ill（生病的）等字，都只能放在連綴動詞後。

・換你試試看，找出句子中的形容詞！

1. The teacher is so nice.
2. Amanda is a smart student.
3. William is a naughty boy.
4. Simon likes this blue paints.
5. There's something wrong.
6. Do you have anything red?
7. The plum tastes sour.
8. The coffee smells bitter.

・你完成了嗎？

1. The teacher is so nice .
2. Amanda is a smart student.
3. William is a naughty boy.
4. Simon likes this blue paints.
5. There's something wrong .

6. Do you have anything red ?
7. The plum tastes sour .
8. The coffee smells bitter .

‖ 形容詞的順序

　　當同一個句子中，有兩個以上的形容詞時，我們習慣照下面的順序排列。這個順序分別是：數量、評價、尺寸、狀態、年紀、形狀、顏色、來源、材質、目的，例如：

two cute black cats（兩隻可愛的黑貓）
→ 形容詞依照數量、評價、顏色的順序排列。

this old blue watch（這隻老舊的藍色手錶）
→ 若有冠詞或代名指示形容詞，則放在所有形容詞的最前面。

a pretty small square pink Japan purse（一個漂亮又小的方形粉紅色日本錢包）
the silver bread knife（銀製的麵包刀）
→ knife 前的 bread 在這裡也當作形容詞使用，表示「目的」的形容詞，要放在所有形容詞的最後面。

　　若形容詞和評價、尺寸和狀態相關，我們可以在三種形容詞間加上逗號，也可以不加，例如：

a great, lively, famous city（一個很棒、有朝氣又有名的城市）
→ 也可以寫成：a great lively famous city

・換你試試看，排列出正確的形容詞順序！
1. the / soft / wonderful / paper / box
2. sweet / small / delicious / a / chocolate cake
3. beautiful / two / brown / happy / dog
4. wet / white / that / bath / towel
5. smart / angry / this / old / French / woman

· 你完成了嗎？

1. the wonderful soft paper box
   → 冠詞、評價、狀態、材質。
2. a delicious small sweet chocolate cake
   → 數量、評價、尺寸、狀態、材質。
3. two beautiful happy brown dogs
   → 數量、評價、狀態、顏色。
4. that wet white bath towel
   → 指示形容詞、狀態、顏色、用途。
5. this smart angry old French woman
   → 指示形容詞、評價、狀態、年紀、來源。

▎形容詞的比較級和最高級 ▎

在兩個事物間進行比較，稱為比較級。比較級的規則如下：

形容詞的比較級		
一個或兩個音節的形容詞	字尾直接 + er	cold → colder sweet → sweeter
	結尾是 e，直接 + r	brave → braver nice → nicer
	母音加子音，重複子音加 + er	hot → hotter thin → thinner
	結尾是 y，去 y + ier	angry → angrier happy → happier
兩個音節以上的形容詞	more + 形容詞	beautiful → more beautiful important → more important 例外：fun → more fun
不規則變化	×	good → better bad → worse many / much → more

例如：

Amy is taller.（Amy 比較高。）

Today is hotter.（今天比較熱。）
→ hot 中的母音為短母音，因此若要變化為比較級，要重複子音才能加 er。

This bowl is cleaner.（這個碗比較乾淨。）
→ 注意 clean 這個字的結構，雖然最後字尾為母音+子音，但母音前還是母音，兩個母音通常會唸成長音，不符合短母音要重複子音 + er 的規則，因此不用重複子音加 er。

She is more interesting.（她比較有趣。）

若有兩件事物在同一個句型中進行比較，要在比較級後面加 than：

Amy is taller than Nancy.（Amy 比 Nancy 高。）
→ Amy 和 Nancy 間做比較，比較級後面 + than。

This bowl is cleaner than that one.（這個碗比那個碗乾淨。）
→ 相比較的東西一致，後面出現的物體用代名詞即可。

She is more interesting than her sister.（她比他姊姊有趣。）

在非正式的英文中，than 後面可以放受詞；但在正式的英文用法中，只能用主格，例如：

My sister is thinner than I.（我的妹妹比我瘦。）
→ 正確的寫法，同時，主格代名詞後面省略了 be 動詞 am。

My sister is thinner than me.
→ 使用受格，是非正式的英文寫法。

當兩個比較級用 and 連接時，可以表示「越來越…」，例如：

She was angrier and angrier.（她越來越生氣。）
→ ＜比較級 and 比較級＞表示「越來越…」。

The air pollution is getting more and more serious.（空氣汙染越來越嚴重。）
→ 兩個音節以上的形容詞，在前面加 more 表示比較級。

最高級，顧名思義，就是所有的形容詞前面都加上一個「最」字。最高級的行程規則如下表：

形容詞的最高級		
一個或兩個音節的形容詞	字尾直接 + est	cold → coldest sweet → sweetest
	結尾是 e，直接 + st	brave → bravest nice → nicest
	母音加子音，重複子音加 + est	hot → hottest thin → thinnest
	結尾是 y，去 y + iest	angry → angriest happy → happiest
兩個音節以上的形容詞	most + 形容詞	beautiful → most beautiful important → most important 例外：fun → most fun
不規則變化	×	good → best bad → worst

例如：

She is the tallest girl in the class.（她是班上最高的女孩。）
→ 最高級的形容詞前要加 the。

He is the best runner in the world.（他是世界上最棒的跑者。）

The woman is the most beautiful actress I have seen.
（這個女人是我見過最漂亮的演員。）

· 換你試試看，要用原形、比較級還是最高級？

1. Jimmy is the _____ (smart) student in the school.
2. Mandy is _____ (fat) than Amy.
3. Mimi is a _____ (cute) cat.
4. She is _____ (fun) than Ivy.
5. Albert is the _____ (handsome) man in the world.
6. Justin is _____ (happy) than Tracy.

7. To watch a baseball game is _____ (exciting) than to watch a golf game.
8. This woman is the _____ (old) in this town.

・你完成了嗎？

1. Jimmy is the <u>smartest</u> student in the school.
2. Mandy is <u>fatter</u> than Amy.
3. Mimi is a <u>cute</u> cat.
4. She is <u>more fun</u> than Ivy.
5. Albert is the <u>most handsome</u> man in the world.
6. Justin is <u>happier</u> than Tracy.
7. To watch a baseball game is <u>more exciting</u> than to watch a golf game.
8. This woman is the <u>oldest</u> in this town.

▍什麼是副詞

副詞在句子中，扮演修飾動詞、形容詞或其他副詞的角色，例如：

Leo runs fast.（Leo 跑得很快。）
→ 副詞 fast 修飾動詞 run。

He is very smart.（他很聰明。）
→ 副詞 very 修飾形容詞 smart。

He sings very well.（他唱歌唱得很好。）
→ 副詞 very 修飾副詞 well。

▍副詞的種類

副詞根據表達的功能不同，可以分為五種類別：

⑴ 時間副詞
　　時間副詞，就是在句子中點出時間的語詞，通常在句子的最後，也可以放在句首，例如：

She called Ivy yesterday.（她昨天打電話給 *Ivy*。）
→ 時間副詞 yesterday 在句尾。

Yesterday she called Ivy.
→ 時間副詞放在句首。

時間副詞常見的如：yesterday（昨天）、today（明天）、yesterday（昨天）、then（當時）、now（現在）、this week（這週）、last week（上週）、next week（下週）等。

有一些介係詞和時間結合為一個詞組時，也會構成時間副詞，例如：for one hours（一個小時）、since 3 o'clock（從三點開始。）、until 7 o'clock（直到七點）等，關於介係詞和時間的詳細用法，請參考第三篇介係詞。

(2) 地方副詞

地方副詞表示事件發生的地方。地方副詞多在動詞後出現，例如：

He lives here.（他住在這裡。）
→ 地方副詞 here 在動詞 live 後面。

She walked here yesterday.（她昨天走來這裡。）
→ 當句子中同時有地方副詞和時間副詞時，要先寫地方副詞。

地方副詞常見的有：here（這裡）、there（那裡）、near（近地）、far（遠地）、up（向上）、down（向下）、forwards（向前地）、backwards（向後地）等。

(3) 頻率副詞

頻率副詞，用來表示動作發生的頻率或次數。頻率副詞可以細分為定期發生和不定期發生，例如：

He drinks two cups of coffee every day.（他每天喝兩杯咖啡。）
→ every day 代表每天都會發生的頻率，是定期發生的頻率副詞。

He always drinks Cappuccino.（他總是喝 *Cappuccino*。）
→ always 強調喝 Cappuccino 的頻率，但並不一定是每天或每週等規律的發生頻率。

　　一般而言，定期發生的頻率副詞可以放在句首或句尾，不定期發生的頻率副詞多出現在動詞前，少部分時候會出現在句首。

　　常見的頻率副詞有：daily（每天）、every day（每天）、once a week（每週一次）、annually（每年）、every two hours（每兩小時）、always（總是）、usually（通常）、often（時常）、sometimes（有時）、seldom（很少）、never（從不）等。

⑷ 表示程度的副詞

　　表示程度的副詞，目的在加強語氣，通常會放在動詞的前面，例如：

I really want to go to the playground.（我真的很想去遊樂場。）
→ 程度副詞 really 修飾動詞，加強「想要」的程度。

She only plays the piano once a week.（她一個星期只練一次鋼琴。）
→ 這個句子中有兩個副詞，only 修飾動詞 play，once a week 表示時間。

　　可以修飾動詞的程度副詞，常見的有：almost（幾乎）、really（真地）、hardly（幾乎不）、only（只有）、nearly（將近）、also（也）、much（很）、slightly（稍微地）、entirely（完全地）、enough（充分地）、quite（相當地）等。

　　enough 是個例外，在修飾動詞時，要放在動詞的後面，例如：

Do you talk enough?（你說夠了沒？）
→ enough 在動詞的後面作修飾。

This cake is not baked enough.（這個蛋糕烤得不夠。）

　　除了修飾動詞，程度副詞也可以用來修飾形容詞或副詞，例如：

The baby panda is very cute.（熊貓寶寶非常可愛。）
→ 副詞 very 修飾形容詞 cute。

Stop talking so loudly.（不要在這麼大聲說話。）
→ 副詞 so 修飾副詞 loudly。

用來修飾形容詞或副詞的程度副詞，常見的有：very（非常）、so（很）、quite（相當地）、too（太）、enough（足夠地）、pretty（相當地）、simply（僅僅地）、a little（一點）、almost（幾乎）、more（更）、absolutely（絕對地）等。

(5) 情狀副詞

表示動作處於某種狀態的副詞，稱為情狀副詞，例如：

The student answered the question carefully.（這位學生小心翼翼地回答問題。）
→ 副詞 carefully 修飾動詞 answer，表示當時回答問題的情緒狀態。

He fell down the stairs suddenly.（他突然摔下樓梯。）
→ 副詞 suddenly 修飾動詞 fell down 的狀態。

・換你試試看，判斷句中的副詞是屬於哪一類？

1. She sings very well.
2. He seldom walks to school.
3. My dad likes reading the newspaper every morning.
4. She almost finished the assignment last Saturday.
5. He has never gone there since he was five years old.

・你完成了嗎？

1. She sings very well.
   → 情狀副詞。
2. He seldom walks to school.
   → 頻率副詞。
3. My dad likes reading the newspaper every morning.
   → 頻率副詞，
4. She almost finished the assignment last Saturday.
   → 時間副詞。
5. He has never gone there since he was five years old.
   → 頻率副詞、地方副詞、時間副詞。

▌副詞的位置

副詞在句中的位置，根據修飾語詞的不同而改變：

⑴ 在動詞之後修飾動詞

He sings well.（他唱歌唱得很好。）

He plays the drum badly.（他打鼓打得很差。）
→ 如果有受詞，副詞要放在受詞的後面。

⑵ 在形容詞之前修飾形容詞

His girlfriend is very beautiful.（他的女朋友很漂亮。）

This novel is so interesting.（這本小說很有趣。）

⑶ 在其他副詞之前修飾副詞

The rabbit runs very fast.（兔子跑得很快。）

The turtle walks very slowly.（烏龜走得很慢。）

⑷ 放在句首修飾整個句子

Surely, she likes Jerry.（想必她喜歡 Jerry。）
→ 副詞 surely 在句首修飾後面的句子 she likes Jerry。

Suddenly, the phone rang.（突然地，電話響了。）

▌副詞的比較級和最高級

副詞的比較級和形容詞的比較級幾乎一模一樣，看看下列的表格：

副詞的比較級		
一個或兩個音節的副詞	字尾直接 + er	fast → faster
	結尾是 e，直接 + r	late → later
	結尾是 y，去 y + ier	early → earlier
兩個音節以上的副詞或結尾是 ly 的副詞	more + 副詞	often → more often
		kindly → more kindly
不規則變化	×	well → better
		badly → worse
		much → more

例如：

She runs faster.（她跑得比較快。）

He sings better.（他唱得比較好。）

和形容詞一樣，若有兩者進行比較時，要在副詞的比較級後面加 than：

She runs faster than Jimmy.（她跑的比 Jimmy 快。）

He sings better than Amy does.（他唱得比 Amy 好。）

My sister dances better than I do.（我的妹妹跳舞跳得比我好。）

→ 和動詞連用，than 後面的代名詞只能用主格 I，而不能用受格 me。

副詞的最高級和形容詞最高級的規則一樣，請看下面的表格：

副詞的最高級		
一個或兩個音節的副詞	字尾直接 + est	fast → fastest
	結尾是 e，直接 + st	late → latest
	結尾是 y，去 y + iest	early → earliest
兩個音節以上的副詞或結尾是 ly 的副詞	most + 副詞	often → most often
		kindly → most kindly
不規則變化	×	well → best
		badly → worst
		much → most

和形容詞最高級不一樣的地方是，副詞的最高級前面不用加 the，例如：

He runs fastest in his class.（他是他班上跑最快的。）
→ fastest 前面不用加 the。

·換你試試看，這些句子的英文怎麼說？

1. Jimmy 開車比 Tim 快。
2. Garcia 英文講得比 Kevin 差。
3. Nina 是世界上跳舞最美的人。
4. Eric 是班上表現最勇敢的男孩。

·你完成了嗎？

1. Jimmy drives faster than Tim does.
2. Garcia speaks English worse than Kevin does.
3. Nina dances most beautifully in the world.
4. Eric behaves most bravely in the class.

二、好學好用的句型

▍好學好用的形容詞／副詞句型 ▏

> 1. A + be 動詞 + 倍數 + 比較級 + than B = A 是 B 的…倍

例如：

The football field is five times larger than the basketball court.
（足球場是籃球場的五倍大。）
→ 倍數的規則就是在數字後面加上 times。

Jimmy is twice heavier than Tim (is).
（*Jimmy* 是 *Tim* 的兩倍重。）
→ 兩倍的時候可以用 two times 或是 twice；than 後面的 be 動詞可以省略。

This villa is four times bigger than that house.
（這棟別墅是那棟房子的四倍大。）

這句話也可以用＜倍數＋as＋形容詞＋as...＞的句型改寫：

This villa is four times as big as that house.
→ 記得在 as... as... 前要加上倍數。

Amanda owns twice more dolls than Kathy does.
（*Amanda* 擁有比 *Amy* 多兩倍的娃娃。）
→ 也可以將 be 動詞改成一般動詞。

· 我們可以這樣說

　　購買 3C 產品時，我們可以利用這個句型來比較電腦的記憶體容量，例如：

The memory of this computer is twice larger than that one.
（這個電腦的記憶體容量是那台電腦的兩倍大。）

· 換你試試看，兩種句型的改寫練習！

1. The skyscraper is three times taller than the building.
2. Nancy's hair is four times longer than Amy's.
3. This bag is three times cheaper than that one.

· 你完成了嗎？

1. The skyscraper is three times as tall as the building.
2. Nancy's hair is four times as long as Amy's.
3. This bag is three times as cheap as that one.

2. the ＋ 比較級 ＋ 主詞 ＋ 動詞 , the ＋ 比較級 ＋ 主詞 ＋ 動詞 ＝ 越…，就越…

　　例如：

The more you study, the smarter you will be. （你讀越多書，你就會越聰明。）

The more vegetables you eat, the healthier you will be.
（吃越多青菜，你就會越健康。）

The less money you spend, the richer you will be.
（花錢花得少，你就會越有錢。）
→ less 表示和 more 相反的情況。

The higher up, the greater the fall.（爬得越高，摔得越重。）
→ 在比較級後面，不一定要接＜主詞＋動詞＞所構成的子句。

The sooner, the better.（越快越好。）
→ 我們也可以只保留 the ＋ 比較級，省略後面的主詞和動詞。

More haste, less speed.（欲速則不達。）
→ 在慣用語中，定冠詞 the 也可以被省略。

・我們可以這樣說

　　這個句型可以用來表示叮嚀，例如：

The less you smoke, the healthier you will be.
（你菸抽得越少，就會越健康。）

・換你試試看，排列出正確的順序！

1. The farther you see jump, the higher you can.
2. The they get together more, the painful more they will be.
3. The angrier he waited, the longer he became.

・你完成了嗎？

1. The higher you jump, the farther you can see.
2. The more they get together, the more painful they will be.
3. The longer he waited, the angrier he became.

> 3. 主詞 + would rather +動詞 (1) + than + 動詞 (2) = 寧可⋯，也不⋯

　　例如：

I would rather watch TV at home than go mountain climbing.
（我寧願待在家看電視，也不要去爬山。）
→ would rather 後面的動詞要用原形動詞。

She would rather study math than study English.
（她寧願念數學也不要唸英文。）

would rather 可以分開，因此上面這個句子可以改寫成：

She would study math rather than study English.

She prefers to study math than study English.
→ would rather 也可以用＜prefer to...＞代替。

Kim would rather tell the truth.（Kim 寧願說實話。）
→ 當句子語意清楚時，也可以省略 than 後面的句子。

・我們可以這樣說
　　假日當家人問你要不要去大賣場逛逛時，如果你真的不想去人擠人，你可以這樣說：

I would rather to stay at home.（我寧願待在家裡。）

・換你試試看，寫出完整的句子！
1. He / play computer games / play board games / his little brother
2. This child / eat carrots / eat spinach
3. The manager / get fired / lie to the customers

・你完成了嗎？
1. He would rather play computer games than play board games with his little brother.
2. The child would rather eat carrots than eat spinach.
3. The manager would rather get fired than lie to the customers.

---

4. be 動詞 + not so much A as B = 與其說 A，不如是 B

例如：

She is not so much happy as excited.
（與其說她很開心，不如說她很興奮。）
→ not so much 和 as 後面連接的語詞詞性要一致。

He is not so much stupid as stubborn.（與其說他笨，不如說他很固執。）

這個句型可以用＜less...than...＞代換，因此，上面的句子可以改寫成：

He is less stupid than stubborn.

‧我們可以這樣說

這個句型可以用來表示讚美。當你的家人或是朋友完成了艱難的任務，你可以這樣說：

You are not so much as intelligent as talented.
（與其說你聰明，不如說你天才。）

‧換你試試看，利用這個句型練習造句！

1. He / writer / poet
2. She / dancer / street performer
3. She / angry / furious

‧你完成了嗎？

1. He is not so much a writer as a poet.
2. She is not so much a dancer as a street performer.
3. She is not so much angry as furious.

---

5. 主詞 + had better + 動詞 = 最好⋯

例如：

You had better quit smoking.（你最好戒菸。）

→ had better 後面的動詞要用原形動詞。quit 後面的動詞要改成動名詞。

The student had better follow the teacher's instruction.（學生最好遵守老師的教誨。）

You had better not call her right now.（你最好不要現在打電話給她。）

→ 在 had better 後面加 not，就可以構成否定句。

這個句型可以延伸另一個句型＜主詞 + know better than + 不定詞＞，表示「明白做某事是不好的，所以不會去做」：

I know better than to drive after drinking alcohol.（我知道不能酒醉駕車。）

→ 英文句子中雖然沒有否定詞，卻帶有否定涵義。

・我們可以這樣說

如果忘記繳帳單，可能因此會被停止使用或需要額外繳交滯留金，因此，快到帳單到期的日子時，我們可以這樣表示提醒：

You had better not forget to pay the bill.（你最好不要忘記繳帳單。）

・換你試試看，這句英文怎麼說？

1. 你要多吃青菜。
2. 你要守規矩。
3. 你不要看太多電視。
4. 你不要去外面，雨很大。

・你完成了嗎？

1. You had better eat more vegetable.
2. You had better behave yourself.
3. You had better not watch too much TV.
4. You had better not go outside. The rain is heavy.

---

6. the last + 名詞 + 不定詞 = 最不可能…

例如：

I believe he is the last person to lie me.（我相信他不會騙我。）
→ the last 後面的名詞可以省略，因此這句可以改寫成：I believe he is the last to lie me.

Jim is the last (boy) that I want to talk to.（*Jim* 是我最不想說話的男孩。）
→ the last 後除了接不定詞，也可以銜接子句。

My best friend is the first (person) to help me.（我的好朋友一定會幫我。）
→ the first 是 the last 的相反，表示「最有可能的」。

・我們可以這樣說

當你想要表示某件事是你最不喜歡的，你可以用這個句型來表達，例如，你非常不喜歡榴槤的味道，你可以這樣說：

Durian is the last fruit that I want to eat.（我一點都不想吃榴槤。）

・換你試試看，這種狀況的英文怎麼說？

1. 我非常喜歡打躲避球。
2. 我非常不喜歡下西洋棋。
3. 我非常想要讀這部小說。
4. 我很不想跟 Sandy 玩。

・你完成了嗎？

1. The dodge ball is the first sport I want to play.
2. The chess is the last board game I want to play.
3. This novel is the first book I want to read.
4. Sandy is the last person I want to play with.

---

7. as + 形容詞／副詞 + as = 像⋯一樣

例如：

Jimmy is as a good student as Jason.（*Jimmy* 像 *Jason* 一樣，是個好學生。）

→ ＜as... as...＞可以用來比較兩個不同的主詞。

She writes English as well as speaks.（她英文寫得和說得一樣好。）
→ 修飾動詞時，要將形容詞改為副詞。

Jimmy is as stubborn as Jason is conservative.
（*Jimmy* 固執的程度就和 *Jason* 保守的程度一樣。）
→ 比較的內容也可以不一樣。

· 我們可以這樣說

當工作很忙的時候，我們可以用這個句型表達：

I am as busy as a bee. I really want to take a vacation.
（我像蜜蜂一樣忙，我真希望可以去度假。）

· 換你試試看，排列出正確的句子順序！

1. She speaks English well as speaks as Chinese.
2. He does newspaper as fast as his father reads.
3. He is as puppy as the cute.
4. She is smart as he is.

· 你完成了嗎？

1. She speaks English as well as speaks Chinese.
2. He reads newspaper as fast as his father does.
3. He is as cute as the puppy.
4. She is as smart as he is.

‖ 好學的形容詞／副詞諺語 ‖

· 你來試試看，可以找出正確的中文意思嗎？

1. Love is blind.
2. Men are blind in their own cause.
3. The price of wisdom is above rubies.
4. Better late than never.
5. A good medicine tastes bitter.

6. All is well that ends well.

7. A rolling stone gathers no moss.

8. Honesty is the best policy.

9. In at one ear and out at the other.

10. Let sleeping dog lie.

11. Comparisons are odious.

12. Action speaks louder than words.

13. Being happy is the priority of living, if you want to be sad, be sad for something that's worth it.

14. Two heads are better than one.

15. What is worth doing is worth doing well.

16. Wine in, truth out.

A. 智慧勝過一切。

B. 結果好，一切都好

C. 滾石不生苔。

D. 愛是盲目的。

E. 人比人，氣死人。

F. 一人計短，兩人計長。

G. 值得做的事就值得做好。

H. 良藥苦口。

I. 遲做總比不做好。

J. 誠實為上策。

K. 左耳進，右耳出。

L. 珍惜你所擁有的，慶幸所曾發生的。

M. 酒後吐真言。

N. 別自找麻煩。

O. 行動勝於空談。

P. 切身之人皆盲目。

· 你找到了嗎?

1. Love is blind. 愛是盲目的。

2. Men are blind in their own cause. 切身之人皆盲目。

3. The price of wisdom is above rubies. 智慧勝過一切。

4. Better late than never. 遲做總比不做好。

5. A good medicine tastes bitter. 良藥苦口。

6. All is well that ends well. 結果好，一切都好。

7. A rolling stone gathers no moss. 滾石不生苔。

8. Honesty is the best policy. 誠實為上策。

9. In at one ear and out at the other. 左耳進，右耳出。

10. Let sleeping dog lie. 別自找麻煩。

11. Comparisons are odious. 人比人，氣死人。

12. Action speaks louder than words. 行動勝於空談。

13. Being happy is the priority of living, if you want to be sad, be sad for something that's worth it. 珍惜你所擁有的，慶幸所曾發生的。

14. Two heads are better than one. 一人計短，兩人計長。

15. What is worth doing is worth doing well. 值得做的事就值得做好。

16. Wine in, truth out. 酒後吐真言。

三、文法糾正篇

1. 形容詞和副詞的混淆

大部分的副詞結尾為 ly，但有些形容詞的結尾也有 ly，因此常常和副詞產生混淆，例如：

He is very friendly.（他很友善。）
→ 正確的用法。

He talks to me friendly.
→ 誤將 friendly 當成副詞修飾動詞，錯誤的用法。

這類的形容詞有：friendly（友善的）、lovely（可愛的）、lonely（寂寞的）、likely（很有可能的）、lively（活潑的）、ugly（醜的）、deadly（致命的）、cowardly（膽小的）、silly（愚蠢的）等。

有些結尾為 ly 的語詞，可以同時做形容詞或副詞使用，例如：

A weekly magazine is published weekly.（週刊每週都會出版。）
→ 第一個 weekly 為形容詞，修飾名詞 magazine；第二個 weekly 為副詞，修飾動詞 publish。

這類形容詞和副詞都是 ly 結尾的語詞如：daily（每天的／地）、weekly（每週的／地）、monthly（每月的／地）、yearly（每年的／地）、early（早的／地）等。

---

2. 動詞和形容詞或副詞一起使用，有不同的意思

這類的動詞如：be 動詞、appear（顯現／出現）、sound（聽起來／聽）、taste（嘗起來／嚐）、feel（感覺／觸摸）、look（看起來／看）、smell（聞起來／聞）等，在和形容詞或副詞一起使用時，會代表不同的意思，例如：

He looks happy.（他看起來很快樂。）
→ look 和形容詞 happy 一起使用，中文翻成「看起來…」。

He looks at the dog happily.（他快樂地看著這條狗。）
→ look 和副詞 happily 一起使用，中文翻成「看」。

再看一個例子：

The cake tastes sweet.（蛋糕嚐起來很甜。）
→ taste 和形容詞 sweet 一起使用，中文翻成「嚐起來」。

She tasted the cake quickly.（她很快地品嘗了一下蛋糕。）
→ taste 和副詞 quickly 一起使用，表示「品嘗」的動作。

---

3. 只能放在動詞後面的形容詞

有些形容詞只能出現在動詞後面，例如：

The child is afraid.（這個小孩很害怕。）

→ afraid 在動詞的後面。

The afraid child is Tom.（X）
→ 將 afraid 放在名詞前修飾名詞，是錯誤的用法。

The frightened child is Tom.（這個感到害怕的小孩是 *Tom*。）
→ 若想要修飾名詞，可以用 frightened 取代 afraid。

這些形容詞有：awake（醒著的）、afloat（漂浮著的）、afraid（害怕的）、alike（相像的）、alight（點亮著的）、alive（活著的）、alone（單獨的）和 asleep（睡著的）等。

通常，這些形容詞也不會和 very 一起使用，例如：

The boy is very awake.（X）
→ 用 very 來修飾 awake，是錯誤的用法。

The boy is wide awake.（這個小男孩徹底醒了。）
→ 用 wide 來修飾 awake 的狀態。

The baby is very asleep.（X）
→ 不會用 very 來修飾 asleep。

The baby is fast asleep.（小寶寶很快睡著了。）
→ 用 fast 來修飾 asleep。

---

4. 分詞的位置不同，意思也不同

我們已經瞭解了分詞有現在分詞和過去分詞兩種。現在分詞多半帶有主動意味，過去分詞則表示被動意味，例如：

an interesting movie（令人感到有趣的電影）
→ 現在分詞表示主動。

a broken window（被打破的窗戶）
→ 過去分詞表示被動。

若分詞在句子中的位置不同，代表的涵義也會略也改變，例如：

the students laughing in the classroom（在教室笑的學生們）
→ 現在分詞 laughing 放在名詞 students 後面，不僅可以讓我們知道學生在笑，也讓我們可以感受到在笑的動作。

a glass broken yesterday（昨天打破的玻璃杯）
→ 過去分詞 broken 放在名詞 glass 後修飾，不僅讓我們知道杯子打破了，也幫助我們聯想到杯子打破的動作。

這種在句子中又像形容詞，又像動詞的分詞，可以表達狀態，也可以讓我們聯想到動作本身，使句子更具有動感。

5. how / so / too 和名詞連用時，要有不定冠詞

當 how、so 和 too 與形容詞一起使用時，後面若有名詞，名詞前面要有不定冠詞 a 或是 an，例如：

How pretty a woman she is!（她是多美的一個女人啊！）
→ woman 前有不定冠詞 a。

How pretty woman she is!（X）
→ woman 前沒有不定冠詞，是錯誤的寫法。

再看一個例子：

It is so cold a day that you had better put on your sweater.
（今天很冷，你最好穿上你的毛衣。）
→ day 前面有不定冠詞 a。

It is so cold day that you had better put on your sweater.（X）
→ day 前面沒有不定冠詞，是錯誤的寫法。

6. 副詞位置的混淆

副詞在句中的位置，常常產生混淆，比較看看下面的句子：

We often play badminton in the afternoon.（我們通常都在下午打羽毛球。）

→ 句中有動詞，副詞要放在動詞的前面。

She speaks Japanese well.（她日文說得很好。）
→ 若動詞後有受詞，副詞應放在受詞的後面。

She speaks well Japanese.（X）
→ 先寫副詞才寫受詞，是錯誤的寫法，也是常犯的錯誤。

She is often early.（她通常都會早到。）
→ 句中有 be 動詞，副詞放在 be 動詞的後面。

You will never see me again.（你將不會再看到我。）
→ 句中有助動詞，副詞放在助動詞後。

但下列三種情形，副詞可以放在助動詞或動詞的後面，也可以放在前面：

I must always do the laundry.（我總是必須要洗衣服。）
→ 一般習慣將副詞放在助動詞的後面。

I always must do the laundry.
→ 副詞放在助動詞 must 的前面，也是正確的寫法。

must 可以用＜have to＞代換，因此副詞也可以變換位置：

I always have to do the laundry.
→ 正確的寫法。

I have always to do the laundry.
→ 正確的寫法。

除了助動詞，當動詞是 used to 時，副詞的位置可以改變：

We always used to go to the movies on weekends.
（我們總是習慣週末去看電影。）
→ 副詞放在動詞 used to 的前面。

We used always to go to the movies on weekends.
→ 將 always 放在動詞 used 的後面，也是正確的寫法。

7. 副詞的特殊位置

時間副詞，通常會放在句子的最後，例如：

He went to the library yesterday.（他昨天去圖書館。）
→ 時間副詞放在句尾。

He yesterday went to the library.（X）
→ 將時間副詞放在一般動詞前，是很常見的錯誤。

地方副詞也多放在句子的最後面，但若句子中同時有時間副詞怎麼辦呢？看看下面這個句子：

They went there yesterday.（他們昨天去那裡。）
→ 先寫地方副詞，在寫時間副詞。

表示規律的頻率副詞，也多習慣放在句尾，例如：

They have a meeting weekly.（他們每週開一次會。）
→ weekly 是規律性的頻率副詞，放在句尾。

They weekly have a meeting.（X）
→ 將 weekly 等副詞放在一般動詞前，是錯誤的用法。

表示不定時間的頻率副詞，可以放在句中，例如：

She seldom goes to the movies.（她很少去看電影。）
→ seldom 並非規律的頻率副詞，因此放在句子中間。

She goes to the movies seldom.（X）
→ seldom 放在句尾是錯誤的用法。

We often rent videos.（我們常常租影片。）
→ often 表示不定時間的頻率，可以放在句子中間。

We rent videos very often.
→ 但是我們卻習慣將 very often 放在句尾。

有些表示評價的副詞，通常也會出現在句子的後面，例如：

You sing well.（你唱得很好。）
→ 正確的寫法。

You well sing.（X）
→ 錯誤的寫法。

再看一個例子：

She dances badly.（她跳舞跳得很差。）
→ 正確的寫法。

She badly dances.（X）
→ 錯誤的寫法。

・換你試試看，形容詞和副詞的綜合練習，判斷句子是否正確！

1. The baby sleeping on the bed is his daughter.
2. My elder sister called Amy.
3. Amy is elder than I.
4. The old man is an ill person.
5. Today is so hot day that I want to go swimming.
6. He likes very much scuba diving.
7. She runs faster her brother.
8. He is taller than his small brother.
9. She can play well the piano.
10. Jimmy eats his breakfast quickly.
11. He usually drinks a cup of coffee in the morning.
12. He daily writes an English article.
13. Annie is too funny girl.
14. She last night called me.
15. The necklace is beautifuler than that one.
16. Andy is tallest boy in his class.

・你完成了嗎？

1. The baby sleeping on the bed is his daughter.

→（O），這句的意思是：睡在床上的嬰兒是他的女兒。

2. My elder sister called Amy.

→（O）形容詞 elder 多放在名詞前修飾名詞。這句的中文翻譯是：我的姐姐叫做 Amy。

3. Amy is elder than I.

→（X）上一題有提到，elder 多放在名詞前修飾名詞，在動詞後面，通常會用 older 來表示「比較大的」，因此本句應寫成：Amy is older than I. 中文翻譯為：Amy 比我大。

4. The old man is an ill person.

→（X）ill 不會和名詞一起使用，多半放在動詞的後面。因此本句應寫成：The old man is ill.或是 The old man is a sick person. 中文翻譯為：這位老先生生病了。和 ill 同樣用法的還有 well，也是不能和名詞一起使用。

5. Today is so hot day that I want to go swimming.

→（X）有 so 修飾的形容詞，若後面有名詞，名詞前要有不定冠詞。本句應寫成：Today is so hot a day that I want to go swimming. 中文意思是：今天真是熱，我想要去游泳。

6. He likes very much scuba diving.

→（X）句子中的動作有受詞，應將副詞放在受詞的後面，本句應寫成：He likes scuba diving very much. 中文翻譯為：他非常喜歡潛水。

7. She runs faster her brother.

→（X）比較級中若有兩者進行比較，則中間要加入 than。本句正確的寫法為：She runs faster than her brother. 中文翻譯為：她跑得比她的弟弟快。

8. He is taller than his small brother.

→（X）一般習慣用 little 加名詞，動詞加 small，因此本句正確的寫法應為：He is taller than his little brother. 中文翻譯是：他比他的弟弟還高。

9. She can play well the piano.

→（X）表示評價的副詞，習慣上會放在句尾，本句正確的寫法是：She can play the piano well. 中文翻譯為：她鋼琴彈得很好。

10. Jimmy eats his breakfast quickly.

→（O）本句翻譯為：Jimmy 吃早餐吃得很快。

11. He usually drinks a cup of coffee in the morning.

→（O）不定期的頻率副詞放在句中，時間副詞放在句尾。本句中文翻譯為：他通常在早上喝一杯咖啡。

12. He daily writes an English article.

→（X）定期的頻率副詞放在句尾，本句應改寫成：He writes an article daily.，中文翻譯為：他每天寫一篇英文文章。

13. Annie is too funny girl.

→（X）too 修飾形容詞，後面的名詞前要有不定冠詞，本句應寫成：Annie is too funny a girl.，中文翻譯為：Annie 真是個有趣的女孩。

14. She last night called me.

→（X）時間副詞要放在句尾，本句應寫成：She called me last night.，中文翻譯為：她昨晚打電話給我。

15. The necklace is beautifuler than that one.

→（X）兩個音節以上的形容詞，變成比較級，應在形容詞前面加 more，本句應寫成：The necklace is more beautiful than that one.，中文翻譯為：這條項鍊比那條項鍊漂亮。

16. Andy is tallest boy in his class.

→（X）最高級前面要加 the，本句應寫成：Andy is the tallest boy in his class. 中文翻譯為：Andy 是他班上最高的男生。

NOTE

01 CHAPTER

02 CHAPTER

03 CHAPTER

04 CHAPTER

05 CHAPTER

06 CHAPTER

07 CHAPTER

08 CHAPTER

09 CHAPTER

10 CHAPTER

05
CHAPTER
把句子連接起來：連接詞、連接副詞和關係代名詞

一、概念篇

‖ 連接詞

在字與字、句子與句子中起聯接作用的詞，稱為連接詞。

連接詞分為對等連接詞和從屬連接詞。

對等連接詞，顧名思義，連接對等的語詞或句子，同時，前後連接的語氣也要一致，例如：

I like cats and she likes cats, too.（我喜歡貓，而她也喜歡。）

→ and 前面是句子，後面也是句子，在語氣上，也都是肯定句。

常見的對等連接詞有：

對等連接詞	
單字型對等連接詞	and、but、or、so、nor、yet
片語型對等連接詞	both...and...、neither...nor...、not only...but also...

從屬連接詞，連接具有從屬關係的兩個句子，例如：

I am tired because I didn't sleep well last night.
（我很累因為我昨晚沒睡好。）
→ because 連接前後的因果關係，為從屬連接詞。

從屬連接詞非常多，我們可以依表達的涵義將其分為七種類型：

從屬連接詞	
表示時間	when、while、before、after、as、as soon as、since、until
表示地點	where、wherever
表示條件	if、unless、providing / provided that、in case
表示原因	because、since、as
表示結果	so...that、so that
表示讓步	though、although
表示比較	than、no sooner than

▌換你試試看，選出正確的連接詞！

(1) _____ he is rich, he isn't happy.
　　(A) And　(B) But　(C) Because　(D) Even though

(2) _____ my sister _____ my brother likes this cartoon.
　　(A) Neither...nor...　(B) Both...and...　(C) Neither...or...　(D) Both...or...

(3) She can't come to your party _____ she is sick.
　　(A) so　(B) or　(C) and　(D) because

(4) This movie is funny, _____ I like it very much.
　　(A) but　(B) and　(C) though　(D) so

(5) Jimmy _____ Tim is handsome.
　　(A) although　(B) and　(C) as well as　(D) or

(6) He didn't study hard. _____, he got bad grades.
　　(A) However　(B) Therefore　(C) Although　(D) Even though

01 CHAPTER
02 CHAPTER
03 CHAPTER
04 CHAPTER
05 CHAPTER
06 CHAPTER
07 CHAPTER
08 CHAPTER
09 CHAPTER
10 CHAPTER

・你選對了嗎？

(1)(D)　(2)(A)　(3)(D)　(4)(D)　(5)(C)　(6)(B)

‖ 連接副詞 ‖

連接副詞屬於副詞的一種，但其表達的意思與從屬連接詞相似，也可以在語氣上連接兩個句子。

‖ 連接副詞的基本類型 ‖

常見的連接副詞可以歸類為下列四種類型：

連接副詞	
表示因果關係	therefore、thus、hence、as a result、as a consequently、consequently、then
表示語氣轉折	besides、however、even so、nevertheless、nonetheless、otherwise
表示換句話說	in other words、that is、that is to say
表示情況相反	on the other hand、on the contrary
表示舉例	for example、for instance

連接副詞的基本句型為＜主詞＋動詞；連接副詞，主詞＋動詞＞，例如：

He lied to me again; therefore, I won't believe him anymore.
（他又對我說謊；所以，我不會再相信他了。）

雖然連接副詞具有連接前後句子語氣的功用，但在文法規則中，並不具有連接詞的功能，因此連接副詞前的標點符號應為分號或句號。

He lied to me again. Therefore, I won't believe him anymore.
→ Therefore 帶領一個新的句子。

· 換你試試看，找出連接副詞！

1. The bracelet is made by gold. Hence, it is very expensive.
2. Burt studied hard. Thus, he got great grades.
3. I want to go to the theater. However, my sister wants to stay at home.
4. Nancy decided to learn the flute. On the other hand, her sister decided to learn the piano.

· 你完成了嗎？

1. The bracelet is made by gold. Hence , it is very expensive.
2. Burt studied hard. Thus , he got great grades.
3. I want to go to the theater. However , my sister wants to stay at home.
4. Nancy decided to learn the flute. On the other hand , her sister decided to learn the piano.

▌關係代名詞

　　在了解關係代名詞前，我們要先知道什麼是先行詞。先行詞就是在關係代名詞前面的名詞，是關係代名詞帶領的句子所要修飾的名詞，例如：

I don't know the girl who is standing by the tree .
（我不認識那個站在樹邊的女孩。）
→ 關係代名詞 who 前的名詞 girl 是先行詞，who 所帶領的句子用來修飾 girl。

那麼，什麼是關係代名詞呢？
顧名思義，關係代名詞，就是**代**替前面的**名詞**和句子產生**關係**的語詞。例如：

I know the girl. （我認識這個女孩。）

The girl is an American. （這個女孩是美國人。）

這兩個句子都是在討論 the girl，因此我們可以把這兩個句子合併。
首先，先找到句子的主角，這兩句重複出現的語詞是 the girl，我們可以判

定，主要就是 the girl。再來，我們要選定關係代名詞，代表人物的關係代名詞是 who，我們可以用 who 來代換 the girl，：

I know the girl ~~the girl~~ is an American.
→ 第二個 the girl 用 who 代替
→ *I know the girl who is an American.*

你有沒有發現，關係代名詞除了具有代表前面名詞的作用，也具有連接詞的作用，可以把兩個句子連接起來，相當於 and：

I know the girl | *and the girl* | *is an American.*
　　　　　　　　　//
I know the girl | *who* | 　　　　　 *is an American.*

由關係代名詞所帶領的句子，稱為關係子句，也可以稱為形容詞子句，目的在修飾前面的先行詞，而形容詞子句則是放在名詞的後面：

The pretty singer is my idol.（這位漂亮的歌手是我的偶像。）
→ 形容詞 pretty 放在名詞 singer 的前面作修飾。

The singer who sings beautifully is my idol.（這位唱歌很優美的歌手是我的偶像。）
→ who 帶領的形容詞子句放在 singer 後面作修飾。

· 換你試試看，找出短文裡的關係代名詞！

Wendy is the girl who has three cats. One cat whose name is Mimi is a naughty girl. She always plays the pens and erasers on Wendy's desk and makes Wendy angry. Another cat that likes sleeping on the shelf is Du-Du. The other cat, which likes to chat with Mimi is Mei-Mei. Wendy loves her cats very much!

· 你找到了嗎？

Wendy is the girl **who** has three cats. One cat **whose** name is Mimi is a naughty girl. She always plays the pens and erasers on Wendy's desk and makes Wendy angry. Another cat **that** likes sleeping on the shelf is Du-Du. The other cat, **which** likes to chat with Mimi, is Mei-Mei. Wendy loves her cats very much!

▌關係代名詞的種類

　　關係代名詞依據先行詞的種類，可以分為代替人的 who、代替動物或事物的 which 和同時代替這三種的 that。和人稱代名詞一樣，關係代名詞也可以分為主格、所有格和受格：

關係代名詞			
	主格 (1)	所有格 (2)	受格 (3)
人	who	whose	whom
動物、事物	which	whose	which
人、動物、事物	that	----	that

(1) 作為主格的 who、which 和 that，後面接續動詞：

The boy who is sitting next to me is Albert.（坐在我旁邊的男孩是 *Albert*。）
→ who 加動詞 is sitting。

The cat, which ate the fish last night, is very naughty.
（這隻昨晚吃了魚的貓咪非常頑皮。）
→ which 加動詞 ate。

上面的兩個句子，也可以用 that 取代 who 或是 which：

The boy that is sitting next to me is Albert.

The cat that ate the fish last night is very naughty.

作為主格的關係代名詞，在其引導的句子中，具有扮演主詞的作用，因此，動詞要根據先行詞做適當的變化：

He is the man who has ten dogs.（他就是擁有十隻狗的那個男人。）
→ who 代替前面的 man，為第三人稱，因此動詞為 has。

There are three cats which are sleeping on the sofa.
（有三隻貓正睡在沙發上。）
→ cats 為複數，動詞也要配合使用 are。

關係代名詞作為主詞使用時，不可以省略；若和 be 動詞一起使用時，則兩者可以同時省略，以上述的句子為例：

He is the man who has ten dogs.
→ who 為主格關係代名詞，後接一般動詞，不可省略。

There are three cats which are sleeping on the sofa.
→ which 為主格關係代名詞，後接 be 動詞，兩者可以一起省略。
因此這句可以改寫成：*There are three cats sleeping on the sofa.*

一般而言，先行詞是人物時，要用 who 作為關係代名詞，但如果先行詞是集合名詞或人物與動物的組合時，要用 that 作為關係代名詞，例如：

That's the school team that won the basketball game.
（那就是贏得籃球比賽的校隊。）
→ school team 為集合名詞，後面的關係代名詞用 that 不用 who。

May saw Jimmy and his dog (that were) walking in the park.
（*May* 看到 *Jimmy* 帶著狗在公園散步。）
→ Jimmy and his dog 是人加動物的組合，關係代名詞用 that。

⑵ 作為所有格的 whose，後面接續名詞：

I like the girl whose eyes are brown.（我喜歡這個有棕色眼睛的女孩。）
→ whose 後面加名詞 eyes。

The cat whose color is black named Ruru.（這隻黑色的貓叫做 *Ruru*。）
→ whose 後面接名詞 color。

Whose 和後面的名詞，可以作為其所引導的關係子句中的主詞或受詞，例如：

He has a friend whose dad is a professor.
（他有一個爸爸是教授的朋友。）
→ whose dad 是關係子句中的主詞。

The building whose owner you talked to is David.
（這位和你說話的建築物擁有者叫做 David。）
→ whose owner 是動詞 talked to 的受詞。

(3) 作為受格的 whom、which 和 that，後面接續主詞與動詞：

The boy whom you like is my friend.（你喜歡的男孩是我的朋友。）
→ whom 後面接主詞 you 和動詞 like；whom 雖然代替前面的名詞 boy，但但同時也作為 like 的受詞。

The cat which you are holding is very cute.（你正抱著的貓很可愛。）
→ which 後面接主詞 you 和動詞 are holding。

上面的兩個句子，也可以用 that 代替 whom 或是 which。
關係代名詞 which 和 that 的主格與受格是同一個字，所以在使用上要小心混淆，試比較下面兩句：

The novel, which is about vampires, is very exciting.
（這本關於吸血鬼的小說非常刺激。）
→ which 後面接動詞，which 是主格的關係代名詞。

The novel, which my mom bought me, is very exciting.
（這本我媽媽買給我的小說非常刺激。）
→ which 是 bought 的受詞，為受格的關係代名詞。

在口語中，作為受格的關係代名詞常常可以省略，因此，上述句子也可以省略 which，改寫成：

The novel my mom bought me is exciting.

· 換你試試看，要用什麼格的關係代名詞呢？

1. This is the man _____ wants to meet you.
2. This is the man _____ my parents want to see.
3. Is this the pen _____ Tim is looking for?
4. She has a glass _____ material is crystal.
5. She finally met the man _____ she loves.
6. He is the student _____ Miss Yang spoke to yesterday.
7. I don't know the old woman and her cat _____ are sitting over there.
8. This is a pair for the pants _____ I bought in the department store.
9. The boy _____ is watching TV is Jane's brother.
10. Tina doesn't like the boy _____ has green eyes.

· 是不是很簡單呢？

1. This is the man who wants to meet you.
   → 關係代名詞後面是動詞，因此用主格的 who。
2. This is the man whom my parents want to see.
   → 關係代名詞是接受動詞 see 的受詞，用受格的 whom。
3. Is this the pen which / that Tim is looking for?
   → 關係代名詞代表錢的東西 pen，同時也是 look for 的受詞。
4. She has a glass whose material is crystal.
   → 關係代名詞後面銜接名詞，要用所有格的 whose。
5. She finally met the man whom she loves.
   → whom 作為 loves 的受詞。
6. He is the student whom Miss Yang spoke to yesterday.
   → whom 作為 spoke to 的受詞。
7. I don't know the old woman and her cat that are sitting over there.
   → 有人和動物的組合，關係代名詞要用 that。
8. This is a pair for of the pants which / that I bought in the department store.
   → which / that 是 bought 受詞。
9. The boy who is watching TV is Jane's brother.
   → 關係代名詞 who 後面接動詞 is。
10. Tina doesn't like the boy who has green eyes.
    → 關係代名詞 who 後面接動詞 has。

‖ 關係代名詞 that 的特殊用法 |

前文提到，若先行詞是人和動物的組合，關係代名詞必用 that，除此之外，有些時候也必用 that，這些狀況有：

(1) 先行詞前有最高級的形容詞時：

Steven is the shortest boy that I have known.
（*Steven* 是我認識的男生中最矮的。）
→ 先行詞 boy 前有最高級 the shortest，關係代名詞要用 that。

(2) 先行詞前有序數時：

Nancy is the fast girl that has sat down.（*Nancy* 是第一個坐下的女孩。）
→ 先行詞 girl 前面有序數 the last，關係代名詞要用 that。

(3) 先行詞前有 all、any、the only、the same、the very 時：

He lost all the money that he made.（他遺失了所有他賺的錢。）

Helen is the only girl that has short hair.（*Helen* 是唯一有短髮的女孩。）

We have the same pencil boxes that we bought in England.
（我們有在英國買、相同的鉛筆盒。）

This is the very dress that I want to buy.（這就是我一直想買的洋裝。）

(4) 先行詞本身是 thing 或 one 結尾的語詞時：

He complained everything that he met.（他抱怨他所遇到的每一件事。）
→ everything 是帶有 thing 的語詞，關係代名詞要用 that。

He invited everyone that he met on the street.
（他邀請他在街上遇到的每個人。）
→ everyone 是帶有 one 的語詞，關係代名詞要用 that。

⑸ 疑問詞是 who 或 which 開頭時：

Who is the boy that is standing in front of the door?
（那個站在門前的男孩是誰？）
→ 為了避免和疑問詞 who 重複，關係代名詞用 that。

Which is the dog that you brought home?（哪一隻是你撿回來的狗？）
→ 避免和 which 重複，關係代名詞用 that。

二、好學的連接句型

▌好學的連接詞句型 ▌

1. A and B = A 和 B

當句子出現兩個語法結構相似的語詞，同時，這兩個語詞的語氣是一致的時候，我們可以用 and 來連接。例如：

The apple is big and red.（這顆蘋果又大又紅。）
→ and 用來連接單字與單字，兩者詞性皆為形容詞。

I like cats and she likes cats, too.（我喜歡貓，而她也喜歡。）
→ and 前面是句子，後面也是句子，在語氣上，也都是肯定句

David likes hot dogs, hamburgers and potato chips.
（David 喜歡熱狗、漢堡和洋芋片。）
→ 要記得，and 放在最後的兩個語詞之間。

若句子中列舉很多例子，我們習慣將列舉的單字由字母少到字母多排列，例如 book and dictionary（書和字典）、ruler and pencil case（尺和鉛筆盒），但是，有些單字的組合是固定的，例如：knife and fork（刀叉）、bread and butter（奶油麵包）、fish and chips（炸魚薯條）。

· 我們可以這樣說

　　and 可以用來連接語氣順接或是相似的單字，比如說，在餐廳點菜時，想要漢堡，也想要汽水和蘋果派，我們可以這樣說：

I would like a hamburger, apple pie and soda, please.
（我想要漢堡、蘋果派和可樂。）

　　這個句型也可以用於金錢的數量，例如，當有人問你 You've got money?（你身上有錢嗎？），你就可以回答：

I have two thousand five hundred and ten dollars.（我有兩千五百一十元。）

---

2. 主詞 + 動詞 + but + 主詞 + 動詞 = 但是

例如：

I like cats, but she doesn't like cats.（我喜歡貓，但她不喜歡貓。）
→ but 也是對等連接詞，但在語氣上是相對的。

but 還有一種特殊用法，比較看看下面的句子：

I will not tell anyone but you.（除了你，我不會告訴任何人。）
→ but 在否定句中，如果和 any 開頭的複合字，例如 anything、anyone、anybody 等一起使用，具有 except（除了…）的意思。

I will tell no one but you.（除了你，我不告訴任何人。）
→ 如果和 no 的複合字，如 nobody、nothing、no one 等連用，則具有 only（只有）的涵義。

　　你有沒有發現，使用 any 或 no 開頭的複合字，也會影響句子的肯定或否定形式呢？關於這兩個複合字的用法，我們會在第六篇否定句中加以討論。

　　另外要特別注意的是，在這類的句型中，but 後面連接的人應為受詞，若是連接動詞，則動詞要為原形動詞：

My younger sister did nothing but cry.
（我的妹妹除了一直哭，什麼都沒做。）

· 我們可以這樣說

but 表示語氣的轉折。在日常生活中，如果有人要求你做你真的不想要做的事情，你可以說：

I know it is good for me, but I really do not want to do it.
（我知道這樣做對我很好，但是我真的不想要這麼做。）

如果你遇到需要反駁對方意見的時候，but 也是很好用的句型唷!假設對方一直邀請你喝咖啡，你實在不想喝，你就可以說：

But I have drunk coffee today.（但是我今天已經喝過咖啡了。）
→ 這在文法中，不是非常正確的用法，但在口語中，我們可以這樣說。

---

3. both A and B＝A 和 B 兩者都⋯
   neither A nor B＝A 和 B 兩者都不⋯

---

both...and... 也是前後語詞和語氣都要一致的連接詞，例如：

She can play both tennis and badminton.（她會打網球和羽毛球。）
→ 在 both 與 and 後面，都是連接單字。

She can both play tennis and play badminton.（她會打網球和羽毛球。）
→ both 和 and 後面都是＜動詞＋名詞＞。

這個句子，也可以用＜**not only A but also B**＞的句型表達，例如：

*She can play **not only** tennis **but also** badminton.*
（她不僅會打網球，還會打羽毛球。）
→ not only 和 but also 後面接的語詞結構也要一致

neither...nor... 表示「兩者都不⋯」，在語氣上與 both...and... 相反，例如：

She can play neither tennis nor badminton.
（她不會打網球，也不會打羽毛球。）
→ neither 和 nor 後面接的語詞結構要一致。

這三種句型若和人稱一起應用時，動詞該怎麼辦呢？比較看看下面三個句子的 be 動詞：

Both Dad and Mom are not at home.（爸爸媽媽都不在家。）
→ both...and... 因為強調兩者，動詞用複數形

Neither Dad nor Mom is at home.（不論爸爸或媽媽都不在家。）
→ 動詞要以靠近的人稱為主。

Not only Dad but also Mom is not at home.（不僅爸爸，連媽媽也不在家。）
→ 動詞要以靠近的人稱為主。

在第二個和第三個句子中，不在家的共有兩個人，但是卻不能用表示複數 be 動詞 are，而要用第三人稱 mom 的 be 動詞 is。

・我們可以這樣說

我們可以利用這個句型來強調「兩者都不…」的狀況，例如，你的男性朋友邀請你和你的女性朋友參加生日派對，但是你們真的很不想去，你可以強烈的表達你的想法：

Neither my friend nor I want to go to your birthday party!
（不論是我朋友或是我，都不想去你的生日派對！）

相反的，若是你們都很想參加，就可以說：

Both my friend and I want to go to your birthday party.
（我和我朋友都想參加你的生日派對。）

在派對上，和新認識的朋友討論到搖滾樂和爵士樂，你也可以這樣說：

Both rock music and Jazz music are my cup of tea.

（搖滾樂和爵士樂都是我的菜。）

4. either A or B = A 或 B 兩者擇一的

想要表示有選擇性的時候，可以用 either...or... 這個句型，這個句型中所提到的兩件事物，僅有一件會發生：

You can either watch the TV at home or walk the dog with me.
（你可以留在家裡看電視，或是跟我一起去遛狗。）
→ either 和 or 後面的詞語結構要一致，watch 和 walk 都是動詞。

We can play either dodge ball or badminton.
（我們可以打躲避球或羽毛球。）
→ either 和 or 後面都是接名詞。

當這個句型和人稱一起應用時，動詞要跟著最近的人稱做變化，舉例來說：

Either Kelly or Kevin are the best musician.（X）
→ be 動詞靠近 Kelly，應該要根據 Kelly 來變化。

Either Kelly or Kevin is the best musician.（O）
（最棒的音樂家不是 *Kelly* 就是 *Kevin*。）
→ be 動詞靠近第三人稱 he，所以雖然句子中提到兩個人，但還是只能用 is。

‧我們可以這樣說

這個句型主要在提供選項給對方參考。日常生活中，當我們和朋友聚餐時，如果朋友拿不定主意要點些什麼，你可以這樣建議：

You can order either the pizza or the pasta.（你可以點披薩或是千層麵）。

5. A as well as B = A 還有 B

這個句型類似之前提到的 and，表示前後的語詞或是句子同時發生，例如：

Dave can speak Chinese as well as English.（*Dave* 會說中文和英文。）
→ as well as 也是對等連接詞，前後語詞要一致。

但和上個句型不同的是，as well as 前面的名詞才是句子的重點，因此，動詞要根據 as well as 前面的名詞而變化：

Dave as well as I is good at speaking English.
（*Dave* 和我會說流利的英文。）
→ as well as 前面的人稱為第三人稱單數，be 動詞用 is。

・我們可以這樣說

在社交場合中，難免會需要介紹朋友相互認識，為了讓朋友們可以更加了解彼此，在介紹的時候，也可以稍微稱讚一下對方，你可以說：

Betty is my best friend. She is a talented dancer as well as an excellent Yoga teacher.
（*Betty* 是我最好的朋友，她不但是很有天分的舞者，還是優秀的瑜珈老師。）

6. though / although / even though = 雖然、即使

though、although 和 even though 多半放在主詞的前面，表示「雖然、即使」，看看下面的句子，這三句都表示「雖然正在下雨，我還是出門兜風」：

Though it is raining, I go outside for a ride.
→ though 所表達的語氣最不強烈，偏向口語。

Although it is raining, I go outside for a ride.
→ although 是書面正式的用法。

Even though it is raining, I go outside for a ride.
→ even though 的語氣最為強烈。Even though 中的 even 是副詞，用於強調 though，因此不能將單獨將 even 當連接詞使用。

雖然 though、although 和 even though 在意思或用法上大致相同，但也有不

一樣的地方，舉例來說，我們可以將 though 放在句尾，表示「然而、但是」，但卻不能將 although 放在句尾：

This isn't an interesting book. I enjoy it, although. → （X）
This isn't an interesting book. I enjoy it, though. → （O）
（這不是一本很有趣的書。但我滿喜歡的。）

在句尾出現的 though 當作副詞，具有強調語氣的效果，這種用法，在口語中常常出現：

She is not very pretty; I think I fall in love with her, though.
= She is not very pretty, but I think I fall in love with her.
（她不是很漂亮，但我想我愛上她了。）

你有沒有發現？當我們將 though 放在句尾時，兩個句子中間的標點符號要改為分號，也可以用句點表示。標點符號會有這樣的差別，是因為位於句尾的 though，扮演強調語氣的作用，而非連接的作用。

在某些句子中，我們會發現 though 或 although 前會加逗號，有些則不加逗號。是否加逗號，關鍵在於。試比較下列句子：

He is positive although he is blind.
（雖然他看不見，但他保持正面的態度。）
→ although 連接的兩句是具有獨立意義的兩個句子，不用逗號。

He may be fired, although I am not sure.
（他可能會被裁員，但我不是很確定。）
→ although 後面的句子是補充說明前面句子的狀況，所以 although 前面要加逗號。

・我們可以這樣說

這種句型會給人說話者表示讓步的感覺，比如說，有人邀請你喝咖啡，雖然你不喜歡喝咖啡，但是因為對方盛情難卻，你可以用這樣的句型表達，讓對方知道你是因為他／她才願意做這件事：

I can go with you, although I don't like coffee very much.
（我可以和你一起去，雖然我沒有很喜歡喝咖啡。）

　　這種句型也可以用來強調主詞心中的欲望和實際條件之間的不平等關係，例如，有時候會忍不住看到衣服就想買，但是買太多又會被家人碎念，雖然心中知道要省錢，但是嘴巴還是忍不住會說：

Even though I make little money, I still want to buy this dress.
（雖然我賺的錢很少，但是我還是想要買這件洋裝。）

7. 主詞 + 動詞 + because + 主詞 + 動詞 = 因為…

例如：

He didn't go to work <u>because</u> <u>he was sick</u>.（他沒有去上班，因為他生病了。）

Because he was sick, he didn't go to work.
→ 若將 because 置於句首，兩個句子中要加逗號。

　　在中文的語法中，常會有「因為…所以…」的句子出現，但若將 because 和 so 置於同一個句子中，在英文的語法是錯誤的。

<u>Because</u> he was sick, <u>so</u> he didn't go to work.→（X）
because 和 so 不能在同一個句子出現。

He didn't go to work <u>because</u> he was sick. →（O）

He was sick, <u>so</u> he didn't go to work.→（O）
當 so 作為連接詞連接兩個句子時，前面要加上逗號將兩個句子區分開來。

　　because 除了不能和 so 一起使用外，也要小心和 because of 產生混淆，試比較下列句子：

He didn't go to work <u>because of sickness</u>. →（O）
（他沒有去上班，因為他生病了。）

He didn't go to work <u>because of being sick.</u> → （O）

He didn't go to work <u>because of he was sick.</u> → （X）
because of 後面不能連接句子。

because of 是介詞片語，後面要接名詞或代名詞，若是兩個句子，則只能用 because 來連接：

He didn't go to work <u>because he was sick.</u> → （O）

He didn't go to work <u>because being sick.</u> → （X）
because 後面不能單獨連接名詞。

・我們可以這樣說

這個句型主要表示事件的因果關係，有時候，另一半會要求我們替他們做一些事情，你可以利用這個句型甜言蜜語一下：

I can do everything for you because I love you.
= I love you, so I can do everything for you.
（我可以為你做任何事，因為我愛你。）

---

8. in case / if + 主詞 + 動詞 = 假設…

in case 和 if 都可以表示假設的狀況，但是，if 強調事情的條件，而 in case 則是強調事情的可能性，例如：

You need to take an umbrella if it rains.
（如果下雨的話，你需要帶一把傘。）
→ 用 if 來連接，表示如果有下雨的話，你需要傘，相反地，如果沒有下雨，你就不需要雨傘。

You need to take an umbrella <u>in case</u> it rains.
（你需要帶把傘以防下雨。）
→ 用 in case 作連接，表示有下雨的可能，所以最好帶把傘。

in case 和 in case of 也常常產生混淆，例如：

You need an umbrella in case it rains.（你需要一把雨傘以防下雨。）
→ in case 是連接詞片語，後面加子句（主詞＋動詞）

You need an umbrella in case of rain.（萬一下雨，你會需要一把雨傘。）
→ in case of 是介系詞片語，後面連接名詞

In case of rain, you need an umbrella.
→ In case of 若置於句首，則兩個子句中要以逗點區分。

・我們可以這樣說

　這個句型帶有些許警告和提醒的意味，可以利用這個句型來表示叮嚀：

In case it is getting cold, you need to wear the coat.
（你最好穿件外套以免天氣變冷。）

If it is getting cold, don't forget to put on the coat.
（如果天氣變冷了，不要忘了加件外套。）

---

9. as ＋ 形容詞 ＋ as 名詞 ＝ 像…一樣…
　 as ＋ 名詞 ＝ 按照…

　例如：

She runs as fast as a rabbit.（她跑步像兔子一樣快。）

Do as what I told you.（按照我跟你說的做。）

・我們可以這樣說

　我們可以用這樣的句型來形容狀態，例如，當自己非常忙的時候，可以說：

I am as busy as a bee.（我像蜜蜂一樣忙 ＝ 我非常忙碌。）

　有時，也可以將這個句型用於尋求對方的同意：

As you know, he is such a sleepy head.（如你所知，他就是一個貪睡蟲。）

---

10. as / when / while 主詞 + 動詞 = 當⋯

as、when 和 while 都用來連接兩個句子的時間，例如：

It started to rain as we were leaving the restaurant.
= *It started to rain when we were leaving the restaurant.*
= *It started to rain while we were leaving the restaurant.*
（當我們離開餐廳時，開始下雨。）

雖然 as、when 和 while 都可以表示「當⋯」，但在用法上有些許差異。若句子中有兩個動作出現，when 主要連接短暫的動作，while 連接具有持續性的動作，as 可以連接短暫或持續性的動作，試比較下列兩句：

When the phone rang, I was taking a shower.（當我洗澡時，電話響了。）
→ when 加短暫性的動作。

While I was taking a shower, the phone rang.
→ while 加持續性的動作。

但是論及兩件同時發生，並持續一段時間的動作，我們通常會用 while。若兩個句子具有對比的意味時，也多用 while。

She arrived the restaurant at 8 o'clock while I arrived at 7.
（她八點才到餐廳，而我是七點就到了。）

若句子中有講到和年紀有關的時間，連接詞多用 when。

I have been to Japan when I was eleven years old.
（我十一歲時去過日本。）

若兩個句子中的動作具有相互影響的關係，或是兩個句子中的情況正在改變時，連接詞用 as。

As Tom gets older, he is braver.（Tom 年紀越大越勇敢。）

· 我們可以這樣說

　　這樣的句型多用於表達事件發生時，兩件事情的時間關聯。日常生活中，可以運用在向對方描述所發生的事：

The story is, the phone rang while she was taking the shower and you know what happened.
（事情是這樣的，當她在洗澡時電話響了，然後你知道接下來發生什麼事了。）

· 換你試試看，連接詞的綜合練習！

A. 請找出本篇文章中的連接詞

David and Kelly dined out to celebrate their wedding anniversary.

(In the restaurant)

Waiter: Are you ready to order?

Kelly: What do you recommend?

Waiter: Well...we are famous not only for the steaks but also for the hamburgers. Some of our guests like our sandwiches as well.

Kelly: I would like a hamburger, but I don't want mayonnaise. I am allergic to the onions, so please make sure there aren't any onions in the hamburger.

Waiter: OK. And you, Sir?

David: I would like steak, please.

Waiter: How would you like your steak to be cooked?

David: I would like a medium well steak, please.

Waiter: Would you like some dessert? You can choose either cheesecake or apple pie. Both of them are delicious.

Kelly: I would like a piece of cheesecake, please.

David: Even though I don't like dessert, I take the apple pie. We also want a cup of coffee and a cup of black tea. We don't want sugar both the tea and the coffee. Thank you very much.

Waiter: Because we make the dishes after ordering, it may take you a few minutes.

Kelly: It's OK. Thanks you.

· 你找到了嗎？

David **and** Kelly dined out to celebrate their wedding anniversary.

(In the restaurant）

Waiter: Are you ready to order?

 Kelly: What do you recommend?

Waiter: Well...we are famous **not only** for the steaks **but also** for the hamburgers. Some of our guests like our sandwiches as well.

 Kelly: I would like a hamburger, **but** I don't want mayonnaise. I am allergic to the onions, **so** please make sure there aren't any onions in the hamburger.

Waiter: Ok. And you, Sir?

 David: I would like steak, please.

Waiter: How would you like your steak to be cooked?

 David: I would like a medium well steak, please.

Waiter: Would you like some dessert? You can choose **either** cheesecake **or** apple pie. Both of them are delicious.

 Kelly: I would like a piece of cheesecake, please.

 David: **Even though** I don't like dessert, I take the apple pie. We also want a cup of coffee **and** a cup of black tea. We don't want sugar **both** the tea **and** the coffee. Thank you very much.

Waiter: **Because** we make the dishes after ordering, it may take you a few minutes.

 Kelly: It's OK. Thank you.

B. 翻譯看看這些句子！

1. 我想要兩份潛艇堡、一杯拿鐵和一杯巧克力牛奶。

2. 拿鐵和巧克力牛奶都要熱的。

3. 其中一份潛艇堡要加番茄醬，但不要加洋蔥。

4. 一份潛艇堡不加洋蔥，也不加番茄醬。

5. 因為我感冒了，拿鐵請不要加糖。

· 你想到怎麼寫了嗎？

（1）I want two subs, one latte and a cap of chocolate milk.

（2）I would like both a Latte and chocolate milk that are hot.

（3）One of the subs with ketchup, but do not add any onions.

(4) The other one adds neither onions nor ketchup.

(5) Because I have a cold, I want my latte with no sugar.

‖ 好學的連接副詞句型 ‖

1. In addition,

   Besides,　　主詞 + 動詞 = 除此之外⋯

   Moreover,

　　例如：

Mr. Lee is a Chinese teacher. Besides, he is a busker.

（李先生是一位國文老師，此外，他還是一位街頭藝人。）

→ 利用這個句型介紹身分。

Smart Phone is harmful to children's eye. In addition, it makes the children distractive.

（智慧型手機對小孩的眼睛不好，此外，也讓小孩分散注意力。）

→ 利用這個句型加強自己的觀點。

She shows mercy to the old. Moreover, she is a volunteer for community service.

（她對老年人展現憐憫心，此外，她還是社區服務的義工。）

→ 利用這個句型補充說明。

・我們可以這樣說

　　在自我介紹的時候，要多多介紹自己的優點，讓人留下深刻的印象，你可以說：

I can play the piano well. In addition, I play the jazz piano at bar sometimes.

（我鋼琴彈得很好，此外，我有時會在酒吧裡演奏爵士鋼琴。）

・換你試試看，完成句子！

1. take a walk after dinner / good for health / aid digestion

2. have a pet / make you laugh / release the pressure

3. study / get knowledge / make you smarter

· 你完成了嗎？

1. To take a walk after dinner is good for health. In addition, it aids digestion.

2. To have a pet makes you laugh. Besides, it can release the pressure.

3. To study will help you get knowledge. Moreover, it can make you smarter.

---

2. Personally, 主詞 + 動詞 = 就個人而言…
　　In my opinion,

這個句型可以用來表達個人的意見，例如：

Personally, I don't like Cappuccino.
（就我本人而言，我不是很喜歡卡布奇諾。）

In my opinion, the actress must do the plastic surgery.
（我認為，這個女演員一定有整形。）

· 我們可以這樣說

有些場合需要表達自己的意見，但又不希望冒犯到別人時，我們可以在自己的想法前面使用這個句型，例如：

In my opinion, this story is awful.
（我認為，這個故事真是糟透了。）

Personally, I don't like this movie at all.
（就我個人而言，我一點都不喜歡這部電影。）

· 換你試試看，這個情況你會怎麼說？

1. The durian is stinky

2. This novel is interesting.

3. No one can sing beautifully as this singer.

4. My neighbor holds a party all the time.

5. To drink too much coffee will make you insomnious.

・你完成了嗎？

1. The durian is stinky. Personally, I don't like durian at all.
2. This novel is interesting. In my opinion, it is a great novel.
3. No one can sing beautifully as this singer. In my opinion, she is the best signer in the world.
4. My neighbor holds a party all the time. Personally, it is annoying.
5.. To drink too much coffee will make you insomnious. In my opinion, it is not good for your health.

---

3. In other words,

That is,　　　　主詞 + 動詞 = 換句話說…

That is to say,

例如：

Henry is the naughtiest student in the class. In other words, he is naughtier than any other student.
（*Henry* 是班上最頑皮的學生，換句話說，他比其他學生都要頑皮。）

He performs on the street. That is to say, he is a busker.
（他在街頭表演，也就是說，他是個街頭藝人。）

Albert is thirty years old. That is, he was born in 1983.
（*Albert* 三十歲，也就是說，他是在 *1983* 年出生的。）

・我們可以這樣說

和朋友相約吃晚餐，朋友說想吃又酸又辣的東西，你可以說：

You want something tastes spicy and sour? That is to say, you want to eat the Thai food.
（你想吃些又辣又酸的東西？那就是想吃泰國菜嘛！）

・換你試試看，練習換句話說！

1. Jessie can eat a horse.
2. Mandy has a green thumb.
3. Justin gets ants in his pants.

4. Joyce has a sweet tooth.

5. Jeff is a candy person.

1. Jessie can eat a horse. In the other words, she is very hungry.

2. Mandy has a green thumb. That is, she is good at gardening.

3. Justin gets ants in his pants. That is to say, he feels anxious.

4. Joyce has a sweet tooth. In the other words, she likes eating dessert.

5. Jeff is a candy person. That is, he likes eating candy very much.

---

4. On the other hand,
　　However,　　主詞 + 動詞 = 另一方面…

這個句型可以用來說明兩種可能的情況，例如：

She knows she needs to be on a diet. On the other hand, she can't help but eat a lot.

（她知道她必須要控制飲食，然而另一方面她卻忍不住吃很多。）

→ 用這個句型說明的兩種情況，常常是相反的。

Sandy is tired. However, she still works until the time for off work.

（Sandy 很累。然而，她仍然工作到下班時間。）

還有一個例子：

I want to eat fast food. My husband, on the other hand, wants to eat Chinese food.

（我想要吃速食，另一方面，我先生則想吃中國菜。）

你有沒有發現，on the other hand 也可以放在句子的中間呢？記得當你這樣做的時候，前後要有逗點。

・我們可以這樣說

　　結婚周年紀念日的晚上，老闆突然交付了隔天要開會的資料，那真是糟糕呀!面對生氣的另一半，我們只好這樣說：

I know tonight is important. My job, on the other hand, is important, too.
（我知道今晚很重要，另一方面，我的工作也很重要。）

I do love you. However, I need to finish my job.
（我是愛你的。然而，我必須完成我的工作。）

・換你試試看，練習造句吧！

1. short hair / make your face look smaller
2. diet / looks slim / undernourished
3. play video game / exciting / harmful to the eyes

・你完成了嗎？

1. You look great with short hair. On the other hand, it makes your face look smaller.
2. To diet make you look slim. However, it make you undernourished, too.
3. To play video game is exciting. On the other hand, it is harmful to the eyes.

5. On the contrary, Conversely,	主詞 + 動詞 = 恰好相反地…

這個句型用來表示完全相反的兩種狀況，例如：

I think it will rain today. On the contrary, it is a sunny day.
（我以為今天會下雨。相反地，是晴天。）
→ rain 和 sunny 是對比的天氣。

Tim thought she would be angry. Conversely, she convulsed with laughter.
（Tim 以為她會生氣。相反地，她捧腹大笑。）

・我們可以這樣說

當朋友工作遇到挫折時，用這個句型來鼓勵他吧！你可以說：

You didn't screw it up. Conversely, I think you did pretty well.
（你才沒有搞砸，相反地，我覺得你做得很好。）

・換你試試看，將句子換句話說！

1. Helen is more popular than Jimmy on the class.
2. Tracy is taller than Mia.
3. To ride bikes is more interesting to play baseball.
4. You look prettier in this red dress than in the black one.
5. This fairy tale is more romantic than that one.

・你完成了嗎？

1. Helen is more popular than Jimmy on the class.

   → Helen is popular in the class. On the other hand, Jimmy is not **as** popular **as** Helen.

   → as...as... 表示像…一樣…，形容詞要放在兩個 as 的中間，類似的用法有 as busy as a bee（像蜜蜂一樣忙）、as soon as possible（盡快）。

2. Tracy is taller than Mia.

   → Tracy is tall. Conversely, Mia is short.

3. To ride bikes is more interesting to play baseball.

   → To ride bikes is interesting. On the other hand, to play baseball is boring.

4. You look prettier in this red dress that in the black one.

   → You look pretty in this red dress. Conversely, you look ugly in the black one.

5. This fairy tale is more romantic than the story.

   → The fairy is romantic. On the other hand, the story is not as romantic as the fairy tale.

▌ 好學的關係代名詞句型 │

和關係代名詞有關的小技巧，可以讓你的英文更道地！

1. 關係代名詞用不定詞取代

如果句子的意思帶有「必須、最先、最後」的涵義時，可以用不定詞取代關係子句，例如：

I was the first student that came here this morning.
（我是今天早上第一個到的學生。）

句子中的 the first 使句子具有「最先」的涵義，因此可以用不定詞將這句改寫成：

I was the first student to come here this morning.

・我們可以這樣用

每到十二月份，公司都要對整年度的工作進行評估，並對來年編列預算和計畫，這時候是大家最忙碌的時候，如果有人邀約你在這段期間聚餐，你可以說：

I am sorry, but I have many things <u>to do</u>.（我很抱歉，但我有很多事要做。）

這句原本應為：*I am sorry, but I have a lot of thing <u>that I must do</u>.*
因為 must 帶有「必須」的意味，因此可以將關係子句用不定詞改寫。改寫完後，是不是變得比較簡短又順口呢？

2. 關係代名詞 + have / has 的組合可以用 with 取代

例如：

Look at the boy <u>who has</u> curly hair.（看看這個有捲髮的男孩。）

Who has 可以用 with 取代，這句可以改寫為：

Look at the boy <u>with</u> curly hair.

・我們可以這樣說

在朋友的聚會上認識了一位長髮披肩的女孩，這個女孩時在太漂亮了，忍不住想跟朋友說：

I met a girl <u>with</u> long hair last night. She is so beautiful that I can't take my eyes off her.
（我昨晚遇見了一個長髮女孩，她太漂亮了，我根本沒辦法把視線從她身上移開。）
→ 這個句子中，with 取代了關係代名詞 who 和動詞 has。

---

3. 先行詞＋關係代名詞的組合可以用 what 取代

例如：

This is the book which my sister wants to buy. （這就是我妹妹想要買的書。）

book 和 which 可以用 what 代替，因此這句可以改寫為：

This is what my sister wants to buy.

這種 what 所引導的句子為名詞子句，和一般關係代名詞所引導的形容詞子句不同，複合關係代名詞 what 所引導的句子，可以用做名詞、補語或受詞，以上面句子為例：

This is what my sister wants to buy.
→ what 引導的名詞子句作為受詞使用。

What you do to me makes me surprise. （你對我做的事讓我感到震驚。）
→ what 引導的名詞子句為主詞。

．我們可以這樣說

為了讓業績更好，我們會要求員工針對讓業績變好的方法腦力激盪，但有些員工提出的建議實在太天馬行空時，你可以說：

What you said is nonsense! （你所說的話完全沒有道理！）

這個句子中的 what，是取代先行詞 the thing 和關係代名詞 that 而來。

．換你試試看，關係代名詞的綜合練習！試著把句子合併或改寫！

1. I met a girl. The girl wants to talk to you.
2. The boy is playing badminton. The boy is my cousin.
3. The man likes playing the violin. The man is in the classroom.
4. Anna had a necklace. The necklace was broken by Kevin yesterday.
5. The man is Daniel. You can't trust Daniel.

6. Ivy is the first girl that graduated from the school.

7. Justin is the boy who has beautiful eyes.

8. I bought this computer last week. This computer is broken.

9. The thing that your parents said is right.

10. I love the man who has messy hair.

・是不是很簡單呢？

1. I met a girl. The girl wants to talk to you.

   I met the girl who wants to talk to you.

2. The boy is playing badminton. The boy is my cousin.

   The boy who is playing badminton is my cousin.

3. The man likes playing the violin. The man is in the classroom.

   The man who likes playing the violin is in the classroom.

4. Anna had a necklace. Kevin broke the necklace yesterday.

   Anna had a necklace which / that was broken by Kevin yesterday.

5. The man is Daniel. You can't trust Daniel.

   Daniel is the man you can't trust.

6. Ivy is the first girl that graduated from the school.

   Ivy is the first girl to graduate from the school.

7. Justin is the boy who has beautiful eyes.

   Justin is the boy with beautiful eyes.

8. I bought this computer last week. This computer is broken.

   The computer I bought last week is broken.

9. The thing that your parents said is right.

   What your parents said is right.

10. I love the man who has messy hair.

    I love the man with messy hair.

三、文法糾正篇

▌ 和連接詞有關的錯誤 ▏

---
1. 對等連接詞連接的語詞不對等

例如：

She wants some coffee and happy.（她想要咖啡和快樂。）（*X*）

在 and 前後連接的語詞結構應該一致，若是單字對單字，詞性也應相等。本句 and 前連接 coffee，為名詞，則後面的 happy 不能以形容詞的狀態出現，應該為 happiness：

She wants some coffee and happiness.（*O*）
→ 名詞 + 名詞，結構正確。

She wants some coffee and wants to be happy.（*O*）
→ and 前後都是＜動詞 + 名詞＞，結構正確。

在這種句型中，除了注意詞性要一致，也要注意類型是否對等。以上述句子來看，咖啡和快樂是完全不相干的名詞，所以雖然在文法結構上沒有問題，但在語意邏輯上卻顯得怪怪的。

She wants coffee and milk.（她想要咖啡和牛奶。）

She wants to be a smart and pretty girl.（她想要當一個聰明又漂亮的女孩。）

這兩句是不是合理許多呢？

---
2. neither...nor... 不可以和 not 一起使用

請你想想看，當你看到這兩個句子，你會怎麼連接呢？

I don't like reading detective novels.（我不喜歡閱讀偵探小說。）

My sister doesn't like reading detective novels.（我妹妹不喜歡閱讀偵探小說。）

你想到了嗎？

I don't like reading detective novels, and my sister doesn't like, either.
（我和妹妹都不喜歡閱讀偵探小說。）
→ 用連接詞 and 將兩句連接

Both my sister and I don't like reading detective novels.
→ 使用＜both...and...＞的句型，記得在動詞前加上 not 表示否定。

當然也可以用＜neither...nor...＞改寫，但下面這個句子是錯誤的寫法：

Neither my sister nor I don't like reading detective novels.（X）
→ neither 和 nor 已表示否定，不用在 like 前面加上 not。

neither 和 nor 本身就具有否定的意涵，若再加入表示否定的 not，就會形成雙重否定的句子，因此正確的寫法為：

Neither my sister nor I like reading detective novels. →（O）
（不論我妹妹或是我都不喜歡閱讀偵探小說。）

3. because 和 so 不能在同一個句子中出現

例如：

Because I was tired, so I went to bed early last night.（X）
→ 在英文語法中，在一個句子中同時使用 because 和 so 是錯誤的。

這個句子可以這樣寫：

Because I was tired, I went to bed early last night.
（因為我很累，昨晚我很早就上床睡覺了。）
→ 用 because 表示原因

I was tired, so I went to bed early last night.
（我很累，所以我昨晚很早就睡了。）
→ 用 so 表示結果

---

4. although 不能置於句尾

though 表示「雖然」，位置多放在句子的結尾。although 和 though 意思相似，若置於句子中間，兩者可以代換，但 although 不可以放在句尾，看看下面的例句：

I drank some coffee yesterday, <u>although</u> I don't like coffee actually.
= *I drank some coffee yesterday, <u>though</u> I don't like coffee actually.*
（雖然我不是很喜歡咖啡，但我昨天還是喝了一些。）
→ though 和 although 都在句子中間，可以互相代換。

I drank some coffee yesterday, <u>but</u> I don't like coffee actually.
= *I drank some coffee yesterday, I don't like coffee <u>though</u>.*
（我昨天喝了一些咖啡，但是其實我不喜歡咖啡。）
→ though 放在句尾，除表示「雖然」，更強調「但是」的語氣

I drank some coffee yesterday, I don't like coffee <u>although</u>. → （X）
→ 將 although 放在句尾是錯誤的用法。

---

5. 容易混淆的 despite / in spite of 和 though / although

though 和 although 是連接詞，後面要連接完整的句子，但 despite 和 in spite of 則是介系詞，後面要接名詞或是名詞的相關語。其基本句型為＜despite / in spite of + 名詞 / 代名詞 / V-ing＞＝「儘管」

In spite of <u>what I said</u>, I still love you very much.
（不論我說過什麼，但我還是很愛你。）
→ in spite of 後面接疑問詞開頭的名詞片語 what I said。

I didn't get up early this morning, in spite of <u>having lots of things to do</u>.
（儘管有很多事情要做，我今天還是沒有早起。）
→ in spite of 後面接動名詞 having。

My little brother loves his toy car, in spite of <u>its oldness</u>.
（即使這台玩具車很老舊，我的弟弟還是對它愛不釋手。）
→ in spite of 後面接名詞 oldness。

因為 despite / in spite of 和 though / although 的意思非常接近，很容易在用法上產生混淆，試比較下列各句：

I didn't get up early this morning, in spite of <u>having lots of things to do</u>.（O）
I didn't get up early this morning, in spite of <u>I have</u> lots of things to do（X）
→ despite / in spite of 連接名詞或動詞轉化為名詞型態的動名詞

I didn't get up early this morning, although <u>I have</u> lots of things to do.（O）
（儘管有很多事情要做，我今天還是沒有早起。）
→ though / although 連接句子

▌和連接副詞有關的錯誤

6. 標點符號的誤用

標點符號於連接詞和連接副詞中的使用常常產生混淆。

對等連接詞中，若舉例兩個語詞以上，則最後的語詞前要加上連接詞，連接詞前要有逗號，例如：

She likes apples, bananas<u>, and</u> watermelons.（她喜歡蘋果、香蕉和西瓜。）
→ 連接詞 and 前有逗號

Which one do you want, coffee, tea<u>, or</u> juice?（你想要咖啡、茶還是果汁？）
→ 連接詞 or 前有逗號

但若只有兩樣語詞，則不用逗號。

I love cats and rabbits.（我喜歡貓咪和兔子。）
→ 連接詞 and 前沒有逗號

I won't tell anyone but you.（除了你以外，我不會告訴任何人。）
→ 連接詞 but 前沒有逗號

當連接詞連接兩個具有主詞的句子，連接詞前要加上逗號，例如：

My dad is a doctor, and my mom is a nurse.
（我爸爸是醫生，我媽媽是護士。）
→ 兩個句子中有主詞，連接詞前要加逗號。

because 是一個例外，雖然連接的兩個句子都有主詞，但位於句子中間的 because 前不用加逗號，只有將 because 放在句首時，才需要用逗號將兩個句子隔開：

I don't want to talk to her anymore because she is so selfish.
= Because she is so selfish, I don't want to talk to her anymore.
（我再也不想跟她說話，因為她太自私了。）

連接副詞在意思上可以使兩個句子發生關連，但應用分號或句號將其分隔，同時，應於連接副詞後加上逗點：

I was sick; however, I went to work yesterday.
= I was sick. However, I went to work yesterday.
（我昨天不舒服；然而，我還是去工作。）

---

7. even though 和 even so 不要搞錯了

請看下面的句子，這三句都是表示「即使下雨，我還是要去兜風」：

I go for a ride even though it is raining outside.（*O*）
→ even though 是連接詞，可以連接兩個句子。

I go for a ride even so it is raining outside.（*X*）

→ Even so 連接兩個句子錯誤的用法。

I go for a ride. Even so, it is raining outside. → （*O*）

→ even so 做連接副詞使用時，只能與一個句子連接。

▌ 和關係代名詞有關的錯誤

> 8. 有加逗點的是非限定用法（補述用法）
>   沒有加逗點的是限定用法

　　在關係代名詞前面加上逗號，表示針對先行詞補充說明，稱為非限定用法或補述用法；關係代名詞前沒有加上逗號，表示限定用法，試比較下列兩個句子：

My brother, who is in Japan, will come back next week.
（我的哥哥，他住在日本，下周要回來。）

My brother who is in Japan will come back next week.
（我住在日本的哥哥下周要回來。）

　　第一句的關係代名詞前面有加逗號，是補充說明哥哥住在日本的補述用法，因為是補充說明，如果省略，對句子結構不構成影響；第二句中的關係代名詞前面沒有逗號，是限定用法，說明哥哥不只有一個，而是有好多個，下周要回來的是住在日本的哥哥。

> 9. 介係詞可以放在受格的關係代名詞前，但不能放在 that 前。

　　例如：

Jason is the student (whom) I talked of last night.
（這就是昨晚我提到的學生 Jason。）

→ whom 為 talked of 的受詞，可以省略。

可以將介係詞 of 放在關係代名詞的前面，這時候的 whom 不可以省略。

Jason is the student of whom I talked last night.

通常，我們可以用 that 取代 whom，但若前面有介係詞，則不能以 that 進
行取代：

Jason is the student that I talked of last night. →（O）
Jason is the student of that I talked last night. →（X）

·換你試試看，綜合練習，這個句子是正確的嗎？

1. We both like to play badminton and play dodge ball. →（　　）
2. What would you like, ice cream and milk shake? →（　　）
3. I can't play the piano, but she. →（　　）
4. Not only David but also Jimmy will join the school team. →（　　）
5. Because hungry, I went out to grab a bite. →（　　）
6. Neither David nor Kelly is happy. →（　　）
7. Both she and I don't like spiders. →（　　）
8. You cannot eat neither ice cream nor French fries because you are sick.
　　→（　　）
9. Neither I nor my sister watch romantic movies. →（　　）
10. Both she and I want to see this movie. →（　　）
11. Because she won the lottery, so she bought a sport car. →（　　）
12. He doesn't believe because her lie. →（　　）
13. She went to Japan because her boss asked her to manage the branch company.
　　→（　　）
14. My girl friend was angry, so I bought her a bouquet of flowers. →（　　）
15. My mom is busy, therefore I need to prepare the dinner by myself. →（　　）
16. I am not hungry although I didn't eat anything since last night. →（　　）
17. The movie isn't popular. I like it, although. →（　　）
18. Neither Kelly or David got up early in the morning. →（　　）
19. He can't play the piano or the violin →（　　）
20. I studied hard. But I didn't get good grades. →（　　）
21. The teacher to whom he spoke is an English teacher. →（　　）
22. The house in that he lives in is very big. →（　　）

23.The girl about whom they are talking is Gina. → （　　）
24.The dog that you looked at is mine. → （　　）
25.The man to that the teacher spoke is Jason's father. → （　　）

‧你答對了嗎？

1. We both like to play badminton and play dodge ball.
→（O）本句中文為：我們都喜歡打羽毛球和躲避球。And 是對等連接詞，前後語詞結構要一致，本句 and 前後都是動詞加受詞，使用正確。本句也可以寫成：We like to play both badminton and dodge ball.

2. What would you like, ice cream and milk shake?
→（X）本句中文為：你想要冰淇淋或是奶昔？and 表示兩者都要，雖然 and 的前後都是名詞，符合文法，但本句的意思是希望對方在兩者之間進行去捨，故應使用表示「或者」or。

3. I can't play the piano, but she.
→（X）but 是對等連接詞，若前面為句子，後面連接的也應該是句子，本句 but 後面只有主詞，不能構成句子，是錯誤的文法。正確應寫成 I can't play the piano, but she can play the piano.（我不會彈鋼琴，但是她會彈鋼琴。）

4. Not only David but also Jimmy will join the school team.
→（O）本句中文為：不僅 David，Jimmy 也將加入校隊。Not only...but also... 是對等連接詞，本句都連接人名，是正確的句子。

5. Because hungry, I went out to grab a bite.
→（X）本句中文為：因為肚子餓了，我出門吃些東西。Because 是從屬連接詞，表示「因為…」。because 後面要連接句子，本句應於 hungry 前加上主詞 I 和動詞 was，若不接句子，則應將 because 改為 because of，hungry 改為 hunger。本句正確的寫法是：
Because I was hungry, I went out to grab a bite. →（O）
Because of hunger I went out to grab a bite. →（O）

6. Neither David nor Kelly is happy.
→（O）本句中文為：不論 David 或是 Kelly 都不快樂。Neither 和 nor 已經具有否定意味，不需要再將 is 改為 isn't。

7. Both she and I don't like spiders.
→（O）本句中文為：她和我都不喜歡蜘蛛。本句中，both...and...中間的

語詞都是人稱，結構一致，表示「兩個人都…」，為主詞，後面連接肯定句或否定句皆可。

8. You cannot eat neither ice cream nor French fries because you are sick.

→（X）本句中文為：因為你生病了，不論冰淇淋或炸薯條都不可以吃。因為 neither 和 nor 已經表示否定，不需在前面的動詞使用否定形態。本句應寫成：You can eat neither ice cream nor French fries because you are sick.

9. Neither I nor my sister watch romantic movies.

→（X）本句中文為：不論是我或是我姐姐，都不喜歡愛情電影。在 neither...nor... 的句型中，動詞應依據較為靠近的人稱做變化。本句的動詞 watch 靠近 my sister，應將 watch 做第三人稱單數的動詞變化。這句應寫成：Neither I nor my sister watches romantic movies.此外，若有兩個以上的人稱出現，一般習慣將第一人稱放在最後，故這句最為正確的寫法是：Neither my sister nor I watch romantic movies.

10. Both she and I want to see this movie.

→（O）本句中文為：她和我都想看這部電影。Both...and... 所連接的語詞一致，文法正確。

11. Because she won the lottery, so she bought a sport car.

→（X）Because 和 so 不能在同一個句子中使用。本句應改寫成 Because she won the lottery, she bought a sport car. 或是 She won the lottery, so she bought a sport car.

12. He doesn't believe because her lie.

→（X）Because 後面應連接句子，若要連接名詞，則應於 because 後面加上 of。本句可以寫成 He doesn't believe because she lies. 或是 He doesn't believe because of her lie.

13. She went to Japan, because her boss asked her to manage the branch company.

→（X）because 前面不可以有逗號，應將逗點去掉。若希望用逗號將兩個句子分隔，應將 because 置於句首，例如：Because her boss asked her to manage the branch company, she went to Japan.

14. My girl friend was angry, so I bought her a bouquet of flowers.

→（O）若用 so 表示兩個句子的因果關係，so 的前面要有逗點。

15. My mom is busy, therefore I need to prepare the dinner by myself.

→（X）therefore 是連接副詞，用於連接句子時，前面的標點符號應為分

號或是句號，同時，在連接副詞的後面要加上逗號。本句正確的寫法為
My mom is busy; therefore, I need to prepare the dinner by myself. 或是
My mom is busy. Therefore, I need to prepare the dinner by myself.

16. I am not hungry although I didn't eat anything since last night.

→（O）本句的語法正確，although 也可以用 even though 代換，語氣更為
強烈。

17. The movie isn't popular. I like it, although.

→（X）although 雖然和 though 在意思上可以互相代換，但是若 though 表
示「但是」且置於句尾時，不可以用 although 代換，應將 although 改為
though。

18. Neither Kelly or David got up early in the morning.

→（X）neither 和 nor 為一組的連接詞，不可以個別單獨使用。這句應該
這樣寫：Neither Kelly nor David got up early in the morning.

19. He can't play the piano or the violin

→（O）若想表示「兩者都不…」的概念，除了用 neither...nor...，也可以
用 cannot...or...。這句也可以寫成：He can neither play the piano nor play the
violin.

20. I studied hard. But I didn't get good grades.

→（X）在口語的使用下，連接詞若單獨帶領一個句子，具有強調的效
果，但在正確的文法中，連接詞無法單獨帶領一個句子。因此在本句中，
but 帶領一個單獨的句子是錯誤的用法，應寫成 I studied hard, but I didn't
get good grade. 若想將兩個句子分別獨立開來，卻又保持從屬的關係，可
以使用連接副詞。因此，這句也可以寫成 I studied hard. However, I didn't
get good grades. 或是 I studied hard. Nevertheless, I didn't get good grades.

21. The teacher to whom he spoke is an English teacher.

→（O）在介係詞後面，關係代名詞要用受詞。

22. The house in that he lives in is very big.

→（X）應改為 The house that he lives in is very big. 或把 that 改成 which，
寫成 The house in which he lives is very big.

23. The girl about whom they are talking is Gina.

→（O）在介係詞後面，關係代名詞用受詞。

24. The dog that you looked at is mine.

→（O）動物的關係代名詞原本為 which，但也可以用 that 代替。

25.The man <u>to that</u> the teacher spoke is Jason's father.

→（X）這句應把 to 放在 spoke 後面，或把 that 改為 whom。

PART 2

好用好學的
句型

06
CHAPTER
否定句

一、概念篇

▌什麼是否定句

　　如果某件事不是真的，或是沒有發生，我們可以用否定句來表示。最簡單的否定句，是在 be 動詞或是助動詞後面加上 not，例如：

I am not tired.（我不累。）
→ be 動詞後面加 not 構成否定句。

He does not like sandwiches.（他不喜歡三明治。）
→ 助動詞後面加 not 構成否定句。

　　有些句子本身具有情態助動詞，直接在情態助動詞後加上 not，也可以構成否定句型：

He will go to America.（他將要去美國。）

He will not go to America.（他將不會去美國。）
→ 直接在情態助動詞後加上 not。

但是如果句子裡沒有助動詞，該怎麼改成否定句？

有一個口訣是，句子裡面有動詞，變成否定句找助動詞幫忙，例如：

Jimmy likes swimming. （*Jimmy* 喜歡游泳。）

這個句子沒有 be 動詞或助動詞，但是有動詞 like，所以想要寫成否定句，要找助動詞來幫忙。要找哪一個助動詞，由主詞來決定。主詞 Jimmy 是第三人稱單數的 He，所以助動詞要用 does，因此這句的否定句會寫成：

Jimmy does not like swimming. （*Jimmy* 不喜歡游泳。）

要記得，助動詞後面的動詞，一定要使用原形動詞。

· 換你試試看，把句子改寫成否定句！

1. I am a dentist.
2. The steak is delicious.
3. She likes playing volleyball.
4. I would like a cup of tea.
5. He should tell her the truth.

· 你完成了嗎？

2. I am a dentist.

   I am not dentist.

3. The steak is delicious.

   The steak is not delicious.

4. She likes playing volleyball.

   She does not like playing volleyball.

5. I would like a cup of tea.

   I would not like a cup of tea.

6. He should tell her the truth.

   He should not tell her the truth.

‖ 否定句的縮寫 ‖

not 和 be 動詞或助動詞一起使用，可以縮寫為 n't 的形式，例如：

He doesn't like sandwiches.
→ doesn't 是 does 和 not 的縮寫。

He won't go to America.
→ won't 是 will 和 not 的縮寫。

幾乎所有的 be 動詞和助動詞都可以和 not 構成縮寫，但在正式英文中，not 不能和 am 縮寫。

· 換你試試看，要怎麼縮寫？

1. are not	_____	11. can not	_____
2. is not	_____	12. could not	_____
3. was not	_____	13. will not	_____
4. were not	_____	14. would not	_____
5. do not	_____	15. shall not	_____
6. does not	_____	16. should not	_____
7. did not	_____	17. must not	_____
8. have not	_____	18. might not	_____
9. has not	_____	19. ought not	_____
10. had not	_____		

· 你寫對了嗎？

1. are not	aren't	11. can not	can't
2. is not	isn't	12. could not	couldn't
3. was not	wasn't	13. will not	won't
4. were not	weren't	14. would not	wouldn't
5. do not	don't	15. shall not	**shan't**
6. does not	doesn't	16. should not	shouldn't
7. did not	didn't	17. must not	mustn't
8. have not	haven't	18. might not	mightn't
9. has not	hasn't	19. ought not	**oughtn't**
10. had not	hadn't		

是不是很簡單呢？只要在 be 動詞或助動詞後加 n't，就是縮寫的形式。

但是，如果句子中，主詞已經和 be 動詞或助動詞縮寫，那麼 not 就不能再進行縮寫，例如：

He is not hungry.（他不餓。）

He's not hungry.

→ 主詞和 be 動詞縮寫，not 要自己獨立出來。

He'sn't hungry.（X）

→ 把主詞、be 動詞和一起縮寫，是錯誤的寫法。

· 換你試試看，這個句子有沒有錯？

1. She's not a nurse.
2. They'ren't going to the park.
3. He doesn't have a chance to study abroad.
4. She hasn't finished it yet.
5. I'mn't tired.

· 你找到了嗎？

1. She's not a nurse.（O）
2. They'ren't going to the park.（X）
   → 正確的寫法為 They're not going to the park. 或
   　　　　　　　They aren't going to the park.
3. He doesn't have a chance to study abroad.（O）
4. She hasn't finished it yet.（O）
5. I'mn't tired.（X）
   → 正確的寫法為 I'm not tired.。am 和 not 沒有縮寫式。

大部分否定句中都有 not，但是不一定要有 not 才能構成否定句。如果句子中有其他的否定詞，也可以作為否定句使用。

▌什麼是否定詞

否定詞是在否定句中代表否定意味的語詞。否定詞有：

否定詞				
neither	no	none	no one	nothing
never	nor	not	nobody	nowhere

例如：

I have never been to Canada.（我從來沒有去過加拿大。）
→ never 是否定詞，可以使整個句子帶有否定意味。

同一個句子中，不可以出現兩個否定詞。如果出現兩個否定詞，稱為雙重否定，在文法上是不合邏輯的，例如：

I have not never been to Canada.（X）
→ 句子中出現兩個否定詞，是錯誤的寫法。

還有一些語詞具有「並非完全否定」的涵義，這些不完全否定的語詞，我們統稱為**廣義否定詞**。這些廣義的否定詞有：hardly（簡直不）、seldom（很少）、scarcely（幾乎不）、rarely（很少）和 barely（幾乎沒有）。
和否定詞的位置一樣，我們習慣將這些廣義否定詞放在 be 動詞或助動詞後，如果句子中沒有 be 動詞或助動詞，可以將廣義否定詞放在一般動詞前，請看下面的例子：

He could hardly believe his eye.（他幾乎沒辦法相信他看到的。）
→ 否定詞放在助動詞後。

This restaurant is seldom empty.（這家餐廳很少是空空的。）
→ 否定詞放在 be 動詞後。

He rarely speaks to his sister.（他很少和他的妹妹說話。）
→ 否定詞放在一般動詞前。

要特別注意的是，否定詞並不是助動詞，除非句子中有助動詞，不然即便有否定詞，動詞還是要作適當的變化。

有時候為了加強語氣，我們可以在這些廣義的否定詞前加上 so、very、too、pretty 等語詞表示程度：

He so rarely speaks to his sister.（他超少和他妹妹說話。）

・換你試試看，用否定詞將句子完成並做適當的變化！

1. She / seldom / make dinner for her family.
2. He / will / never / tell / secret
3. I / rarely / visit / uncle Sam
4. The teacher / scarcely / hear / student
5. No one / home
6. I / want / cookies / but / none / left

・你完成了嗎？

1. She seldom makes dinner for her family.
2. He will never tell anyone this secret.
3. I rarely visit uncle Sam.
4. The teacher scarcely hears the student.
5. No one at home.
6. I wanted some cookies but there was none left.

除了否定詞可以構成否定句，有些特別的字綴也會使語詞具有否定意涵。通常這些字綴會出現在字首或是字尾的地方：

帶有否定字綴的語詞	
un-	uneasy、unfit、unfair、unnecessarily、untruth 等
in-	invalid、infinite、inaccurate、invisible、insoluble 等
il-	illicit、illogical、illegible、illiterate、illegal 等
im-	immoral、impolite、imbalance、impossibility 等
ir-	irregular、irrational、irresponsible、irresolvable 等
dis-	dislike、disbelief、disfavor、disown、dissimilar 等
non-	nonage、nonpayment、nonstop、nonprofit 等
-less	useless、helpless、hopeless、odorless 等

二、好學好用的句型篇

‖ 和否定有關的句型 ‖

---
1. not + very + 形容詞＝不是很…

這個句型是語氣較為婉轉的否定句型，例如：

She is not very intelligent.（她不是很聰明。）

→ 不好意思用 stupid 來形容，就可以用 not + very，減輕否定的感覺。

The man is not very handsome.（這個男的沒有很帥。）

The test is not easy.（這項測驗沒有很簡單。）

·我們可以這樣說

這種句型目的在於減經否定的程度，希望顯得客氣一點，但並不表示就只能用在貶損的時候。有時候和朋友聚餐，朋友怕喝了咖啡睡不著覺，你就可以說：

The coffee is not very strong. It won't make you insomnious.
（這杯咖啡不會很濃，不會讓你失眠。）

·換你試試看，這個問題怎麼回答？

1. Excuse me; is the shopping mall far from here?
2. Do you think Miss Tang is a good secretary?
3. Are you sure?
4. Is Sam fat?
5. Are Nancy and Sunny easygoing?

·你完成了嗎？

1. Excuse me; is the shopping mall far from here?

   → No, the park is not very far from here.

2. Do you think Miss Tang is a good secretary?

   → No, I think Miss Tang is not a very good secretary.

3   Are you sure?

   → No, I am not very sure.

4. Is Sam fat?

   → No, Sam is not very fat.

5. Are Nancy and Sunny easygoing?

   → No, they are not very easygoing.

---

2. not + 形容詞，not + 形容詞＝不會⋯也不會⋯
**　 not just + 形容詞 but 形容詞＝不只⋯還⋯**

使用 not 放在兩個對比的形容詞前，可以表示剛剛好的狀態，例如：

The driver drives the bus steadily, not fast, not slow.
（這位司機穩穩地駕駛公車，不會太快，也不會太慢。）
→ fast 和 slow 是對比的形容詞。

如果在這個句型中加入 but，具有補充說明和加強語氣的作用，例如：

The movie is not just interesting but funny.（這部電影不僅有趣，還很好笑。）
→ interesting 和 funny 是同性質的形容詞。

This restaurant is not just delicious but amazing!
（這家餐廳不僅好吃，而且讓人吃驚！）

・我們可以這樣說

和朋友相約喝下午茶，你點的紅茶溫度剛剛好，你可以說：

The black tea tastes good, not hot, not cold.
（這杯紅茶真好喝，不會太燙，也不會太涼。）

喝完了下午茶，在購物中心逛一逛吧！這時候，朋友試穿一件洋裝，看起來真漂亮，你可以稱讚她：

You look not just beautiful but elegant.（你看起來不僅漂亮，還很有氣質。）

・換你試試看，下面的語詞要用哪一種句型呢？

1. cat / cute / fat / thin
2. novel / scary / terrified
3. work / boring / tedious
4. soup / delicious / salty / spicy

・你完成了嗎？

1. The cat is cute, not fat, not thin.
2. This novel is not just scary but terrified.
3. This work is not just boring but tedious.
4. The soup is delicious, not salty, spicy.

---

3. not + 帶有否定意味的詞＝強調事物有還不錯的地方

我們在第一篇學到了帶有否定字綴的字，這些字和 not 一起使用，表示描述的事物事實上仍有不錯的地方，例如：

The computer is not useless.（這部電腦並非沒有用。）
→ 雖然 not 和 useless 都是帶有否定意味的字，但卻是表示電腦是有用的。

這種句型雖然是將否定詞和有否定字綴的語詞一起連用，但並非雙重否定，要小心被混淆。

Justin is not helpless.（Justin 並非沒有幫上忙。）
Cheer up! It is not hopeless.（打起精神來！並不是完全沒有希望的！）

・我們可以這樣說

這個句型的語氣也是較為客氣的語氣，比較不像單純使用否定詞的否定句那麼絕對，我們可以用這樣委婉的語氣表示事情的可能性，例如：

It is not impossible to solve the problem.（要解決這個問題也不是不可能。）

· 換你試試看，利用單詞照樣造句！

1. John / insupportable
2. Henry / undesirable
3. James / irresponsible
4. Mia / impatient
5. Vicky / unthankful

· 你完成了嗎？

1. John is not insupportable.
2. Henry is not undesirable.
3. James is not irresponsible.
4. Mia is not impatient.
5. Vicky is not unthankful.

---

4. 主詞 + never + 動詞＝絕對不⋯

例如：

Patty never arrives late.（Patty 從來不遲到。）
→ never + 動詞 arrive。

She will never play the drum anymore.（她再也不會打鼓了。）

Never forget to turn off the light when you leave.
（當你離開時絕對不要忘記關燈。）
→ never 也可以放在句首做祈使句使用。

· 我們可以這樣用

當和另一半吵架時，這個句型可以幫助我們表達心中的氣憤，例如：

I will never talk to you.（我絕對不會再跟你說話。）

當然，能夠不要吵架是最好的，我們也可以用這個句型向情人甜言蜜語：

I will never leave you alone.（我永遠都不會放你一個人。）

1. John hates eating pineapple.
2. Sandra hates traveling.
3. Kim hates rock music.

1. John never eats pineapple.
2. Sandra never travels.
3. Kim never listens to rock music.

5. not + any = 沒有任何…

any 或 any 開頭的字，例如 anything、anybody、anyone 等，可以和 not 一起使用，例如：

There aren't any books on the table.（在桌上沒有任何書。）
→ not 和 any 一起使用。

There isn't any ice cream in the bowl.（碗裡面沒有任何冰淇淋了。）

You don't need to say anything.（你什麼都不用說。）
→ not 和 anything 一起使用。

She can't go anywhere.（她哪裡都不能去。）
→ not 和 anywhere 一起使用。

和姊妹淘聊天，難免會說些八卦，如果你的朋友要告訴你一個天大的秘密，並要你保證絕對不能告訴別人，你可以說：

I never tell anyone about your secret.（我絕不會把你的秘密告訴任何人。）

1. 家裡沒有任何人。
2. 水壺裡沒有任何水。

3. 她什麼都不知道。
4. 他哪裡都不能去。

・你寫完了嗎？

1. There isn't anyone at home.
2. There isn't any water in the bottle.
3. She doesn't know anything.
4. He can't go anywhere.

---

6. no 開頭的否定詞 + but，but 具有 only 的涵義

no 開頭的否定詞，例如 nothing、no one、nobody 或 nowhere，可以自己構成否定句，例如：

There's nothing we can do.（我們什麼都不能做。）
→ 句子中不需要 not 就具有否定意味。

No one in this classroom likes David.（教室裡沒有人喜歡 David。）

I went nowhere in summer vacation.（我暑假哪裡都沒有去。）

若這些否定詞和 but 一起使用，but 表示「只有…」，例如：

There is nothing on the shelf but books.（書櫃上除了書什麼都沒有。）
→ nothing 和 but 一起用，but 表示 only。

He has nothing but his cats.（除了貓，他一無所有。）

There is nobody in the restaurant but Sandy.（餐廳裡除了 Sandy 沒有別人。）

・我們可以這麼說

除了和情人要甜言蜜語，朋友之間也是需要互相稱讚的，你可以這樣說，讓朋友知道她在你心目中的地位：

I have no friends but you.（除了你，我沒有朋友了。）

・換你試試看，改寫這個句子！

1. He only saw Jenny.
2. She only drank water yesterday.
3. There's only a cat on the sofa.
4. He only went to swimming pool last night.
5. My brother only reads detective novels.

・你完成了嗎？

1. He saw nobody but Jenny.
2. She ate nothing but water yesterday.
3. There's nothing on the sofa but a cat.
4. He went nowhere but swimming pool last night.
5. My brother reads nothing but detective novels.

---

7. no + 名詞 = 沒有…

no 放在名詞的前面，表示某物並不存在，例如：

We have no time.（我們沒有時間。）
→ no 後面的 time 是名詞，兩者一起使用，表示「沒有時間」。

除了 no 和名詞的組合，否定詞 not 和 any 一起連用時，也表示「沒有…」：

The poor man can't see any hope.（這個可憐的男人看不到任何希望。）
→ not 和 any 組合等於 no + 名詞。

這句可以改寫成：
The poor man sees no hope.

・我們可以這樣說

馬上就要開會了，今天輪到你作會議報告，上台前，你可以這樣鼓勵自己：
I wish I could make no mistake in this presentation.
（我希望我的報告沒有任何錯誤。）

・換你試試看，這句英文還可以怎麼說？

1. Mr. Jones doesn't have any children.
2. He solved this math question easily.
3. There isn't anyone in the mall at midnight.
4. There weren't any players hit the baseball in this game.
5. There's any difference between these pencils.
6. The government doesn't have money to build a new sport center.

・你寫對了嗎？

1. Mr. Jones doesn't have any children.

   → Mr. Jones has no children.

2. He solved this math question easily.

   → He had no difficulty solving this math question.

3. There isn't anyone in the mall at midnight.

   → There's no one in the mall at midnight.

4. There's any difference between these pencils.

   → There's no difference between these pencils.

5. The government doesn't have money to build a new sport center.

   → The government has no money for building a new sport center.

---

8. neither...nor... = 兩者都不…

這個句型表示兩者都不可能的情況。neither...nor... 是屬於對等連接詞，因此前後銜接的語詞要一致，例如：

Neither Sam nor I like this movie.
（不論是 *Sam* 或是我，都不喜歡這部電影。）
→ 在 Neither 和 nor 後面的 Sam、I 都是代表人的名詞。

Neither 可以單獨於答句中使用，表示「兩樣都不要」

A: Would you like some tea or juice?（你想要來點茶或果汁嗎？）
B: Neither.（我兩個都不要。）

Neither 也具有「既不是這個，也不是那個」的涵義，例如：

Neither hamburger is delicious.（這兩個漢堡都不好吃。）
→ 雖然 neither 表示兩者都不⋯，但後面的名詞和動詞都使用單數。

這句也可以改寫成：

Neither of the hamburgers is delicious.
→ 當 neither 後有加 of 時，名詞前要有冠詞，名詞也要變複數。

這種句子一般習慣動詞使用單數動詞，但若使用複數動詞也不能說不正確。

・我們可以這樣說
還記得剛剛朋友逛街試穿的新洋裝嗎?除了可以稱讚她穿的洋裝很漂亮，你也可以稱讚她的身材真不錯：

You are neither too fat nor too thin.（你不會太胖也不會太瘦，剛剛好。）

・換你試試看，這句英文怎麼說？
1. Owen 和 Alvin 都沒有受到邀請。
2. Kevin 不會太高，也不會太矮。
3. 鉛筆盒裡沒有尺，也沒有橡皮擦。
4. 爸爸媽媽都不在家。
5. 她沒有錢也沒有食物。

・你完成了嗎？
1. Neither Owen nor Alvin was invited.
2. Kevin is neither too tall nor too short.
3. There is neither a ruler nor an eraser in the pencil case.
4. Neither Dad nor Mom is at home.
5. She has neither money nor food.

> 9. There is no use + V-ing = 做⋯是沒用的
>   There is no + V-ing = 做⋯是不可能的

這兩個句型非常相似，但是差了一個 use，意思就會差了十萬八千里，因此在使用上，要特別小心唷！

有加 use 的句型，表示「做⋯是沒用的」，例如：

There is no use crying.（哭是沒有用的。）

沒有加 use 的句型，表示「做⋯是不可能的」，例如：

There is no telling the weather in the future.（判斷未來的天氣是不可能的。）

這種句型可以用＜It is impossible to + 動詞原形＞改寫：

It is impossible to tell the weather in the future.

・我們可以這樣說

當我們遇到朋友為了工作不順心而發脾氣，我們可以這樣鼓勵她：

There is no use being angry.（生氣是沒有用的。）

There's no denying that you did well.（不可否認的，你做得很好。）

・換你試試看，練習改寫！

1. It's impossible to deny that he loves her very much.
2. It's useless to do these things for her.
3. It's impossible to believe him again.
4. It's useless to shout.

・你完成了嗎？

1. There is no denying that he loves her very much.
2. There is no use doing these things for her.
3. There is no believing him again.

4. There is no use shouting.

---

10. far from + 名詞 / 動名詞 = 完全不…

例如：

The secretary's report is far from perfect.（這個秘書的報告一點也不完美。）
→ far from 後面接名詞。

Far from being rude, he is very gentle.（他不但不粗魯，還非常溫柔。）
→ far from 後面加動名詞。

・我們可以這樣說

當小朋友拿著段考成績單回來，你發現他考的實在差強人意時，你可以
說：

Your grade is far from satisfactory.（你的成績完全不令人滿意。）

・換你試試看，利用單詞造句！

1. girl / beauty
2. her dress style / elegant
3. his trick / amazement

・你完成了嗎？

1. The girl is far from beauty.
2. Her dress style is far from elegance.
3. His trick is far from amazement.

11. It doesn't matter to 某人 that / what / how... = 對某人來說，做…無所謂

例如：

It doesn't matter to me that he loves Ella.
（對我而言，他愛 *Ella* 跟我沒關係。）
→ it doesn't matter 加 that 領導的子句。

It doesn't matter to me what you wear today.
（你今天穿什麼，我都無所謂。）
→ it doesn't matter 加 what 領導的子句。

It doesn't matter to Jason how his girlfriend feels.
（對 Jason 而言，他女朋友怎麼覺得不重要。）
→ it doesn't matter 加 how 領導的子句。

· 我們可以這樣說

和情人吵架的時候，我們可以用這個句型表達自己心中的氣憤：

It doesn't matter to me what you said.（對我而言，你說什麼我都無所謂。）

· 換你試試看，試著翻譯看看！
1. 對她而言，誰掌管這間公司一點也不重要。
2. 對 Justin 而言，吃什麼一點也不重要。
3. 對我而言，事情怎麼發展一點一不重要。
4. 你覺得你不會在意輸掉比賽嗎？

· 你完成了嗎？
1. It doesn't matter to her that who charges this company.
2. It doesn't matter to Justin what to eat.
3. It doesn't matter to me how things are going.
4. Do you think it doesn't matter to you to lose the game?

‖ 好學的否定句諺語 ‖

否定句型常常被應用於諺語中，換你試試看，可以猜出這些諺語是什麼意思嗎？

1. Never twice without three times.
2. No rose without a thorn.
3. No smoke without some fire.
4. Nothing succeeds like success.
5. Nothing ventured, noting won.
6. No time like the present.
7. Waste not, want not.
8. You cannot eat your cake and have it.
9. You cannot see the wood for the trees.
10. There's no eel so small but it hopes to become a whale.
11. No sin is hidden to the soul.
12. A clear conscience shines not only in the eyes.

A. 沒有罪惡可以藏在靈魂裡
B. 不入虎穴，焉得虎子
C. 歷史會重演
D. 一事成，事事順
E. 魚與熊掌不可兼得
F. 有苦必有樂
F. 人小志氣高
H. 良心不只在眼睛裡閃耀
I. 捨本逐末
J. 不浪費，不愁缺
K. 無火不生煙
L. 現在最寶貴

· 你找到了嗎？

1. Never twice without three times.（C. 歷史會重演。）
2. No rose without a thorn.（F. 有苦必有樂。）
3. No smoke without some fire.（K. 無火不生煙。）
4. Nothing succeeds like success.（D. 一事成，事事順。）
5. Nothing ventured, noting won.（B. 不入虎穴，焉得虎子。）
6. No time like the present.（L. 現在最寶貴。）
7. Waste not, want not.（J. 不浪費，不愁缺。）
8. You cannot eat your cake and have it.（E 魚與熊掌不可兼得。）
9. You cannot see the wood for the trees.（I. 捨本逐末。）
10. There's no eel so small but it hopes to become a whale.（F. 人小志氣高。）
11. No sin is hidden to the soul.（A. 沒有罪惡可以藏在靈魂裡。）
12. A clear conscience shines not only in the eyes.（H. 良心不只在眼睛裡閃耀。）

▌好學的會話小短句

1. I can't believe it! 我真不敢相信！

A: I won the lottery!（我中樂透了！）

B: Really? I can't believe it!（真的嗎？我真不敢相信！）

2. I can't agree more! 我完全同意！

A: Dogs are human's best friends.（狗是人類最好的朋友。）

B: I can't agree you more!（我完全同意！）

3. I didn't mean it! 我不是故意的！

A: Why you spill the coffee on the floor?（你為什麼把咖啡潑在地上？）

B: I didn't mean it!（我不是故意的）

4. I don't think so. 我才不這麼認為！

A: Nancy is really a pretty woman.（Nancy 真是個漂亮的女人。）
B: Well, I don't think so.（嗯，我才不這麼認為！）

5. I don't have a clue. 我一點也不知道。

A: Do you know where my keys are?（你知道我的鑰匙在哪裡嗎？）
B: I don't have a clue about it.（我一點也不知道。）

6. I have no choice. 我也沒辦法。

A: Why you tell Mom my secret?（你幹嘛跟媽媽說我的秘密？）
B: I am sorry, but she threatened me to deduct my allowance. I have no choice.
（我很抱歉，但她威脅要扣我的零用錢，我也沒辦法。）

7. I have no idea. 我不知道。

A: Do you know why Annie broke up with her boyfriend?
（你知道 Annie 為什麼和她男朋友分手嗎？）
B: I have no idea.（我不知道。）

8. I am not finished. 我還沒好。

A: Did you finish the report for the meeting?（你完成會議記錄了嗎？）
B: I am not finished! I am so busy this week.（我還沒弄完！我這星期超忙。）

9. It won't work. 沒有用的。

A: We can fix the motorcycle by ourselves.（我們可以自己來修理摩托車。）
B: It won't work. We don't know anything about motorcycle.
（行不通的，我們一點都不懂摩托車。）

10. Wouldn't I know? 我還會不知道嗎？

A: You can't get through the red light.（你不可以闖紅燈。）
B: Wouldn't I know?（我還會不知道嗎？）

---

11. Not a chance! 絕不可能！

A: Could you lend me ten thousand dollars?（你可以借我一萬元嗎？）
B: Not a chance!（想都別想！）

---

12. Nothing. 沒什麼事。

A: You look pale. What happened?（你看起來臉色很蒼白，發生什麼事了？）
B: Nothing.（沒什麼事。）

三、文法糾正篇

1. not 的位置會影響句子的涵義

not 在句子中的位置會影響整個句子的涵義，比較看看下面的句子：

He tried not to lose the game.

He didn't try to lose the game.

你發現有什麼不同了嗎？

He tried not to lose the game.
→ tried not 翻譯成「試著不要…」，這句的中文翻譯是「他試著不要輸掉比賽。」

He didn't try to lose the game.
→ didn't try 是「沒有試著…」，這句的中文翻譯是「他沒有試圖輸掉比賽。」

　　但有些動詞不論 not 放在什麼位置，都不影響句子的意思。這類的動詞常見的有：appear（顯現）、intend（試圖）、except（除了）、wish（希望）、want（想要）、seem（似乎）、happen（發生）等，例如：

I wish not to lose the game.（我希望不要輸掉比賽。）

也可以說成：

I don't wish to lose the game.

---

2. 部分否定不代表完全沒有

　　若句子裡有 very、always、every 和 not 一起使用時，表示部分否定，例如：

The American doesn't speak Chinese very well.
（這個美國人中文說得不是很好。）
→ not very well 代表「不會不好，但也沒有很好」的涵義。

The rich man is not always happy.（這位有錢人並不是總是感到快樂。）

　　在概念篇中提到的廣義否定詞，也具有部分否定的涵義，但卻不是完全的否定：

He rarely makes breakfast for his daughter.（他很少做早餐給女兒吃。）
→ 很少不代表沒有。

She seldom plays basketball.（她很少打籃球。）

　　還有一種句型＜almost + no / never＞，也可以代表部分否定，例如：

There is almost no coffee in the cup.（杯子裡幾乎沒有咖啡。）
→ 幾乎沒有不代表完全沒有。

I almost never play dodge ball.（我幾乎沒有打躲避球。）

3. I don't think 而不是 I think you don't

例如：

I think she isn't at home.（X）
→ 句子中有 think 和 not 的時候，習慣將 think 改為否定使用。

I don't think she is at home.（我不認為她在家。）
→ think 改為否定語意，句子正確。

這類用法的動詞有：believe（相信）、suppose（推測）、imaging（想像）。再舉一個例子：

He believes he hasn't met Tracy.（X）
→ believe 要改為否定型。

He doesn't believe he has met Tracy.（他不相信他見過 *Tracy*。）
→ 正確的句型。

這些動詞也可以用在簡答句中，例如：

I suppose not.（我想不是。）
→ suppose 後面直接加 not，形成否定簡答。

She believes not.（她相信不會。）

4. any 開頭的否定詞 + but，but 具有 except 的涵義

在好學的否定句型 (6) 中，我們了解 no 開頭的否定詞加 but，but 具有 only 的涵義，但是 any 開頭的否定詞和 but 一起使用，卻有不同的意思：

I can't speak any language but English.（我除了英文，什麼語言都不會說。）
→ any 開頭的否定詞和 but 一起使用時，but 代表「除了…」。

He didn't talk to anyone but this young lady.
（他除了和這位年輕小姐說話，沒有和任何人說話。）

・換你試試看，否定句的綜合練習，判斷句子是否正確！

1. I don't eat nothing but a hamburger.

2. She knows nothing.

3. I won't believe you anymore.

4. He drank anything but beer.

5. He drank nothing but beer.

6. I think she isn't stupid.

7. The Japanese can't speak Chinese very well.

8. He doesn't never ask Mia out.

9. The boss is far from satisfied.

10. There is no use write this letter to her.

11. Neither the comic book nor the magazine are funny.

12. Hurry up! We have not time.

・你完成了嗎？

1. I don't eat nothing but a hamburger.
→（X）如果要使用 nothing，就不可以使用 don't，若寫成 I eat nothing but a hamburger.，表示「除了漢堡，我什麼都沒有吃。」若想保留 don't，則要把 nothing 改成 anything，寫成 I don't eat anything but a hamburger.，表示「我什麼都沒有吃，只吃了漢堡。」

2. She knows nothing.
→（O）nothing 和否定詞不能同時使用，這個句子的意思是：她什麼都不知道。

3. I won't believe you anymore.
→（O）any 和 any 開頭的字可以和否定詞一起使用，這個句子的意思是：我再也不會相信你了！

4. He drank anything but beer.
→（X）如果要使用 anything，則句子中要加否定詞 not 改寫成：He didn't drank anything but beer 中文意思為：他除了啤酒，什麼都沒有喝。

5. He drank nothing but beer.
→（O）有 no 開頭的字，就可以將句子改變為否定句，不需要另外加 not。這句的意思是：他什麼也沒有喝，只有喝啤酒。

6. I think she isn't stupid.

→（X）I think 連接的子句中有否定，則應將 think 改為否定，這個句子正確的寫法是：I don't think she is stupid.，中文翻譯為：我不認為她很笨。

7. The Japanese can't speak Chinese very well.

→（O）否定句中的 very，可以讓整句話的語氣較為完婉轉。本句的中文翻譯是：這個日本人的中文說得不是很好。

8. He doesn't never ask Mia out.

→（X）句子中出現兩個否定詞，就不具有否定句的涵義。本句應改寫為：He doesn't ask Mia out. 或是 He never asks Mia out.，但兩句的中文意思略有不同，前者表示「他沒有邀請 Mia 出去」，後者表示「他從不邀請 Mia 出去」。

9. The boss is far from satisfied.

→（X）far from 後面要接名詞或動名詞，本句應改寫為：The boss is far from satisfaction.，中文翻譯為：老闆並不滿意。

10. There is no use write this letter to her.

→（X）There is no use 後面的動作要變成動名詞，這句應改寫為 There is no use writing this letter to her. 中文翻譯為：寫信給她沒有用。

11. Neither the comic book nor the magazine are funny.

→（X）neither...nor... 的動詞根據名詞的單複數決定，這個句子中的 comic book 和 magazine 都是單數，be 動詞也要使用單數動詞。本句正確的寫法為：Neither the comic book nor the magazine is funny. 中文翻譯為：不論漫畫或雜誌都不有趣。

12. Hurry up! We have not time.

→（X）＜no + 名詞＞才具有「沒有…」的涵義，本句正確的寫法應將 not 改為 no：Hurry up! We have no time. 中文翻譯為：快一點，我們沒有時間了！

07
CHAPTER
表示疑問和徵詢的句型：問句、間接問句和附加問句

一、概念篇

‖ 什麼是疑問句 |

用來表示疑問或徵詢的句子，就稱為疑問句，例如：

Are you a lawyer?（你是律師嗎？）

What are you doing?（你正在做什麼？）

依照回答的方式，可以將疑問句分成兩個種類，一個是回答以 Yes 或 No 開頭的疑問句，另一個是以疑問詞開頭的疑問句：

⑴ 回答以 Yes 或 No 開頭的疑問句
這類的疑問句，目的在詢問資訊，例如：

Is he your boyfriend?（他是妳的男朋友嗎？）
→ 詢問資訊。

Do you like scuba diving?（你喜歡潛水嗎？）

Will you go to the concert?（你會去演唱會嗎？）

有時，這類的疑問句，也可以用來表達建議或其他狀況，特別是當句子中有助動詞時，例如：

Shall we dance?（來跳舞吧？）
→ 表示建議。

Could you pass the salt to me?（你可以把鹽遞給我嗎？）
→ 表示詢問。

Would you like some coffee?（你要來一些咖啡嗎？）
→ 表示邀請。

May I borrow your cell phone?（我可以借用你的手機嗎？）
→ 表示徵求同意。

以 Yes 或 No 開頭的疑問句的形成方式很簡單，看看下面的例子：

He is a doctor.（他是一位醫生。）
→ 句子裡面有 be 動詞，變成問句，把 be 動詞放句首。

Is he a doctor?（他是醫生嗎？）
→ be 動詞放句首，後面的語序不變，最後的標點符號要改成問號。

He plays the basketball every day.（他每天都打籃球。）
→ 句子裡面有動作，變成問句，要找助動詞幫忙。

Does he play basketball every day?（他每天都打籃球嗎？）
→ he 的助動詞為 does，助動詞後面的動詞要使用原形動詞。

I will call you later.（我晚點會打給你。）
→ 句子中已經有助動詞，變成問句，直接把助動詞放在句首。

Do you will call me later? （X）
→ 一個句子中使用兩個助動詞，是錯誤的用法。

Will you call me later?（你晚點會打給我嗎？）
→ 正確的寫法。

在完成式的句子中，特別容易忽略句子中的助動詞，例如：

She has been to China.（她去過中國。）
→ has 在完成式中，扮演助動詞的角色，所以變成問句的時候，不需要用另外的助動詞來形成問句。

Does she have been to China?（X）
→ 同時使用 does 或 have 兩個助動詞，是錯誤的寫法。

Has she been to China?（她去過中國嗎？）
→ 正確的寫法。

・換你試試看

A. 將句子改成問句

1. She helps her mom with those books.
2. I have eaten French fries.
3. We practice volleyball every Monday and Wednesday.
4. Jacky is going to the supermarket.
5. Mike and Jill went camping last weekend.

B. 這個狀況的問句怎麼說?

1. 你想和 Jeff 借筆記本。
2. 你提議休息五分鐘。
3. 你邀請 Bob 一起去看電影。
4. 你看到火車上有空位，想要坐下來。
5. 你請人留下聯絡的電話。

・你完成了嗎？

A. 將句子改成問句

1. Does she help her mom with those books?
2. Have you eaten French fries?
   → 記得改寫時，人稱也要作適當的變化。
3. Do you practice volleyball every Monday and Wednesday?
4. Is Jacky going to the supermarket?

5. Did Mike and Jill go camping last weekend?

　→ 如果動詞是過去式，變成問句的助動詞也要使用過去式。

B. 這個狀況的問句怎麼說?

1. 你想和 Jeff 借筆記本。

　→ May I borrow your notebook?

2. 你提議休息五分鐘。

　→ Shall we take a break for five minutes?

3. 你邀請 Bob 一起去看電影。

　→ Would you like to go to the movie with me?

4. 你看到火車上有空位，想要坐下來。

　→ May I sit here?

5. 你請人留下聯絡的電話。

　→ Could you leave your phone number?

(2) 以疑問詞開頭的疑問句

　疑問詞如 what（什麼）、who（誰）、which（哪一個）、whose（誰的）、where（哪裡）、when（何時）、why（為什麼）和 how（如何），例如：

What are you watching?（你在看什麼？）

Who is that person?（那個人是誰？）

Which sweater is yours, the red one or the blue one?
（哪一件毛衣是你的，紅色或藍色的？）
→ which 具有選擇性的涵義，後面通常會提供選擇的選項。

Whose pencil is it?（這是誰的鉛筆？）
→ whose 後面一定會銜接名詞。

Where is the toyshop?（玩具店在哪裡？）

When will you go to the bank?（你什麼時候要去銀行？）

Why are you crying?（為什麼你要哭？）

How are you?（你好嗎？）

　　從上面的例句中，你有沒已發現，形成以疑問詞開頭的疑問句的方法，只需要將疑問時放在疑問句前就好，例如：

I am watching the talk show.（我正在看脫口秀。）
→ 原本的直述句。

Are you watching the talk show?（你正在看脫口秀嗎？）
→ 將 be 動詞移到句首變疑問句，人稱和 be 動詞要作適當的變化。

What are you watching the talk show?
→ 疑問詞放在句首，但已經問「正在看什麼」，如果還寫出 the talk show 很奇怪。

What are you watching?（你正在看什麼？）
→ 正確的寫法。

　　和以 Yes 或 No 開頭的疑問句一樣，如果句子中有動詞，變成疑問句找助動詞幫忙；如果句子中本身有助動詞，將助動詞移到疑問詞的後面，例如：

Where did he go last night?（他昨晚去哪裡了？）

What will you do next Saturday?（你下星期六要做什麼？）

　　有些疑問詞會和其他語詞形成慣用語，常見的有：

What time is it?（現在幾點？）

What kind of sport do you like?（你喜歡什麼類型的運動？）

How often do you exercise?（你多常運動？）

How long will you stay in America?（你在美國會待多久？）

How much money is this coat?（你這件外套多少錢？）

How old are you?（你幾歲？）

How far is the supermarket?（超市離這裡有多遠？）

How many books do you have?（你有幾本書？）

what 和 for 一起使用，可以用來詢問意圖，例如：

What is this book for?（這本書用來做什麼？）

What did you buy this book for?（你為什麼買這本書？）
→ ＜What...for?＞的句型，可以用 why 改寫：Why did you buy this book?

What 和 like 一起使用，是用來詢問某事物的好壞程度，例如：

What was the movie like?（這部電影如何？）

What is your girlfriend like?（你女朋友個性如何？）

但是下面這個句子卻是用來詢問喜好，試試看找出和上面句子不同的地方：

What does your girlfriend like?（你女朋友喜歡什麼？）
→ 當使用助動詞時，like 為一般動詞，表示「喜歡」。

下面兩個句子的意思也很常被混淆：

How is Monica?（*Monica* 好嗎？）
→ 問 Monica 的狀況。

What is Monica like?（*Monica* 的個性如何？）
→ 問 Monica 是怎麼樣的人。

‧換你試試看，選擇正確的疑問詞！

1. A: ＿＿＿＿ is Annie?
   B: She is in the living room.
2. A: ＿＿＿＿ color do you like, white or black?
   B: I like black.
3. A: ＿＿＿＿ ＿＿＿＿ is it?
   B: It's twelve o'clock.
4. A: ＿＿＿＿ is the woman talking to you?
   B: She is my English teacher.

5. A: _____ _____ do you play video games?

   B: Once or twice a week.

6. A: _____ don't you talk to Jimmy?

   B: Because I am mad at him.

7. A: _____ bag is it?

   B: It's Wendy's bag.

8. A: _____ is the man like?

   B: He is very nice.

・你完成了嗎？

1. A: <u>Where</u> is Annie?

   B: She is in the living room.

2. A: <u>Which</u> color do you like, white or black?

   B: I like black.

3. A: <u>What time</u> is it?

   B: It's twelve o'clock.

4. A: <u>Who</u> is the woman talking to you?

   B: She is my English teacher.

5. A: <u>How often</u> do you play video games?

   B: Once or twice a week.

6. A: <u>Why</u> don't you talk to Jimmy?

   B: Because I am mad at him.

7. A: <u>Whose</u> bag is it?

   B: It's Wendy's bag.

8. A: <u>What</u> is the man like?

   B: He is very nice.

▋ 什麼是間接問句 ▏

　　將疑問詞領導的疑問句，放在句子中間，作為前面動詞的受詞，稱為間接問句，例如：

　　Who is she?（她是誰？）

　　→ 疑問句領導的疑問句。

I don't know who she is.（我不知道她是誰。）
→ Who she is 是間接問句，作為動詞 know 的受詞。

She doesn't know what Jimmy's address is.（她不知道 Jimmy 的地址。）
→ what 領導的間接問句，主詞要先寫才寫動詞。

Tell me who told you the secret.（告訴我誰告訴你這個秘密的。）
→ 如果間接問句中的疑問詞是主詞，後面可以直接銜接動詞。

間接問句的標點符號，要看主要子句的語氣是肯定句還是疑問句，例如：

I don't know which is yours.（我不知到哪一個是你的。）
→ I don't know 是否定句，最後的標點符號用句號。

Do you know what is under the table?（你知道在桌子下的是什麼嗎？）
→ Do you know 為疑問句，最後的標點符號要用問號。

間接問句中，疑問詞和其所領導的子句，可以改寫成＜疑問詞＋不定詞＞，將疑問詞與不定詞結合，可以加強疑問詞的涵義：

Can you tell me where I can buy the same bag?
（你可以告訴我哪裡可以買到相同的袋子嗎？）

Can you tell me where to buy the same bag?
→ 原本的子句代換成不定詞，加強了「哪裡買」的語氣。

這類的用法例如：what to do（該怎麼辦）、which one to buy（要買哪一個）、who to believe（要相信誰）、how to do it（該如何做）、when to leave（何時離開）等。

・換你試試看，合併成間接問句！

1. I don't know.
   Who is this woman?
2. Ask Jimmy.
   Where is the newsstand?
3. Tell me.
   How to go to Will's house?

4. Do you know?

When will she hold a concert?

5. Do you understand?

What is he talking about?

・你完成了嗎？

1. I don't know who this woman is.
2. Ask Jimmy where the newsstand is.
3. Tell me how to go to Will's house.
4. Do you know when she will hold a concert?
5. Do you understand what he is talking about?

‖ 什麼是附加問句 ‖

附加問句是用於直述句後面的問句，目的是用來叮嚀對方或是徵詢對方的意見：

He is a professor, isn't he *?*（他是一位教授，不是嗎？）
→ isn't he 是附加問句。

She doesn't like dogs, does she *?*（她不喜歡狗，不是嗎？）
→ does she 是附加問句。

在語調上，如果是叮嚀對方，語調下降；若是徵詢對方的意見，語調上升。

附加問句的形成方式有幾項原則：

⑴ 前後相反，否定縮寫

前後相反的意思是，當前面的直述句是肯定句時，後面的附加問句要使用否定句，反之亦然，若是否定句，則要用縮寫式：

She isn't a nurse, is she?（她不是護士，是嗎？）
→ 直述句是否定句，間接問句用肯定句。

She is a nurse, isn't she?（她是一位護士，不是嗎？）
→ 直述句是肯定句，間接問句用否定句，否定要用縮寫式。

否定式的縮寫，可以參考第六篇否定句。

⑵ 主詞變成代名詞
　　間接問句的主詞一定要使用代名詞，例如：

<u>Nancy</u> is a teacher, isn't <u>she</u>?（*Nancy* 是一位老師，不是嗎？）
→ 間接問句用代名詞 she 取代 Nancy。

John and Willie are good friends, aren't they?（*John* 和 *Willie* 是好朋友，不
是嗎？）
→ 間接問句用代名詞 they 取代 John and Willie。

⑶ be 動詞、助動詞不變，只有動詞找助動詞幫忙
　　如果直述句中使用 be 動詞或助動詞，附加問句也使用相同的 be 動詞或助
動詞：

The cat <u>is</u> cute, <u>isn't</u> it?（這隻貓很可愛，不是嗎?）
→ be 動詞不變。

She <u>can</u> make cookies, <u>can't</u> she?（她會做餅乾，不是嗎？）
→ 助動詞不變。

若是直述句中有動詞，附加問句要找助動詞來幫忙，例如：

Bob <u>likes</u> swimming, <u>doesn't</u> he?（*Bob* 喜歡游泳，不是嗎？）
→ 直述句中用動詞，附加問句要使用助動詞，助動詞要隨著人稱不同而變
化。

⑷ 特殊用法
Do something, will you?（做些什麼，好嗎？）
→ 祈使句的附加問句要用 will you。

Come with me, won't you?（跟我來，好嗎？）
→ 表示邀請的附加問句，習慣用 won't you。

Let's go shopping, shall we?（我們去購物吧，好不好？）
→ let's 句型的附加問句要用 shall we。

Let's not watch TV, OK?（我們不要看電視了，好不好？）
→ let's 句型的否定句，附加問句習慣用 OK 或是 all right。

The coffee is too bitter to drink, isn't it?（咖啡喝起來很苦，不是嗎？）
→ ＜too...to＞的句型表示「太…以至於…」，雖然中文具有否定的涵義，但在英文句子中仍是肯定句，間接問句要使用否定形。

・換你試試看，附加問句要怎麼寫？

1. You are a clerk.
2. He will marry to Jane.
3. We don't go to the party.
4. She is her best friend.
5. They love each other.
6. Let's have some tea.
7. Sit down.
8. Let's not talk to Jerry.
9. The lemon is too sour to eat.
10. Sandy didn't go to the park.

・你完成了嗎？

1. You are a clerk, aren't you?
2. He will marry to Jane, won't he?
3. We don't go to the party, do we?
4. She is her best friend, isn't she?
5. They love each other, don't they?
6. Let's have some tea, shall we?
7. Sit down, will you?
8. Let's not talk to Jerry, all right / OK?
9. The lemon is too sour to eat, isn't it?

10.Sandy didn't go to the park, did she?

▍疑問句的回答 ▏

　　疑問句回答的原則很簡單，只要記住三個方法：「是就是 Yes，不是就是 No」、「用什麼問，用什麼回答」和「前面有 No，後面有 not」，例如：

Is he a dentist?（他是牙醫嗎？）

<u>*Yes, he is.*</u>（是，他是。）
→ 是就說 Yes，問句用 be 動詞問，答句用 be 動詞回答。

<u>*No, he is not.*</u>（不，他不是。）
→ 不是就說 No，前面有 no，後面的答案要加上 not。

換你想想看，這個問句的回答是什麼？

<u>*Do you like cats?*</u>（你喜歡貓嗎？）

你想到了嗎？有肯定和否定的回答方式：

<u>*Yes, I do.*</u>（是，我喜歡。）
→ 是就說 Yes，問句用助動詞問，答句用助動詞回答。

<u>*No, I don't.*</u>（不，我不喜歡。）
→ 不是就說 No，前面有 no，後面的答案要加上 not。

簡答句可以寫成縮寫，但一定要記得，逗號後面要有兩個以上的字，例如：

<u>*No, she isn't.*</u>
→ 逗點後面要有兩個字。

Yes, she's.
→ 若將 she is 縮寫成 she's，逗號後面就只有一個字，是錯誤的寫法。

這些回答的原則，通用於所有的疑問句，包含否定開頭的疑問句或附加問

句：

Don't you come with me?（你不和我一起來嗎？）
→ 肯定回答：Yes, I do.（要，我和你一起去。）
→ 否定回答：No, I don't.（不，我不去了。）

Don't you come with me, do you?（你不跟我一起來，對吧？）
→ 肯定回答：Yes, I do.（要，我和你一起去。）
→ 否定回答：No, I don't.（不，我不去了。）

這類的問題，不要因為否定疑問詞和中文的邏輯影響了答案，寫成：*No, I do.*（不，我要跟你一起去。）或是 *Yes, I don't.*（對，我不跟你一起去。）這兩個都是錯誤的寫法。

二、好學好用的疑問句句型

1. How + 助動詞 + 主詞 + 動詞原形 = …如何？

例如：

How do you go to school?（你是如何去學校的？）

How does he solve this problem?（他是如何解決這個問題的？）
→ 助動詞要跟著人稱不同而改變。

How did she look yesterday?（她昨天看起來如何？）
→ 如果是過去式，助動詞也要變成過去式。

How is the ice cream?（冰淇淋嘗起來如何？）
→ 除了助動詞，也可以用 be 動詞。

How often do you play the drum?（你多久打一次鼓？）
→ 在助動詞前，how 也可以做變化。

・我們可以這樣說

當你看到朋友買了一條很漂亮的項鍊時，你可以這樣表達你的讚嘆：

How do you get this? It's so beautiful.（你怎麼得到這個的？好漂亮！）

・換你試試看，用這個句型完成句子！

1. you sweep the floor
2. you feel yesterday
3. the cappuccino
4. you know

・你完成了嗎？

1. How do you sweep the floor?
2. How did you feel yesterday?
3. How is the cappuccino?
4. How did you know?

2. What on earth + 助動詞 + 主詞 + 原形動詞 = 究竟…

例如：

What on earth did she tell you?（她究竟告訴你什麼？）

What on earth are you thinking?（你究竟在想什麼？）

What in the world did you find?（你究竟在找什麼？）

What in the world are you yelling?（你究竟在大叫什麼？）

・我們可以這樣說

這個句型可以用來表示不耐煩的語氣，例如，當你和朋友約好要聚餐，到了要出門的時候，卻發現另一半還坐在電腦前悠哉的上網，你可以這樣說：

What on earth are you doing? We have no time.
（你究竟在做什麼？我們沒有時間了。）

01 CHAPTER
02 CHAPTER
03 CHAPTER
04 CHAPTER
05 CHAPTER
06 CHAPTER
07 CHAPTER
08 CHAPTER
09 CHAPTER
10 CHAPTER

· 換你試試看，將句子排列成正確的順序！

1. What are earth you on crying?
2. in What the world do you did?
3. What on him did she ask earth?
4. What is in he the laughing world?

· 你完成了嗎？

1. What on earth are you crying?
2. What in the world did you do?
3. What on earth did she ask him?
4. What in the world is he laughing?

---

3. How about + 名詞? = …如何？

這類的句型，多用來表示建議或邀請，例如：

How about some cake?（要來些蛋糕嗎？）

How about watching TV after lunch?（吃完午餐要不要來看電視？）
→ about 後面的動詞要改成動名詞的形式。

How about going to the theme park next Sunday?
（下星期天要不要去遊樂園玩？）

· 我們可以這樣說

遇到不想下廚的時候，就到外面餐廳打打牙祭吧，你可以這樣表示邀請：

How about dining out tonight? I know a wonderful Chinese restaurant.
（今天晚上要不要出去吃飯？我知道一間很棒的中國餐館。）

· 換你試試看，這些動作怎麼表示邀請？

1. 打排球
2. 一杯茶
3. 登山
4. 下午來做餅乾

・你完成了嗎？

1. How about playing volleyball?
2. How about a cup of tea?
3. How about going mountain climbing?
4. How about making some cookies in the afternoon?

---

4. How come + 主詞 + 動詞? = 怎麼會…？

例如：

How come you broke the vase?（你怎麼會把花瓶打破？）

How come you forgot to turn off the light?（你怎麼會忘記關燈？）

How come you didn't lock the door?（你怎麼會沒有鎖門？）
→ 想表達「沒有做…」，在動詞前可以加入助動詞和 not 形成否定。

How come he quarreled with his wife?（他怎麼會和太太吵架？）

How come 可以 why 來代替，當用 why 形成問句時，要記得加入助動詞：

Why did he quarrel with his wife?

・我們可以這樣說

如果家人超過的約定的時間才回家，你可以這樣表達不滿：

How come you came home so late?（你怎麼這麼晚回家？）

・換你試試看，改寫下列句子！

1. Why did she get hurt in the game?
2. Why did you lose your keys?
3. Why did she buy a birthday gift for you?
4. Why did he kidnap these children?

・你完成了嗎？

1. How come she got hurt in the game?

2. How come you lost your keys?

3. How come she bought a birthday gift for you?

4. How come he kidnaped these children?

---

5. Why not + 原形動詞? = 為什麼不…？

例如：

Why not ask her out?（為什麼不邀她出去？）

Why not quit your work?（為什麼不辭掉工作？）

Why not take your daughter to the zoo?（為什麼不帶你女兒去動物園？）

這個句型也可以用 why don't 來代替，例如：

Why don't you take your daughter to the zoo?

・我們可以這樣說

　　當家人為了工作，沒日沒夜的努力，連假日也不好好休息，你可以這樣表示叮嚀：

Why not enjoy your life?（為什麼不享受你的生活呢？）

・換你試試看，改寫這些句子！

1. Why don't you take a break for ten minutes?

2. Why don't you come with us?

3. Why don't you go to the movies?

4. Why don't you have a party?

・你完成了嗎？

1. Why not take a break for ten minutes?

2. Why not come with us?

3. Why not go to the movies?

4. Why not have a party?

6. Are you sure + 主詞 + 動詞? = 你確定…嗎？

例如：

Are you sure you want to wear this?（你確定你要穿這件衣服嗎？）

Are you sure they will break up?（你確定他們要分手了嗎？）

Are you sure Tom didn't tell a lie?（你確定 *Tom* 沒有說謊嗎？）

・我們可以這樣說

當你遇到別人跟你講了一件不可思議的事，你可以表達你的驚訝：

Are you sure?（你確定嗎？）

・換你試試看，利用單詞完成句子！

1. She / be going to / leave
2. It / will / a sunny day
3. She / be going to / stare / movie

・你完成了嗎？

1. Are you sure she is going to leave?
2. Are you sure it will be a sunny day?
3. Are you sure she is going to stare this movie?

7. Can you believe that + 主詞 + 動詞 = 你相信…嗎？

這個句型用來表示驚訝，例如：

Can you believe that Tim lost the game?（你相信 *Tim* 輸掉這場比賽嗎？）

Can you believe that Albert won the lottery?（你相信 *Albert* 贏了樂透嗎？）

Can you believe that the teacher punished the student with a stick?
（你相信這個老師用棍子處罰學生嗎？）

·我們可以這樣說

你可以利用這個句型來強調自己獨力完成了工作，例如，當你完成了一桌的菜，你可以說：

Can you believe that I made all these by myself?
（你相信這全部都是我做的嗎？）

·換你試試看，排列出正確的順序！

1. Can you survived that firefighter believe this in the accident?
2. Can believe you in that the forest guide left us the tour?
3. Can that the cost ten believe thousand you dress dollars?

·你完成了嗎？

1. Can you believe that this firefighter survived in the accident?
2. Can you believe that the tour guide left us in the forest?
3. Can you believe that the dress cost ten thousand dollars?

---

8. Do you by any chance know + 疑問詞 + 主詞 + 動詞…? = 你碰巧知道…嗎？

例如：

Do you by any chance know why she left me?
（你碰巧知道她為什麼離開我嗎？）
→ Do you by any chance know + 疑問詞領導的間接問句。

Do you by any chance know how to fix the bicycle?
（你碰巧知道怎麼修裡這台腳踏車？）

Do you by any chance know who Tom is? （你剛好認識 *Tom* 嗎？）

這個句型也可以用＜Do you happen to know...＞來代替：

Do you happen to know who Tom is?

・我們可以這樣說

當需要問路時，用這個句型可以讓人覺得更加客氣，你可以說：

Do you by any chance know where the supermarket is?
（你剛好知道超市怎麼去嗎？）

・換你試試看，用這個句型把句子完成！

1. Why is she angry?
2. How to get to the theater?
3. What can I do?

・你完成了嗎？

1. Do you by any chance know why she is angry?
2. Do you by any chance know how to get to the theater?
3. Do you by any chance know what I can do?

---

9. Do you mind if + 主詞 + 動詞? = 你介意…嗎？

例如：

Do you mind if I close the window?（你介意我關窗戶嗎？）

Do you mind closing the window?
→ mind 後面若接動詞，要改為動名詞的形式。

Do you mind mopping the table?（你介意擦一下桌子嗎？）

・我們可以這樣說

好不容易在百貨公司的美食街看到了一個位子，但是卻已經有人坐了同一張桌子的其他位子，你可以這樣客氣的詢問：

Do you mind if I sit here?（你介意我坐在這裡嗎？）

・換你試試看，這個狀況怎麼說？

1. 你想要在這裡抽菸。

2. 你想請家人幫忙倒垃圾。

3. 你想邀請朋友一起吃晚餐。

4. 你詢問另一半可不可以和朋友去夜店玩。

・你完成了嗎？

1. Do you mind if I smoke here?

2. Do you mind taking out the trash?

3. Do you mind having dinner with me?

4. Do you mind if I go to the night club with friends?

‖ 好學好用的疑問句小短句 ‖

---

1. How about you? 那你呢？

A: I would like a latte. How about you?（我想要點拿鐵，那你呢？）

B: I would like a cappuccino.（我想要點卡布奇諾。）

---

2. How could that be? 怎麼會這樣？

A: I got fired.（我被炒魷魚了。）

B: How could that be?（怎麼為這樣？）

---

3. What's so funny? 什麼事這麼好笑？

A: What's so funny?（什麼事這麼好笑？）

B: John choked by his saliva.（John 被口水嗆到了。）

---

4. Where were we? 我們說到哪了？

A: Where were we?（我們說到哪了？）

B: I forgot.（我忘了。）

> 5. Why didn't you say so?　為什麼你剛剛不說？
>
> A: I can't find my wallet.（我找不到我的皮夾。）
> B: I saw you leave it on the table.（我看見你忘在桌上了。）
> A: Why didn't you say so?（你剛剛為什麼不說？）

三、文法糾正篇

> 1. 疑問句中的助動詞順序錯誤

　　助動詞在疑問句中的位置，是放在句首或是疑問詞的後面，這是一個很簡單的概念，但在使用上卻常常發生錯誤，例如：

You do want to take a trip?（你想要去旅行嗎？）
→ 錯誤的語序，助動詞要放句首。

Do you want to take a trip?
→ 正確的寫法。

What he <u>did</u> go last night?（他昨晚去哪裡了？）
→ Did 應放在疑問詞的後面，這句是錯誤的寫法。

What did he go last night?
→ 正確的寫法。

　　但是在間接問句中，疑問詞帶領的子句卻要用直述句的語序：

I know <u>what he had done</u>.（我知道他做了什麼。）
→ ＜what + 主詞 + 動詞＞是間接問句正確的寫法。

I know <u>what had he done</u>.
→ 錯誤的用法。

2. 疑問句中沒有助動詞

當句子中只有動詞時，變成問句要找助動詞幫忙，不同的人稱和時態，助動詞也會隨著改變，例如：

She plays the badminton every week?（她每星期打羽毛球嗎？）
→ 疑問句中，應將助動詞置於主詞的前面，本句的文法錯誤。

Does she play the badminton every week?
→ she 的助動詞為 does，當句子中有助動詞時，後面的動詞要使用原形動詞。

上述的句子：She plays the badminton every week? 我們不能說是錯誤的寫法，因為在非正式的場合或口語中，直述句若結尾的語調上揚，也可以表示疑問的口吻，但這不是正確的文法，在書面或正式的場合，要謹慎使用。

若加入疑問詞時，要記得疑問詞後面也要有助動詞：

What you eat for breakfast?（你早餐吃什麼？）
→ 應在疑問詞後加入助動詞 do 或是 did，本句的文法錯誤。

What did you eat for breakfast?
→ 助動詞用過去式的 did，表示問發生過的動作。

What do you eat for breakfast?
→ 助動詞用現在式的 do，表示問習慣或事實。

3. 助動詞和情態動詞一起出現

當句子中已經有情態動詞時，變成疑問句不需要在加入助動詞，例如：

Leo can speak English well.（Leo 的英文說得很好。）
→ can 本身就是助動詞，直接移到句首就可以形成疑問句。

Can Leo speak English well?
→ 正確的寫法。

Does Leo can speak English well?
→ does 和 can 在同一個句子中出現，是錯誤的用法。

完成式的句子特別容易犯這種錯誤，例如：

You have called your mom?（你已經打電話給你媽媽了嗎？）
→ have 是助動詞，移到句首即構成疑問句。

Do you have called your mom?
→ 句子中不能有兩個助動詞。

Have you called your mom?
→ 正確的寫法。

再看一個例子：

He has gone to Thailand?（他去泰國了嗎？）
→ Has 應放在句首構成疑問句。

Does he have gone to Thailand?
→ 錯誤的寫法。

Has he gone to Thailand?
→ 正確的使用。

---

4. 疑問句的主詞是 who、what 和 which 時，不用助動詞

例如：

Who left the cell phone on the table?（誰把手機留在桌上？）
→ who 扮演主詞的角色，直接加動詞。

What happened?（發生什麼事了？）
→ what 是句子中的主詞，後面銜接動詞。

Which is Mike's coat?（哪一件是 Mike 的外套？）
→ which 當主詞，後面直接加動詞。

但是，當這些疑問詞做為受詞時，還是要和助動詞一起使用，例如：

Who do you want to invite?（你想要邀請誰？）
→ who 是動詞 invite 的受詞。

What do you want?（你想要什麼？）
→ what 是動詞 want 的受詞。

Which one do you like?（你喜歡哪一個？）
→ which one 是動詞 like 的受詞。

---

5. 主要子句用什麼助動詞，附加問句也要用相同的助動詞

例如：

You don't like hamburger, do you?（你不喜歡漢堡，對吧？）
→ 主要子句中的助動詞用 do，附加問句的助動詞也要用 do。

You don't like hamburger, will you?
→ 主要子句和附加問句的助動詞不一致，是錯誤的寫法。

再舉一個例子：

He can't play dodge ball, can he?（他不會打躲避球，對吧？）
→ 主要子句中的助動詞用 can，附加問句的助動詞也要用 can。

She is very nice, isn't she?（她人真好，不是嗎？）
→ be 動詞也要一致。

但是若主要子句中沒有助動詞，附加問句的助動詞一律用 do、does 或 did：

You like reading, don't you?（你喜歡閱讀，不是嗎？）

He wants to go to the party, doesn't he?（他想要去這個派對，不是嗎？）

She went to the concert last night, didn't she?
（她昨晚去聽演唱會了，不是嗎？）

‧換你試試看，疑問句的綜合練習，判斷下列句子是否正確！

1. He didn't go to the library, does he?
2. Who called you this morning?

3. Doesn't Larry can speak Spanish?

4. Vicky does plays the piano well?

5. Do you happen to know who is she?

6. Can you believe that she invited her ex-boyfriend to the party?

7. Do you mind turn the TV down?

8. What on earth he did give you?

9. Let's play soccer, shall we?

10. Let's not go to the movies, shall we?

11. Do you think who he is?

12. Tell me what going on is.

13. Kitty is a cook, isn't Kitty?

‧你完成了嗎？

1. He <u>didn't</u> go to the library, <u>does</u> he?
   → （X）附加問句和主要子句的助動詞要一致，本句正確的寫法為：He didn't go to the library, did he? 中文翻譯為：他沒有去圖書館，對嗎？

2. Who called you this morning?
   → （O）疑問詞若當主詞，後面可直接加動詞。本句中文翻譯為：今天早上是誰打電話給你？

3. Doesn't Larry <u>can</u> speak Spanish?
   → （X）疑問句中不可以有兩個助動詞，本題有兩種寫法，第一種是：Doesn't Larry speak Spanish? 中文翻譯為：Larry 不說西班牙文嗎？第二種寫法是：Can Larry speak Spanish? 中文翻譯是：Larry 會說西班牙文嗎？

4. Vicky <u>does plays</u> the piano well?
   → （X）本句的語序錯誤，疑問句中的助動詞應放在主詞前面，同時，句中的動詞要改成原形動詞，本句正確的寫法為：Does Vicky play the piano well? 中文翻譯為：Vicky 的鋼琴彈得好嗎？

5. Do you happen to know <u>who is she</u>?
   → （X）間接問句中，要先寫主詞再寫動詞，本句正確的寫法為：Do you happen to know who she is? 中文翻譯是：你剛好知道她是誰嗎？

6. Can you believe that she invited her ex-boyfriend to the party?
   → （O）本句中文翻譯為：你相信她邀請她前男友去參加派對嗎？

7. Do you mind turn the TV down?

→（X）mind 後面若加動詞，要使用動名詞的形式，本句正確的寫法是：Do you mind turning the TV down? 中文翻譯為：你介意把電視轉小聲嗎？

8. What on earth he did give you?

→（X）疑問句中的助動詞要寫在主詞的前面，本句正確的寫法為：What on earth did he give you? 中文翻譯為：他到底給了你什麼？

9. Let's play soccer, shall we?

→（O）本句中文翻譯為：讓我們一起踢足球，好嗎？

10. Let's not go to the movies, shall we?

→（X）祈使句若使用否定型態，附加問句習慣用 OK 或是 all right 來表達，本句正確的寫法是 Let's not go to the movies, OK / all right? 中文翻譯為：我們不要去看電影，好嗎？

11. Do you think who he is?

→（X）當句子的動詞是 think 或 believe，形成間接問句時，要將疑問詞移到句首，本句正確的寫法為：Who do you think he is? 中文翻譯是：你覺得他是誰？

12. Tell me what going on is.

→（X）疑問詞也可以做附加問句的主詞，當疑問詞為主詞時，後面直接銜接動詞，本句正確的寫法為：Tell me what is going on? 中文翻譯是：告訴我發生了什麼事？

13. Kitty is a cook, isn't Kitty?

→（X）附加問句中的主詞要使用代名詞，本句正確的寫法為：Kitty is a cook, isn't she? 中文翻譯為：Kitty 是一位廚師，不是嗎？

NOTE

01
CHAPTER

02
CHAPTER

03
CHAPTER

04
CHAPTER

05
CHAPTER

06
CHAPTER

07
CHAPTER

08
CHAPTER

09
CHAPTER

10
CHAPTER

08
CHAPTER
加強語氣的句型：祈使句、感嘆句和倒裝句

一、概念篇

▌祈使句

什麼是祈使句

祈使句是日常生活中，使用非常頻繁的句型，幾乎是以原形動詞或是 Don't 作為句子的開頭。

Listen to me.（聽我說！）
→ listen 不作任何動詞變化

Don't go.（別走。）
→ don't 放在動詞前面表示否定。

祈使句的口氣可以很嚴厲，也可以很客氣婉轉，主要用來發出命令、表示請求、禁止某件行為的發生、提出建議或忠告，也可以用來鼓勵對方和表示祝願，例如：

Look at the picture.（看這張照片。）
→ 發出命令，要求別人做「看照片」的動作。

Say something.（說些什麼吧。）
→ 表示請求，希望對方說些什麼。

Don't talk.（不要說話。）
→ 禁止對方做「說話」的動作。

Don't you come with us?（你不跟我們來嗎？）
→ 提出建議，邀請對方一起來。

Have a nice day.（祝你有美好的一天。）
→ 表示祝願，希望對方有美好的一天。

　　看了上面的例句，你有沒有發現，所有的句子前面都沒有主詞，這是祈使句的一個特色。當說話的對象很明確時，可以省略掉主詞：

You look at the picture.（你看這張照片。）
→ 對方很明確知道你是要求他／她看這張照片，可以把 You 省略，寫成 Look at the picture.

　　但想要表達特別的情緒時，例如暗示對方你快要生氣了，或是希望對方一定要按照你所說的去做，也可以把 You 留在句子中，如果再加上逗號，語氣又更為強烈，例如：

Get out of here !（滾出去！）
→ 單純要求對方離開。

You get out of here!（你滾出去！）
→ 強調是「你」離開。

You, get out of here.（就是你！給我滾出去！）
→ 加上逗號，語氣停頓，強烈的命令「你」離開。

　　當然，也不是所有的祈使句的主詞都是 You。在聽者不一定知道自己就是你講話的對象時，也可以使用主詞，舉例來說：

Maggie , stay here; John , go there.（*Maggie* 留在這裡；*John* 去那裡。）
→ Maggie 和 John 都是人名。

Everyone , sit down.（大家都坐下。）
→ everyone 是代名詞，表示「每個人」。

這種代名詞為主詞的祈使句，也可以把人物放在句子的尾端：

Sit down, everyone.
→ 人物放在句尾，前面記得加上逗號。

如果是使用人名的話，不論位置在哪裡，名字的前面都要加上逗號，例如：

Open the door, Jimmy.（*Jimmy*，把窗戶打開。）
= *Jimmy, open the window.*

在使用代名詞做為祈使句的主詞時，很多人會因為代名詞是第三人稱的關係，而將動詞做變化加上 s 或是 es，但對於祈使句而言，這是錯誤的用法，不管是第幾人稱或是單複數，動詞都要用原形動詞。

Everyone stands up.（X）
→ stand 要用動詞原形。

Everyone, stand up.（O）
（大家站起來。）

・換你試試看，判斷是不是祈使句！

1. Shut the door.
2. Don't do that.
3. Open the box, Daniel.
4. Lisa sleeps in the bed.
5. Somebody answer the door.
6. You don't want to go to the movies.

7. Why do you stand on the table?

8. You go to your room.

9. Tracy stand up.

10.Do you want to grab a bite?

・你判斷對了嗎？

1. Shut the door.

　　→ 原形動詞開頭，是肯定祈使句。

2. Don't do that.

　　→ Don't + 原形動詞開頭，是否定祈使句。

3. Open the box, Daniel.

　　→ 肯定祈使句；人名前面要加逗號。

4. Lisa sleeps in the bed.

　　→ 由動詞加 s 可以判斷，本句為一般陳述句，並非祈使句。

5. Somebody answer the door.

　　→ answer 為原形動詞，是祈使句；若將 somebody 放在句尾，前面要加逗號。

6. You don't want to go to the movies.

　　→ 這個句子只是一般的否定句，並非祈使句。

7. Why do you stand on the table?

　　→ 本句是疑問句，並非祈使句。

8. You go to your room.

　　→ 本句含有命令的意味，是祈使句。

9. Tracy stand up.

　　→ 本句的動詞原形，可以判斷為祈使句，但是人名不管在句首或是句尾，都要加上逗號，所以應該要寫成 Tracy, stand up.。

10.Do you want to grab a bite?

　　→ 這個句子也只是一般的問句，並非祈使句。

　　除了看看句子是不是有命令要求的語氣外，也可以藉由動詞的位置和有沒有作動詞變化來判斷句子是否為祈使句，如果在動詞前面有出現人稱、人名或是代名詞，我們可以把這三種詞類放在句尾或是句首，如果語意都是通順的，那麼可以肯定一定是祈使句。以上面練習題的第 4、5、6 題為例：

4 *.Lisa sleeps in the bed.*

→ 把 Lisa 放到句尾：Sleeps in the bed Lisa. 語意不通順，不是祈使句。

5 *Somebody answer the door.*

→ 把 somebody 放到句尾：Answer the door, somebody. 語意通順，為祈使句。

6 *You don't want to go to the movies.*

→ 把 you 放到句尾：Don't want to go to the movies you. 語意不通順，不是祈使句。

‖ 祈使句的附加問句 ‖

祈使句用來表達請求或命令，為了確定對方有聽到你所說的，可以在祈使句後面加上附加問句，這裡的附加問句不是當做真正的問句使用，而是具有確認的語感。祈使句的附加問句可以區分為幾種類型：

祈使句的附加問句	
(1) 表示建議	shall we / all right / Ok?
(2) 表示請求	will / can / would / could you?
(3) 表示邀請	will / won't you?
(4) 表示生氣或是不耐煩	will / won't / can you?
(5) 希望能對方配合你	will you?

(1) 表示建議：

Let's go for a walk, shall we / all right / OK?（要不要一起去散步？）

(2) 表示請求：

Be an honest girl, would you?（當個誠實的女孩，好嗎？）

(3) 表示邀請：

Have a cup of tea, won't you?（喝杯咖啡，好嗎？）

(4) 表示生氣或不耐煩：

Don't make noise, can you?（可以不要製造噪音嗎？）

(5) 希望對方能配合你：

Do me a favor, will you?（你會幫我吧？）

・換你試試看，填入適當的附加問句！

1. Let's go swimming in the river, _____?
2. Come over for lunch, _____?
3. Wake me up at 6:00, _____?
4. Don't take away the book, _____?
5. Stop shouting, _____?

・你寫對了嗎？

1. Let's go swimming in the river, shall we / all right / OK?
2. Come over for lunch, will / won't you?
3. Wake me up at 6:00, will / can / would / could you?
4. Don't take away the book, will you?
   → 以 Don't 開頭的祈使句，後面的附加問句多用 will you。
5. Stop shouting, will / won't / can you?

▌動詞以外的祈使句

　　我們對於原形動詞構成的祈使句並不陌生，但也有以其它詞性組合而成的祈使句，例如：

動詞以外的祈使句	
名詞	Danger!（危險！）/ Patience!（有點耐心！）
形容詞	Careful!（小心點！）/ Quiet!（安靜！）/ Louder!（大聲點！）
副詞	Quickly!（快點！）/ Forward!（前進！）
名詞＋副詞	Hands up!（手舉起來！）/ Hats off!（脫帽致敬！）
代名詞＋副詞	All aboard!（請上船／上船／登機！）
介係詞片語	At ease!（稍息！）

‖ 感嘆句 ‖

「感嘆」語氣的使用，可以分為感嘆句和感嘆詞。

‖ 什麼是感嘆句 ‖

感嘆句可以用來表達驚訝、喜悅或傷悲的強烈情感，這樣的句型多半以驚嘆號作為結尾，例如：

What a beautiful dress!（多漂亮的洋裝呀！）
→ 驚嘆號代表強烈的語氣。

How sweet!（多貼心啊！）

You look so great!（你看起來很不錯！）

He is such a nice person!（他真是一個好人！）

從上述的句子，我們可以發現，除了句尾的標點符號是驚嘆號外，感嘆句的句型大多是以 what 或是 how 作為句子的開頭。這兩種用法在感嘆句中沒有原本作為疑問詞的意思，而僅僅表達「多麼…啊！」；而 so 和 such 也可以用來加強說話的語氣，但並非所有含有 so 或 such 的句子都是感嘆句，還是要依照句子的內容做判斷。

・換你試試看，這是感嘆句嗎？

1. How old are you?
2. What a nice watch!
3. How amazing!
4. He is so boring!
5. The tea is so hot that I can't drink it.
6. It is such an interesting book!
7. What are you doing?
8. Such were his words.
9. So! Why you didn't tell me?
10. So do I.

· 你判斷出來了嗎？

1. How old are you?

   → （X）how 為疑問詞，本句不是感嘆句。

2. What a nice watch! → （O）

3. How amazing! → （O）

4. He is so boring! → （O）

5. The tea is so hot that I can't drink it.

   → （X）so that 表示「因為⋯以至於⋯」，本句不是感嘆句。

6. It is such an interesting book! → （O）

7. What are you doing?

   → （X）what 是疑問詞，本句不是感嘆句。

8. Such were his words.

   → （X）such 是代名詞，在這句中表示「他所說的話」。

9. So! Why you didn't tell me? → （O）

10. So do I.

   → （X）這句中的 so 是副詞，表示「⋯也如此」，後面要用倒裝的句型。

▌什麼是感嘆詞

　　除了一個完整的句子，在日常生活中，我們也可以用簡短的字來表示強烈的情感，這些語詞稱為感嘆詞，和句子中其他語詞於文法結構上沒有關係，只在意思上有加強情感表達的作用，因此，感嘆詞即使被省略，句子的意思也不受影響，例如：

Oh! The coffee smells good!（噢！咖啡聞起來真香！）
→ Oh 是獨立於句子之外，即使省略也不會影響理解句子的涵義。

Alas! I can't find me cell phone.（哎呀！我找不到我的手機！）

感嘆詞的位置通常放在句子的前面，有時，也會出現在句子的中間：

<u>*Wow!*</u> *Your cat is cute!*（哇！你的貓咪好可愛！）
→ 感嘆詞在句子的前面。

The girl sits next to you, oh, is beautiful!
（坐在你旁邊的女孩，噢，真是太美了！）
→ 感嘆詞在句子的中間。

一般而言，和感嘆詞一起使用的標點符號為驚嘆號，但有時也會因想要表達的意思不同，而使用問號或逗號。若感嘆詞和句子相連，或是後面銜接人名、代名詞、Yes 和 No 時，也可以不加標點符號，但這是比較少見的用法，例如：

Hi, nice to meet you.（嗨，很高興見到你。）
→ 用逗號，情緒不如驚嘆號強烈。

Oh my god!（我的天哪！）
→ 和句子相連的感嘆詞，標點符號可以省略。

‖ 常用的感嘆詞 ‖

感嘆詞非常多，同一個感嘆詞也可以表達不同的情緒：

常用的感嘆詞	
Oh	用來表示驚訝、興奮或滿意
Ha	用來表示驚訝、歡樂或懷疑
Aha	用來表示滿足、愉快、嘲笑或得意
Hey	用來表示驚訝或喜悅，多半希望引起對方注意
Alas	表示悲痛、焦急、憐憫或遺憾
Ouch	疼痛時發出的聲音
Eh	表示疑問或懷疑，有時也用於徵求對方同意時
Gosh	表示驚奇，有「唉呀、糟了」的涵義
Tush	表示不贊成或輕蔑的態度
Wow	表示驚訝、愉快或痛苦

除了擬聲的感嘆詞，名詞、動詞或形容詞也可以用來作為感嘆詞，例如：

名詞作為感嘆詞使用			
Nonsense	胡說	Shit	胡扯（非禮貌）
Thief	小偷	Congratulation	恭喜
Shame	真丟臉	Danger	危險
動詞作為感嘆詞使用			
Help	救命	Hush	安靜
Stop	站住	Welcome	歡迎光臨
Listen	仔細聽	Look	注意
形容詞作為感嘆詞使用			
Quiet	安靜	Excellent	太優秀了
Great	太好了	Ridiculous	真荒謬
Wonderful	太棒了	Strange	奇怪了

另外，我們比較常見的 well，是副詞作為感嘆詞使用，可以表示安心、讓步、疑問或是猶豫的語氣：

Well, I am not sure.（嗯，我不是很確定。）
→ well 表示猶豫的語氣。

Well, maybe it's true.（好吧！也許這是真的。）
→ well 表示讓步的感覺。

・換你試試看，什麼感嘆詞比較適合呢？

1. Alas / Great / Eh! What a pity!
2. Ridiculous / Ha / Ouch, I won the lottery.
3. Ha / Help / Hey, are you OK?
4. Ouch / Excellent / Shame, that hurts.
5. Tush / Wow / Shit! You chicken!
6. Stop / Listen / Help, how can you do this to me?
7. Danger / Hush / Welcome! my dear friend!
8. Strange / Look / Hush, where did I put my wallet?

・你選對了嗎？

1. <u>Alas</u>! What a pity!

2. <u>Ha</u>, I won the lottery.

3. <u>Hey</u>, are you OK?

4. <u>Ouch</u>, that hurts.

5. <u>Tush</u>! You chicken!

6. <u>Stop</u>, how can you do this to me?

7. <u>Welcome</u>, my dear friend!

8. <u>Strange</u>, where did I put my wallet?

▌倒裝句

什麼是倒裝句

在英文的語法中，當我們講述一個句子時，會先講主角（主詞），再講發生什麼事（動詞），然後才補充說明發生的地點或是時間，例如：

I go to school at 7 o'clock.（我七點上學。）

→ I 是主詞，go 是動作，school 和 7 o'clock 是表示目的地和方向。

I am a teacher.（我是一位老師。）

→ I 是主詞，teacher 是補充說明 I 的身分，am 是 be 動詞，表示狀態。

如果我們把句子的排列順序作變動，將動詞放到主詞的前面，就稱為倒裝句。

因此在寫倒裝句時，最重要的要先將動詞找出來：

I am a teacher.

→ 動詞是 am，將 am 放到主詞 I 的前面。

Am I a teacher?

→ 這就是一個簡單的倒裝句型。

再來看看另一個句子：

I go to school at 7 o'clock.
→ 動詞是 go。

但是當我們把 go 放到主詞 I 的前面時，語意就會變得很奇怪，所以我們要請助動詞（do / does）來幫助動詞變成倒裝的句型：

Do I go to school at 7 o'clock?
→ I 的助動詞是 do，放在句子的開頭。

不論在上述哪一個例句中，問自己是不是一位老師或是不是七點上學在邏輯上都沒有道理，所以我們要把 I 改成 you（你），才會是語意通順的問句。

從這兩個例子可以發現，問句其實就是最簡單的倒裝句，當句子裡有 Be 動詞時，將 be 動詞放到句首；當句子裡有動作時，請助動詞來幫忙，將助動詞放在句首，就會形成問句。

有了問句的概念，你可以了解，在句子中，若主詞的位置在動詞的後面，就可以稱為倒裝句。

▌倒裝句的使用時機

為什麼要使用倒裝句呢？就像上面的問句一樣，倒裝句具有轉換句子功能或強調語氣的作用。除了寫成問句形式的倒裝句，還有哪些時候會用到倒裝句呢?以下幾種情形，我們習慣使用倒裝句。

(1) 可以表示假設語氣

假設語氣的基本句型是＜If + 主詞 + 動詞過去式，(I would) + 動詞原形＞。變成倒裝句時，只要將 if 省略，將動詞放在主詞前面即可，例如：

If I were you, I would make some cakes.（如果我是你，我會做一些蛋糕。）
→ 假設語氣的句型。

Were I you, I would make some cakes.
→ 省略 if 的倒裝句型。

再看一個例子：

If I were you, I would tell the truth.（如果我是你的話，我會說實話。）
→ 假設語氣的句型。

Were I you, I would tell the truth.
→ 省略 if 的倒裝句型。

(2) 可以用來引用格言

中文有一句話叫「俗話說得好」，英文寫成＜Well runs / goes a saying, ＋格言＞。

Well runs a saying, "No pain, no gain."
（俗話說得好，「一分耕耘，一分收穫。」
→ A saying 是主詞，go 是動詞，well 是修飾動詞的副詞。

Well goes a saying, "Man proposes, God disposes."
（俗話說得好，「謀事在人，成事在天。」）

(3) 主詞太長的句子用倒裝句來寫

有時主詞太長時，我們可以先寫主詞補語再寫主詞，例如：

To stay healthy is important.（保持健康很重要。）
→ To stay healthy 是這個句子的主詞，因為太長，我們可以將其放到句尾。

Important is that to stay healthy.
→ 先點出某件事很重要的概念。

(4) 感嘆句也可以使用倒裝句型

感嘆句的倒裝形式可以分為肯定和否定兩種句型：

Am I thirsty!（我好渴！）
→ 這句原形為：I am thirsty.在美式英語中，這樣的說法很常見。

Haven't you grown!（你長大好多呀！）
→ 這句原形為：You have grown a lot.這個句子是否定疑問句倒裝後當作感嘆句使用。

二、好學好用的句型

好學的祈使句句型

> 1. 原形動詞 + …
>   Don't + 原形動詞 + …
>   Never + 原形動詞 + …

將主詞省略，用原形動詞開頭的句子，就是祈使句：

~~You~~ have a piece of cake.（請用蛋糕。）
→ 把 You 省略，動詞 have 放到句首。
→ Have a piece of cake.

有時候，單單動詞也可以構成祈使句，例如：

Relax!（放輕鬆！）

將 don't 置於句首就是否定的祈使句，表示強烈禁止，例如：

Don't watch TV now!（現在別看電視了！）

在這個句型中，要小心把表示助動詞的 Don't 和作為動詞的 do 混淆：

Don't do it!（不要這樣做！）
→ 助動詞 don't 用來作為 do 的否定。

否定的祈使句，也可以用＜Never + 原形動詞 + …＞。Never 表示「絕不…」，在語氣上不像 don't 具有禁止的涵義，但也表現出強烈堅決的態度，比較看看這兩種不同的用法：

Never give up!（絕不放棄！）
→ never 強調不要使「give up」這件事發生。

01 CHAPTER 02 CHAPTER 03 CHAPTER 04 CHAPTER 05 CHAPTER 06 CHAPTER 07 CHAPTER 08 CHAPTER 09 CHAPTER 10 CHAPTER

Don't give up!（不可以放棄！）

→ Don't 是要求不可以使「give up」這件事發生

否定的祈使句，還常常和被動語態一起使用，＜Don't ＋ be 動詞 / get ＋ 過去分詞＞是表示被動式的句型。

Don't be fooled by the salesman.（不要被店員騙了。）

→ be ＋ 過去分詞表示「被⋯」。

Don't be led your nose by others.（不要被別人牽著鼻子走。）

・我們可以這樣用

我們想要專心做某樣事情時，周圍的人一直大聲講話，我們可以說：

Be quiet!（安靜點！）

如果大家還是很吵，我們可以加重語氣說：

Shut up!（閉嘴！）

這樣的情況，也可以使用否定句的方式：

Don't talk!（不要說話！）

或是帶有一點警告意味：

Never talk when I am studying!（在我唸書時，絕對不要說話。）

・換你試試看，遇到這種情形怎麼說？

1. 同事很緊張，因為她馬上就要去見總經理。
2. 下屬看到你，馬上站起來。
3. 房間太悶了，需要透風。
4. 和老朋友相約下次再聚。
5. 小朋友說出不雅的話。

6. 警告別人絕對不能再這樣做。

・你想到了嗎？

1. 同事很緊張，因為她馬上就要去見總經理。
   Take it easy. / Relax. / Calm down.
2. 下屬看到你，馬上站起來。
   Sit down. / Have a seat. / Take the seat.
3. 房間太悶了，需要透風。
   Open the window. / Let the window open.
4. 和老朋友相約下次再聚。
   Remember to call me.
5. 小朋友說出不雅的話。
   Don't say that! / Don't talk like that!
6. 警告別人絕對不能再這樣做。
   Never do that again! / Don't do it again.

　　是不是很簡單呢？因為祈使句僅需要原形動詞就是完整的結構，因此同樣的意思也會有很多不同的表達方式。

2. Always + 原形動詞 + …＝千萬要 …

　　在原形動詞前加上 always 可以加強語氣，表示「千萬要…」，例如：

Always remember to be a nice person.（一定要記得當個善良的人。）
→ always 放在動詞前面加強語氣，後面連接原形動詞 remember。

Always allow your eyes to rest after reading.（閱讀後千萬要讓眼睛休息。）

・我們可以這樣說

　　這個句型帶有一點提醒的意味，可以用在教導人做某事上，例如，當你要分享你的獨家甜點食譜時，你可以強調：

Always use the whole milk while you are making the cup cakes.
（當你在做杯子蛋糕時，一定要記得使用全脂牛奶。）

・換你試試看，試著翻譯看看！

1. 千萬要檢查帳單。

2. 出門前千萬要檢查瓦斯。

3. 千萬要記得吃足夠的蔬菜。

・你完成了嗎？

1. Always make a careful check of bills.

2. Always check the oven before you leave.

3. Always remember to eat enough vegetables.

---

3. Please + 原形動詞 + …＝請 …

　 Please don't + 原形動詞 + …＝請不要 …

祈使句不只具有要求、命令的意味，有時也可以用來表示請求；為了使語氣更加客氣，我們可以在祈使句的句首或是句尾加上 please，例如：

Please stand up.（請起立。）

→ Please 放在原形動詞前。

Stand up, please.

→ please 放在句尾時，前面要加上逗號。

和肯定祈使句一樣，否定的祈使句若想要表達客氣的請求時，也可以在句首或句尾加上 please，只是，在句尾的 please 前要加上逗號：

Please don't drink on the MRT.

= Don't drink on the MRT, please.

（請不要在捷運上喝飲料。）

・我們可以這樣用

有朋友在我們正在洗碗時打電話來，我們可以客氣的請對方過五分鐘再打來：

Please call me five minutes later.（請五分鐘後再打給我。）

‧換你試試看，把句子改寫成客氣的句子！

1. Open the door.
2. Pass him the handout.
3. Read the story to me.

‧是不是很簡單呢？

只要在句子的前面或後面加上 please 就可以了！

1. Please open the door. / Open the door, please.
2. Please pass him the handout. / Pass him the handout, please.
3. Please read the story to me. / Read the story to me, please.

---

4. Do + 原形動詞 + …

Do 開頭的祈使句，有強調原形動詞的作用，因此有時候也會被應用到抱怨或是道歉的句子中，試比較下列各句：

Do pay attention to your teacher.
（千萬要認真聽老師上課！。）
→ Do 用來強調動作 pay attention。

Do try to make fewer mistakes in spelling, students.
（同學們，拼字時，試著少犯錯誤好嗎？）
→ do 用來強調動詞 make fewer mistake，帶有抱怨的情緒。通常這種語氣很容易和形容詞的比較級一起使用。

Do forgive my child. He doesn't mean it.
（請原諒我的小孩，他不是有意的。）
→ Do 強調 forgive 的動作，一起使用可以表示十分抱歉的語氣。

除了強調動作，Do 也是比 please 更為禮貌的用法，例如：

Do have a seat.（請坐下。）
→ Do 表示非常客氣的要求。

這樣的句型，在英式英文中較為常用。

· 我們可以這樣說

邀請朋友來家裡吃飯，我們可以說：

Do come! We will have lots of fun.（你一定要來！會很好玩的！）

· 換你試試看，這樣的句子對不對？

1. Do remember to charge your cell phone.
2. Does listen to the consultant.
3. Do help me prepare for the party.
4. Do do me a fever.

· 你答對了嗎？

1. Do remember to charge your cell phone. → （O）
2. Does listen to the consultant.

   → （X），要把 does 改成 do。

3. Do help me prepare for the party. → （O）
4. Do do me a favor.

   → 這句在文法結構上是正確的，但是為了避免重複出現相同的字，可以把 do me a favor 代換成 help me 或是 give me a hand。

---

5. May you + 原形動詞 + … !

這是一個祈求、祝福的句型，可以用來表示希望擁有對方好運等，通常這種句型會以驚嘆號結尾：

May you have a nice weekend!（祝你有美好的周末！）
May you have a wonderful day!（祝你有美好的一天！）
May you get well soon!（希望你早日康復！）

· 我們可以這樣說

朋友要去面試新的工作，為了表示祝福，我們可以說：

May you get this job!（希望你得到這個工作！）

・換你試試看，這種情形怎麼辦？

　1. 另一半買了樂透。

　2. 朋友生病感冒了。

　3. 同事要去度假。

・你想到了嗎？

　1. 另一半買了樂透，你可以說：

　　May you win the lottery!

　2. 朋友生病感冒了，你可以說：

　　May you get well / better soon.

　3. 同事要去渡假，你可以說：

　　May you have a wonderful vacation!

---

6. be 動詞 + 形容詞

　Don't + be 動詞 + 形容詞

　例如：

　Be quiet.（安靜。）

　→ be 加上形容詞 quiet。

　Be kind to your little brother.（對你弟弟好一點。）

　→ 接受形容詞的對象，中間要用 to 連接。

　也可以在 be 動詞後面加上名詞，讓句子的意思更完整：

　Be a good boy.（當個好男孩。）

　→ 形容詞 good 放在名詞 boy 前面。

　只要在＜be 動詞 + 形容詞＞前面加上 Don't，就構成否定句。be 動詞通常不會和助動詞 do 一起使用在句子中，但祈使句是例外。

　Don't be rude.（不可以無禮。）

01 CHAPTER
02 CHAPTER
03 CHAPTER
04 CHAPTER
05 CHAPTER
06 CHAPTER
07 CHAPTER
08 CHAPTER
09 CHAPTER
10 CHAPTER

如果想要強調 rude 的程度，可以在前面加上 so，例如：

Don't be <u>so</u> rude.
→ 用 so 強調 rude 的程度。

· 我們可以這樣說

當另一半在管教小孩的時候，越來越失去耐心，我們可以提醒對方：

Hey! calm down. Be patient!（嘿！冷靜一點，要有耐心！）

· 換你試試看，利用單字照樣造句！

1. good teacher
2. happy
3. angry
4. rude person
5. nice to each other

· 你寫對了嗎？

1. good teacher
   <u>Be a good teacher.</u>
2. happy
   <u>Be happy!</u>
3. angry
   <u>Don't be angry.</u>
4. rude person
   <u>Don't be a rude person.</u>
5. nice to each other
   <u>Be nice to each other.</u>

---

7. Let's + 動詞原形
   Let's + not + 動詞原形（美式用法）
   Don't let's + 動詞原形（英式用法）

這個句型具有邀請的意味，多用於表示提議或是勸誘，例如：

Let's go mountain climbing.（我們去爬山吧！）

＜Let's＋動詞原形＞的句型也可以用＜Shall we＋動詞原形…?＞或是＜Why don't we＋動詞原形…?＞代換，因此這句也可以寫成：

Shall we go mountain climbing?
= Why don't we go mountain climbing?
→ 當用 shall we 或是 why don't we 作為句子的開頭，標點符號要改成問號。

如果變成否定，只要在 Let's 後面加上 not，或是在 let's 前加上 don't：

Let's not go mountain climbing.
= Don't let's go mountain climbing.
（讓我們別去爬山吧！）

・我們可以這樣用

小朋友不喜歡洗澡的時候，為了引起他們的興趣，我們可以說：

Let's take bubble bath!（我們來洗泡泡澡吧！）

在洗澡時，小朋友一直把水潑的到處都是，只好向另一半求救：

Don't let him / her do this!（不要讓他／她這樣做！）

・換你試試看，用 let 改寫句子！

1. Shall we dance?
2. Why don't we go to the movies?
3. Please don't be upset.

・你寫好了嗎？

1. Shall we dance?
   Let's dance.

2. Why don't we go to the movies?

Let's go to the movies.

3. Please don't be upset.

Let's not be upset.

‖ 好學的祈使句諺語 ‖

除了祈使句的句型，也有很多和祈使句有關的諺語，我們可以把這些諺語牢牢記熟，不僅在文章裡看到時，可以馬上了解意思，也可以應用在生活口語中，讓別人覺得你很有學問唷！

1. Do at Rome as the Romans to.　入境隨俗。
2. Out of sights, out of mind.　眼不見為淨。
3. Wine in, truth out.　酒後吐真言。
4. Think today and speak tomorrow.　今日思明日語。
5. Practice what you preach.　以身作則。
6. Soon got, soon spent.　來得快，去得快。
7. Spare the rod, spoil the child.　不打不成器。
8. Strike the iron while it is hot.　打鐵趁熱。
9. Penny wise, pound foolish.　因小失大。
10. Look before you leap.　三思而後行。
11. Lay it up for a rainy day.　未雨綢繆。
12. Let sleeping dog lie.　別自找麻煩。
13. Live and let live.　寬以待人如代己。
14. Like father, like son.　虎父無犬子。

‖ 好學的祈使句小短句 ‖

1. Get off my back.　別煩我。

A: Can you read me a story?（你可以說故事給我聽嗎？）

B: Get off my back. I'm cleaning the kitchen.（別煩我，我正在整理廚房。）

2. Leave me alone! 讓我一個人靜一靜！

A: Do you want to talk about it?（你想要談一談嗎？）

B: Leave me alone! I don't want to talk to anyone.
（讓我一個人靜一靜，我不想和任何人說話。）

3. Give me a break. 饒了我吧！

A: Give me a break. I don't believe Jack cheated on his wife.
（饒了我吧。我不相信 Jack 對他的太太不忠。）

B: Believe it or not.（信不信隨你。）

4. Go for it! 勇敢去試！

A: Go for it! I know you can make it!
（勇敢去試吧.我知道你可以做到的！）

B: Thank you. I will do my best.（謝謝你，我會盡力去做。）

5. Give me a hand. 幫我一下。

A: Could you give me a hand?（你可以幫我一下嗎？）

B: Sure, what can I do for you?（當然可以，你希望我做些什麼？）

6. Let me get this straight. 讓我搞清楚。

A: Do you know? Jason fell in love with Amanda!
（你知道嗎？Jason 愛上 Amanda 了！）

B: What? Let me get this straight, you mean Jason want to break up with his wife?
（什麼？讓我搞清楚，你是說 Jason 想要和他太太分手？）

7. Let's chew the fat. 讓我們來聊天吧！

A: Let's chew the fat.（來聊天吧！）

B: Sorry, but I'm busy right now.（抱歉，我現在真的很忙。）

01 CHAPTER
02 CHAPTER
03 CHAPTER
04 CHAPTER
05 CHAPTER
06 CHAPTER
07 CHAPTER
08 CHAPTER
09 CHAPTER
10 CHAPTER

---

8. Put it in my hands. 交給我吧！

A: I don't know how to deal with this problem.
（我不知道怎麼處理這個問題。）
B: Put it in my hands.（交給我吧！）

---

9. Stop picking on me. 別再挑我毛病了。

A: Why you wear this yellow dress? It makes you fat.
（為什麼你要穿這件黃色洋裝?讓你看起來很胖！）
B: Stop picking on me. This is me.（別再挑我毛病了，這就是我呀！）

---

10. Get to the point. 講重點！

A: Come on. Get to the point!（拜託，講重點！）
B: Okay.（好啦。）

‖ 好學的感嘆句句型 ‖

---

8. What a + 形容詞 + 名詞！= 多麼…呀！

例如：

What a spread!（多麼豐富的饗宴呀！）

What an honest child!（多麼誠實的孩子呀！）
→ a 或 an 要看後面的形容詞而定，若形容詞是母音發音開頭，則用 an。

What cute children!（多可愛的小孩們呀！）
→ 是主詞的單複數決定要不要加 a 或是 an。
也可以在名詞後面，加上主詞和動詞，例如：

What a good teacher he is!（他真是個好老師！）
→ 在名詞 teacher 後面加上主詞 he 和動詞 is。

‧我們可以這樣說

這種句型可以作為稱讚使用，例如，另一半難得下廚，煮了你最喜歡的牛肉麵，不管菜餚是否美味，為了體恤對方，你可以說：

What delicious beef noodles!（牛肉麵好好吃！）

‧換你試試看，改寫成 What 開頭的感嘆句吧！

1. She is a snobbish woman.
2. He opened the window rudely.
3. They are wearing strange hats.
4. I am stupid to believe her.
5. The ghost story is terrible.

‧你成功了嗎？

1. She is a snobbish woman.
   What a snobbish woman (she is). / What a snob!
2. He opened the window rudely.
   What a rude man (he is).
3. They are wearing strange hats.
   What strange hats they are wearing!
   → 主詞 they 是複數，因為不可能一起戴一頂帽子，所以 hat 也要改為複數。
4. I am stupid to believe her.
   What a fool I am to believe her.
   → 在感嘆的部分後面加入不定詞，表示原因，以這個句子為例，「我」是個 fool 才會「相信」她。
5. The ghost story is terrible.
   What a terrible ghost story!

---

9. How + 形容詞！= 多麼…呀！

例如：

How surprise!（多麼驚訝啊！）
How hot!（多麼熱呀！）

這個句型和 What 開頭的感嘆句一樣，可以在形容詞後面加入主詞和動詞，例如：

How proud Dad and Mom are of you!（爸爸媽媽多以你為榮呀！）
→ 形容詞 proud 後面加入主詞 Dad and Mom 和動詞 are。

甚至，也可以將形容詞省略，這種句型中的 how 就具有表示程度的意味：

How I love you!（我多麼愛你呀！）

如果是要感嘆某種動作時，我們要將形容詞換成修飾動詞的副詞，例如：

How well you play the piano!（你鋼琴彈得多好呀！）
→ 副詞 well 用來修飾動作 play。

How 作為感嘆句的開頭，後面也可以接續完整的句子，表示「多麼…呀」，例如：

How I wish I could live in Japan.（我多麼希望我可以住在日本呀！）
→ How 後面接完整的句子

How you have changed these years!（你這些年變得好多！）

·我們可以這樣說

這個句型除了可以表示驚訝、驚喜，也可以用來感嘆某件事的發生，例如，見到好久不見的親戚小孩，你可以說：

How the boy has grown!（這個小男孩長得多快呀！）

· 換你試試看，改寫成 How 開頭的感嘆句吧！

1. She is so sweet.
2. My mom is considerate to bring me lunch.
3. Wen can cook many dishes and all of them are delicious.
4. To marry you is so lucky!
5. The police officers are very brave.

· 是不是很簡單呢？

1. She is so sweet.

   How sweet (she is)!

2. My mom is considerate to bring me lunch.

   How considerate my mom is to bring me lunch!

3. Wen can cook many dishes and all of them are delicious.

   How well Wen cooks!

4. To marry you is so lucky!

   How lucky (I am) to marry you!

5. The police officers are very brave.

   How brave the police officers are!

---

10. such + a + 形容詞 + 名詞 = 真是個⋯
    so + 形容詞 = 太⋯

　　Such 的用法和 What 開頭的感嘆句有點類似，後面加上＜a + 形容詞 + 名詞＞；而 so 則和 How 開頭的感嘆句一樣，後面要加上形容詞，例如：

My mom is such a good teacher.（我的媽媽真是個好老師。）
→ such 主要強調名詞 a good teacher。

這句也可以改寫成：

What a good teacher my mom is.
→ What 也是強調名詞 a good teacher。

My sister is so beautiful.（我的妹妹很漂亮。）
→ so 強調形容詞 beautiful。

若用 How 改寫，會寫成：

How beautiful my sister is.
→ How 也用來強調形容詞。

· 我們可以這樣說

　　有時候和朋友聊天時，講到有趣好玩的事情，但又不想要像 How 或 What 句型一樣這麼誇張，我們可以用 so 或是 such 來代替，例如：

The movie is so interesting.（這部電影超有趣的！）
This is such a marvelous novel.（這本小說真是太棒了！）

· 換你試試看，要怎麼改寫呢？

1. How naughty my cats are!
2. What a smart man Albert is!
3. What a pity to miss the train.
4. How surprise to see you!
5. How happy to win the baseball game.

· 你完成了嗎？

只要記得 so 和 How 是一組、such 和 What 是一組，就很簡單了唷！

1. How naughty my cats are!
   My cats are so naughty!
2. What a smart man Albert is!
   Albert is such a smart man.
3. What a pity to miss the train.
   It's so bad to miss the train.
   → pity 是名詞，因此要改為 so 的句型時，要選擇符合 pity 的形容詞。
4. How surprise to see you!
   I am so surprised to see you!

4　How happy to win the baseball game.

I am so happy to win the baseball game!

---

11. Fancy + 動詞-ing! = 真沒想到…！

Fancy 具有想像、幻想的涵義，這個句型在口語中，可以用來表示「真沒想到…、難以想像…」，後面若是接動詞，動詞要轉換為動名詞的形式，例如：

Fancy standing in the sun at noon!（真沒想到要在正午時站在太陽底下！）

→ 動詞 stand 要加上 ing。

Fancy her saying so rudely!（真沒想到她說話這麼無禮！）

→ 動詞 say 轉換為動名詞，表示「所說的話」。

・我們可以這樣說

如果在餐廳碰到好久不見的同學，可以說：

Fancy meeting you in the restaurant!（真沒想到在這家餐廳碰到你！）

・換你試試看，這樣的情況怎麼說？

1. She sings beautifully.
2. He goes to the movies very often.
3. I have seven cats.
4. The children behave well yesterday.
5. The news surprised me.

・你說對了嗎？

1. She sings beautifully.

　→ Fancy her singing beautifully!

2. He goes to the movies very often.

　→ Fancy his going to the movies so often!

3. I have seven cats.

　→ Fancy your having seven cats!

4. The children behave well yesterday.

→ Fancy their behaving well yesterday!

5. The news surprised me.

→ Fancy hearing the news!

▌好學的感嘆句小短句

1. Adorable! 好可愛！

A: Here is a doll for you.（這個娃娃給你！）

B: Adorable! Thank you so much!（好可愛，太謝謝你了！）

2. Amazing! 不可思議！

A: Amazing! This is the greatest church I've ever seen.

（太不可思議了！這是我看過最偉大的教堂！）

B: It was built in 1300.（這是在 1300 年建造的。）

3. Awesome! 了不起！

A: The fire fighter saved the old woman from the fire.

（這位消防隊員從火場裡把這位老太太救了出來。）

B: Awesome!（太了不起了！）

4. Awful! 糟透了！

A: How are you recently?（你最近如何？）

B: Awful.（糟透了！）

5. Fantastic! 了不起！

A: Look! This is my new painting!（你看！這是我的新作品！）

B: Fantastic!（了不起！）

6. How time flies!　光陰似箭呀！

A: That is my son. He is thirteen years old. （那是我的兒子，他今年十三歲。）

B: How time flies. （時間過得真快！）

7. What a bummer!　真倒楣！

A: We planned to see the movie, but the ticket was sold out!
　（我們本來計畫要看電影的，但是電影票都賣光了。）

B: What a bummer! （真倒楣！）

8. What a pity!　太可惜了！

A: We lost the game. （我們比賽輸了。）

B: What a pity! （太可惜了。）

9. What a day!　真是…的一天呀！

A: We finally finished this job! （我們終於把工作完成了！）

B: What a day! Do you want to grab a bite?
　（真是辛苦的一天呀！要不要去吃些東西？）

A: I can't believe I picked up one thousand dollars. What a day!
　（我不敢相信我撿到一千元。多幸運的一天呀！）

B: You are a lucky guy. （你真是幸運的人！）

10. What a drag!　好無聊！

A: Do you want to visit Aunt Nancy with me?
　（你想要跟我一起去拜訪 Nancy 阿姨嗎？）

B: What a drag! I don't want to go. （好無聊唷！我不想去。）

01 CHAPTER
02 CHAPTER
03 CHAPTER
04 CHAPTER
05 CHAPTER
06 CHAPTER
07 CHAPTER
08 CHAPTER
09 CHAPTER
10 CHAPTER

▌好學的倒裝句型 ▏

> 1. 否定詞 + 助動詞 + 主詞 + 動詞 = 不…
>   否定詞 + 動詞 + 主詞

　　否定詞就是本身帶有否定意味的語詞，常見的否定詞在第六篇否定句中有詳細的介紹，當否定詞置於句首時，後面的句子要倒裝：

Never have I heard this song.（我從來沒聽過這首歌。）
→ 這句話的原形是：I have never heard this song. never 是否定詞，當 never 放在句首時，後面的助動詞要先寫。

Not only is the cat big in size, but it weights over 5 kilograms.
（這隻貓不僅體型很大，體重也超過五公斤。）
→ 這句話的原形是：The cat is not only big in size, but weights over 5 kilograms. 如果句子中沒有助動詞，則將動詞移到主詞前面。

Not one thing did he remember.（他沒有一件事是記得的。）
→ 這句的原形是：He did not remember one thing. 當句子中有 not 時，要一起將 not 和受詞一起移到句首。

・我們可以這樣說

　　這類的句型具有強烈的否定意味，目的在強調沒有發生過的事或是經驗。在日常生活中，如果我們遇到自己的男女朋友懷疑我們說謊，我們就可以強烈的表示反對：

Never have I lied to you.（我從來沒有對你說過謊。）

如果對方還是不相信，我們可以再進一步的說些甜言蜜語：

Not until I met you did I realize who the true love in my life is.
（直到遇見你，我才知道我生命中的真愛是誰。）

・換你試試看，寫出這些句子的否定句！

1. He has never felt so angry in his life.
2. We didn't leave any trash in the classroom.
3. The theory is not correct anymore.

・你完成了嗎？

1. Never has he felt so angry in his life.
2. No any trash did we leave in the classroom.
3. No longer is the theory correct.

---

2. only + 說明 only 的狀況 + 助動詞 + 主詞 + 動詞 = 只有⋯

例如：

Only by studying hard can you get good grades.
（你要得到好成績就只有用功念書。）
→ 這句原本為：You can get good grade only by studying hard. 句子中的 by studying hard 是用來說明 only 的狀況，在文法上稱為副詞子句或副詞片語，強調「只有這樣作，才可以⋯」。

Only on weekends can Dad take a rest at home.
（爸爸只有在周末才可以在家休息。）
→ 這句的原形是：Dad can take a rest at home only on weekends.

Only his students get good grades is the teacher happy.
→ 這句原形為：The teacher is happy only his students get good grades. 若是句子中的動詞是 be 動詞，則將 be 動詞放在主詞的前面。

・我們可以這樣說

這種句型因為有談條件的感覺，所以我們可以將這個句型運用在叮嚀提醒上。

例如，小朋友很喜歡看電視，但是不可以顧著看電視而不寫功課，我們可以這樣說：

Only finish your homework can you watch TV.

01 CHAPTER
02 CHAPTER
03 CHAPTER
04 CHAPTER
05 CHAPTER
06 CHAPTER
07 CHAPTER
08 CHAPTER
09 CHAPTER
10 CHAPTER

（只有寫完功課才可以看電視。）

1. Jimmy saved his money only when he was a child.
2. May goes to the supermarket only when she wants to eat candy.
3. Tracy studies only the exam is coming.

·你完成了嗎？
1. Only he was a child did Jimmy save his money.
2. Only when she wants to eat candy does May go to the supermarket.
3. Only the exam is coming does Tracy study.

---

3. So + 助動詞 + 主詞 = …也是
   neither + 助動詞 + 主詞 = …也不是

So 和 neither 分別表示「也」和「也不」。

You like apples, and I like apples, too.（你喜歡蘋果，我也喜歡蘋果。）
→ 原本的句子重複出現 like apples，可將第二句中的 like apples 用助動詞 do 代替。

You like apples, and I do, too.
→ 用 do 代替 like apple 的動作。

You like apples, and so do I.
→ 如果不用 too 表示，也可以用 so 代替。So 帶領的句子要倒裝，因此 do 要寫於 I 之前

否定用法的 neither 也要倒裝，只是 neither 本身具有否定意味，故不用再強調 not：

You don't like apples, and I don't like apples, either.
You don't like apples, and I don't, either.
You don't like apples, and neither do I.

（你不喜歡蘋果，我也不喜歡。）

我們可以這樣說

　　這樣的句型強調對另一個說話者的認同。和朋友聊天時，談到彼此間的興趣，如果對方說: *I love shopping so much!*（我超級喜歡購物！），如果你也很喜歡對方提出的活動，你就可以說：

So do I!（我也是！）

　　如果對方說的是否定的句子：I don't love shopping.（我不喜歡買東西。），而你剛好也不喜歡，你就可以附和地說：

Neither do I!（我也不喜歡！）

・換你試試看，改寫成倒裝句！

1. I don't like bananas. Tim doesn't like bananas, either.
2. Nancy love chocolate milk. I like chocolate, too.
3. Anna has a beautiful bag. Gina has a beautiful bag, too.

・你寫對了嗎？

1. I don't like bananas, and neither does Tim.
2. Nancy love chocolate milk, and so do I.
3. Anna has a beautiful bag, and so does Gina.

---

4. so + 形容詞／副詞 + 倒裝句（+that）+子句
   such + 倒裝句（+that）+子句　　＝ 如此…以至於

　　和上一個的 so 表達意思不同，這裡的 so 後面加形容詞，具有「太~」的意思，後面要和形容詞連用，例如：

Jack's book is <u>so great</u> that I love it very much.
（*Jack* 的書寫得太好了，因此我非常喜歡。）
→ so + 形容詞 great

若要改成倒裝句，把 so great 移到句首，後面要先寫動詞：

So great is Jack's book that I love it very much.

再看看另一個例子：

Such is her anger that she doesn't want to talk to me anymore.
（她是如此生氣，以至於她不想再跟我說話了。）
→ 這句原形為：Her <u>anger</u> is <u>such</u> that she doesn't want to talk to me anymore.
記得 such 後面銜接的為名詞。

・我們可以這樣說

這個句型強調因果關係，因為某件事發生以至於另一件事情也發生。我們可以用這種句型來強調自己心情和所發生的事之間的關係。例如，讀完一則很可怕的鬼故事，結果睡不著覺，要強調那則故事真的很可怕，可怕到害我睡不著覺，我們可以這樣說：

So horrible is the story that I can't fall asleep.
（那個故事太可怕了，以至於我睡不著覺。）

・換你試試看，練習將句子倒裝！

1. The little girl is so cute that every one can't help but kiss her.
2. His proposal is so great that the clients like it very much.
3. The teacher's anger is such that no one dares to speak.
4. The man's happiness is such that we don't want to tell him the truth.

・你答對了嗎？

1. So cute is the little girl that every one can't help but kiss her.
2. So great is his proposal that the clients like it very much.
3. Such is the teacher's anger that no one dares to speak.
4. Such is the man's happiness that we don't want to tell him the truth.

5. 地方副詞 + 動詞 + 主詞

例如：

Down fell the building.（這棟建築物倒了。）
→ 這句原形為：The building fell down. 若將 down 置於句首，後面的句子要先寫動詞才寫主詞。

特別要注意的是，這類的句型若主詞為代名詞時，不能倒裝，例如:

Here it is.（這裡有一枝鉛筆。）
→ 這句的原形是：Here is a pencil.句子中 pencil 是可以用 it 代替，使用代名詞時不可以倒裝。

表示時間的字，我們稱作時間副詞。為了加強語氣，有時也會將時間放在句首，此時，和時間副詞的方式一樣，將主詞和動詞的位置互換：

After the storm comes the calm.（否極泰來。）
→ 時間副詞放句首，後面句子倒裝。

・我們可以照樣說

這類的句型要強調的是地點或是時間。當我們要特別說明地點或時間時，可以運用這樣的句型，例如：

In Taipei lived Tom and his parents.
（*Tom* 和他的父母一起住在台北。）

In 2010 moved Tom and his parents to Taipei.
（*Tom* 和他的父母在 *2010* 年搬到台北。）

・換你試試看，改寫為倒裝句型！

1. A beautiful girl is sitting under the tree.
2. The cat lay on the bed.
3. Your key is here.

4. Nicole is coming.

5. The man is leaving.

·你完成了嗎？

1. Sitting under the tree is a beautiful girl.

2. On the bed lay a cat.

3. Here is your key.

   → Here 句子中的主詞若為代名詞，則不能倒裝，例如：Here it is.

4. Here comes Nicole.

5. There goes the man.

   → There 句子中的主詞若為代名詞，也不可以倒裝，例如：There he goes.

三、文法糾正篇

祈使句錯誤用法

> **1.＜Why don't we...?＞和＜Why don't you...?＞不一樣**

在使用＜Why don't we + 動詞原形…?＞時，要特別小心人稱的使用：如果將 we 改成 you 時，會產生完全不一樣的意思，試比較下面的句子：

Why don't we marry?（為什麼我們不結婚呢？）
→ why don't we 用於建議你和我之間來做某事。

Why don't you marry him?（為什麼你不嫁給他呢？）
→ why don't you 用於向對方提出建議。

·換你試試看，要怎麼翻譯呢？

1. 要不要一起去購物？

2. 你何不穿這件紅色的洋裝呢？

3. 要不要去游泳？

4. 你何不喝一些牛奶呢？

・你答對了嗎？

1. 要不要一起去購物？

   <u>Why don't we go shopping?</u>

2. 你何不穿這件紅色的洋裝呢？

   <u>Why don't you wear this red dress?</u>

3. 要不要去游泳？

   <u>Why don't we go swimming?</u>

4. 你何不喝一些牛奶呢？

   <u>Why don't you drink some milk?</u>

2. Let's 和 Let 不一樣

　　Let's 是 let us 的縮寫，表示包含說話者在內的一群人；而 Let 表示「讓⋯」，後面要接受詞，比較看看下面的句子：

Let's go to the party.（讓我們參加派對吧！）

→ Let's 表示說話的人和說話的對象都要去。

Let me go to the party.（讓我參加派對。）

→ Let me 表示只有說話的人要去，正在請求聽者的同意。

　　如果是否定句的話，只要加 Don't 放在 let 的前面，例如：

Don't let him wait too long.（不要讓他等太久。）

・換你試試看，這個句子正確嗎？

1. Let me sweep the floor.
2. Let's watching TV.
3. Don't let she open the door.
4. Don't let Jimmy drinks too much coffee.
5. Let Tracy do the presentation.

・你判斷對了嗎？

1. Let me sweep the floor. →（O）

2. Let's watching TV.

　　→（X）Let 後面的動詞要用原形動詞。這句正確的寫法為：Let's watch TV.

3. Don't let she open the door.

　　→（X）let 後面的人稱若是代名詞要改為受格。這句正確的寫法是：Don't let her open the door.

4. Don't let Jimmy drinks too much coffee.

　　→（X）let 後面的動詞要用原形動詞。這句正確的寫法為：Don't let Jimmy drink too much coffee.

5. Let Tracy do the presentation. →（O）

---

3. No 後面的動詞要加上 ing

　　No 加上動詞，可以用來表示強烈的禁止，但要記得動詞要改為現在分詞的形式：

　　No parking!（禁止停車！）
　　→ 動詞 park 接在 No 後面要加 ing。

　　No 後面加名詞，也表示強烈的禁止，這時候的名詞不需要特別的變化：

　　No way!（不行！）

・換你試試看，怎麼說出強烈禁止的句子呢？

1. spit
2. smoke
3. pets
4. camera
5. nap

・是不是很簡單呢？

1. spit

　　No spitting!

→ 動詞 spit 加 ing，因為動詞結尾的兩個字母是母音加子音，因此要重複子音加 ing。

2. smoke

<u>No smoking!</u>

→ 動詞 smoke 結尾的字母是 e，要去 e 加 ing。

3. pets

<u>No pets.</u>

→ pets 為名詞，前面直接加 No 即可。

4. camera

<u>No camera!</u>

5. nap

<u>No napping!</u>

---

4. 和 and / or 一起的特別用法

和祈使句一起使用的 and 和 or，具有談論條件的意味，and 和 or 表示相反的語氣，例如：

Study hard, <u>and you will</u> succeed one day.
（認真讀書，有一天一定會成功。）
→ 只要認真念書，一定會成功，and 承接前一句的語氣。

Study hard, <u>or you will</u> get bad grade.
（認真念書，否則你將會得到壞成績。）
→ or 表示「否則」，用來連接前後對立或是具有因果關係的狀況。

你發現了嗎？儘管 and 和 or 表示的語氣不同，它們所帶領的句子，都要用未來式。

・換你試試看，是 and 還是 or？

1. Don't do that again, _____ you will be in trouble.
2. Work hard, _____ you will be the general manager someday.
3. Put your coat on, _____ you will get sick.
4. Hurry up, _____ you can get on the train.

5. Hurry up, _____ you will miss the school bus.

· 你完成了嗎？

1. Don't do that again, <u>or</u> you will be in trouble.

2. Work hard, <u>and</u> you will be the general manager someday.

3. Put your coat on, <u>or</u> you will get sick.

4. Hurry up, <u>and</u> you can get on the train.

5. Hurry up, <u>or</u> you will miss the school bus.

---

5. 祈使句的 go，可以直接加原形動詞

在祈使句中，如果有兩個動作，中間要用 and 將兩個動作分開，例如：

Wait <u>and</u> see!（走著瞧！）
→ 兩個動作用 and 相連。

<u>Open</u> your student book <u>and</u> <u>turn</u> to page 11.（打開課本並翻到第十一頁。）
→ 兩個祈使句用 and 相連。

但是，若其中的動作有 go，則可以不用加 and，例如：

<u>Go and take</u> a shower.
→ *Go take a shower.*（去洗澡。）

· 換你試試看，可以怎麼說？

1. Go and fetch your sister.

2. Go and pick up the ball.

3. Go and grab a bite.

· 你說對了嗎？只要把 and 省略就好了！

1. Go fetch your sister.

2. Go pick up the ball.

3. Go grab a bite.

▌ 感嘆句的錯誤用法 ▏

> **1. What 和 How 開頭的感嘆句，主詞要在動詞前面**

　　在這樣的句型裡，我們很容易把 What 和 How 想成疑問詞，而把後面的動詞和主詞的位置顛倒，然而，應該要先將主詞置於動詞前才是正確的寫法：

What a strong man is he.（X）
→要把主詞 he 放在動詞 is 的前面。

What a strong man he is. →（O）
（他是一個多麼強壯的男人啊！）

How pale look you!（X）
→要把主詞 you 放在動詞 look 前。

How pale you look! →（O）
（你看起來好蒼白呀！）

・換你試試看，這樣寫對不對？

1. How generous is he to pay the bill.
2. What a lousy movie it is!
3. How gracefully the ballerina dances!
4. What a performance!
5. What a studious student is he!

・你找到錯誤了嗎？

1. How generous is he to pay the bill.（X）
　　→ 應改寫成 How generous he is to pay the bill.
2. What a lousy movie it is! →（O）
3. How gracefully the ballerina dances! →（O）
4. What a performance! →（O）
5. What a studious student is he!（X）
　　→應改寫成 What a studious student he is!

01 CHAPTER
02 CHAPTER
03 CHAPTER
04 CHAPTER
05 CHAPTER
06 CHAPTER
07 CHAPTER
08 CHAPTER
09 CHAPTER
10 CHAPTER

> **2. What 後面要有 a 或是名詞變為複數**
> **How 後面要緊連著形容詞或副詞**

What 開頭的感嘆句，如果名詞為單數，後面要有不定冠詞 a 或是 an；如果名詞為複數，則不寫不定冠詞，例如：

What polite girl! → （X）

這句有兩種改法，可以在 polite 前加上 a，或是在 girl 後面加上 s：

What a polite girl!（多麼有禮貌的女孩呀！）
→（O）女孩只有一個。

What polite girls!（這一群女孩多有禮貌呀！）
→（O）女孩有好多個。

How 開頭的感嘆句，後面要銜接形容詞或副詞，而不能將主詞和動詞置於形容詞或副詞之前，例如：

How the grapes are sweet! → （X）

How 後面應該先寫形容詞 sweet，才寫主詞 the grapes 和動詞 are：

How sweet the grapes are!（葡萄多甜啊！）→（O）

・換你試試看，找出下列句子的錯誤！

1. How your mom is graceful!
2. What nice person.
3. What a naughty boys!
4. How the music is beautiful!
5. What love puppets!
6. How hot is it!
7. What a exciting race!
8. How he performed well!

· 你找到錯誤了嗎？

1. How your mom is graceful!

    → 形容詞要放在 How 的後面，正確寫法為：How graceful your mom is!

2. What nice person.

    → person 是單數，要在 nice 前面加上 a，正確寫法為：What a nice person! 也可以把 person 改為複數 people：What nice people!

3. What a naughty boys!

    → 不能同時有 a 又用複數名詞，本句可以寫成：What a naughty boy! 或是 What naughty boys!

4. How the music is beautiful!

    → 形容詞要放在 How 的後面，正確寫法為：How beautiful the music is!

5. What love puppets!

    → puppets 前面要放形容詞，因此要將 love 改為 lovely。

6. How hot is it!

    → 本句的形容詞放在 How 後面正確，但後面的主詞和動詞順序卻顛倒了，應該要先寫主詞 it，在寫動詞 is。

7. What a exciting game!

    → 形容詞 exciting 是母音開頭的單字，前面的 a 要改成 an。

8. How he performed well!

    → 副詞要放在 How 的後面，正確寫法為：How well he performed!

‖ 倒裝句的錯誤用法

1. 倒裝的順序錯誤

　　當句子中有助動詞時，應將助動詞置於主詞前，而非動詞置於主詞前，例如：

I have never read this book before.（我之前從來沒有讀過這本書。）

→ 原本的句子中有否定詞 never，可以倒裝。

Never have read I this book before.（X）

→ 助動詞＋動詞＋主詞，是錯誤的倒裝句型。

Never read I have this book before.（X）

→ 動詞 + 主詞 + 助動詞，是錯誤的倒裝句型。

Never have I read this book before.（O）

→ 助動詞 + 主詞 + 動詞，才是正確的倒裝。

2. Only 或否定詞的倒裝，改寫時應加入助動詞

例如：

Kevin feels easy only at home.（只有在家時，*Kevin* 才覺得自在。）

→ 原本的句子。

Only at home feels Kevin easy.（X）

→ 錯誤的倒裝句型。這個句子中有 only，但沒有助動詞，變成倒裝時，要加入配合人稱的助動詞。

Only at home does Kevin feel easy.（O）

→ 記得助動詞後面的動詞要使用原形動詞。

再來看一個例子：

I rarely hear my sister sing this song.（我很少聽到我姐姐唱這首歌。）

→ 原本的句子。

Rarely hear I my sister sing this song.（X）

→ 句子中有否定詞 rarely，要在倒裝時加入適當的助動詞。

Rarely do I hear my sister sing this song.（O）

→ 加了助動詞後才是正確的倒裝句型。

3. 否定詞本身具有否定意味，改寫時要特別注意 not 的使用。

例如：

I don't like watching TV at all.

→ 原本的句型。

Not at all don't I like watching.（*X*）
→ 句子中有兩的 not，是錯誤的文法。

Not at all do I like watching TV.（*O*）
→ Not 移到句首形成倒裝句，後面的助動詞的 not 要刪掉。

再看一個例子：

I didn't realize what had happened until I read the newspaper.
（我不知道發生什麼事，直到我讀了報紙。）
→ 原本的句子。

你可以判斷哪一個句子是正確的嗎？
Not until did I read the newspaper did I realize what had happened.（　　）
Not until I read I the newspaper did I realize what had happened.（　　）

你答對了嗎？第一個句子才是正確的句型。同時，你有沒有發現，這兩個句子倒裝得地方不一樣？當句子中有兩個子句的時候，主要的子句才要倒裝：

Not until did read I the newspaper did I realize what had happened.
→「不知道發生什麼事」是主要陳述的內容，這個句型倒裝的地方錯誤。

Not until I read the newspaper did I realize what had happened.
→ 有兩個句子時，在主要子句進行倒裝。這樣是正確的寫法

4. 不是問句卻用了問號

在倒裝句中，雖然有助動詞置於主詞之前的情況，但仍為一般陳述句，而非問句。故標點符號應為句號而非問號，例如：

You can't go into my room without my permission.
（沒有我的允許，你不可以進我的房間。）
→ 原本的句子。

By no means can you go into my room without my permission?（*X*）
→ 以為助動詞在助詞前是問句而加了問號是錯誤的。

By no means can you go into my room without my permission.（O）
→ 倒裝句仍是一般的陳述句，用句號即可。

・換你試試看，加強語氣的綜合練習，判斷句子是不是正確！

1. Stop jerk me around.
2. What girl beautiful.
3. What amazing she is.
4. How well she plays the piano.
5. Opens the book and turns to page 10.
6. Don't be silly.
7. Let she do what she wants.
8. Don't let me laugh.
9. Let's not talk to him.
10. How exciting!
11. Not didn't Tom call until seven o'clock.
12. Only whisky Dad will drink.
13. Only that time I realize the difficulty of being parents.
14. What Jane needs is love.
15. Fill with their heart, patriotism is.

・你完成了嗎？

1. Stop jerk me around.
   →（X）stop 後面的動詞要變成動名詞，本句正確的寫法是：Stop jerking me around. 中文翻譯為：不要再騙我了。
2. What girl beautiful.
   →（X）本句正確的寫法有兩種，一種是：What a beautiful girl.，另一種寫法是：What a beautiful girl she is.，中文翻譯是：多漂亮的女孩呀！
3. How amazing she is.
   →（O）中文翻譯：她真是不可思議呀！
4. How well she plays the piano.
   →（O）感嘆句也可以用來形容動作，若修飾動詞，要使用副詞。本句翻譯為：她鋼琴彈得真好！
5. Opens the book and turns to page 10.

→（X）祈使句用動詞原形，本句正確的寫法是：Open the book and turn to page 10.，中文翻譯為：把書本打開並翻到第十頁。

6. Don't be silly.

　　→（O）中文翻譯為：別傻了。

7. Let she do what she wants.

　　→（X）let 後面的人稱代名詞要使用受詞，本句正確的寫法是：Let her do what she wants.，中文翻譯為：讓她做她想做的事。

8. Don't let me laugh.

　　→（O）中文翻譯是：別讓我笑。

9. Let's not talk to him.

　　→（O）不定詞的否定句，要將 not 放在 let 的後面，本句中文翻譯為：我們不要和他說話。

10. How exciting!

　　→（O）中文翻譯為：多刺激呀！

11. Not didn't Tom call until seven o'clock.

　　→（X）本句正確的寫法是：Not until seven o'clock did Tom called.，倒裝的時候，until 引導的名詞片語要和 not 一起移到句首，本句中文翻譯為：直到七點，Tom 才打電話來。

12. Only whisky Dad will drink.

　　→（O）only 移到句首時，後面的句子可以倒裝也可以不倒裝，本句的另一種寫法是：Only whisky will Dad drink.，中文翻譯為：爸爸只喝威士忌。

13. Only that time do I realize the difficulty of being parents.

　　→（O）本句翻譯為：只有在這個時候，我才了解身為父母的辛苦。

14. What Jane needs is love.

　　→（O）本句翻譯為：Jane 需要的就是愛。

15. Fill with their heart the strong patriotism is.

　　→（X）動詞要在主詞的前面，本句正確寫法為：Fill with their hearts is the strong patriotism.，中文翻譯為：充滿他們內心的，是強烈的愛國心。

09
CHAPTER
假設句

一、概念篇

∥ 什麼是假設句 ∣

假設句可以用來表示願望、假想、推測或是虛擬的狀況，有時，假設句也可以用來表示請求或建議，例如：

I wish I were a musician.（我希望我是一位音樂家。）
→「希望是」代表在事實中不是，這個句子表示願望或虛擬的狀況。

If I were you, I will order the steak.（如果我是你的話，我會點牛排。）
→「我」不可能是「你」，表示虛擬的狀況，同時也表示建議。

He sings as if he were a super star.（他唱歌的樣子彷彿他是巨星一樣。）
→「他」不是巨星，表示與事實相反的虛擬狀況。

∥ 假設語氣的形成方式 ∣

假設句的構成，可以依發生的時間和可能性的不同，分為三種類型：

⑴ 和現在事實相反

假設過去式，是表示和現在事實相反的假設，例如：

If he knew, he wouldn't leave her alone.（如果他知道，他就不會留她一個人。）
→ 所有假設過去式的動詞都要用過去式。

If I were you, I wouldn't go to America.（如果我是你，我不會去美國。）
→ 如果是 be 動詞，不分人稱都用 were。

If she was / were rich, she would buy a villa.
（如果她有錢，她會買一棟別墅。）
→ 在非正式用法中，第一人稱或第三人稱單數也可以用 was 代替 were。

If it were raining, I would stay at home.（如果還在下雨，我會待在家裡。）
→ 基本句型是＜If + 主詞 + 過去式動詞, 主詞 + would + 動詞原形＞。這個句型中，兩個子句中的主詞不一定相同。

If it were raining, I might stay at home.
→ would 也可以用 might、should、could 代替。

If it were raining, I would stay at home.
→ ＜were + 現在分詞＞的假設，表示持續的動作。

⑵ 和過去事實相反

假設過去完成式，表示和過去事實相反，例如：

If she had eaten the apple, she wouldn't have been hungry.
（如果她當時有吃蘋果，她就不會餓了。）
→ 所有假設過去完成式的動詞都是＜had + 過去分詞＞。

If I had been there, I would have solved the problem.
（如果當時我在那裡，我就可以解決問題。）
→ 基本句型是＜If + 主詞 + had + 過去分詞，主詞 + would + have + 過去分詞＞

If he had driven slowly, he wouldn't have gotten a speeding ticket.
（如果他當時開車慢慢地，他就不會接到超速罰單。）

→ would 除了可以用 could、should、might 代換，也可以加 not 變成否定句型。

If I had cleaned my room, Mom wouldn't have been angry.
（如果當時我有整理房間，媽媽就不會生氣。）
→ 兩個子句中的主詞不一定要相同。

若動作有持續性，也可以用＜had been + 現在分詞＞，例如：

If I had been standing here, the drinker might have hit me.
（如果當時我一直站在這裡，我可能會被這個醉漢打到。）
→ had been standing 是持續性的動作。

(3) 表示未來可能發生的假設
　　表示未來可能發生的假設，可以分成三個部分，分別是非事實的未來、不確定的未來和可能的未來。
　　非事實的未來，指的是對未來會發生的事實持相反的假設或想像：

If I were to go, I would bring some cookies.
（如果我可以去，我將會帶一些餅乾。）
→ 表示「非事實的未來」的基本句型是＜主詞 + were to + 動詞原形, 主詞 + would + 原形動詞＞。

If you were to try, you might be successful.
（如果你試試看，也許你將會成功。）
→ would 也可以用 might、could、should 代替。

不確定的未來表示對未來會發生的事實持不確定會發生的態度：

If he should be free tomorrow, he would come.（如果他有空，他將會來。）
→ 表示「不確定的未來」的基本句型是＜主詞 should + 動詞原形, 主詞 + would + 原形動詞＞。

If she should play the piano hard, she will be a musician.
（如果她練習很努力練習鋼琴，她將會成為音樂家。）

→ would 除了可以使用 should、could、might，也可以用 will、shall、can 或 may 代替。

If you should meet John, tell him to call me.
（如果你看到 *John*，叫他打電話給我。）
→ 主要子句除了用主詞加 would 外，也可以用祈使句的句型。

可能的未來則代表假設未來的事情有可能會發生：

If I drink too much coffee, I will be insomnious.
（如果我喝太多咖啡，我會失眠。）
→ 表示「可能的未來」的基本句型為＜主詞 + 現在式動詞, 主詞 + will + 原形動詞＞。

If it rains, he can ask me to bring an umbrella for him.
（如果下雨，他可以叫我帶雨傘給他。）
→ will 可以代換成 can、shall 或是 may，但要特別注意，這裡不可以用 would 等字。

看完這些例句，是不是已經被搞糊塗了呢？下面的表格可以幫助你更加清楚假設語氣的基本句型：

假設句的構成	
和現在事實相反的假設	＜If + 主詞 + 過去式動詞, 主詞 + would + 原形動詞＞
和過去事實相反	＜If + 主詞 + had + 過去分詞, 主詞 + would + have + 過去分詞＞
表示未來可能發生的假設	不可能發生： ＜主詞 + were to + 動詞原形, 主詞 + would + 原形動詞＞
	有可能發生，但可能性很小： ＜主詞 should + 動詞原形, 主詞 + would / will + 原形動詞＞
	在某種狀態下，有可能會發生： ＜主詞 + 現在式動詞, 主詞 + will + 原形動詞＞

· 換你試試看，練習將句子寫成假設句！

1. I / you / follow the direction
2. rain / tonight / I / stay at home（用可能性不大的未來寫假設句）
3. the little boy / wings / fly like a bird
4. you / come / I / happy
5. I / make / money / a millionaire
6. he / go to Japan / be a famous dancer（用不可能的未來寫假設句）
7. you / watch too much TV / be nearsighted（用可能性大的未來寫假設句）

· 你完成了嗎？

1. If I were you, I would follow the direction.
2. If it rains tonight, I will stay at home.
3. If the little boy had wings, he would fly like a bird.
4. If you come, I will be happy.
5. If I had made a lot of money, I would have be a millionaire.
6. If he were to go to Japan, he would be a famous dancer.
7. If you watch too much TV, you will be nearsighted.

‖ If 也可以省略

　　假設句主要由兩個子句組成，第一個由 if 帶領的子句稱為條件句，第二個句子稱為主要子句。當我們將 if 省略時，要記得將條件句進行倒裝，也就是動詞或助動詞，要放在主詞的前面：

　　If I were you, I would take a trip to Italia.
　　（如果我是你，我會去義大利旅行。）
　　→ 條件句 + 主要子句。

　　Were I you, I would take a trip to Italia.
　　→ 省略 if，先寫 be 動詞 were，再寫主詞 I。

　　再看另一個例子：

If he had worked hard, he would have be a manager.
（如果他當時努力工作，他就會成為主管了。）
→ 原本的句子。

Had he worked hard, he would have be a manager.
→ 省略 if，助動詞 had 要放在主詞 he 前。

· 換你試試看，練習省略 if 的假設句！

1. If I were you, I would buy this pink bag.
2. If he should come, he will arrive at seven o'clock.
3. If she had learnt Japanese, she would have spoken Japanese fluently.
4. If he were free, he would spend all day playing video games.
5. If I had a villa, I would invite all my friends and have a party.

· 你完成了嗎？

1. Were I you, I would buy this pink bag.
2. Should he come, he will arrive at seven o'clock.
3. Had she learnt Japanese, she would have spoken Japanese fluently.
4. Were he free, he would spend all day playing video games.
5. Had I a villa, I would invite all my friends and have a party.

▌If 也可以用別的字代替

　　條件句中的 if，可以用其他連接詞代替，這些語詞如：if only（但願）、suppose（假使）、supposing（假使）、in case（假使）、as long as（只要）、on condition（倘若）等，例如：

In case he should call, tell him to wait.（假使他打來，叫他等一下。）
→ if 被 in case 取代。

Supposing I were you, I would marry him.（假設我是你，我會嫁給他。）
→ if 被 supposing 取代

As long as you should break the record, I will buy you a PS3.
（只要你可以打破紀錄，我就買一台 PS3 給你。）
→ if 被 as long as 取代。

二、好學的假設語氣句型

---
1. I wish + 主詞 + were / 過去式動詞 = 但願…可惜沒有…

這個句型表示「和現在事實相反」的假設，例如：

I wish I saved the money.（我希望我把錢存了下來。）
→ 用過去式動詞表示和現在事實相反：希望存錢，但實際沒有存。

I wish my husband were here to share my honor.
（我希望我的丈夫能在這裡和我一起分享榮耀。）
→ 兩個主詞不一定要相同，但不管人稱，be 動詞都是用 were。

I wish I studied the medical science.（我希望我可以讀醫。）

I wish I had saved all the money I earned.
（我希望我之前有把賺的錢都存起來。）
→ had + 過去分詞，表示和過去事實相反：過去希望存錢，但過去沒有存。

How I wish I had saved all the money I earned.
（我多麼希望之前有把賺的錢存起來。）
→ 用 how 可以加強語氣，表示「多希望…呀」。

If only I had told her the good news.（我希望我有告訴她這個好消息。）
→ 可以用 if only 代替 I wish。

Would that I had told her the good news.
→ 也可以用 would that 代替 I wish。

・我們可以這麼說

說謊以後被拆穿，除了道歉，你也可以這樣說表示你心中的愧疚：

I wish I didn't lie.（我真希望我沒有說謊。）

I wish I didn't make this mistake.（我真希望我沒有犯下這樣的錯。）

・換你試試看，利用單詞造句！

1. spill the coffee

2. gotten a haircut like this
3. were an actress
4. taken the note during the class

· 你完成了嗎？

1. I wish I didn't spill the coffee.
2. I wish I hadn't gotten a haircut like this.
3. I wish I were an actress.
4. I wish I had taken the note during the class.

---

2. 主詞 + would have + 過去分詞 = 本來可以…但卻沒…

例如：

She would have told you the truth, but she didn't.
（她本來可以告訴你真相，但她沒有。）
→ ＜主詞 + would have + 過去分詞＞。

I should have celled you last night.
（我昨天晚上應該要打電話給你的。）
→ would 也可以用 could 或 should 代替。

若假設句中的助動詞後面加上 not，句子的意思就會改變為「本來不該做…卻…」，看看下面的例句：

She would not have told you the secret, but she did.
（她不應該告訴你這個秘密的，但她說了。）

I should not have called you at midnight.
（我不應該昨天半夜打電話給你的。）

這個句型也可以用來表示對過去事件的推測：

He could have slept at ten o'clock last night.
（昨天晚上十點他應該已經睡了。）
→ could have slept 可以代表「當時可能睡了」的假設。

She should have left the office when I called her.
（當我打給她的時候，她應該已經離開辦公室了。）

· 我們可以這樣說

為了公司的產品發表會，已經熬夜好幾天了，你可以這樣抱怨一下：

I should have taken a rest after working for several hours.
（我在工作這麼久以後本來應該休息一下的。）

· 換你試試看，用這個句型改寫句子！

1. We have gone to the movies.
2. He has lent his brother some money.
3. You haven't smoked and drunk the beer.
4. I haven't fought with my little brother.

· 你完成了嗎？

1. We should have gone to the movies.
2. He should have lent his brother some money.
3. You couldn't have smoked and drunk the beer.
4. I wouldn't fought with my little brother.

---

3. It is time that + 主詞 + 過去式動詞 = 該是…的時候（但還沒做）

這個句型用來表示「是時候去做…」，實際上，這件事還沒有發生，例如：

It's time that we spent time with the kids.（該是花時間陪小孩的時候了。）
→ 用過去式動詞，表示與現在事實相反。

It's about time that you cleaned your room.（你該去整理房間了。）
→ 在 time 前面加 about 或 high，可以加強語氣。

It's time for me to study.（我該去唸書了。）
→ 若想說明「對誰來說該…」，可以用介係詞 for，記得後面的人稱要用受格。

It's time for a birthday party.（該舉辦生日派對了。）
→ for 後面也可以接名詞。

It's time for paying the bill.（是付帳單的時候了。）
→ for 後面的動作要記得改為動名詞的形式。

這種句型也可以用來表示建議，當 that 子句中加了 should，後面的動詞要變回原形動詞：

It's time that you should apologize to them.（你該向他們道歉了。）
→ 雖然還沒做，但預計要做，所以不用和現在事實相反的過去式動詞，而是用 should + 原形動詞，此時的 should 不可以省略。

・我們可以這樣說
家事怎麼做都做不完，當想要請另一半幫貓咪洗澡的時候，你可以這樣說：

It's time that you gave Mimi a bath.（你該幫 Mimi 洗澡了。）

・換你試試看，用這個句型把句子完成！
1. You fixed the bike.
2. I stopped fooling around.
3. He fed the pet.
4. We kept quiet.

・你完成了嗎？是不是很簡單呢？
1. It's time that you fixed the bike.
2. It's time that I stopped fooling around.
3. It's time that he fed the pet.
4. It's time that we kept quiet.

---

4. 主詞 + 動詞 + as if + 主詞 + were / 過去式動詞 = …彷彿是…

例如：

The little boy dances as if he <u>were</u> a dancer.
（這個小男孩跳舞的樣子彷彿他是舞者。）
→ 假設句用過去式動詞，表示和主要子句的動作是同時發生的，從這個句子來看，小男孩是「一邊跳舞，一邊覺得自己是舞者」。

The little girl screams as if someone <u>had hit</u> her.
（這個小女孩尖叫的樣子，像是剛剛有人打她。）
→ 假設句用＜had ＋ 過去分詞＞，表示動作比主要子句的動作還要早發生，也就是說，小女生是先覺得有人打她才尖叫的。

　　除了假設句的動詞變化會影響句子的意思，主要子句的動詞變化，同樣也會改變句子的涵義，試比較看看下面兩個句子：

She <u>talks</u> as if she were a teacher.（她講話的樣子像個老師。）
→ 主要子句用簡單式動詞，表示是當下發生的動作；假設句用過去式動詞，表示這兩個子句中的動作是同時發生的。

She <u>talked</u> as if she were a teacher.（她當時講話的樣子像個老師。）
→ 主要子句用過去式動詞，表示事過去發生的動作。

　　再看另一個例子：

He <u>looks</u> as if he <u>had eaten</u> a fly.（他看起來像吃了一隻蒼蠅。）
→ 主要子句用簡單式動詞，表示是當下發生的動作；假設句用＜had ＋ 過去分詞＞，表示比 look 還要早發生。

He <u>looked</u> as if he <u>had eaten</u> a fly.（他當時看起來像吃了一隻蒼蠅。）
→ 主要子句用過去式動詞，表示事過去發生的動作。

・我們可以這樣說
　　看到朋友或同事臉色不好的時候，我們可以用這個句型表達關心，你可以說：

What's wrong with you? You look as if you had butterfly in your stomach.
（你怎麼了？你看起來很焦慮！）

・換你試試看，把句子完成！

1. He / go up in the air / someone / steal / money
2. She / have a red face / her boyfriend / kiss
3. He / run / dog / chase
4. She / cry / her life / totally ruin

・你完成了嗎？

1. He goes up in the air as if someone had stolen his money.
2. She has a red face as if her boyfriend had kissed her.
3. He runs as if a dog chased after him.
4. She cries as if her life were totally ruined.

---

5. Without + 名詞, 主詞 + would + 動詞原形 = 若沒有…就…

例如：

Without your help, I wouldn't solve this problem.
（沒有你的幫助，我就不能解決這個問題。）
→ would 後面也可以加上 not 表示否定。

除了用 without，也可以用 but for 或 If it were not for 代替，例如：

Without his warming, she would bump into the tree.
（沒有他的提醒，她就會撞到樹。）
→ 原本 without 的句型。

But for his warming, she would bump into the tree.
→ but for 代替 without。

If it were not for his warming, she would bump into the tree.
→ if it were not for 代替 without。

Without your teaching, we couldn't pass the exam.
（沒有你的教導，我們不可能通過考試。）
→ would 也可以用 could、might 代替。

Without the guide, we wouldn't have walked out the desert.
（沒有這位嚮導，我們當時不可能走出沙漠。）
→ 若想表示「和過去事實相反」，則主要子句的動詞用＜would have + 過去分詞＞。

・我們可以這樣說

要常常和另一半說些甜蜜的話，感情才會越來越加溫唷，你可以這樣說：

Without your love, I would die.（沒有你的愛，我就會死。）

・換你試試看，利用這個句型翻譯看看！

1. 沒有這個藥，他就不會好得這麼快。
2. 沒有他的鼓勵，她不會成功。
3. 沒有她的父母，她不可能撐下去。
4. 沒有你的話，我之前可能就放棄了。

・你完成了嗎？

1. Without the medicine, he wouldn't recover his health so soon.
2. Without his encouragement, she wouldn't success.
3. Without her parents, she couldn't hang on any more.
4. Without you, I wouldn't have given up.

---

6. If it had not been for 名詞, 主詞 + would have + 過去分詞 = 若非…就…

這個句型和第五個句型是一樣的中文意思，但是要小心這個句型的主要子句要用＜would have + 過去分詞＞，表示和過去事實相反的狀況，例如：

If it had not been for the attack, his uncle would have lived.
（若非這件襲擊事件，他的舅舅可能還活著。）

If it had not been for the rain, we would have gone mountain climbing.
（若不是下雨，我們就會去爬山了。）

If it had not been for the fact that she was tired, she would have gone with you.
（若非她很累，她就會跟你一起去了。）

→ if it had not been for 後面除了加名詞，也可以接 the fact that 帶領的子句，在 that 子句中的動詞要用過去式動詞。

If it had not been for waiting here, I wouldn't have met you.
（若不是待在這裡，我就不可能會遇見你。）
→ if it had not been for 後面也可以接動名詞。

‧我們可以這樣說

　　快下班的時候，主管卻臨時丟了很多文件要處理，面對家人的抱怨，我們可以這樣說：

If it had not been for the extra job, I would have been home earlier.
*(*若不是這些額外的工作，我可能可以早一點到家。）

‧換你試試看，利用單詞完成句子！

1. the advertisement / the product / not sold well.
2. the fact that / I / shouted loudly / you / not found / thief behind you
3. his cheat / they / married

‧你完成了嗎？

1. If it had not been for the advertisement, the product wouldn't have sold well.
2. If it had not been for the fact that I shouted loudly, you wouldn't found the thief behind you.
3. If it had not been for his cheating, they would have married.

---

7. what if + 主詞 + 動詞 = 萬一⋯的話怎麼辦？

　　這個句子中的事件，多半是指不好的狀況，例如：

What if he bumps into the car?（如果他撞到車子怎麼辦？）
→ 動詞可以用簡單式的動詞。

What if I lost?（如果我迷路了怎麼辦？）
→ 動詞若用過去式動詞，語氣較為禮貌。

What if you had been caught?（如果你當時被抓了怎麼辦？）
→ 用過去完成式的動詞變化，表示過去未曾發生的事。

What if I have a stomachache?（如果我胃痛怎麼辦？）

但這個句子也可以用來表示建議，例如：

What if we paint the wall pink ?
（如果我們把牆壁刷成粉紅色如何？）

・我們可以這樣說

　　每天都在家裡煮飯，雖然健康又衛生，但有時候還是想要打打牙祭，你可以這樣建議：

What if we dine out tonight?（今天晚上要不要出去吃飯？）

・換你試試看，把句子的順序重組！
1. What the ladder the fall boy if down from?
2. If what injury she suffered?
3. What if had he ankle sprained his?
4. What you if slip fall and?

・你完成了嗎？
1. What if the boy fall down from the ladder?
2. What if she suffered injury?
3. What if he had sprained his ankle?
4. What if you slip and fall?

---

8. weather + 主詞 + 動詞 + or + 主詞 + 動詞 = 不管⋯還是⋯

例如：

Whether the wind blows or it rains, we will go on a picnic.
（不管颱風還是下雨，我們都要去野餐。）

→ whether 和 or 之後銜接＜主詞＋動詞＞。

Whether you agree or not, I will buy this computer.
（不管你同意或是不同意，我都要買這台電腦。）
→ 若兩個動詞是一樣的，且表達相反的意思，可以省略第二個動詞，直接在 or 後面加上 not。

Whether or not you agree, I will buy this computer.
→ 如果子句很短，可以把 or not 放在 whether 的後面。

Whether American or Chinese, we are the people on earth.
（不論是美國人還是中國人，都是地球上的人。）
→ whether 和 or 之後也銜接名詞。

Whether you eat potato chips or hot dogs, you can't get enough nutrition.
（不論你吃薯片或是熱狗，都不能獲得足夠的營養。）
→ 若兩的動詞是一樣的，可以省略第二個動詞。

‧ 我們可以這樣說

對情人的甜言蜜語，總是要越肉麻越好，你可以這樣表達你的真心：

Whether you get older or fatter, I still love you.
（不論你變老或變胖，我都愛你。）

‧ 換你試試看，用這個句型練習造句！

1. Mom / Dad / help you
2. Typhoon comes or not / she / work
3. He / take the bus / MRT / late
4. She / wear / dress / make up / look pretty.

‧ 你完成了嗎？

1. Whether Mom or Dad, they can't help you this time.
2. Whether the typhoon comes or not, she still needs to work.
3. Whether he takes the bus or the MRT, he will be late.
4. Whether she wears this dress or makeup, she still looks pretty.

---

9. given that + 主詞 + 動詞 = 考慮到⋯來說

例如：

Given that you behave well, you can eat the lollipop.
（考慮到你表現很好，你可以吃棒棒糖。）

Given his age, he can't see this movie.
（考慮到他的年紀，他不能看這部電影。）
→ 除了接 that 引導的子句，也可以接名詞。

Given his health, he isn't allowed to smoke.
（考慮到他的健康，他不能抽菸。）

Given the condition of the laptop, its performance surprises me.
（考量到這部筆電的狀況，它還可以運作讓我很驚訝。）

・**我們可以這樣說**
　　小朋友喜歡吃糖，但吃完糖用不刷牙，結果滿嘴蛀牙，考量到小朋友的牙齒狀況，當小孩又要吃甜食時，你可以這樣說：

Given your decayed tooth, you can't eat much candy.
（考慮到你的蛀牙，你不可以吃太多糖果。）

・**換你試試看，這句英文怎麼說？**
1. 考慮到他感冒，他需要盡可能的多喝熱水。
2. 考慮到你的支持，我才有更多勇氣撐下去。
3. 考慮到她的身材，她決定要節食。
4. 考慮到成本，這個商人決定提高商品的價錢。

・**你完成了嗎？**
1. Given his cold, he needs to drink as much hot water as he can.
2. Given your support, I have more courage to hang on.
3. Given her figure, she decides to diet.
4. Given the cost, the merchant raises the price of this merchandise.

10. unless + 主詞 + 動詞 = 除非…

unless 引領的子句用來表示某事可能發生，但尚未發生的情況，例如：

Have a cup of tea unless you would like a soda.
（來杯茶吧？除非你想要汽水。）
→ 不論式茶或汽水都還沒有喝，這兩個動作都是未來有可能會發生的狀況。

Let's play poker card unless you want to sleep.
（來玩撲克牌吧？除非你想睡覺。）
→ unless 子句中的動詞用簡單式，代表未來有可能會發生的動作。

Don't wake me up unless Jane calls.
（除非 Jane 打電話來，不然不要叫醒我。）

You won't get good grades unless you study hard.
（除非你認真念書，不然你不會得到好成績。）

‧我們可以這樣說

如果不小心和另一半吵架了，為了展現自己道歉的誠意，你可以這樣說：

I will keep calling unless you talk to me.
（除非你跟我說話，不然我會一直打電話來。）

‧換你試試看，排列出正確的句子順序！

1. He buy the he house will broken unless is.
2. She breaks will the for up unless bicycle game sign she her leg.
3. The won't raise leave the boss workers promises to the pay unless.

‧你完成了嗎？

1. He will buy the house unless he is broken.
2. She will sign up for the bicycle game unless she breaks her leg.
3. The worker won't leave unless the boss promises to raise the pay.

---

11. had better + 動詞原形 = 最好⋯

例如：

We had better go home before ten o'clock. （我們最好在十點前回家。）
→ had better 後面直接加原形動詞。

She would rather go hiking. （她寧願去健行。）
→ 也可以用 would rather 代替 had better，表示「寧願⋯」。

She would go hiking rather than go to the movies.
（她寧願去健行也不要看電影。）
→ 若有兩件事在比較的時候，可以將 rather than 放在兩件事情的中間。

He would sooner die rather than eats vegetable. （他寧願死也不要吃蔬菜。）

・我們可以這樣說

遇到小朋友說謊的時候，你可以語帶警告的說：

You had better tell the truth. （你最好說實話。）

・換你試試看，這句英文怎麼說！
1. 她最好吃一些水果。
2. 我寧願買這條手環也不要買那條項鍊。
3. 他最好停止喝咖啡。

・你完成了嗎？
1. She had better eat some fruit.
2. I would buy this bracelet rather than that necklace.
3. He had better quit coffee.

‖ 好學的假設句小短句 |

---

1. If I could. 如果我可以。

A: Will you arrive home before dinner? （你會在晚餐前回家嗎？）

B: I have lots of work today. I will back home before dinner if I could.
（我今天有很多工作要做，如果我可以我會在晚餐前回家。）

2. If it is convenient for you. 如果對你方便的話。

A: May I borrow your dictionary? If it is convenient for you.
（我可以跟你借字典嗎？如果對你來說方便的話。）
B: Sure, here you are.（沒問題！拿去吧！）

3. If I were you. 如果我是你。

A: I don't know what to order.（我不知道要吃什麼。）
B: I'd have the special if I were you.（如果我是你的話，我會點特餐。）

4. God willing. 如果情況允許的話。

A: Try to be on time, OK?（試著準時，好嗎？）
B: God willing.（如果情況允許的話。）

5. Just to be on the safe side. 以防萬一。

A: Do you remember that Miss Yang asked us to preview chapter 3 or 4?
（你記得楊老師要我們預習第三章還是第四章？）
B: We can preview both of them. Just to be on the safe side.
（我們可以兩章都預習，以防萬一。）

C、文法糾正篇

1. If 子句中可以有 would 或 will 嗎？

一般而言，if 引導的子句中不可以出現 would 或 will，例如：

If I were he, I would cycling around Taiwan.
（如果我是他，我會騎腳踏車環島。）
→ would 在主要子句中出現。

If she had got up earlier, she wouldn't missed the bus.
（如果她早一點起床，她就不會錯過巴士。）
→ if 子句中沒有 would。

但若是表示主詞的意願或某種堅持，if 子句中可以有 would 或 will：

If he would lend me ten thousand dollars, I would be thankful.
（如果他肯借我一萬元的話，我會對他心存感激的。）
→ 在 if 子句中的 would 代表主詞 he 的意願。

If she will practice the piano every day, she would be a great musician.
（如果她堅持每天練習鋼琴，她會是一個偉大的音樂家。）

---

2. As if 後面若接簡單式動詞，和假設語氣沒有關係

例如：

It seems as if the typhoon will hit Taiwan the day after tomorrow.
（看起來颱風會在後天登陸台灣。）
→ as if 子句中的動詞使用簡單式，表示實際上會發生的事，而非假設的狀況。

再看一個例子：

The train has left; it looks as if we will have to take the bus.
（火車開走了，看來我們只好搭公車了。）
→ will have to take 也表示未來將會發生的動作。

有時候，我們可以把 as if 後面的主詞和動詞省略，例如：

He raised his hand as if to speak.（他舉手彷彿有什麼話要說。）
→ 這句原本寫成 He raises his hand as if he wants to speak.省略了 as if 後面的主詞和動詞。

---

3. 搞不清楚到底是和現在事實相反還是和過去事實相反

在假設句中，常常讓人困擾得就是搞不清楚到底是和現在的事實相反，還是和過去的事實相反。有一個小訣竅就是，把假設句的時間往後推一格，什麼意思呢？例如：

If I were you, I wouldn't talk back to my parents like that.
（如果我是你，我不會向我父母這樣頂嘴。）
→ 假設句的動詞是過去式，過去式往後推一格時間，就是現在，所以這個句子是和現在事實相反。

If I had taken the note, I wouldn't forget to do homework.
（如果當時我有抄筆記，我就不會忘記要寫功課。）
→ 還記得完成式嗎?我們在討論完成式的時候，有提到當句子中有兩個動作，比較早完成的動作要用完成式，因此，在這個句子中，比較早完成的是抄筆記的動作，把時間往後推一格，就是過去式。這樣就可以判斷，這個句子和過去事實相反。

・換你試試看，假設句的綜合練習，這個句子正確嗎？

1. He would rather buy the bag.
2. If I were him, I sing a song for Lisa.
3. She looks shock as if a mouse will run in front of her.
4. If I had watched this talk show, I would know what they said.
5. If I would study Japanese hard, I could speak Japanese fluently.
6. If Mom should be free on weekend, she will take us to the zoo.
7. If Dad drinks too much beer, he would feel uncomfortable.
8. If I arrived home before six o'clock, I would help her make dinner.
9. If she was here, she would know what to do.
10. If you looked at Jimmy, you couldn't help but laugh.

‧你完成了嗎？

1. He would rather buy the bag.
   → （O）這句的意思是：他寧願買這個包包。

2. If I were him, I sing a song for Lisa.
   → （X）這句的意思是：要是我是他，我會唱一首歌獻給 Lisa。這個句子錯誤的地方有兩個，一個是受詞 him 要改為 he，因為 be 動詞後面接主詞補語，但受詞並不能作為主詞補語，但在現在口語的英文中，常常有 him 代替 he 的狀況出現。另一個錯誤是主要子句中少了助動詞 would，本句的正確寫法應該是：If I were he, I would sing a song for Lisa.

3. She looks shock as if a mouse will run in front of her.
   → （X）這句的意思是：她看起來很震驚，彷彿有老鼠從她前面跑過。as if 後面銜接的若為假設語氣，應將 will run 改為過去式動詞，本句正確的寫法是：She looks shock as if the mouse ran in front of her.

4. If I had watched this talk show, I would have known what they said.
   → （O）這句的意思是：如果當時我有看這個脫口秀節目，我就會知道他們在講什麼。

5. If I would study Japanese hard, I could speak Japanese fluently.
   → （O）這句的意思是：如果我認真學習日文，我可以講出流利的日文。

6. If Mom should be free on the weekend, she will take us to the zoo.
   → （O）這句的意思是：如果媽媽周末有空的話，她會帶我們去動物園。

7. If Dad drinks too much beer, he would feel uncomfortable.
   → （X）這句的意思是：如果爸爸喝太多啤酒，他會覺得不舒服。如果假設句用簡單式動詞，那麼主要子句的助動詞一般習慣用 will，本句正確的寫法應該是：If Dad drinks too much beer, he will feel uncomfortable.

8. If I arrived home before six o'clock, I would help her make dinner.
   → （O）這句的意思是：如果我六點之前到家，我會幫她做晚餐。

9. If she was here, she would know what to do.
   → （X）這句的意思是：如果她在這裡，她會知道該怎麼做。我們之前有提到，假設句中的 be 動詞，不論人稱都用 were，只有在非正式用法中才會有使用 was 的情況出現，因此，這個句子比較好的寫法是：If she were here, she would know what to do.

10. If you looked at Jimmy, you couldn't help but laugh.
    → （O）這句的意思是：如果你看著 Jimmy，你會忍不住笑出來。

NOTE

01 CHAPTER
02 CHAPTER
03 CHAPTER
04 CHAPTER
05 CHAPTER
06 CHAPTER
07 CHAPTER
08 CHAPTER
09 CHAPTER
10 CHAPTER

10
CHAPTER
被動句

一、概念篇

▍什麼是被動句

到目前為止，我們練習的句型都是屬於主動語態，例如：

The cat drinks the milk.（貓咪正在喝牛奶。）
→ 主詞＋動詞＋受詞，是主動語態的語序。

在中文裡，我們可以把這個句子換句話說：「牛奶被貓咪喝完了。」同樣地，英文也可以把這句話倒過來說，也就是所謂的被動句：

The milk is drunk by the cat.
→ 原本的主詞和受詞的位置交換，動詞也要做被動語態的變化。

再看一個例子：

The teacher teaches the students.（老師教導學生。）
→ 主動語態。

The student is taught by the teacher.（學生被老師教。）

→ 被動語態。

被動句可以用來表示被動的動作或是狀態，例如：

The juice was drunk by May this morning.（果汁今天早上被 *May* 喝掉了。）
→ 表示被喝掉的動作。

The movie was made by this movie company.
（這部電影由這個電影公司製作。）
→ 表示被製作的動作。

This story is written in Japanese.（這個故事是由日文寫成的。）
→ 表示書的狀態。

The door is opened.（門被打開了。）
→ 表示門的狀態。

‖ 被動句的形成方式

Jimmy ate the cookies yesterday.（*Jimmy* 昨天吃了餅乾。）
→ 主詞 + 動詞 + 受詞

你可以試試看把這個句子變成被動句嗎?首先，先找到原本句子的受詞 the cookies，接著找出原本句子中的主詞 Jimmy，將這兩個語詞的位置顛倒：

The cookies ate *Jimmy* yesterday.

然後，將動詞做被動語態的變化，變動語態的動詞為＜be 動詞 + 過去分詞＞：

The cookies were eaten Jimmy yesterday.
→ 因為原本句子中的動詞是過去式，因此 be 動詞也要使用過去式。

最後，在給予動作的人前面加上 by，就是完整的被動句型了：

The cookies were eaten by Jimmy yesterday.（餅乾昨天被 *Jimmy* 吃掉了。）

‖ 被動語態的種類 ‖

被動語態根據時間的不同，可以區分為七種類型：

(1) 現在時間的被動語態

Tom is caught by the police.（Tom 被警察抓到了。）
→ ＜is＋過去分詞＞是現在式的被動語態。

The magazines are read by these teenagers.（雜誌被這些青少年閱讀。）
→ 如果主詞是複數，be 動詞也要改為表示複數的 are。

I am loved by my family.（我被我的家人愛著。）
→ 如果主詞是第一人稱，be 動詞要改成 am。

除了簡單式的被動，現在進行式也可以改為被動語態，例如：

The cookie is been eating by the dog.（餅乾正在被小狗吃。）
→ ＜is＋been＋V-ing＞是現在進行式的被動句，＜is＋been＋V-ing＞是
＜is＋過去分詞＞和＜is＋eating＞的合併，been 是 be 動詞的過去分詞。

These books are been reading by the children.（書本正在被小孩閱讀。）
→ 如果是複數，be 動詞用 are。

現在完成式也可以寫成被動式，例如：

She has been told what happened.（她已經被告知發生了什麼事。）
→ ＜has＋been＋過去分詞＞，是現在完成式的被動語態。

The two books have been read by May.（這兩本書已經被 May 讀完了。）
→ 如果主詞是複數，要使用表示複數的 have。

(2) 過去時間的被動語態

The trunk was bumped by the motorcycle.（卡車被摩托車撞了。）
→ ＜was＋過去分詞＞是過去式被動語態的基本句型。

These two dresses were sold by the sales clerk.（這兩件洋裝被售貨員賣掉了。）
→ 如果主詞是複數，be 動詞要改為表示複數的 were。

和現在式的被動語態一樣，過去進行式也可以有被動語態，只要將 be 動詞改為 was 或 were 即可，例如：

The student was been teaching by the teacher.（學生當時正在被老師教。）
→ ＜was＋been＋V-ing＞是過去進行式的被動句

The color books were been drawing by the children.（著色本當時正在被小孩畫。）
→ 主詞是複數的話，將 be 動詞改為 were。

那過去完成式的被動語態，你知道怎麼寫了嗎？沒錯，就是將完成式中的 have 改成過去式的 had，就構成了＜had＋been＋過去分詞＞：

Jimmy had been bitten by a dog.（*Jimmy* 當時被一隻狗咬到。）

(3) 含助動詞的被動語態

The supermarket will be opened at eleven o'clock.
（超市將會在十一點開門。）
→ 助動詞放在被動式的動詞前，be 動詞要用原形。

The necklace will have been sold by the end of the auction.
（項鍊將會在拍賣會結束的時候被賣出。）

This cup of coffee must be drunk by Mom.

（這杯咖啡一定是被媽媽喝掉的。）

‖ by 可以省略 ‖

一般的被動句，除非需要強調，可以不用寫出施予動作的人，例如：

The theater is reopened.（戲院重新開張了。）
→ 句子中沒有寫出讓戲院重新開張的人物。

當遇到下面幾種狀況的時候，也可以將 by 省略：

Taiwanese is spoken by Taiwanese in Taiwan.
（台語在台灣被台灣人民使用。）
→ 做動作的人泛指多數人的時候，可以將 by 和作動作的人一起省略。這句可以寫成 Taiwanese is spoken in Taiwan.

He was shot by ... in the war.（他在戰爭裡被射中。）
→ 不知道誰做動作的時候，也可以省略 by。這句話可以寫成 He was shot in the war.

Dad was fined twelve hundred dollars by the police for drunk driving.
（爸爸因為酒駕被罰款 1200 元。）
→ 大家都清楚某動作必由某些特定的人所做時，可以省略 by。這句可以寫成：Dad was fined twelve hundred dollars for drunk driving.

‖ 除了 by 也可以用其他的介係詞 ‖

I am pleased to have this opportunity to talk to Mr. Wang.
（我很高興有機會和王先生說話。）

The writer is known to everyone in the town.
（這個作家在這個小鎮裡很有名。）

The cake is made from flour, milk and eggs.
（蛋糕是由麵粉、牛奶和雞蛋做成的。）

She was born of American parents.（她出生在美國家庭。）

I am engaged in cleaning the house.（我正忙於整理家裡。）
The lion was caught in the cage.（獅子被困在籠子裡。）
The bed is covered with white bed sheet.（床被白色的床單罩著。）

類似這樣的常用語有：be made of（由⋯製成的）、be known for（以⋯聞名）、be married to（結婚）、be drowned in（溺斃）、be based on（以⋯為基礎）、be trained to（被培養成）等。

二、好學的被動句句型

1. get + 過去分詞 = 被⋯

被動式的動詞是＜be 動詞 + 過去分詞＞例如：

The cookies are baked in the kitchen.（餅乾在廚房被烘焙。）
The news will be announced tomorrow.（這則消息會在明天被宣布。）
The house was built in 1982.（這棟房子在 1982 年被建造。）

但也可以用 get 代替 be 動詞：

The thief got caught by the police officer.（小偷被警察抓到了。）

用 get 代替 be 動詞，是比較不正式的用法，通常用於突然發生的意外，或是不預期的事件：

The vase got broken by the cat.（花瓶被貓咪打破了。）
They got married.（他們結婚了。）

常常和 get 一起使用的動詞有：get dressed / changed（換衣服）、get washed（清洗）、get engaged（訂婚）、get married（結婚）、get divorced（離婚）、get started（開始）、get lost（迷路）等。

· 我們可以這樣說

和朋友聚餐快遲到了，沒想到另一半還坐在沙發上打電動，你可以這樣提醒他：

We're late. You'd better get dressed.（我們要遲到了，你趕快換衣服。）

· 換你試試看，利用單詞完成句子！

1. Kenny / hurt / car accident.
2. My bicycle / steal / a few weeks ago.
3. They / lose / in the mountain.
4. Charlie / surprised / he / invite / her party.

· 你完成了嗎？

1. Kenny got hurt in the car accident.
2. My bicycle got stolen a few weeks ago.
3. They got lost in the mountain.
4. Charlie was surprised that he got invited to her party.

---

2. 主詞 + have + 某事 + done = 使某人做…

這個句型用來表示「請某人做…」，比較看看下面兩個句子：

Keri cleaned the bathroom.（Keri 清裡了浴室。）
→ Keri 自己清理浴室。

Keri had the bathroom cleaned.（Keri 請人來清理浴室。）
→ Keri 請人來做清理浴室的動作。

再來看一個例子：

Dad repaired the roof.（爸爸修理屋頂。）
→ 爸爸自己修理屋頂。

Dad had the roof repaired.（爸爸請人來修理屋頂。）
→ 爸爸請人來做修理屋頂的事。

Mom had the car serviced last month.（媽媽上個月將汽車送修。）
Larry had his hair cat in the beauty salon.（*Larry* 在這家理髮店剪頭髮。）

我們也可以用 get 來代替 have，例如：

May got her dress cleaned.（*May* 將洋裝送洗。）
→ 這句原本的寫法是：May had her dress cleaned.

但是，＜have + 某事 + done＞可能會有完全不同的意思，例如：

He had his leg broken in the race.（他在比賽中摔斷腿。）
→ 不是他請人讓他摔斷腿。

Nancy had her passport stolen.（*Nancy* 的護照被偷了。）
→ 不是 Nancy 請人偷護照。

從上面兩個例子可以發現，並非所有＜have + 某事 + done＞的句型，都是代表「使某人來做…」，通常這樣的用法，多表示某人發生了某件出乎意料的事，而這件事多半是不愉快的經驗。

・我們可以這樣說

看到同事換了新造型，你可以用這個句型來表示稱讚：

You look great! Where did you have your hair cut?
（你看起來好極了！你在哪裡剪頭髮的？）

・換你試試看，這句英文怎麼說？

1. Jane 的錢昨晚被偷了。
2. 她請人將房間漆成粉紅色。
3. 這個男孩請人清理地板。
4. 這個男人很少請人幫他刮鬍子。

・你完成了嗎？

1. Jane had her money stolen last night.

2. She had her room painted in pink.

3. The boy is having the carpet cleaned.

4. The man seldom has his beard shaved.

> **3. 主詞 + be 動詞 + given = 被給予某物⋯**
> **某物 + be 動詞 + given to... = 某物被給予⋯**

例如：

Opportunities are given the people who are ready.（機會是給準備好的人。）

Sandy was given a bunch of flowers.（Sandy 收到了一束花。）

有時，主詞和受詞在句子中交換位置，代表的意義略有不同，比較看看下列兩個句子：

The students are given useful training.（學生受到有用的訓練。）
→ 重點是 the students。

The useful skill is given to the students.（有用的技巧被教給學生。）
→ 重點是 useful skill，同時，be given 後面要加表示方向的 to。

・我們可以這樣說

和老同學聚會，可以藉機炫耀一下老公有多疼你，你可以說：

I was given a diamond bracelet by my husband last night.
（我昨天晚上收到老公送的鑽石手鍊。）

・換你試試看，練習用兩種方式完成句子！

1. woman / a pink dress

2. good salesmen / extra bonus

3. May / money

・你完成了嗎？

1. The pink dress is given to the woman.

2. Extra bonuses are given to the salesmen.

3. The money is given to May.

---

4. It's said that... = 據說…

例如：

It's said that Jimmy is in love with Nancy.（據說 *Jimmy* 和 *Nancy* 戀愛了。）

It's said that the workers will get pay raise.（據說工人們會得到加薪。）

It's said that Simon is in a diet.（據說 *Simon* 正在節食。）

It's thought that children need to eat enough vegetables.
（人們認為，孩童們需要攝取足夠的蔬菜。）
→ 除了 said，也可以用 thought 來表示同樣的意思。

It's reported that coffee will make people insomnious.
（據報導，咖啡會造成人們失眠。）
→ report 也有類似的涵義，表示「據報導…」。

・我們可以這麼說

熬個雞湯替工作辛苦的家人打打氣，你可以這樣說：

It's said chicken soup may revive tired people.
（據說雞湯可以幫助疲累的身體恢復元氣！）

・換你試試看，把句子完成！

1. Jimmy / purpose / Nancy

2. Her husband / cheat / her

3. The dress code / party / ocean

・你完成了嗎？

1. It's said that Jimmy purposed to Nancy.

2. It's said that her husband cheats on her.

3. It's said that the dress code to the party is about an ocean.

---

5. It's supposed to... = 據說…

例如：

It's supposed to be exciting.（這應該會很令人興奮。）

It's supposed that to eat vegetable is healthy.（據說吃蔬菜很健康。）
→ It's supposed 後面可以接 that 引導的子句。

It's supposed that the music of Mozart is good to babies.
（據說莫札特的音樂對嬰兒很好。）

Suppose 也可以表示不同的涵義，例如：

Nancy is supposed to bite the boy, but I don't think so.
（據說 Nancy 咬了這個男孩，但我不相信。）
→ 表示推測。

The news is supposed to be a secret.（這個新聞本來應該是個祕密。）
→ 表示原本的安排。

She is supposed to go to America.（她打算要去美國。）
→ 表示未來的計畫。

但是，如果在 suppose 前面加了 not，表示「不被允許…」：

She is not supposed to go to America.（她不被允許去美國。）
→ 這句話也可以寫成：She is not allowed to go to America.

· 我們可以這樣說

邀請朋友一起吃飯，我們可以用這個句型加強說服力，你可以說：

Let's eat in this restaurant. It's supposed to be delicious.
（讓我們去這家餐廳吃飯吧！據說很好吃唷！）

如果小朋友考試考不好，或是功課還沒寫完，你可以這樣說：

You're not supposed to play the computer game.
（你不准打電腦遊戲。）

・換你試試看，這句英文怎麼說？
　1. 他不准把他的車停在這裡。
　2. 她被認為會贏得冠軍。
　3. 據說，他們住在墨西哥。
　4. 我本來要打給我媽媽，但是我忘了。

・你完成了嗎？
　1. He's not supposed to park his car here.
　2. She is supposed to win the champion.
　3. It's supposed that they live in Mexico.
　4. I was supposed to call my mom, but I forgot.

---

6. be 動詞 + 主詞 allowed... = 可以…嗎？

　例如：

Are children allowed to go out with friends at midnight?
（小孩們可以在半夜和朋友出門嗎？）

Are we allowed to smoke in the lobby?（我們可以在大廳抽菸嗎？）

Is smoking allowed in the lobby?（可以在大廳抽菸嗎？）

Is Jason allowed to pay for the dinner?（Jason 可以付晚餐錢嗎？）

Is the secretary permitted to visit that company?
（秘書可以去拜訪這間公司嗎？）
→ permit 比 allow 更正式。

・我們可以這樣說
　晚上想和朋友去夜店時，我們可以用這個句型來詢問：

Am I allowed to go to the night club with Anna?
（我可以和 *Anna* 去夜店嗎？）

・換你試試看，這個狀況怎麼說？

1. 小狗想要進房間。
2. 爸爸想要喝啤酒。
3. 大家忍不住闖紅燈。
4. 小女孩想要幫媽媽煮晚餐。

・你完成了嗎？

1. Is the dog allowed in the room?
2. Is Dad allowed to drink beer?
3. Are people allowed to get through the red light?
4. Is the girl allowed to help her mom make dinner?

---

7. 主詞 + be 動詞 + forced to... = 不得不做…

例如：

Charlie is forced to leak the news.（*Charlie* 不得不透漏這個消息。）
→ to 後面要用動詞原形。

She is forced to open the window.（她不得不把窗戶打開。）

The plane is compelled to land in the meadow.
（這架飛機不得不停在草坪上。）
→ 除了 be forced to，也可以用 be compelled to。

He was obliged to apologize to the customer.（他不得不向客戶道歉。）
→ be obliged to 也具有同樣的意思。Be 動詞要根據時間的不同而變化。

・我們可以這樣說

　　本來預約一家有名的餐廳，想和另一半好好享受一頓美食，但沒想到要臨時要加班，你可以這樣說：

I am forced to cancel the reservation tonight. I need to work until midnight.
（我不得不取消今晚的預約，我需要工作到半夜。）

· 換你試試看，用單詞完成句型！

1. He / leave / hometown
2. She / give up / dance / because / knee / hurt
3. She / ask / fellow worker / help

· 你完成了嗎？

1. He was obliged to leave his hometown.
2. She is forced to give up dancing because she had her knee hurt.
3. She is forced to ask her fellow worker to help her.

---

8. 主詞 + be 動詞 + fed up with... = 我難以忍受⋯

這個句型可以用來表示對某事難以忍受或感到厭煩，例如:

I am fed up with waiting for you.（我對一直等你感到很煩。）
→ 如果 with 後面接動詞，要改為動名詞的形式。

She is fed up with waking her son up in the morning.
（她對於早上要叫兒子起床感到很厭煩。）

I am fed up with your nagging.（我已經無法忍受你的嘮叨。）
→ with 後面也可以接名詞。

He is fed up with his boss.（他已經無法忍受他的老闆了。）

Sandra is bored with the game.（Sandra 對這項遊戲感到厭煩了。）
→ ＜be bored with＞也可以表示感到厭煩的意思。

＜be pleased to＞是這個句型的相反意思，表示「很樂意做⋯」，例如:

I am pleased to do this job.（我很高興可以做這份工作。）
→ to 後面的動詞要使用原形動詞。

He is pleased to skiing.（他很喜歡滑雪。）
→ to 後面也可以接名詞。

She is pleased to bungee jumping.（她很喜歡高空彈跳。）

・我們可以這樣說

　　家事做累了，可以尋求家人的幫助，你可以這樣說：

I am fed up with sweeping the floor. Could you give me a hand?
（我實在對掃地感到很煩，你可以幫我一下嗎？）

・換你試試看，排出正確的順序！

1. He is mopping fed the up with floor.
2. She is fed up the with playing flute.
3. I up this copy am with fed machine. It broken is again.

・你完成了嗎？

1. He is fed up with mopping the floor.
2. She is fed up with playing the flute.
3. I am fed up with this copy machine. It is broken again.

---

9. It is hoped that... = 希望…

　　例如：

It is hoped that Tracy could win the game.（希望 Tracy 可以贏得比賽。）

It is hoped that Jane would be a doctor.（希望 Jane 可以成為醫生。）

It is hoped that there was no one get hurt in the gun battle.
（希望在這場槍戰裡面沒有人受傷。）

It is hoped that you could get promoted in the company.
（希望你可以在公司裡獲得晉升。）

・換你試試看，這句英文怎麼說？

1. 希望政府對促進我們的經濟能有因應的政策。
2. 希望流浪動物都有甜蜜的家。
3. 希望你可以盡快恢復健康。

・你完成了嗎？

1. It is hoped that the government takes measure to improve our economy.
2. It is hoped that all stray animals could have a sweet home.
3. It is hoped that you can recover your health soon.

---

10. It is well known to everyone that... = 眾所周知…

例如：

It is well known to everyone that she loves her husband very much.
（眾所周知，她很愛她的老公。）

It is well known to everyone that cats like fish.
（大家都知道，貓咪喜歡吃魚。）

It is well known to everyone that once bitten, twice shy.
（大家都知道，一朝被蛇咬，十年怕草繩。）

・我們可以這樣說

你可以用這個句型來表示叮嚀，例如：

It is well known to everyone that tomorrow never comes.
You need to value your time.
（大家都知道，不可以依賴明天，你一定好好珍惜你的時間。）

・換你試試看，完成句型！

1. She is a dentist.
2. He treats his cat as a child.
3. It rains in summer afternoon.
4. Saying is one thing and doing is another.

・你完成了嗎？

1. It is well known to everyone that she is a dentist.
2. It is well known to everyone that he treats his cat as a child.
3. It is well known to everyone that it rains in summer afternoon.
4. It is well known to everyone that saying is one thing and doing is another.

01 CHAPTER
02 CHAPTER
03 CHAPTER
04 CHAPTER
05 CHAPTER
06 CHAPTER
07 CHAPTER
08 CHAPTER
09 CHAPTER
10 CHAPTER

---

11. 某事 be used for... = 被用來⋯

例如：

The yeast is used for making bread.（酵母被用來做麵包。）
→ for 後面的動詞要變成動名詞。

The razor is used for shaving beard.（刮鬍刀被用來刮鬍子。）

Your time should be used for enjoying the life.
（你的時間應該用來享受人生。）

The workbook is used for students to do some exercises.
（習作被用來給學生做練習題。）
→ for 後面也可以接名詞，若要接動詞，可以使用不定詞。

・我們可以這樣說

如果你的好朋友向你尋求建議，問你時間可以怎麼運用，你可以這樣說：

Your leisure should be used for learning another language.
（你的空閒時間應該用來學習另一個語言。）

・換你試試看，完成這個句子！

1. Helmet / protect / head
2. Machine / doctor / find out / disease
3. Eraser / erase / mistake

・你完成了嗎？

1. The helmet is used for protecting the head.
2. The machine is used for doctor to find out the disease.
3. The eraser is used to erase the mistake.

‖ 好學的祈使句諺語 ‖

01 CHAPTER
02 CHAPTER
03 CHAPTER
04 CHAPTER
05 CHAPTER
06 CHAPTER
07 CHAPTER
08 CHAPTER
09 CHAPTER
10 CHAPTER

・換你試試看,你知道這個句子是什麼意思呢?

1. A tree is known by its fruit.
2. No sin is hidden to the soul.
3. Books are well written, or badly written. That's all.
4. What can be cured must be endured.
5. Rome was not built in a day.
6. Once bitten, twice shy.

A. 書只有好壞,沒有善惡。
B. 羅馬不是一天造成的。
C. 逆來順受。
D. 一朝被蛇咬,十年怕草繩。
E. 觀其人,知其行。
F. 沒有罪惡可以藏在靈魂裡。

・你找到了嗎?

1. A tree is known by its fruit.(E.)觀其人,知其行。
2. No sin is hidden to the soul.(F.)沒有罪惡可以藏在靈魂裡。
3. Books are well written, or badly written. That's all.(A.)書只有好壞,沒有善惡。
4. What can be cured must be endured.(C.)逆來順受。
5. Rome was not built in a day.(B.)羅馬不是一天造成的。
6. Once bitten, twice shy.(D.)一朝被蛇咬,十年怕草繩。

‖ 好學的祈使句小短句 ‖

1. I am impressed by... 我對…印象很深刻。

A: I am impressed by the ending. It's awesome!
（我對結局印象深刻。實在是太了不起了!）
B: You can say that again.（我非常同意你。）

---

2. It can't be helped. 沒有辦法。

A: How can I fix this washing machine?（我要怎麼修理這台洗衣機？）

B: It can't be helped.（沒有辦法。）

---

3. My hands are tied. 我很忙。

A: Do you want to go shopping?（你想要去購物嗎？）

B: I would like to, but my hands are tied.（我很想，但是我很忙。）

三、文法糾正篇

1. 授與動詞的順序錯誤

你還記得在動詞篇中提到的授與動詞嗎？授與動詞的句型有兩種：

My mom bought me a dress.（我媽媽買了一件洋裝給我。）
→ ＜授與動詞＋間接受詞＋直接受詞＞。

My mom bought a dress for me.（我媽媽買給我一件洋裝。）
→ 先寫直接受詞時，在間接受詞前要有介係詞。

但是，當這種句型變成被動式時，很容易在順序產生混淆，試比較看看下列的句子，你能判斷哪一句才正確嗎？

A dress was bought for me by Mom. → （　　）

A dress was bought by Mom. → （　　）

I was bought a dress by Mom. → （　　）

上面的句子中，第一句和第二句是正確的句子，但第三句的語序是錯誤的。

再看看另一個例子：

Amy sang Jack a song.（*Amy* 為 *Jack* 唱了一首歌。）

Amy sang a song for Jack.

改成被動式：

A song was sung by Amy.

A song was sung for Jack by Amy.

→ 被授與的對象要放再給予動作的人前面。

---

2. by + 給予動作的人
   with + 做某動作使用的工具

例如：

Tim was hit by Jason.（*Tim* 被 *Jason* 打。）
→ by + 給予動作的人

Tim was hit with a stone.（*Tim* 被一顆石頭打到。）
→ with + 做某動作使用的工具

再看另一個例子：

The thief was shot by a police officer.（小偷被警察射擊。）

The thief was shot with a gun.（小偷被手槍射擊。）

The thief was shot by a police officer with a gun.

（小偷被警察用手槍射擊。）

→ 如果同時有給予動作的人和做某動作使用的工具，要先寫 by 再寫 with。

3. 不是所有的動詞都可以改為被動語態

　　不及物動詞因為沒有受詞，如果改成被動語態，就沒有可以做主詞的語詞，所以不及物動詞沒有被動語態，例如：

She walks.（她走路。）

Is walked by her.（她被走路。）
→ 人不可能被走路，是錯誤的寫法

He arrived.（他到了。）

Was arrived by him.（他被到了。）
→ 人不可能被到了，是錯誤的寫法。

有些及物動詞，特別是表示狀態的動詞，也不行改成被動語態，例如：

He is a wise man.（他是一個睿智的男人。）
→ be 動詞表示狀態，這種用法沒有被動語態。

They have a beautiful garden.（他們有一個漂亮的花園。）
→ have 雖然是及物動詞，但表示擁有的狀態，不能有被動語態。

The garden is had by them.（花園被他們有。）
→ 錯誤的用法。

The dress doesn't fit me.（這件洋裝不符合我的尺寸。）
→ fit 表示合適與否，也是表示狀態的一種。

I wasn't fit by the dress.（我不被這件洋裝符合。）
→ 錯誤的用法。

4. 現在分詞表示主動，過去分詞表示被動

　　例如：

a sleeping baby（正在睡覺的嬰兒）
→ 現在分詞表示主動語態。

a crying boy（正在哭的男孩）

a broken glass（被打破的玻璃杯）

→ 過去分詞表示被動語態。

the invited children（被邀請的小孩）

有些過去分詞，仍然是主動語態，例如：

a retired woman（退休的女人）

→ 雖然 retired 是過去分詞，但卻不帶有被動的涵義。

a fallen ball（掉落的球）

→ fallen 也是具主動意味的過去分詞。

有時，同一個語詞會同時有現在分詞和過去分詞的型態，例如：

This movie is interesting.（這部電影很有趣。）

→ interesting 是現在分詞，中文翻譯成「令人覺得有趣的」。

She is interested in this movie.（她對於這部電影很感興趣。）

→ interested 是過去分詞，中文翻譯成「（某人）感到有趣的」。

The baseball game is exciting.（這場棒球賽很令人興奮。）

The baseball game is exciting to Amanda.

（這場棒球賽很令 *Amanda* 感到興奮。）

→ 使用現在分詞時，想要描述人物為何時，使用介係詞 to。

She is excited about the baseball game.（她對於這場棒球賽感到很興奮。）

→ 過去分詞後面通常會銜接介係詞，每個過去分詞搭配的介係詞不一樣。

Amy is interesting to me.（我覺得 *Amy* 很有趣。）

→ 人也會令人覺得有趣，所以現在分詞的主詞可以是人物。

但是不能這樣用：

The baseball game is interested.（棒球比賽感到有趣。）

→ 事物不會感到有趣，所以將無生命的語詞做為過去分詞的主詞是錯誤的

用法。

這類的語詞例如：boring（令人厭煩的）／bored with（感到厭煩的）、surprising（令人驚訝的）／surprised at（感到驚訝的）、tiring（令人厭煩的）／tired of（感到厭煩的）、exciting（令人興奮的）／excited about（感到興奮的）、 interesting（令人覺得有趣的）／interested in（感到有趣的）、impressing（令人印象深刻的）／impressed by（感到印象深刻的）、frightening（令人害怕的）／frightened at（感到害怕的）等。

---

5. 分辨不出主動或是被動語態

你可以分辨出來下面的句子是主動或被動嗎？

She is asking a question. → （　　）
She has asked the question. → （　　）
She is asked by the students. → （　　）

你分辨出來了嗎？

She is asking a question.（她正在問一個問題。）
→ ＜be 動詞＋現在分詞＞表示現在進行式，是主動語態。

She has asked the question.（她已經問完了問題。）
→ ＜has＋過去分詞＞是現在完成式，也是主動語態。

She is asked by the students.（她被學生問問題。）
→ ＜be 動詞＋過去分詞＞才是被動語態。

再來比較看看另一個句子：

She is called by the teacher.（她被老師叫過去。）
→ 正確的寫法。

She is calling by the teacher.
→ 雖然中文句子表示「正在被叫」，但卻不能用現在分詞。

當句子中有做形容詞用的過去分詞時，特別容易搞不清楚主動或被動：

I am frightened of cockroaches.（我對蟑螂感到害怕。）
→ 雖然中文沒有翻出「被…」的被動語態，但這樣才是正確的寫法。

I am frightening of cockroaches.
→ 錯誤的寫法。

・換你試試看，被動句的綜合練習！

A. 判斷是否為被動式

1. She was playing the violin.
2. The violin was played by Emily.
3. He was interested in the video game.
4. The clothes was washed.
5. The bookstore is closed.
6. He has eaten the breakfast.
7. The bread was eaten.
8. The shoes are selling well.

B. 這個句子正確嗎？

1. There are a lot of things to be done.
2. He is to be congratulated.
3. There is a cried baby.
4. The window is broken.
5. The book had written many years ago.
6. Bob was hurt with a knife.
7. I was given a diamond ring by my husband.
8. A love letter was written to her by her boyfriend.

・你答對了嗎？

A. 判斷是否為被動語態

1. She <u>was playing</u> the violin.
   → ＜was + V-ing＞為過去進行式，不是被動語態。

2. The violin was played by Emily.

　→ ＜was + 過去分詞＞為被動語態。

3. He was interested in the video game.

　→ ＜was + 過去分詞＞為被動語態，這個句子中的過去分詞做形容詞用。

4. The clothes was washed.

　→ ＜was + 過去分詞＞是被動語態。

5. The bookstore is closed.

　→ ＜is + 過去分詞＞也是被動語態。

6. He has eaten the breakfast.

　→ ＜has + 過去分詞＞是現在完成式，不是被動語態。如果要把這個句子改成被動，應該要在 has 和過去分詞中加入 been。

7. The bread was eaten.

　→ ＜was + 過去分詞＞是被動語態。

8. The shoes are selling well.

　→ 少數動詞儘管寫成主動形式，但卻帶有被動語態的涵義，這些動詞如 sell（賣）、read（讀）、wash（洗）等，這個句子雖是主動，但卻是被動語態。

B. 這個句子正確嗎？

1. There are a lot of things to be done.

　→（○）這個句子也可以寫成：There are a lot of things to do. 中文翻譯為：有很多事情要做。

2. He is to be congratulated.

　→（○）除了 to be congratulated，to be seen（被看見）、to be continued（被持續）和 to be found（被發現）也是常常使用被動語態，本句的中文翻譯為：他被恭喜。

3. There is a cried baby.

　→（Ｘ）要把 cried 換成 crying 才對，中文翻譯為：有一個嬰兒正在哭。

4. The window is broken.

　→（○）中文翻譯為：窗戶被打破了。

5. The book had written many years ago.

　→（Ｘ）had 和 written 中間要加入 been 才是被動語態，這句正確的寫法

為：The book had been written many years ago. 中文翻譯為：這本書在幾年前（被）寫完。

6. Bob was hurt with a knife.

　　→（O）本句翻譯為：Bob 被刀子刺傷。

7. I was given a diamond ring by my husband.

　　→（X）這個句子的語序錯誤，正確的寫法為：A diamond ring was given to me by my husband.，中文翻譯為：一個鑽石戒指被我丈夫送給我。（更好的翻譯是：我的丈夫給了我一個鑽石戒指。有時，英文是被動語態，但中文翻成被動語態會不太適合。）

8. A love letter was written to her by her boyfriend.

　　→（O）本句翻譯為：一封情書被她男朋友寫給她。（更好的翻譯是：她男朋友寫了一封情書給她。）

好書報報－生活系列

BEST BOOKS
Best Publishing

愛情之酒甜而苦。兩人喝，是甘露；
三人喝，是酸醋；隨便喝，要中毒。

精選出偶像劇必定出現的**80**個情境，
每個情境－必備單字、劇情會話訓練班、30秒會話教室
讓你跟著偶像劇的腳步學生活英語會話的劇情，
輕鬆自然地學會英語!

作者：伍羚芝
定價：新台幣349元
規格：344頁 / 18K / 雙色印刷

全書中英對照，介紹東西方節慶的典故，
幫助你的英語學習－學得好、學得深入!

用英語來學節慶分為兩大部分－東方節慶&西方節慶

每個節慶共**7**個學習項目：
節慶源由－簡易版、精彩完整版＋實用單字、閱讀測驗、
習俗放大鏡、實用會話、常用單句這麼說、互動單元...

作者：Melanie Venekamp、陳欣慧、倍斯特編輯團隊
定價：新台幣299元
規格：304頁 / 18K / 雙色印刷

用現有的環境與資源，為自己的小寶貝
創造一個雙語學習環境；讓孩子贏在起跑點上!

我家寶貝愛英文，是一本從媽咪懷孕、嬰兒期到幼兒期，
會常用到的單字、對話，必備例句，
並設計單元延伸的互動小遊戲以及童謠，
增進親子關係，也讓家長與孩子一同學習的參考書!

作者：Mark Venekamp & Claire Chang
定價：新台幣329元
規格：296頁 / 18K / 雙色印刷 / MP3

好書報報

心理學研究顯示，一個習慣養成，至少必須重複21次！
全書規劃30天學習進度表，搭配學習，
不知不覺養成學習英語的好習慣！

▲圖解學習英文文法 三效合一！
◎刺激大腦記憶◎快速掌握學習大綱◎複習迅速

▲英文文法學習元素一次到位！
◎**20**個必懂觀念 ◎**30**個必學句型 ◎**40**個必閃陷阱

▲流行有趣的英語！
◎「那裡有正妹！」
◎「今天我們去看變形金剛3吧！」

作者：朱懿婷
定價：新台幣349元
規格：364頁 / 18K / 雙色印刷

要說出流利的英文，就是需要常常開口勇敢說！

國外打工兼職很流行，如何找尋機會？
怎麼做完整的英文自我介紹，成功promote自己？
獨自出國打工，職場基礎英語對話該怎麼說？
不同國家、不同領域要知道那些common sense？
保險健康的考量要更注意，各國制度大不同？

6大主題 **30**個單元 **120**組情境式對話 **30**篇補給站！
九大學習特色：
■主題豐富多元　■多種情境演練　■激發聯想延伸
■增強單字記憶　■片語邏輯組合　■例句靈活套用
■塊狀編排歸納　■舒適閱讀視覺　■吸收效果加倍

作者：Claire Chang & Melanie Venecamp
定價：新台幣469元
規格：560頁 / 18K / 雙色印刷

好書報報-職場系列

漸進式英文文法句型完整KO版

作　　者／黃亭瑋

封面設計／King Chen

內頁構成／菩薩蠻有限公司

發 行 人／周瑞德

企劃編輯／丁筠馨

印　　製／世和印製企業有限公司

初　　版／2013 年 11 月

定　　價／新台幣 349 元

出　　版／倍斯特出版事業有限公司

電　　話／（02）2351-2007

傳　　真／（02）2351-0887

地　　址／100 台北市中正區福州街1號10 樓之 2

E m a i l ／best.books.service@gmail.com

總 經 銷／商流文化事業有限公司

地　　址／新北市中和區中正路752號7樓

電　　話／（02）2228-8841

傳　　真／（02）2228-6939

國家圖書館出版品預行編目(CIP)資料

漸進式英文文法句型完整KO版 / 黃亭瑋著. ― 初
版. ― 臺北市：倍斯特, 2013. 11
　　面；　公分
　　ISBN 978-986-89739-4-7(平裝)

　1. 英語 2. 語法 2. 句法

805.16　　　　　　　　　　　　102020292